Edward Montague Compton Mackenzie was born in West Hartlepool in 1883, the eldest son of the actor-manager Edward Compton and the American actress, Virginia Bateman. He went on from St Paul's School to Magdalen College, Oxford, graduating in History in 1904. In his twenties, like his sister Fay Compton, he went on the stage, but found his true vocation with the publication of *The Passionate Elopement* in 1908. He gained enormous popular and critical success with *Carnival* (1912) and *Sinister Street* (1913) and, also in 1913, he went to live in Capri, haunt of writers and artists and the scene of *Vestal Fire* (1927) and *Extraordinary Women* (1928), both published by The Hogarth Press. He was received into the Roman Catholic Church in 1914.

During the First World War, Mackenzie was a Secret Service agent in the Aegean, but afterwards returned to writing – over a hundred books on everything from cats, tobacco and Bonnie Prince Charlie, to spying, music and country houses; from panoramic novel cycles like *The Four Winds of Love* (1937-45) to farcical entertainments such as *Monarch of the Glen* (1941) and *Whisky Galore* (1947). Even in his eighties he was finishing his ten-volume autobiography *My Life and Times*.

In 1929 he co-founded the Scottish National Party, and still managed to find time to get involved in a spy trial in 1932, to become a popular broadcaster, wage constant battle with the Inland Revenue and to move his vast library from island to island to island. One of the century's most extraordinary characters, he was married three times and died in Edinburgh in 1972, aged eighty-nine.

VESTAL FIRE

Compton Mackenzie

fatalia lumina Vestae
PROPERTIUS

New Introduction by
Sally Beauman

THE HOGARTH PRESS
LONDON

To

JOHN ELLINGHAM BROOKS

Published in 1985 by
The Hogarth Press
Chatto & Windus Ltd
40 William IV Street, London WC2N 4DF

First published in Great Britain by Chatto & Windus 1927
Hogarth edition offset from Chatto 1964 edition
Copyright Compton Mackenzie 1927
Introduction copyright © Sally Beauman 1986

All rights reserved. No part of this publication may be reproduced, stored in a retrieval system, or transmitted in any form, or by any means, electronic, mechanical, photocopying, recording or otherwise, without the prior permission of the publisher.

British Library Cataloguing in Publication Data

Mackenzie, Compton
Vestal fire.
I. Title
823'.912 [F] PR6025.A2526

ISBN 0 7012 0573 3

Printed in Great Britain by
Cox & Wyman Ltd
Reading, Berkshire

INTRODUCTION

Vestal Fire is a novel about an island: set on Capri, which Compton Mackenzie calls Sirene, it re-creates, with careful exactitude, people he encountered during the time that he himself lived on the island – a period that spanned, as does the novel, the First World War. He was to write about Capri again with his next book, *Extraordinary Women*, and in both cases he chose to do so at a considerable distance of time and place.

At the end of July 1926, a time when – as frequently happened – his elaborate life-style had brought about another financial crisis, Mackenzie was about to begin writing a pot-boiler serial for a magazine. He was also planning a gargantuan project, one novel, in seven volumes, running to a million words, and to be called *Our Seven Selves*; with fairly typical Mackenzie optimism he envisaged completing it in two years – if only he could buy himself two years of freedom from debts. *Our Seven Selves* was never written (although his ideas for it influenced his later sequence of novels, *The Winds of Love*), and in the summer of 1926 he put aside both projects to write, instead, *Vestal Fire* – a novel which, as he makes clear in his autobiography, he had been planning for several years.

It was completed on December 19th, some five and a half months later – a fast pace for a long novel beset with technical problems, but a fairly typical one for Mackenzie, who, once launched on a book, could write astonishingly fast. It was finished in that time despite the recurring bouts of sciatica that plagued Mackenzie for most of his life, and – like his other novels – it did not preclude his continuing with the other aspects of his immensely energetic life. He wrote it on the tiny island of Jethou, one of the Channel Islands, which (together with Herm) Mackenzie had leased in 1920, when he finally left Capri. Thus *Vestal Fire*, a novel about an island, and an investigation of human insularity, was written from the fastness of another island – one smaller and more remote than the siren land Mackenzie describes here, and significantly perhaps, one very different in character.

Compton Mackenzie frequently used real events and people as a source for his novels. *Carnival* (1912), his second book and his first major popular success, drew extensively on the experiences of an actress friend in its portrait of Jenny Pearl. *Sinister Street*, the next and the greatest of his novels, had strongly autobiographical elements, and Mackenzie was to use the same technique, mingling fiction and fact, much later in his life, with the Scottish novels (including *Whisky Galore*) that sprang from the years he lived on the island of Barra in the Outer Hebrides. But in *Vestal Fire*, and in *Extraordinary Women*, he took the process much further.

Quite deliberately, Mackenzie set out to re-create not just characters he had known on Capri, but events to which he had been a witness. He took some care to check the accuracy of his memory, consulting notes he had made at the time; and his wife, Faith,* wrote to John Ellingham Brooks (to whom the novel is dedicated) to check a 'long list of dates, epitaphs and details'. J. E. Brooks, husband of the lesbian painter Romaine Brooks (on whom Mackenzie modelled Olimpia Leigh in *Extraordinary Women*) was paid £300 a year by his wife to remain out of her way on Capri. He was an expert on the poetry of Heredia, and shared the Villa Cercola with, intermittently, Somerset Maugham and E. F. Benson. He was thus a fairly typical inhabitant of the period, as well as a close friend, and his help was useful: he had been, as Faith Compton Mackenzie somewhat dryly understated, 'a keen observer of the Capri drama'.

That drama was considerable. Capri, in the first quarter of this century, was one of the most extraordinary places in Europe. Among English dramatists perhaps only Etherege

*Compton Mackenzie married Faith (Stone) in 1905. She died in 1960. In 1962 he married Chrissie (MacSween). After her death he married, in 1965, her sister Lily, the present Lady Mackenzie, who survives him.

could have caught its blend of extravagant hedonism and folly, though both Jonson and Wilde would have relished it, and – among novelists – Firbank and Peacock might have found it an example of life imitating art.

The young Somerset Maugham, visiting Capri for the first time as a young man, found it 'the most enchanting spot' he had ever seen, and 'listened with transport' to exactly the same kinds of conversations – mad, impassioned, eccentric, erudite – that spring from the pages of *Vestal Fire*. He saw two men (one of them presumably J. E. Brooks) 'fly at one another's throats because they disagreed over the poetic merits of Heredia's sonnets', and he thought it grand. Mackenzie, coming to the island slightly later, reacted much as Maugham had done. Like Maugham, he relished a place where there was a constant overlap between the ridiculous and the sublime.

Mackenzie first went to the island in the spring of 1913, on the recommendation of his friend, Norman Douglas, and in the hope that the gentle climate would ease his sciatica. At that time relatively few tourists visited Capri, and it was possible to live there very cheaply. Instead of tourists there were emigrés, refugees from the wilder shores of European and American society, an amazing, cosmopolitan collection of the famous and the infamous: writers, artists, people who already had a past, and others who were energetically creating one. There was a substantial colony of homosexuals, first founded after the Wilde case; there were numerous refugees from the Czar, later to be supplemented by refugees from the Bolsheviks. One of the local doctors (he treated both Mackenzie and his wife) was Axel Munthe; Maxim Gorky had a villa there, and Mackenzie visited him. Visitors to the island, apart from Benson and Maugham, included Scott Fitzgerald, D. H. Lawrence and, of course, Norman Douglas, who first wrote about the island in *Siren Land*, and who was to write about it again, in fictional form, with *South Wind*, published in 1917.

Living side by side with the artists and bohemians were displaced Europeans of grandiloquent title; famous Edwardian beauties; classical scholars; retired English colonels, eking out their pensions in the sun; peripatetic spinsters and widows;

café philosophers . . . a society of *rentiers* and remittance men, many of whom existed on private incomes, like many characters in this novel, or on payouts from families only too glad to wash their hands of them.

Work did feature in the lives of some of the emigrés, and books were actually written on the island as opposed to discussed over *Strega*. Mackenzie's typewriter, for instance, had a distinguished career: it was used to type part of *South Wind*, Mackenzie's *Sylvia Scarlett*, and Maugham's *Our Betters*. It was then borrowed by D. H. Lawrence for *Fantasia of the Unconscious*, after which Lawrence carried it back to Mackenzie's villa on his head.

But such industry, as we see in *Vestal Fire*, was untypical of the island: the main occupation on Capri was gossip, which was elevated to a fine art, and the currency of the place was parties. Parties; parties: a seemingly endless succession of them. Parties for birthdays and parties for funerals; parties to celebrate selling a book or a painting; fancy-dress parties; opium parties; parties on saints' days; parties to celebrate a full moon. 'Life is hardly reasonable,' Faith Compton Mackenzie had written of Capri in her diary: it hardly was, but the parties went on, as if there were no possibility that the kissing would ever have to stop.

Mackenzie established himself on Capri, as he did everywhere, with style. His arrival on the island coincided with the publication of the first part of *Sinister Street* (it came out in two volumes in 1913 and 1914), and sections of that novel were written there. *Sinister Street* was to earn him a lot of money; almost immediately it won him golden opinions. Henry James, an old friend of Mackenzie's father, the actor Edward Compton, called it 'the most remarkable book written by a young man during his [James's] lifetime', and declared that Mackenzie had 'emancipated the English novel'. Ford Madox Ford compared the book to *L'Education Sentimentale* (to which it had obvious similarities) and *Heart of Darkness* (to which it had none). 'Possibly . . .' he wrote, 'a work of real genius.' Mackenzie was thirty; with such plaudits he arrived on Capri on the crest of a wave. The same year the second volume of *Sinister Street* came out, Proust's *Du Côté du Chez Swann* was published (the critic Edmund Gosse gave Mackenzie an early copy); the following year, 1915, D. H. Lawrence's *Women in Love* was published, and, like *Sinister Street*, banned by the circulating libraries.

Always fascinated by houses and gardens – of which, during his long life, Mackenzie bought, leased or created a bewildering succession – he acquired a number of properties on the island, but his chief residence was the rented, and aptly named, Casa Solitaria, a remote and very beautiful villa perched on the edge of cliffs that plunged some three hundred feet to the sea. Designed by Cerio, the Caprese architect, the house is important: Mackenzie's choosing of it is revelatory, both of the man and the writer, and of his attitude to Capri – an attitude that explains much about *Vestal Fire*.

Over the main fireplace at Solitaria, Cerio had had carved, apropos solitude, the words: *Nec tecum nec sine te vivere possum – Neither with thee nor without thee can I live*. Whether or not Mackenzie himself realised it, they were words that might serve as a footnote to his life. For Mackenzie exemplified two deeply opposed characteristics: on the one hand he was gregarious, a famously brilliant conversationalist who loved to hold the floor, and who maintained a wide circle of friends; on the other, he was a solitary, retiring for long hours to write, fuelling himself through the night on Ovaltine and Sanatogen, and deliberately absenting himself, with a writer's sense of self-preservation, from moments of crisis in the lives of those close to him – including that of his wife, Faith. His love of islands was perhaps an expression of that side of his nature (after Capri he was to live on four others, each progressively more remote). Certainly D. H. Lawrence, in his cruelly brilliant story, *The Man Who Loved Islands*, was to portray him as essentially and tragically solitary, ending his days in the exile of self-willed insularity.

That story, published the year after *Vestal Fire*, was based on confidences prised by Lawrence from Faith Compton Mackenzie, and it finally ended Mackenzie's and Lawrence's friendship. Lawrence, presumably aware that the highly detailed portrait was immediately identifiable, swore that, at heart, it was not about Mackenzie at all. Mackenzie threatened legal action if the story was republished. There the matter rested; but the story remains interesting, not just in its own right, but for the light it casts on Mackenzie and on *Vestal Fire*. It was written years after Lawrence and Mackenzie had known each other on Capri, and it is in marked contrast to the things Lawrence wrote about Mackenzie then. Then, far from castigating Mackenzie as a spiritual hermit, Lawrence was directing his characteristic spleneticism at the other side of Mackenzie's nature. Lawrence the puritan found that Monty Mackenzie, dandy and raconteur, set his teeth on edge. He liked him, he wrote, 'but not his island, nor his influence'. He was sick of 'this cat Cranford of Capri'. 'He seems quite rich,' Lawrence wrote, 'and does himself well, and walks with a sort of aesthetic figure . . . in a pale blue suit to match his eyes and a large woman's brown velour hat to match his hair . . .'

If one puts the two portraits together, it becomes clear that, in Capri, Mackenzie had the perfect foil for his gifts. Sybarite and solitary, he was capable simultaneously of being part of Capresi society, and distanced from it. He satirised, but he also sympathized; and it is that duality which gives this fine novel its wit, and its heart.

Vestal Fire has the slenderest of plots; that narrative revelation was not Mackenzie's concern is evident right from the beginning: such plot as there is is almost immediately given away. It tells the story of a betrayal: of two aging American virgins, the Misses Pepworth-Norton, and their trust in and involvement with an exceedingly shady French aristocrat, Count Marsac. These central characters (and most of the peripheral ones) were based on real people, in this case, the Misses Kate and Saidee Wolcott-Perry, and one, Count Jack d'Adelswaerd-Fersen. Compton Mackenzie and his wife were introduced to the Misses Wolcott-Perry, by letter, by Norman Douglas, and the accounts the Mackenzies give, in their respective autobiographies, both of the central story and of other incidents, match almost exactly the fictional version of them in the novel.

But the factual background is a springboard merely. In essence, and deliberately so, *Vestal Fire* is a period piece. It evokes and anatomises a world already distant by 1927 (when the novel was published), and now exceedingly remote. It is a vanished world, this Sirene, and its species are extinct – or so one might feel at first. Then the ghosts grow in substance; they come at times uncomfortably, reproachably, close. Fashions change, and extravagances alter, but the human capacity for self-delusion and for posturing, central to the novel – that, alas, does not.

Vestal Fire contains a series of wicked portraits of monomania. Egotists stalk its pages – and gloriously funny egotists they are, each with his or her own immediately recognizable voice, for Mackenzie's brilliant gift for dialogue is here on triumphant display. Each is of his period, and each transcends it. The scholar who never finishes his definitive book; the artist who does not observe his own decline into a hack; the young exquisite growing old; the gadfly; the gossip; the pansy-puncher; the prude; the canny native on the make and the mildewed ex-pat on the way down – all these were portraits instantly identifiable to anyone who knew Capri then. They are as instantly recognizable now. You can dine with the scholar Scudamore at high table; bump into pretty Nigel Dawson at a private view; encounter the redoubtable Mrs. Ambrogio at an English point-to-point. And Count Marsac, the opium advocate, the fantasist, the bore, he whose actual company would be intolerable, but who, on the page, is one of the chief glories of the book, he whose inevitable decline is treated with such gentleness by Mackenzie that the keen edge of the novel is transmuted, by the end, to one of elegiac poignancy – well, Marsac may seem at first the essence of the *fin-de-siècle poseur*, but he too has an alarming habit of popping up elsewhere. In the late Sixties in San Francisco, for example; tomorrow in New York or Notting Hill. The affectations alter, not the man.

As will now be clear, *Vestal Fire* has a large cast of characters, sometimes – for Mackenzie's imagination was very fertile and, like Count Marsac with his plane-trees, he often refused to prune – too large. The novel, eschewing a hero or heroine, dispensing with a central dominating voice, occasionally falters and loses pace for lack of motor. This was, indeed, one of the chief criticisms levelled at it on publication, by which time younger critics such as Cyril Connolly found Mackenzie *démodé*, and sneered at *Vestal Fire* as a quaint addition to the Capri genre of novels – 'a feeble sequel,' Connolly wrote, in the *New Statesman*, 'to *South Wind*.'

In his eagerness to pigeonhole two very different books together, Connolly argued himself into an equivocating impasse, contriving to combine a patronising pat on the head with a boot up the backside. Damning with faint praise, he found the book 'consistently amusing'; the 'feeble sequel' was somehow also a 'bracing and rather hopeful' new departure for its author. The review was influential, despite its obvious shortcomings, and perhaps partly accounts for the fact that *Vestal Fire* has not received the critical acknowledgement it merits, and was later to languish out of print for many years.

Influenced, perhaps, by Mackenzie's reputation (by 1927 in steady decline), Connolly, like many of his fellow critics, failed to grapple with the novel. He was deceived, maybe, by the book's fluency, by its apparently episodic structure – and this is deceptive. In fact, *Vestal Fire* is one of the most tightly organised and disciplined of Mackenzie's books, and it has one central, unseen protagonist, who gives to the apparent flurry of incidents a cohesion and narrative purpose. That protagonist, announced in the first, fairy-tale, sentence of the book, is time.

Vestal Fire covers a span of some twenty years, from about 1904 to about 1924. Mackenzie does not dwell on the dates, but they are carefully buried in the text. Consider those years: the years in which revolution and war wrenched the whole kilter of Western society. From *Vestal Fire* these key events of the period are excluded. The 1914-18 War, in which Mackenzie himself left Capri to serve with the Army and Intelligence in Greece, happens off-stage. It impinges upon the Capri parties to an extent; it is instrumental in severing friendships, and leads in two cases to the most bitter disillusionment, but for the most part Mackenzie shows it to be merely the excuse for more malice and more posturing. None the less, it occurs, and the novel is carefully structured so that the advent of war, which falls in the penultimate section of the book, coincides with a darkening in its central story. Mackenzie, concerned (as he wrote in *Octave Six* of *My Life and Times*) with what he called 'the architecture of the whole', paced himself so that 'the crisis of the story' was reached at precisely the novel's central point. Thereafter, as Mackenzie intended, the mode shifts. What has been comedy, shot through with rays of farce, transmutes to a powerful and melancholy pathos. It is very delicately done; the temptations of tragedy and sentiment are alike resisted. It is done with a sigh, as it were, with a series of deft flicks of the writer's wrist, with a stoic irony that echoes and justifies the numerous classical quotations Mackenzie has introduced into his text.

The novel has an exquisitely judged dying-fall. Off-stage, the war ends. On-stage, for some of the characters at least, the gaudy nights are over. Even the most alluring of islands cannot provide, ultimately, a refuge from pain. The cemetery of Capri, as firmly fixed from the inception of the novel as the Piazza or the Grande Marina, begins to dominate. Egotism triumphing even in death, the designing of tombs and sepulchres, rather than villas and gardens, becomes paramount. The close of the novel is a sequence of epitaphs, as, one by one, even Sirene numbers its dead.

The party, then, is over, in the aftermath of that unseen war? Well, no: that would be too simple, and this is not a simple book. Compared to the lucidity and Impressionistic grace of the pre-war novels, including *Sinister Street*, *Vestal Fire*, for all its brilliant comedic set-pieces, is a dark novel. Its authorial voice is still recognisably that of an urbane Edwardian, but its timbre has changed; it is also a post-war voice; you can hear a modern disillusionment.

Given the change in Mackenzie's circumstances between 1913, when he first went to Capri, and 1926, when he wrote this book, that is scarcely surprising.

He felt the war changed him: when he left Capri for Gallipoli in 1915, he wrote later, it marked 'the end of a period in my life'. But it was not just the war. In the same period, his life changed deeply in other respects. In 1914 he was received into the Catholic Church. During the war, partly because of infidelities on both sides, a rift opened up in his marriage which was never totally to heal. Finally, the immediate post-war period saw that sharp and viciously swift reversal in his literary fortunes. Mackenzie wrote book after book: *Guy and Pauline; Sylvia Scarlett; The Vanity Girl; Rich Relatives; Poor Relations;* the immensely long High-Anglican trilogy, *The Altar Steps*. They sold, with the exception of the latter, which flopped badly, reasonably but not dramatically well. They received, progressively, lukewarm to dismissive reviews. Mackenzie himself, bitterly aware that everyone was waiting for him to produce 'another *Sinister Street*', described them, with defensive hindsight, as 'marking time'.

With *Vestal Fire* he found form again. All the old virtues are still there: the authenticity of dialogue; the elegance of prose; the vividness of description; the ability to make moral points glancingly, never preaching, never hammering them home. The unusual and intuitive sympathy, with female characters, with servants, with the *demi-monde*, is marked. For Mackenzie's range was wide. He complained, citing E. M. Forster as but one example, that too many of his peers created characters who, regardless of sex, race and class, acted, spoke and thought like middle-class English gentlemen. It was not a criticism that could be levelled against him: here, as in all his novels, there is a Dickensian veracity, and it extends from elderly American spinsters right down the line to Italian peasants.

But there are also new virtues. The novel is held on a tighter rein; when it meanders (and meandering was one of Mackenzie's worst faults) it does so purposefully. There is, perhaps because of the absence of hero or heroine, less authorial self-indulgence, so there is still the celebrated Mackenzie fluency, but there is also control. And, above all, there is that significant alteration in tone. Mackenzie was often to be slightingly described as a 'romantic' author; stress has always been placed on his marked romanticism, the love of lost causes and so on, both as man and as writer. What has been less stressed is his realism, his capacity to present human folly without flinching, glossing it neither with overblown tragedy nor evasive sentiment. It is, simply, there; worse, it will continue to be there. It is that tone: resigned, worldly in the best sense, and sad, which dominates this book.

So Mackenzie knew – and it is implicit in the superbly poised ending of *Vestal Fire* – parties do not end. They just move on.

Sally Beauman, London 1984

si quis tamen tam ambitiose est ut apud illum in nulla pagina Latine loqui fas sit potest epistula vel potius titulo contentus esse.

MARTIAL

My dear Brooks,

There have already been several stories about islands in the Sirenian archipelago, from none of which did the author ever succeed in persuading his friends that his mythology had omitted them. So, warned in advance, I hasten to apologize to Sirenian friends who will be fancying that they recognize themselves in these pages, and who will be convinced that they recognize their neighbours. I apologize with equal fervour to Sirenian friends who will not be fancying that they recognize themselves and who may suffer in consequence a temporary mistrust of their own vividness. You, who know how many years ago I planned to tell this story, will appreciate the reasons that delayed my pen so long. It seemed to me then a story that was wonderfully worth telling, but one that would be difficult to tell, and one that many people would consider never should be told. And that's what I feel about it now. But whether it holds anything of Sirenian life or not, it holds much of my heart, and for that reason I can inscribe it to the memory of the hours you have spent listening to other stories of mine in the making, to many a long talk under the moon and many a long walk in the sun, to the bottles of wine and the glasses of vermouth we have drunk together, to the music and the scandal we have enjoyed, but perhaps most of all to the laughs we have had, of which I hope you will hear a faint echo as you turn over the pages of this book. 'Absit a iocorum nostrorum simplicitate malignus interpres!'

Yours ever,
Compton Mackenzie

Isle of Jethou, March 3, 1927.

*hoc lege, quod possit dicere vita ' Meum est.'
non hic Centauros, non Gorgonas Harpyiasque
invenies: hominem pagina nostra sapit.*

MARTIAL

Contents

BOOK ONE   1

BOOK TWO   139

BOOK THREE   277

BOOK ONE

Vesta coronatis . . . gaudebat asellis
PROPERTIUS

Chapter 1

*protinus a laeva tibi clari fronte Penates
atriaque excelsae sunt adeunda domus.*

MARTIAL

ONCE upon a time it was as much a matter of strict Sunday observance on the island of Sirene for the English and American colony to go to tea at the Villa Amabile in the afternoon as it was for the natives to attend Mass in the morning. People never asked their friends *if* they were going down to the Pepworth-Nortons, though they might occasionally ask what time they were going down in order to suggest sharing a carriage. Such providence had nothing to do with economy. There was only a limited number of carriages that self-respecting foreigners cared to patronize, and the drivers of these, who enjoyed something of the status of private coachmen, had to use the nicest tact to avoid offending their clients. The clients were well aware of this ebb and flow of diplomacy, and since there was always ample to quarrel about in Sirene without quarrelling over one's carriage everything in reason was done to preserve the amenity of the Sunday drive down to the Pepworth-Nortons. Thus, once upon a time you might have heard Mrs. Neave of the Villino Paradiso say to Mrs. Dawson of the Villa Florida, ' Oh, Mrs. Dawson, I was wondering if you'd have any room in your carriage this afternoon and if you'd mind my sharing Peppino with you. My poor Michele sent round in great distress last evening to say that Don Cesare just insisted he must drive down to the Nortons some French count or other who's staying at the Hotel Augusto.'

"Why, surely, Mrs. Neave; I'll only be too perfectly delighted if you'll drive with me. I will be quite alone, because Nigel is going to walk down with a young Harvard philosopher who brought him a letter of introduction from Mr. Maxwell."

"A Harvard man?" Mrs. Neave echoed in a tremor of social excitement. "Well, now, won't Mr. Neave be glad to meet him?"

"How is dear Mr. Neave?"

"Why, I believe he's really a great deal better since his last bad attack."

"Isn't that fine, Mrs. Neave? And how's the translation going along?"

"Oh, I think it's going along very well, Mrs. Dawson. But I must say I do wish sometimes Dante hadn't written quite such a lot. Mr. Neave has been working on it now for twelve years in Sirene, and he was working at it for six years before we came to Europe at all, and he hasn't gotten to the end of the *Inferno* yet."

Mrs. Dawson shook her head compassionately. She was a tall, handsome, beautifully dressed woman of perhaps forty-five, with gleaming pink nails that protruded like the points of daggers from the scabbards of her dry fingers.

"Isn't that discouraging? But I always did say the trouble was they all had too much time on their hands in the old days. Imagine anybody sitting down to write Infernos in these days! Well, good-bye till this afternoon, Mrs. Neave. I told Peppino a quarter of four."

The two Americans parted with what to an English-woman might have seemed an excessive amount of mutual courtesies considering that before the lunches to which they were both bound were fully digested they would be meeting one another again and expending all that fervour of slightly shrill politeness for a second time.

Mrs. Neave was a little blonde with bright weary eyes, who was still pretty enough to make her elderly husband smack his lips at the idea of her being admired by other men. He was one of several Englishmen and Americans on the island engaged with magna opera. There was an American translating Goethe, an Englishman translating the sonnets of Hérédia, and another Englishman wrestling with Mallarmé's *L'Après-midi d'un Faune*. There were novelists who came to Sirene for the Winter in search of quiet, and poets who came there in the Summer to find inspiration. There was a Russian at work on a new system of political economy, and a Swede who was elaborating a theory of health. There was a German writing a history of the Saracens, and there was John Scudamore, an American, who was amassing the material for a history of Roman morals.

When these authors met in Zampone's Café they always enquired most warmly after one another's pregnancies before each began to talk exclusively about his own. But Joseph Rutger Neave was the most indomitable egoist of the lot. He could hitch the wagon of any conversation to the star of Dante with a dexterity that baffled even retired Indian Civilians, and anybody who has chattered feverishly about cabbages and kings to keep retired Indian Civilians from talking about the Punjab will appreciate what that meant. One of the recognized amusements of a Sirene dinner-party was to try to snooker Joseph R. Neave over Dante; but he never failed to find the right angle of the conversational cushion to reach his ball. Most people were sorry for his wife, though some of the American matrons decided that she had married well considering that she hadn't a dollar of her own and that Joseph Rutger Neave belonged to one of the oldest families in the state of New Hampshire. Elsie Neave may have thought that she had obtained the worst of the bargain when she married an elderly hypochondriac, who devoted his whole life to translating the *Divina Commedia* into American. But she was loyalty itself, and the only expression of discontent she allowed herself was for the Villino Paradiso, which was poked away in a maze of ancient overarched alleys that clustered round the base of the Torrione, a steep hill whose summit was jagged with a mediæval fortress and whose southern face, cleft by a yawning cavern, tumbled in fantastic limestone crags eight hundred feet sheer to the sea. Joseph had chosen the stuffy inconvenient little house on account of the name and had promised his wife that they would move when his task was finished. As he had now been working eighteen years on the *Inferno* the prospect of leaving the Villino Paradiso before her blonde hair turned grey was remote indeed. Joseph himself rather liked to hear his wife apologizing for their house. He had no objection whatever to people's knowing that he could if he liked rent the largest villa in Sirene. His choice of a scholar's simple abode became thereby more impressive. Mrs. Neave was now thirty-six, and she was just beginning to think that life was slipping by very fast in the Sirene moonlight. She did not really cherish the hope of a grand passion before it was too late, because she knew that her Joseph with all his eloquence over Paolo and Francesca would take good care that she never did have one.

"Elsie Neave won't find the bathing at Sirene as inflammable as the chaste Laevina found the bathing at Baiæ. She won't forsake Joseph for any young man on this beach. She certainly arrived here a Penelope, but she'll never depart a Helen." Thus John Scudamore, looking up from a translation of one of Martial's wittiest epigrams, which he wanted for a footnote to his history of Roman morals. "Because it's mighty difficult to commit adultery when you have to give your husband his medicine three-quarters of an hour before every meal," he added gravely.

And that's what Elsie Neave herself felt. Still, Penelope had her dreams when the palms glittered like steel in the moonlight and their shadows of black velvet lay across her path. This morning, however, the vivid sunshine of the first of May was not favourable to dreams, and wishing with a sigh that she lived, like Mrs. Dawson, in the fashionable Via Caprera she hurried away across the Piazza and up the steps past the Duomo, smiling to right and left of her as she went at various ragged children and grubby-toed old women to whom she had played Lady Bountiful. She hurried along through the dank smelly twisting alleys, because her conscience was pricking her for having lingered after church to chat with Mrs. Dawson when Mr. Goldfinch, the American painter and doyen of the foreign colony, was lunching at the Paradiso. She hoped that Joseph would not be angry and say something sarcastic in front of Mr. Goldfinch; and by the time she reached her little house she was quite breathless from agitation and haste. The two men were sitting on the balcony, drinking a vermouth which Joseph imported specially from Florence, and which he told everybody was made according to a mediæval recipe.

"I like to play with the idea that Dante himself may have drunk this vermouth," he used to say rosily as he poured out a glass for the guest.

"I'm afraid I'm a little late, Joseph. . . . How d'you do, Mr. Goldfinch . . . a little late, because the minister . . ."

"Chaplain; not minister," her husband interrupted contemptuously. "Elsie prefers our New England expressions, Goldfinch," he turned to explain in an elaborately careful Old English accent.

When the painter nodded and smiled indulgently, shaking his long white curly beard and his white curly hair and showing two rows of teeth like peeled almonds, he exhaled as much wisdom as old Saturn under an oak. We use the word 'patriarchal' lightly; but Christopher Goldfinch was patriarchal in the archigrand style. Christopher Goldfinch would not even have grinned, still less fallen upon his face and laughed as Abraham did on being informed that he at a hundred and Sarah at ninety years old were going to have a son. He would merely have nodded and raised his glass and murmured with a courtly optimism, " Here's trying ! "

The exact age of Christopher Goldfinch was not known ; but he was old enough to be generally credited with eighty years. He had the figure of a man of thirty, and he could wear his beard without being suspected of an attempt to improve his profile, for nobody felt that such a fine aquiline nose was ashamed of the chin beneath. He was a romantic painter, and he belonged to an age when romantic painters considered that they owed it to society to look like what they were. This morning he was celebrating the entry of May by appearing for the first time in white, with a waistcoat of old-rose brocade, buttons of baked topaz, and a tie of crimson sarsenet drawn through a large cameo ring. He had worked in the Villa Adonis nearly forty years, and there he had amassed a large collection of mediæval bric-à-brac from brocades to holy water stoups, a quantity of classical statuary good and bad, and countless photographs and sketches of the women who had loved him. Every Spring, in spite of the chances and changes of fashion, he had contrived to sell enough pictures to maintain himself and shower hospitality for the rest of the year. Sometimes he bought too many suits of clothes or gave too many champagne suppers and ran into debt. When he did, he sold one of his museum pieces to a rich American tourist and gave better parties than ever. He had immense vitality, but few brains ; and there was no reason to suppose that he would not live to a hundred, and, what is more, to the very end be able to count on being suspected of making love to another man's wife. That, as Scudamore used to say, was where painters could always score over writers, for what after all did their day's work entail that a warm bath and a good dinner would not cure ?

Mrs. Neave hoped that her slip over the minister would be pardoned for her news about the young Harvard philosopher; but apparently it was the arrival of the French count that was to be the topic.

"I'm told he's a very delightful fellow," said Joseph, smacking his lips.

"And so rich," the painter added in a reverent voice, showing all his teeth in a smile that only he could have made appear disinterested. "They tell me he's intending to build a villa and is looking for some land. I was wondering if that site of mine on the Anasirene road would suit him. I don't suppose I will ever build there myself now."

Christopher Goldfinch had owned this site for twenty years, and for twenty years he had been showing people the plans of a palace that looked like an illustration in an edition de luxe of the *Arabian Nights*.

"And if this young Frenchman bought my land," he went on, "naturally I'd give him my plans with it."

Joseph brought the conversation back to Dante, because he too had some land on the other side of the island which he was thinking might suit this rich young count. Indeed at this moment there were no less than fifteen people in Sirene who were wondering if various plots of land might not suit the Count, not to mention another dozen who were making up their minds to buy plots of land they had been haggling over for some months in the hope of re-selling at a profit to the stranger.

"Very rich," Goldfinch nodded to himself as he sipped the vermouth. "They tell me he owns large steel-works in the north of France. Lucky fellow!"

"Talking of riches, Goldfinch," said Joseph, "did I ever read you my translation of that passage in the *Inferno* which treats of the punishment of misers?"

"I think you did, Neave; I think you did once. Very fine," said the painter quickly.

But Joseph was not to be put off like this.

"Ah, but I've altered it a good deal since then," he insisted. Then he called his wife and in that slow dusty voice of his began to explain which canto he wanted, which shelf that particular set of folios occupied, how far down in the pile she might expect to find the passage about misers, and . . .

"*La signora è servita*," announced Carmela the maid, appearing on the balcony and snapping off the directions abruptly.

"Joseph, lunch is served," his wife expostulated.

"Ever since Elsie and I were married, Goldfinch," said Joseph, "I have been trying to cure her of a bourgeois attention to the hours of meals. Kindly go and fetch that packet of manuscript," he added viciously to his wife.

"Joseph, it's *ravioli*, and Mr. Goldfinch won't enjoy them if they're cold," she pleaded.

Goldfinch, who had years ago sold his host the only picture he was ever likely to sell him, rose from his chair and offered an exquisitely ceremonious arm to his hostess.

"I daresay the *Inferno* will keep warm till after lunch," he croaked.

The old painter so seldom attempted a witticism, and he was so much amused by his *mot* that he allowed himself to laugh less carefully than usual and set all his magnificent white teeth rattling like dice. Joseph was even baulked of his reading after lunch, because his guest escaped immediately on the plea of having business to attend to before he went down to the Villa Amabile.

"Goldfinch is beginning to show his age a great deal," said Joseph to his wife with the smile of a malignant cherub.

"Poor old boy, I'm afraid he is," she agreed tactfully.

"Let me see," he added, smacking his lips with relish. "What am I? Sixty-three. And my life was despaired of when I married you."

"I know, dear," she assented sympathetically.

"Goldfinch is ten years older than I."

"I thought he was eighty."

"Fiddlesticks!" Joseph snapped.

"I beg your pardon, dear."

"Goldfinch will be seventy-three on his next birthday. Well, we shall see."

"See what, Joseph?"

"If he outlives me."

"Oughtn't you to be getting ready for your afternoon rest?" she suggested timidly.

"I don't think I will lie down this afternoon," the invalid announced.

"Joseph! But Doctor Squillace..."

"Damn Squillace... oh, very well, is my couch ready?"

Mrs. Neave sighed her relief. Joseph's afternoon siesta was one of the things that made life tolerable. It was indeed, though of course she would never have admitted as much even to herself, a daily reminder that he would not live for ever. The grey hair or so she was already beginning to find every month were not nearly so conspicuous when Joseph was tucked away on his couch, a light coverlet spread over his plump form, the various bottles of medicine disposed on the table beside him, the bell-pull brought carefully within reach of his short fat arm, the jalousies closed against the garish sunlight, and the door of his room quietly shut. Those widowed afternoons were very dear to her.

"You'll listen carefully for the signore's bell," she warned Carmela when, after dressing herself not quite so successfully as she might have done if she had not had to perform the whole business on tiptoe, she paused in the doorway of the Villino Paradiso to listen if the scholar were still fast asleep.

"*Non abbia paura*," Carmela reassured her grimly. "*Buon divertimento!*"

"Gratsi, Carmela," she replied in not the best of Italian

11

accents but with a warm grateful smile for her maid's good wishes for an afternoon of pleasure. Then she gathered her petticoats out of the way of the odds and ends of decayed fruit and fishes' heads that strewed the alleys round the Villino Paradiso and hurried down to keep her appointment on the Piazza with Mrs. Dawson. All the favourite carriages were mustered, the spruce little Abruzzi cobs using their pheasants' feathers that were intended to ward off the evil eye to ward off the flies. There, too, were all the favoured coachmen—Luigi, Domenico, Raffaele, Pasquale, Giovanni, Mrs. Dawson's Peppino, and her own Michele, who managed to convey merely by the gesture with which he took off his hat an unimaginable remorse at not being able to drive her down to the Villa Amabile, a resentment against Don Cesare, and an indifference to the French count to drive whom instead of *la signora* cruel fate had condemned him. And in the smile with which she returned his salute Mrs. Neave tried to express the profundity of her own comprehension of all that poor Michele must have suffered on her account.

Herbert Bookham came breezily across the Piazza and bade Mrs. Neave good afternoon. It being Sunday he was in blue serge instead of the knickerbocker suit of dark grey flannel he usually wore. Some of his boisterous British-bulldog manner was tempered by a pair of unexpectedly shifty eyes.

"Splendid collection this morning," he bellowed.

"Why, I'm so glad to hear that, Mr. Bookham," said Mrs. Neave.

"Jolly good collection," he continued to bellow. "In spite of that nincompoop of a chaplain we've got this year."

The feud between Mr. Bookham as churchwarden of the little English church and the various chaplains licensed to it by the Anglican Bishop of Europe was perpetual. Duncan Maxwell used to vow it was because all the chaplains found out that Bookham was sticking to half the collections; but then, Duncan Maxwell, dearly though Mrs. Neave loved to gasp at the outrageous things he said, was a little apt to exaggerate about people. And he did not like the churchwarden.

"Now, Mr. Bookham, you oughtn't to talk like that about our minister—I mean our chaplain. Except that he gabbles a bit over some of the prayers I think he's one of the best we've ever had."

"A beastly milksop," bellowed Bookham. "Excuse my bluntness. But you know what I am. John Blunt. What? Haw-haw. The fellow's simply an effeminate puppy."

"Now do be careful, Mr. Bookham. Somebody will hear what you're saying."

"Don't care if they do, Mrs. Neave. I always speak my mind. Those who don't like it can lump it. Hullo, good afternoon, Major."

Behind Mrs. Neave, craning his long neck like a turkey-cock trying to thrust his beak between feeding hens, stood Major Natt.

"How do, Mrs. Neave? Going down to the Nortons? So am I. Going down to the Nortons, Bookham?" he exhaled in a kind of muffled bark.

This was a tactless question, because about six months ago Miss Virginia Pepworth-Norton had told Mr. Bookham that she never wanted to see his mean, shifty, lying face inside her house again. That was Miss Virginia's way when she quarrelled with anybody. She did not intend to be reconciled, and she never was. She had quarrelled with Bookham over a commission she accused him of taking when she bought an extra piece of land for the Villa Amabile.

"Splendid collection this morning, Major," said the churchwarden, ignoring the question.

"Yes, I had to put in a two-lira piece," the Major grumbled. "Found I'd come out with nothing less. Are you driving down, Mrs. Neave?"

"Mrs. Dawson is kindly giving me a lift."

"Oh, I thought perhaps we might have managed some kind of alliance. Don't see why we shouldn't now. My legs are long, but I can stow them away, don't you know. I mean to say I don't want to charter one of these brigands on my own."

Mrs. Neave would not have chosen Major Natt as her ideal beau for driving down to the Nortons; but ever since Duncan Maxwell had told her that in days gone by he was celebrated as the most ingenious rake in the British Army her New England imagination had been faintly thrilled by Major Natt. He accorded so little with her idea of a rake. She could hear Duncan Maxwell's convincing enthusiasm as now she contemplated the Major.

"My dee-aw woman, he was notorious. Oh yes, he always used black silk sheets to set off the snowy amplitudes of the female form."

"Mr. Maxwell, Mr. Maxwell, how can you say such things in front of Joseph?"

"Oh, but Joseph likes it. Don't you, Joseph? Joseph would like to do the same, wouldn't you, Joseph?"

And Joseph had smacked his lips and smiled that rather uncomfortable smile and said that Maxwell always reminded him of that passage in the *Inferno* where . . .

"Why, I'm sure Mrs. Dawson will be delighted to have you drive down with us, Major Natt."

By this time Bookham had moved on, and the Piazza clock in its crumbling little baroque tower pointed to a quarter of four. From every direction one saw people hurrying toward their carriages.

"I hear this young French fellah is looking out for a site on which to build," the Major was saying. "I've a good mind to offer him the Villa Capo di Monte."

"But where would you go, Major?" Mrs. Neave asked.

"Oh, I'd stow myself away somewhere. Crawl into some wretched corner or other. The place is too large for me. I got carried away when I was building it. I was like one of the Pharaohs with a pyramid. I'm an enthusiastic ass. I saw all those stones lying about, don't you know, and I just kept on heaping them up one on top of another. I'd take 150,000 francs for it, and the fellah'd have it deuced cheap."

One never got a great deal of satisfaction out of laughing at Major Natt, because one always felt that he laughed at himself more than anybody else could. A curious figure. At first sight he seemed the stock half-pay officer that haunts the continent for the sake of cheap living; but presently one discovered that he was intelligent, knew a lot about books, had a splendid library of his own, possessed a rich cynical sesquipedalian wit, was in fact not in the least like a half-pay officer. He was as tall and lean as a maypole, with a dozen or so sandy bristles instead of hair and a dozen or so more for a moustache.

"Is *that* this young French fellah?" he asked, pointing to the companion of Nigel Dawson.

"Why, no indeed," said Mrs. Dawson. "That's Mr. Austin W. Follett, the philosopher from Harvard and Oxford."

Major Natt put up his glass.

"He's rather like me. Memento mori, and all that, poor wretch."

Mrs. Neave had noticed with a twinge of disappointment that Mr. Follett, whose association with Harvard had thrilled her so much, was a lanky young man with light orange hair and a bottle-nose. And he certainly was rather like Major Natt to look at.

The drive down to the Pepworth-Nortons by the road that meanders in such long dusty diagonals from the Piazza to the Porto will be unusually tiresome this afternoon, with Mrs. Neave and Mrs. Dawson trying all the way to avoid Major Natt's stilted legs. It will be more amusing to follow Nigel Dawson and the young bottle-nosed philosopher down by the old wide steps between high mossy walls embowered in lemons and vines and Banksia roses until they reach the Villa Amabile, which hangs like an immense wedding-cake above the huddled blue and white and pink and yellow houses of the Grande Marina.

"Where was it you met Duncan Maxwell?" Nigel Dawson was enquiring in his voice of enthusiastic languor.

"Why, I had the good fortune to meet him in Munich where he is collecting material for a monograph on the snakes of Bavaria," the bottle-nosed philosopher intoned in a nasal treble. "On hearing that I was looking for a place to work at my thesis on the origin of Evil, with which I hope to secure a chair of Moral Philosophy at one of our universities, he had no hesitation in recommending Sirene. That is a very very intellectual man, Mr. Dawson. His mentality was far higher than any mentality with which I came into contact during my unprofitable year at Oxford after I left Harvard."

"He's a very great friend of mine," said Nigel with a smile that came near to being a simper.

Nigel Dawson was a tall, slim, good-looking young man of about twenty-five, whose chief of many vanities was a desire to be taken for eighteen, in which he often succeeded. His mother, left a rich widow in Indianapolis, had brought him to Europe when he was twelve, and he had thrived on the cosmopolitan culture with which she had provided him at the hands of various tutors. His education had been disjointed, because Mrs. Dawson, who was gathering her rosebuds while she might, was capricious and apt to get rid of any tutor as soon as she noticed another she liked better. Only one of them indeed had lasted more than six months, and that was a half-caste Hawaiian whom she engaged in Honolulu on her way round the world and left there on her way back. It was from him that Nigel learnt to dance the hula-hula which was such a feature of parties on Sirene. Mrs. Dawson and her son had settled in the island when Nigel really was eighteen, and since then, though nobody had breathed a word against Mrs. Dawson, several people had hinted at the most extraordinary things about Nigel.

"I envy you that friendship, Mr. Dawson," said Follett earnestly. "Intercourse with such a man must be in the very highest degree stimulating."

"In fact we've only had one real quarrel, and that was when we explored Nepenthe last Summer."

"That must be a very interesting island too," said Follett, gazing through his pince-nez—the owl-eyed cult had not begun at this date—to where on the other side of the bay Nepenthe towered.

"Oh, it is most awfully interesting," Nigel agreed. "It's volcanic," he added, opening his eyes very wide. "We had such jokes about that when I *would* wear my lava-lava on the beach."

"I imagine that when Mr. Maxwell unbends he can be more than usually diverting," said Follett. "But you alluded to a quarrel? I hope you will not credit me with undue inquisitiveness, Mr. Dawson, if I enquire what you quarrelled over."

"It was over the windows."

"The windows?"

"Yes, Duncan *will* shut all his windows at night. He even sticks brown paper over them."

"You astonish me, Mr. Dawson, for I was so immensely struck by the unusual breeziness of his manner."

"And I used to get so stuffy I wanted to scream. I simply couldn't stand it any longer, and I broke the window with my toothbrush and two mosquitoes came surging in and stung Duncan. He was simply furious."

"That is not surprising, Mr. Dawson. Few insects are endowed by nature with such powers to irritate and even exasperate human beings as mosquitoes. I myself find their pertinacious buzzing excessively wearisome, though I am glad to say that something in my physical composition appears to be antipathetic to their appetite so that I am never actually bitten."

Nigel looked critically at his companion's nodulous face. Although it was his habit to shoot his arrows at all he met, he felt as unwilling as a mosquito to sting Follett. Yet here was a man who was making researches into the origin of Evil, and Nigel had an immense respect for Evil. It must be remembered that at this date psycho-analysis had not swept Europe like a mental influenza. At this date young men could not find out all about Evil as easily as they could find out all about piles or strictures. It still possessed for youth a romantic rather than a medical interest. Nigel could still sing with Swinburne, *Come down and redeem us from Virtue, Our Lady of Pain*. Old-fashioned though it must sound, it was genuinely thrilling for him to feel he was tottering on the brink of the Bottomless Pit. The possibility, however faint, that he might spend eternity in such a location provided him with a *frisson* that no endopsychic censor is capable of providing. In spite of Austin Wilbraham Follett's bottle-nose, in spite of his nasal and monotonous treble voice which grated with extra harshness on the ears of an Europeanized American, in spite of his gawkiness and light orange hair, Nigel longed to tempt him with all that was evil in himself and to expose his very soul for the philosopher's dissection, for at this date he had no suspicion that his own subtle and passionate temperament was merely the result of infantile wind.

"Several people have said that I reminded them of the Narcissus in the Naples Museum," he told Follett, hoping that the elfin charm once attributed to him by a sentimental English exile in Naples had lost none of its potency.

"Well, of course, you certainly are both clean-shaven," the philosopher allowed judicially.

Nigel felt that the elfin charm had not worked as well as usual. So he tripped ahead of his companion down the wide steps, waving his arms bacchically.

"I feel so full of life sometimes that I just have to leap like that," he said winningly to Follett when the latter overtook him sitting by the roadside which intersected the stairway about a hundred yards below. "And aren't these flowers *too* wonderful?" he exclaimed, waving a posy of yellow wood-sorrel he had gathered. At this moment one of the carriages on the way down to the Nortons passed, and Nigel leaping to his feet ran beside it and showered the blossoms on old Mrs. Pape who was inside with Angela Pears. Then he turned back to join Follett again and to receive from him the flattery to which he was accustomed. But the philosopher was more anxious to find out who were the ladies in the carriage.

"Mrs. Pape?" he repeated. "Mr. Maxwell did not give me a letter of introduction to her."

"He doesn't give letters of introduction to everybody," Nigel said pettishly. "He gave you one to me because I'm one of his greatest friends."

The philosopher was glad to be assured of this again. When Nigel had leapt forward down the steps and waved his arms bacchically, he had been inclined to wonder if Mr. Maxwell had not been playing a joke on him.

"Mrs. Pape is a nice old thing," Nigel explained. "Very rich and always taking people up. She's thoroughly benevolent."

"That's mighty good hearing," said Follett.

"She has protégés," Nigel continued languidly. "She collects them in America during the Winter and brings them over to Sirene every Spring."

"Was the young lady seated beside her one of her protégés?"

"Good gracious, no. That was Angela Pears, the granddaughter of old Simon Pears."

"Our American poet?" Follett asked, an unusually low note of reverence in his voice.

"If you call *him* a poet," Nigel answered scornfully, "I suppose you'd even call Longfellow a poet."

"Why, I certainly would."

"Good gracious!"

They walked on in silence for awhile, Nigel wondering how a man who thought Simon Pears a poet could possibly suppose that he should be able to discover the origin of Evil, and the philosopher wondering how he could express without discourtesy to Duncan Maxwell's letter of introduction what he thought of snobbish young Europeanized Americans who had the impudence to suppose that Simon Pears was not a poet.

"Has Mrs. Pape any protégés with her this season?" the philosopher enquired to break an awkward silence.

"Yes, but they're all deaf and dumb."

"Deaf and dumb?" Follett gasped.

"Mrs. Pape brought over three deaf and dumb girls this Spring because she wanted them to see Italy. She has them staying with her at the Villa Eolia, but she doesn't take them out to parties yet."

Nigel was giving his information sulkily. He wanted to talk about himself, not Mrs. Pape's latest protégés. It was just like Duncan Maxwell to plant this bottle-nosed bore on Sirene while he himself was away in Bavaria. He was probably chuckling over his letters of introduction at this moment. Wait till he came back. He should have a good dose of Mr. Austin Wilbraham Follett himself.

"And tell me about our hostesses this afternoon, Mr. Dawson?"

Nigel groaned with rage.

"Oh, they were schoolmarms somewhere in the Middle West and they came into money. At least one of them did. They aren't really sisters. One's Miss Virginia Pepworth and the other's Miss Maimie Norton. But they call themselves Pepworth-Norton. It's all *much* too complicated to explain on such a hot afternoon," he sighed.

"If you'll pardon me one moment, Mr. Dawson, I'll take a few notes in my pocket-book. I find it's rather confusing to meet so many people all at once. Have they been resident in Sirene long?"

"I never take notes in pocket-books," said Nigel savagely. "So I'm afraid I can't possibly tell you *how* long they've been here."

The steps crossed the road again, and another carriage rattled by, in which was seated a monumental man with a white moustache and globular eyes, looking straight in front of him.

"And who is that?"

The philosopher was merciless.

"That's Anthony Burlingham. He's an Englishman who lives up at Anasirene with a grand piano on which he practises Chopin day and night. He used to be in the British Dragoons and had . . ." Nigel hesitated. One of the blows to his cosmopolitan pride was his inability to name anybody's income without turning it into dollars and back. "He had £60,000 a year."

"Three hundred thousand dollars. Some income," Follett observed.

"Yes, I suppose it would be three hundred thousand dollars," Nigel murmured coldly. "But he hasn't three thousand dollars a year now. Have you made a note of that?" he asked maliciously. "Because here we are at the Nortons."

The Villa Amabile with its domes and minarets and pinnacles, its loggias and terraces and porcelain-tiled pergolas, appeared beside the road just as Peppino's carriage arrived with Mrs. Dawson, Mrs. Neave, and Major Natt.

"Oh, how do you do, Mrs. Neave?" said Nigel with now an elaborate but quite unenthusiastic languor. "I want you to know Mr. Follett. He's *so* anxious to find out who all the people in Sirene are. So *do* tell him because I'm *simply* tired to death after toiling down all those steps."

"Why, I'm so pleased to meet you, Mr. Follett," she said warmly. "You come from Harvard, I hear." Her eyes shone with hero-worship. *She* would not mind how many questions the philosopher asked, for she loved answering questions, and she looked forward to a really delightful afternoon with this combination of Harvard and inquisitiveness.

Chapter 2

quamvis . . .
et versentur adhuc intra penetralia Vestae.

HORACE

YEARS ago Colonel Orestes Pepworth, the father of Miss Virginia, commanded the garrison of one of the forts in the north-west territories of the United States in the days when Indians still went on the war-path occasionally. He had become a widower early in his married life, and his only daughter lived with him out there, independent of all except the roughest schooling, from the time she was fourteen until she was close on twenty. Tradition (not the tradition of Sirene which gave her a dozen much humbler origins) relates that she was an accomplished, bold, impetuous, but rather cruel horsewoman, and that like an Atalanta of the prairies she was always inviting which of her father's young officers could to overtake and win her. None of them ever succeeded in catching up with her swift white steed, or if any one of them did Virginia must have gone back on her word and flouted him, for when the Colonel retired from military service and brought his daughter to live with him in Washington, D.C., she was heartfree, contemptuously heartfree indeed, and apt to boast of it.

Nobody who visited the Villa Amabile ever had the luck to come across an early portrait of Miss Virginia. If any such existed they were kept under lock and key. It was much likelier, however, that the old lady had destroyed all the evidences of her outward youth, because her indomitable spirit, refusing to accept age, would hate the past as ruthlessly as she hated everything that did not accord with what she was determined the present should be. But nobody who had sat at her table in the Villa Amabile and seen that tall old lady, now a year or two over seventy, with her figure as slim and her form as upright as a girl's, fanning herself Winter and Summer with a fan of painted chicken-skin, and tricked out with furbelows and frills and a sweeping train of old lace, so that her countenance like an eagle's carved from ivory sprang sharp and surprising out of what appeared an overwhelming mass of feminine decoration, nobody who had seen her thus and heard her at the end of a riotous night exclaim when, still fanning herself, she was taking leave of her guests about four o'clock in the morning, " Oh dear, I hate to have folks go! My sakes! Why do perfectly good parties come to an end? Why can't we go on enjoying ourselves for ever? " would not have vowed that she had once been beautiful as a rosy cloud wraith of the Sirene dawn that was breaking now above the villa. And he who believed the authentic story of her girlhood against the pinchbeck confusion of Sirene inventions was fain to picture her galloping over the boundless prairie, and hard on her horse's flowing tail a troop of young officers, every one of them with silky whiskers and every one looking like the faded photograph of Christopher Goldfinch when he was serving in the Federal forces, which he, less proud but more vain than she, always showed his friends.

When Miss Virginia was twenty-three, her father adopted the daughter of a distant cousin who had died in poverty. Maimie Norton was eight years old when she entered the Pepworth family, and from that hour she was the absorbing concern of Miss Virginia's life. It may be that in her refusal to be separated for a moment from her little cousin Miss Virginia did open some kind of a school so that the child's education could be carried on without a parting. Sirene tradition would not be shaken over the school, and yet it must be insisted that neither the spelling of the two old ladies nor their attitude toward life provided the least support for a schoolmarm origin. One would have preferred to believe the story that gave them a beginning in a small-town general store. Anyway, whatever their livelihood, the two cousins grew dearer each to the other than most sisters could have ever grown. They could not bear to be considered anything but actual sisters, and with a passionate sentimentality they hyphenated their two surnames to become Miss Virginia and Miss Maimie Pepworth-Norton. It will be noticed that Miss Virginia gave the prominence to Miss Maimie's name, as if their alliance was to be something even more vital than a marriage in which the name of the wife was lost. Some people, who knew that they were not really sisters, attributed the double name to a kind of pretentiousness. How remote such people were from understanding those two spinsters!

About the year 1890, when Colonel Orestes Pepworth had long been dead, a sum of money came unexpectedly to his daughter from the sale of some land required by a projected railway in Idaho, and from that date onward every year more money came in from unirrigated land which forty or fifty years earlier the Colonel had bought for a trifle. Soon after the first addition to their hitherto small income Miss Virginia and Miss Maimie decided to travel in Europe, and in the course of that trip they visited Sirene. They had no sooner put foot on the island than they recognized that they were at home. The kaleidoscope which had been revolving ever since they sailed from New York had ceased to move. The bright bits of glass that were themselves chinked, and as they fell into place the pattern of their future life was created. They stayed in the old-fashioned Albergo Odisseo, from the *terrazza* of which overhung by an immense wistaria they perceived in the middle of a vineyard that occupied the sloping ground above the inn a small house with three shallow white domes.

"Oh, my," Miss Virginia cried, "wouldn't I just love to settle down in that cunning little cottage while we're still young?" Miss Virginia was then already fifty-six, but Miss Maimie was a mere forty-one.

They made enquiries about the cottage and the land round it, which occupied the whole of the angle formed by the last bend of the road down from the Piazza to the Grande Marina and the tiny port of the island. While they were wondering how they could possibly manage to find money enough to buy the property, news came from America of a fresh addition to their capital.

"Well, I don't know that I ever felt nearer to believing in God than I do at this moment," Miss Virginia declared.

Miss Maimie shook her head. She had no more belief in God than her sister had, but she did not think that it was quite respectable to talk about it so lightly. Miss Virginia's paganism always sounded a little bit frivolous to Miss Maimie, who put into her scepticism the fervour of a narrow and positive creed. But then Miss Maimie had read Colonel Ingersoll's wonderful book and often used to wish that she could argue about it with the Pope—really seriously.

So, the cottage with the three white domes was bought, and thence onward every year the Misses Pepworth-Norton, as in all their invitations—and these were very many—they called themselves, added something to the original building. In some years, when the Colonel's lucky land investments added more than usual to their money, they would build a large and elaborate loggia or two extra rooms; in another year they would be content with hanging glass bunches of grapes to mask the electric bulbs in one of the many pergolas. How they loved light, those old ladies! On evenings when there was a *festa* (none of their parties was awarded a less inclusive name by the Sirenesi) you would stroll from the Piazza on to the columned terrace of the funicular and see five hundred feet below beyond a tangle of orchards and vineyards that the Villa Amabile was ablaze from the pinnacle of the tallest minaret to the humble little gate at the bottom of the garden by which Micheluccio, the owner of the original cottage, disposed of extra vegetables and flowers on his own account. Like so many of the resident *forestieri* in Sirene Miss Virginia and Miss Maimie in addition to buying the property had bought the owner of that property and his family at the same time. They thought it delightful to bring up Micheluccio's sons and daughters one after another to wait at table; at the date of this tea-party to meet Count Marsac, they had already dressed up fat little Agostino aged nine in a white sailor-suit to hand round a dish of cakes, while his elder brothers also in white sailor-suits handed round larger dishes, and his great fat sister Rosina dressed in vivid scarlet handed round the tea. Micheluccio and his family lived in the original cottage which was now buried two and three stories deep by loggias, rooms, towers, and minarets. There was too, separated from the villa, a pleasant little *foresteria* covered in Spring with the yellow trumpets of bignonia flowers, so that if bachelors ever came to stay with them they might be able to feel completely at their ease and not oppressed by the perpetual company of two old maids. Miss Virginia and Miss Maimie made two or three barrels of wine from their own grapes, which cost about four times as much a bottle as the wine they bought already made, but perhaps tasted all the better to the old ladies for that reason. Every two or three years Miss Virginia and Miss Maimie spent a few months in America, not to forget the old folks, as Miss Virginia always said. They used to return primed with the latest slang which must have sounded very inappropriate on their lips to compatriots, inappropriate and perhaps a little shocking. But how glad they always were to be back in the sunshine of their beloved Sirene, and with a *festa* of what boundless prodigality they used to celebrate the occasion.

Of course, they had their quarrels. The expulsion of Mr. Bookham from their friendship was an instance of their fierce side. There had been an Italian lawyer, too, who had swindled them over several transactions. For a long time they refused to listen to a word of warning about him from anybody; but when in the end they discovered his knavery they proceeded against him mercilessly and did not relax their vengeance till he was a broken man sitting in a frayed overcoat over a charcoal brazier in a great bleak barrack of a room and gambling miserably for coppers at one of those incomprehensible Italian card-games. It was Miss Virginia who was considered by most people to be the ruthless one, and to be sure it was always she who did the open fighting; but those who knew Miss Maimie said that she was really more unforgiving than Miss Virginia, and that it was she who provided the fuel for the older woman's flames. Even as they were merciless with passion and hospitable with passion, so too were they generous with passion. No peasant or fisherman appealed to their charity but was granted it; and the bad pictures they had bought from the Sirene painters for sums far in excess of what they were worth or of what they received from other patrons covered the walls of the Villa.

They are dead now—Miss Virginia with her ivory eagle's countenance and eternally fluttering fan, Miss Maimie with her tight intolerant mouth and high cheekbones, her defiant smouldering eyes and her Quaker air. The Villa Amabile stands like a vast wedding-cake that has turned grey and dingy in a shop-window, and there is no sound within those rooms still crowded with inappropriate furniture, still hung with the pink and pale blue ribbons and muslin with which the old ladies were wont to bedeck Gothic windows and Doric columns and Norman arches, no sound within except the chirping of the two canaries which have outlived them. They both lie in the same sprawling rococo tomb which is almost a replica in miniature of their own villa.

The wind sighs in the rusted cypresses all around them instead of the mandolins they used to love; and about four o'clock of a summer day the towering bulk of Monte Ventoso casts a shadow upon their tomb and upon the Villa Amabile a few hundred yards below. It was at this hour that Miss Virginia used to emerge upon her favourite loggia and drink in the *maestrale* that was flecking the azure bay with caps of foam, drink in the welcome coolness of the summer breeze and sigh, " Oh, Maimie, doesn't Vesuvius look a great old boy this afternoon, and my! isn't it good to be alive in this real Italian weather, honey?" And through the romanesque window that is cut in the wall of the cemetery behind their tomb the *maestrale* still blows in upon the last resting-place of those two passionate old ladies.

There was nothing elegiac about the Villa Amabile this afternoon in May once upon a time before the war. Miss Virginia and Miss Maimie were planning to build no tomb as yet, but a summerhouse that was to be an exact replica of the Temple of Vesta. They had spent the month of March in Rome on their way back from America, and guide-book in hand they had explored the city thoroughly. But of all that they saw there they liked the Temple of Vesta most.

"Well," Miss Virginia had exclaimed when they alighted from their carriage and surveyed the relic, "did you ever see a cuter little temple anywhere? Why, it doesn't look like a temple, Maimie. It looks more like a cunning little tea-house. If that isn't just the loveliest little temple . . . what does it tell us about it in the guidebook?"

And while Miss Virginia stood fanning herself under the cloudless Roman sky of March, Miss Maimie read to her a brief account of the Vestal Virgins, of their house in the Via Sacra, and of this innermost fane so many times burnt and rebuilt.

"The circular podium is about ten feet high, and consists mainly of concrete with some foundations of tufa blocks which may belong to the original building. Recent excavations have disclosed a pit in the middle of the podium . . ."

"Well, what is this podium anyway?"

"That's what the book says."

"Why they can't write a guidebook for simple folks without using such crazy words beats me. Read on a bit, honey," said Miss Virginia with a sweep of her fan.

"In the time of Pliny the tholus over the cella—symbolizing the canopy of Heaven—was covered with Syracusan bronze. It's position near the Temple of Castor is mentioned by Martial."

"It is?" Miss Virginia exclaimed sarcastically. "Well, that won't help us any if old Martial doesn't tell us what a tholus is any more than this stupid guidebook."

At this moment a handsome fair young man with rosy cheeks drew near the ladies and, raising his hat, begged in English with a strong French accent to know if he could be of any help.

"Why, you certainly can," said Miss Virginia smiling upon him. "We're just dying to know what a podium is and what a tholus is. We think this is just the sweetest little temple we ever did see, but we don't care one bit for the crazy names."

The young Frenchman, who was extremely voluble, was delighted to give the two ladies all the information he had.

"Oh, a tholus is just a dome? Do you hear that, Maimie? It's just an old dome the same as we've got at the Villa Amabile. And oh, wouldn't it be lots of fun to put up a little Temple of Vesta in our garden? We'd have it just at the end of the new pergola, and when we didn't have folks to tea we might sit under it and drink our tea together. I guess wood alcohol will make an elegant sacred fire."

"I think that is an excessively original idea, Madame,"

said the young Frenchman enthusiastically. "May I present you with my card? And if I can be of any assistance to you in Rome, *je suis à vous*."

Miss Virginia had long outlived her contempt for young men, and she smiled most graciously on the stranger's polite suggestion.

"You will permit me to offer you my card, madame?"

Miss Virginia read *Comte Marsac* and looked up to smile again.

"Why, I'm sorry to say I haven't a card with me, but I'm Miss Pepworth-Norton and this is Miss Maimie Pepworth-Norton and we live on the island of Sirene."

The Frenchman's bright blue eyes danced.

"You are fortunate indeed, mademoiselle. One of my ambitions is to visit Sirene. Indeed I was projecting to visit that *île enchantée* very soon with my friend and secretary Signor Carlo di Fiore."

As the Count spoke a young Italian like Antinous drew near and was presented to the two ladies, who were by no means dismayed when they found he hardly knew a word of English.

"Never mind," said Miss Virginia. "We can understand quite a lot of Italian, because we've lived in Italy getting along for twenty years now. Bella Italia!" she added encouragingly to young di Fiore.

"*Grazie, signora*," he replied with a low bow.

"Oh, Miss Maimie and I, we're just wild about Italy. Isn't that so, Maimie?"

"We certainly are."

"And though we've enjoyed so much seeing Rome we're just pining to be back in our beloved Sirene."

Thus lightly began the famous friendship between Count Marsac and the Misses Pepworth-Norton.

The Count invited them to dine with him at his hotel, a courtesy which they returned by giving him a magnificent dinner at theirs. They discovered that he was a great deal richer than they were, and by this time they were rich enough themselves, thanks to Colonel Orestes Pepworth's investments in land all those years ago. Their new friend assured them that he was tired of Paris, tired of cold and damp and grey skies, and that he was thinking of building himself a villa somewhere in the South. They told him that he must not dream of settling anywhere but in Sirene, and promised him the warmest of weather every day and the warmest of welcomes from everybody. For a week they drove all over Rome and motored to many places in the neighbourhood, listening with the greatest eagerness to Marsac's ceaseless waterfall of information, and smiling the fondest agreement with his rhapsodies about the Campagna as a setting for Carlo's pastoral beauty.

"Well, I think the Count's just a lovely man," said Miss Virginia to Miss Maimie.

And Miss Maimie, who was much less easily moved to enthusiasm, agreed glowingly. Miss Maimie herself was close on sixty now, but the irruption into her life of the handsome young Frenchman (whose father had been half a Dane it turned out, which accounted for his being so much easier to get on with than a full-blooded Frenchman might have been) had rekindled in her eyes the fire of youth. She listened entranced to the tales of his ancestry, flushed crimson when he spoke of a great-great-grandfather on his mother's side who had been a love of the Queen of France, and let his words flower like the golden lilies of his country's flag, for of course Count Bob—thus he became to them in a week—was a royalist. To him the tricolour was a gaudy absurdity. Not merely was he a count of ancient lineage; but he was also the chief owner of immense steel-works on the north-east frontier. Not merely was he an industrial magnate; but he was also a poet. Indeed, besides presenting them with two volumes of verse exquisitely printed on hand-made paper he wrote a sonnet to his new friends, in which he drew a beautiful picture of finding by the Temple of Vesta two of the Sacred Virgins revisiting after many transmigrations their ancient shrine. And he was not yet twenty-five years of age. They admired too so much the way he treated his young Italian secretary.

"He's just a lovely man," said Miss Virginia. "Why, Carlo might be his young brother, the way dear Count Bob looks after him. I'm just mighty glad we took this trip to Rome."

The old ladies went back to Sirene where they set to work at once to build in their garden a model of the Temple of Vesta with plans that the Count had secured for them in Rome.

And now it was the first of May, and the Count, who had dined with them quietly on the night of his arrival, was coming to tea this afternoon at the Villa Amabile to meet all their dear Sirene friends.

Chapter 3

tempus vocandis . . . amicis.
                        AUSONIUS

WHAT the oboe does for an orchestra the American accent not used to excess can do for the sound of conversational chatter that one hears on arriving at a house where a party is in full progress. A whole orchestra of oboes would be as pungent as a roomful of American voices, but judiciously employed the instrument adds a relish which no other can provide. At the Villa Amabile this Sunday afternoon, although the composer had certainly used the oboe generously, the symphony of conversation had a refreshing absence of monotony for anybody accustomed to the gurgling clarinets of an English party or the welter of tenor brass instruments at an exclusively Italian gathering.

The Norton girls, as Duncan Maxwell had nicknamed them, always took care that the food and drink should hold its own in variety and extravagance with the mixture of nationalities they loved to entertain. In most English houses that you visit for tea on Sunday afternoon you are given tea regardless of the fact that you may prefer coffee. You are offered a piece of bread and butter that feels like a damp handkerchief, and sometimes, when cucumber is added to it, like a wet one. There will be two or even three sorts of cake, after you have helped yourself to one of which you will usually wish that you had fumbled in the storeys of the curate's joy for another kind. And that will be your

VESTAL FIRE

tea unless you stay on long enough for your hostess to bribe you to go with a cocktail. In a French house you may get offered port wine and sugar-coated biscuits as an alternative to tea, and in an American house you will always be given a small napkin in addition; but though you will get this you will seldom get anything that resembles tea as you have always known it, and you will remember without surprise the way the people of Boston threw all their tea into the harbour. Ah, but at the Villa Amabile! Yes, you began with triangular napkins, but there the resemblance to any other kind of tea-party in the world ended; and if you had been to tea at the Villa Amabile before you did not wave away the offer of a plate, a fork, and two spoons. You knew very well that the inconvenience of sitting on a chair hardly more substantial than a spider's web and trying to manage on your own little white table a plate, a fork, two spoons, a cup, a saucer, and a napkin would be worth the trouble. You knew that the éclairs of the Villa Amabile would effuse authentic cream and not discharge stale custard like those dreadful waistless middle-aged éclairs you had met in some houses. When you had eaten so many cream cakes that you felt you really must have a drink of water, behold, you were handed a glass of water. Then podgy little Agostino solemnly removed your china plate, and Peppino, his elder brother, presented you with a crystal one, after which fat Rosina carved you an enormous slice of a praliné ice and Costanzo, the eldest brother, suggested a huge piece of sponge-cake that looked like an ottoman on which to rest the tongue from time to time. And when the ice was finished there was crême de menthe frappé, tall, tall glasses of it filled with crushed emeralds. Then Miss Maimie took you round the garden and, because you had to walk up and down several flights of marble steps owing to the slope of the land, when you came back and sank into one of the comfortable wicker chairs that strewed the large terrace paved with tiles of orange porcelain there was as much restorative whisky and soda as you cared to drink.

And on that shady terrace you expanded. You expanded physically owing to the amount you had eaten and drunk; but thanks to the classic beauty of the scene and the Sirenian conversation, which was nearly always sapid and certainly never vapid, you expanded in many other directions as well. You expanded æsthetically as you gazed across a Bay of Naples that was behaving as such famous views usually behave only in railway-posters. You expanded historically as you tried to remember what exactly Nero did at Baiæ, or was it Caligula you asked yourself, and in your mind's eye you rebuilt Minerva's temple on her cape. You looked up at the conical hill of Tiberius on the summit of which, a thousand feet up, you saw the yawning cellars of what had been his mightiest residence, and muttering over to yourself as many lines as you could remember of Shelley's sonnet on Ozymandias you bowed your head before the triumph of time and sipped your whisky. You looked up to where five hundred feet above you beyond the lemon-gardens and lush young vines the Piazza with its baroque tower and crowd of little people like dragon-flies glittered in the clear afternoon air, and you expanded morally, that is you became more elastic. You decided that if there were any mortal follies for which the sun of Sirene was insufficient excuse there was none for which the sun and moon together would not have to bear all the blame.

You looked at Archibald Macadam, who, after a successful social career at Cambridge and a few years of administrative work in the Far East, had come to Sirene and decided there to drink away the rest of his life on his own small income. There might have been times when you had been bored by Macadam's loquacity in Zampone's Café, or when after a dinner party you had had to lead him home and call upstairs to his wife that you would leave Archie sitting on the umbrella-stand till she could get down to attend to him. But at the Amabile you were inclined to think that he had ordered his end wisely.

Archie Macadam was in the Nortons' big *salone* this afternoon, and the two old ladies, who loved nothing so much as to give people what they wanted, loved to give him all the brandy he could drink. This afternoon he had arrived at the stage of well-oiled subtlety when the riddle of the universe appears so perfectly simple to oneself that one longs to explain the Theory of Relativity. In those days the theory had not been invented, so Macadam was trying to get up an argument with Austin Follett whether the monkey goes round the pole or the pole goes round the monkey. Follett, whose politeness will have been noticed, was looking as solemnly interested as if he were listening to a profound exposition of Manicheism that might have been of service to his thesis on the origin of Evil.

"What you observe, Mr. Macadam, is very interesting."

"It is," Macadam agreed gloomily. He was a tall cleanshaven man of the explorer type, always very neatly dressed. "It is interesting, because it's unanswerable. What is unanswerable must by the nature of things be more interesting than what is answerable. Take God for instance. You see what I'm driving at? Of course you do. Well, that's exactly what I mean about this problem of the monkey and the pole."

During this last speech of Macadam's Follett was aware that somebody was digging him in the ribs to an accompaniment of suppressed chuckles. He did not dare to withdraw his eyes from Macadam's glassy stare, because he had reached the point, which one often reaches in an argument with a drunken man, of supposing that it would be extremely imprudent to do so. However, the digs and chuckles became so insistent that at last he had to turn round and risk Macadam's catching him a crack on the head with the decanter. He then discovered that his neighbour was Mrs. Ambrogio, to whom he had been introduced when he came in.

Mrs. Ambrogio was a handsome woman of about forty, ample in the style of feminine beauty that was so much admired when King Edward VII was Prince of Wales. She was the type that used to look so queenly in silver and plush photograph-frames on the occasional tables of houses untainted by æstheticism. Indeed, there were people to assure you that as a young woman she was a rival of the Jersey Lily herself. There was an element of mystery about her which Mrs. Ambrogio, had she wanted to, was incapable of dispelling, because she was incapable of stringing together a sufficiently intelligible long sentence. She had certainly been married before, but whether she divorced her husband or he divorced her, whether she had been a widow when she married Pietro Ambrogio, a Neapolitan lawyer practising in Sirene, or whether she had eloped from England with him nobody on the island had ever discovered. There were twenty legends in Sirene of her origin, which varied from the unrepeatable to the faintly suggestive.

"Talk to me. Talk to me," she spluttered to Follett, her bottlegreen dress of moiré silk swishing an accompaniment to her bubbling ejaculations which issued as from a syphon that from time to time jams and fizzes impotently. "Can't stand Americans. Hate Americans. Not the dear Miss Nortons of course. Bless their hearts, the darling old pets!" This was delivered at the top of her voice, and turning round she blew three or four resonant kisses across the room to where Miss Virginia was fluttering and hovering over each little tea-table like a big pearly moth, and where Miss Maimie with eager watchful eyes was piloting fat Rosina with a tray of crème de menthe. "Hate Americans," she continued, swishing round again to Follett. "Always hunted when I was young. Go over anything. Show you my picture if you like in a riding-habit when I was a girl.

Considered jolly good-looking as a girl. Ugly as sin now. Can't help it. Must grow older. Married an Italian. Peter. Where is he? Want to introduce you to him. Gone out to look over the garden. Mad on gardens. Can't grow anything. Flowers never come up. Loves them just as much. Looks after them like a mother. Only honest lawyer in Italy. Don't know why. Stupid fool, I always tell him. But Peter can't help it. Never make any money. God knows what we shall do."

Macadam, who was not too drunk not to understand that his chance of discussing the problem of the monkey and the pole was gone, had risen rather unsteadily and crossed the room in search of another victim.

"Dear old Macadam! Bless his heart," exclaimed Mrs. Ambrogio, blowing a kiss after him. "Drinks like a fish. Love him just the same. Love all the English. English myself. Always a gentleman, poor old boy. Lives next door to Peter and me. Found him lying on his back in our front garden the other night. Too drunk to get up. Put on his hat and took it off again. Perfect manners. Said 'Good evening, Mrs. Ambrogio, I'm sorry I find myself unable to move out of your way. Would you mind stepping over me?' Always a gentleman. Drinks like a fish and never forgets his manners. Four bottles of brandy a day, but always a gentleman. Hate Americans. Can't stand Americans. Love the dear English. English myself."

"I fear that I have the misfortune to be an American, Mrs. Ambrogio," said Follett.

"Can't help it. Not your fault. Always speak my mind. Always offending people. No brains. Take it or leave it. Can't help it if they don't like me. Love the darling old Nortons."

"I certainly agree that the Miss Pepworth-Nortons must inspire a very great affection in all who have the good fortune to make their acquaintance."

"Love the old pets. *Love* them! Came here over forty

years ago before I was born. Miss Virginia fell in love with a coachman. Stole all her money and ran away. Tell you lots of stories about the foreigners here, but never talk. Peter's sake. Mustn't talk if you marry a lawyer. Used to talk a lot before I married dear old Peter. Never talk now. Bad for his business. Weren't you chatting to Mrs. Neave just now? *Dear* woman! Had an affair with Duncan Maxwell last year. Only repeat what other people tell me. Hate scandal. You walked down with Nigel Dawson. Such a dear boy! One of those. But what does it matter? Why shouldn't he be? Don't care what anybody is. Love everybody."

"I had the good fortune to meet Mr. Maxwell in Bavaria recently," said Follett.

"Isn't he a dear? I like him so much. If you hear that he steals people's geraniums, don't believe it. Don't believe anything you hear in Sirene."

"But why should people accuse a highly intellectual man like Mr. Maxwell of stealing their geraniums?" Follett asked in amazement.

"People here accuse you of anything. I was accused of keeping a disorderly house in Naples. Don't care what they say. Married the only honest lawyer in Italy, so don't care a damn what they say now."

"But geraniums?" Follett persisted.

"Building a house. Making a garden. Must get geraniums somewhere. Engaged three boys with spades and large baskets. Worked all night. Next morning all the geraniums in Sirene growing in Mr. Maxwell's garden. Other people's gardens nothing but feetmarks, footmarks, feetmarks. Don't know which you say. No grammar. No brains. Footmarks everywhere. Major Natt was so angry. That's Major Natt over there. Like him so much. Mean as he can be. Such an old darling. Weighs out the sugar for the kitchen himself every morning. Has hundreds of naughty books. Wish I could read them. Can't read.

Love reading, but can't read. No brains. Let his villa this year—Major Natt, I mean—and the tenants kept chickens in the bathroom."

"Chickens?" Follett gasped. "Why, I could understand keeping ducks in a bathroom, but chickens . . ."

"No water. Driest place in the house. Major Natt cut off the water from the bathroom before he went away. Sells it to the *contadini* at ten centesimi a bottle. Goes to Switzerland every Summer to save money. Say he milks Swiss peasants' cows himself to save paying for his lunch. Don't believe a word of it. Don't you believe it. Such lies. Plenty of cherry brandy when you go there to tea. Love him. There's Peter!" She waved excitably, her face crimsoning, to a neatly dressed little Italian who came in from the garden at that moment. "Peter! Peter! Vous venn, Peter!" She turned back to Follett. "Always speak French to Peter. Peter can't speak English and I can't speak Italian. Servants understand me perfectly and I understand them. Peter made love to my dear Assunta. Turned her out at once. Wouldn't stand it. Caught him kissing her and he said he was spongeing the statue of Venus. Such lies. Hate lies! Most truthful woman in Sirene. Peter! Vous venn! Vous venn!"

The little lawyer approached and was presented by his wife to the American.

"Peter, this is Mr.—didn't hear your name. Never hear names. Doesn't matter. Forget them if I did. No brains."

"Follett."

"This is Peter. That's bang, Peter. Vous va. Parling to Mr. Folly—Fuller—Filly. Vous va. Vous va."

The little lawyer, who somehow understood from this that his wife was engaged in conversation and that he was to go away, again bowed courteously and retired.

"I love my Peter, bless his heart," she cried warmly. "Loves me too, but can't resist fat girls. Can't help it.

Too excitable. Pants. Always know. 'Peter,' I say, and I give him such a look. Went to Mrs. Neave's last week. Thought he was pinching her Carmela. Pinched me instead. How I laughed! Serve him right. All Napolitans the same. Come back to Sirene black and blue after a day's shopping in Naples. There's dear old Mrs. Pape. Kindest woman in Sirene. Brought six blind old women from America to see the island this Summer. Heart of gold."

"Oh, I understood from Mr. Dawson that they were three deaf and dumb girls."

"Perhaps they were. So kind. Rolling in money. Frightfully delicate. Five months child. Brought up in a kind of aquarium and fed with a squirt."

Follett gazed at old Mrs. Pape whose high-domed benevolent head was nodding in amicable conversation with the nebulous and deferential Mr. Cartright, an English painter from Anasirene.

"That's poor old Cartright. Don't care for him much. Painted his wife naked and sent her to the Academy, but don't believe he beat her to death as everybody says. Can't get naked girls in Sirene now. Priests won't let them. Quite right. Can't trust painters. Any excuse. Love my Church. Not a Protestant, thank God. Love my Church. Kept me from going wrong. Sit there in the hot weather. Lovely and cool. Wonder when this French count's coming. Don't believe he's a count at all."

At this moment Miss Virginia called for silence, because Mr. Burlingham had so very kindly consented to play for them.

The monumental man who had passed Follett and Nigel Dawson in a carriage earlier that afternoon rose and proceeded toward the piano.

"So like a policeman," Mrs. Ambrogio whispered. "Used to be in the dragoons. Masses of money. Spent it all on . . ." She stopped. "Don't know you well enough yet to say what he spent it on. Hardly any money left, but still spends it on the same thing."

"I'll play the Polonaise in A," Burlingham announced stolidly, unfastening his big cuffs and turning them back over his sleeves.

"Oh, my dear, how too utterly divine," breathed Nigel Dawson.

Burlingham paid no heed to this ecstasy, but after brushing back his white moustache and fixing the ceiling with his light blue globular eyes immediately began.

"Love music," said Mrs. Ambrogio. "Can't play, but love it. Listen to it for hours. Mr. Burlingham plays so beautifully. Always perspires. Watch his forehead. He'll begin in a minute. Love music. Wish I had a pianola. Can't afford it. Could have once. Always hunted every Winter in . . ."

And then Miss Maimie hushed her severely.

"Dear old soul," Mrs. Ambrogio exploded, blowing a kiss that came out like a champagne-cork.

But now Miss Maimie herself began to fidget, because the sound of carriage wheels was audible, and they must be the wheels of dear Count Bob's carriage. The Polonaise was working up every moment. Mr. Burlingham's globular eyes stared into vacancy. Would he ever forgive her rudeness if she rose and went down to meet the Count? Perhaps the music would stop in time. It surely must stop soon.

"Know he'll burst one hot afternoon," Mrs. Ambrogio declared to Follett. "Wish I could play like that. Get so melancholy sometimes when I think of dear old England."

Everybody had heard the carriage wheels, and everybody was hoping that the Polonaise would stop. Everybody felt that Chopin was a mistake when a rich French count was on the verge of entering Sirene society.

The white sailor-suit of Peppino appeared in the doorway on which every eye was turned. Miss Virginia and

Miss Maimie both hurried forward. The Polonaise swept on, and in came—not the Count, not his Antinous, but of all people in Sirene, beaming like a naughty rosy-cheeked boy, Joseph Rutger Neave.

His wife gave a faint scream.

"Joseph!" she gasped. "Did you take your medicine?"

"No, I didn't," he said, turning on her a cold glance of disapproval. "I felt much too well. Much too well."

No doubt Mrs. Neave was more taken aback than anybody else by this apparition of her husband, but everybody was suffering from the shock. Until this moment Sirene had felt safe against Joseph from half-past three till half-past six. One or two looked across the Bay toward Vesuvius. If Joseph Neave could forgo his nap, were they any longer safe from Vesuvius eighteen miles away? The only imperturbable person in the room was Burlingham, who brought the Polonaise to an end, swung round on his stool, drank a whisky and soda, swung round again, and began a Rhapsody of Brahms.

"Don't paw me about, Elsie," said her husband petulantly. "I'm perfectly capable of finding a chair for myself."

He looked round, smiling complacently and smacking his lips to search for suitable feminine companionship. He decided finally on Miss Dorothy Daynton, the seventeen-year-old granddaughter of old Henry Mewburn, formerly Professor of Italian at Cambridge, who lived with his unmarried daughter Beatrice and three bloodhounds in a large villa halfway up the Torrione. Dr. Mewburn himself was not at the Villa Amabile this afternoon, but Miss Beatrice was, and rather to Joseph's annoyance she came and sat on the other side of him when he took his place by little Dorothy. Beatrice Mewburn was a woman of about forty-five, who must have possessed an exquisite and frail beauty in the days when young women languished before a vase of lilies and dressed in loose green gowns.

She was still beautiful, but she had allowed time and the weather to beat her complexion into numberless fine wrinkles, and the loose gowns that might have become her slim youth looked dowdy now on the angularity to which that slimness had turned. Yet she still diffused on the sensitive observer a fragrance of the romantic 'eighties and made him think of early volumes of Browning he had come across marked here and there in a fine hand beside the poems with dates and the names of fair old towns like Ravenna or Assisi. Indeed, she resembled nothing so much as a roseleaf pressed between the pages of a book, and those who were privileged to enjoy her friendship and sit talking to her in the little study whose windows looked out across olive-orchards to the Salernian gulf never left her company without feeling the richer for it. The walls were crowded with the faded photographs of cinquecento pictures and reproductions of Della Robbia plaques, and the tops of her book-cupboards were thronged with the plaster casts of famous statues. You felt that she had drawn near to beauty along byways of her own and never travelled down the high-road of fashion. Like most people on Sirene she had her eccentricity. It was her habit to take the gloomiest view of everything. She loved to think that people were ill or unhappy or miserable, not because she yearned to sympathize with them or help them, and certainly not from any malice, but purely to indulge a mental luxury of her own. Joseph Neave could not bear her pessimism, which was extreme in the Villino Paradiso where she could revel in the gloomiest forebodings about his own health and at the same time sigh over the anxiety he must be causing to his poor wife, for whom she had a great affection, considering her to be on the whole the most worthy object of compassion in all Sirene.

"I don't think you ought to have got up this afternoon, Mr. Neave," she said in a voice that was like a coronach. "Poor Elsie will be so dreadfully worried. Anything might have happened to you on the way down. It was most lucky the horses didn't bolt."

"And how is little Miss Dorothy?" Joseph enquired, turning away from the aunt to the niece and smacking his lips.

"Not very well, thank you, Mr. Neave," she replied with what she hoped was an interesting and appealing voice.

"Poor little Dorothy," Miss Mewburn broke in with a deep sigh. "She's been feeling the sun a great deal. I do hope she'll get through the Spring without being seriously ill. She may, of course. I beg her to be careful, but she's so impetuous."

"Oh, Auntie," Dorothy protested with a giggle of self-consciousness.

"She *will* run about the garden with the dogs," Miss Mewburn sighed. "She quite wears herself out to give them a little pleasure. She's so unselfish."

"Talking of dogs, Miss Mewburn," said Joseph, "I had a remarkably interesting passage in my work this morning about dogs. You know when Dante . . ."

"*Signorine, signorine,*" Peppino came bursting in to announce. "*È arrivato il signor conte senza carrozza.*"

Immediately behind his herald sounded the self-assured voice of Marsac himself.

"May we come in? We are walking all the way. And I am afraid the temptation to spoliate the Sirene orchards was too strong."

Whereupon Marsac and the Antinous, each carrying branches laden with oranges, their brows garlanded with vine-leaves, marched into the room.

In some places such an entrance would prejudice the social success of newcomers. In Littlehampton or Bognor or in the Isle of Wight a French count, however young and handsome and however rich, would not create a good impression on the life of the place by making his first public appearance disguised like a pulpit at a harvest festival;

but once upon a time there was none of that kind of stuffiness in Sirene. Only about fifteen years before this date an English nobleman made a regular practice of walking down from Anasirene to pay visits in Sirene with nothing on but a top-hat. In fact the tenant of the Villa Parnasso, now owned by Scudamore the American scholar, had grilles put in the seven doors that gave ingress to its hallowed shades so that when she was having a tea-party she could inspect Lord G——'s attire before admitting him. And if any young unmarried girls were present nothing would induce her to let him in, which everybody used to think so sweet and old-fashioned of dear Mrs. W——. Then there was a Slovakian painter called Czcszckz who used to take off all his clothes and sit on the wall of Mrs. Pape's Villa Eolia, reading *The Little Flowers of St. Francis*. Even her benevolence could not stand this, and she sent for Beccafico the *guardia* to dress Czcszckz and take him away. As even in the coldest weather he only wore one of his wife's nightgowns, this should have been easy, but Beccafico had to chase him all over Sirene as a butterfly-hunter pursues his game before he managed to envelop him. Beccafico was so much exhausted by the chase that he drank even more wine than usual to restore himself, with the result that he lay supine for three days and three nights afterwards, during which time no less than six outrages against pudor of a much graver nature were committed in public, and the island was in worse repute than at any time since the days of Tiberius. In these days of course nothing like that could happen. Except for a few Bolsheviks who haunt with terra-cotta nudity the almost inaccessible coves at the foot of Monte Ventoso nobody offends against pudor, and all bathing-dresses must conform to the design approved by the *sindaco* and are not licensed until they have been measured with the municipal tape.

Carlyle once said that Herbert Spencer was the most unending ass in Christendom. He had not met the Count.

Yet Marsac's triumph in Sirene was immediate and conspicuous. People were so much fascinated by the unusual combination of wealth, youth, rank, and good looks that they received the volumes of his poems that he dealt round like a hand at bridge with more respect than they would have accorded to first folios of Shakespeare.

"So handsome," said Mrs. Dawson.

"Such a gentleman," said Joseph Neave.

"So young," said Mrs. Pape.

"And such an old title," said Mrs. Neave.

"So sympathetic," said Nigel Dawson.

"So English," said Mrs. Ambrogio, "and so glad he'll have dear old Peter to give him good advice."

"So intellectual," said Miss Mewburn, who really should have known better.

"Sound fellah," said Major Natt.

"So Latin," said Angela Pears.

"Such a man of the world," said Cartright, who had read Whittaker's Almanack right through, because it was the only book he had.

"So vital," said Ibsen—not the dramatist, but a ladylike Norwegian with the eyes of a pussy-cat, who was to be found wriggling and giggling in a corner of the Villa Amabile every Sunday afternoon.

"He's awfully fascinating," said little Dorothy Daynton.

"And so rich," Christopher Goldfinch declared with the sound of a great Amen.

When all the guests had gone Miss Virginia hugged Miss Maimie.

"Oh, honey, wasn't it a perfect party, and didn't all our dear Sirene friends love our dear boy?"

In spite of the Temple of Vesta whose columns were rising in the moonlight there was about the Villa Amabile that evening the atmosphere of a successful accouchement.

Chapter 4

*frater erat Romae consulti rhetor, ut alter
alteriu sermone meros audiret honores.*
HORACE

locus effusi late maris arbiter.

HORACE

WHEN Duncan Maxwell gave Austin Follett letters of introduction to the Pepworth-Nortons and to Nigel Dawson he gave him at the same time a third introduction which he insisted was the most valuable of all. This was a letter recommending the young philosopher to the good offices of Ferdinando Zampone. Nobody knew better what he was talking about on most subjects than Duncan Maxwell, but on the subject of Sirene he was pre-eminent. Zampone's Café was the focus of the island's life, and the stranger instinctively recognized its power when he saw its situation in a narrow street leading out of the Piazza. There was nothing here to attract the eye. Yet it was crowded with people—tourists, foreign residents, and natives —when the other cafés, with views of the Bay of Naples, neatly-dressed waitresses and reasonable charges, were empty. Inside it consisted of three or four long narrow tables and a dozen or so square ones. The walls were lined with groceries, bottles, and florid paintings of Sirene turned out half a dozen at a time to attract Germans, to whom they were sold like early tomatoes. Outside there was a small terrace raised a few feet above the level of the street and looking out through railings on a blank wall. This held half a dozen tables sheltered by a wistaria vine from the noon-day sun which shone down on them for an hour or two when immediately overhead. Outside the Café doors between his two crowded windows, sat old Don Luigi Zampone himself. He was a fat man in a grey alpaca jacket with a closely-trimmed beard and large hooked nose, and he wore a skull-cap that gave his personality a most definite suggestion of the ghetto. He had none of the joviality one expects from fat men, and even in the tone of his welcome to entering customers there was a kind of cynical contempt as if a huge spider whose web had long been overcrowded by flies was expressing his indifference to new customers. He had amassed wealth in youth by lending money and foreclosing on mortgages. To that wealth he had added by his conduct of the Café, and now he felt rich enough to build the large hotel with which he planned to ruin his lifelong rival Don Cesare Rocco, the owner of the Hotel Augusto. Three times a day he walked slowly up the hill and surveyed the progress of his mighty foundations; stared at the great wooden hoarding, on which was painted in immense letters HOTEL GRANDIOSO; looked down at the flat roofs of the Hotel Augusto; spat contemptuously; and returned slowly to his seat outside the Café, within which in the darkest corner at a table covered with ledgers sat his son Ferdinando, who though hardly out of his twenties was already fatter than his parent. Occupied apparently with the accounts of the business he was all the while being appealed to by the various foreigners for help and advice, which he gave with a quizzical brusqueness that was compounded of insolence, condescension, and good will. Some of his interrogators he fixed with bright dark eyes buried deep as currants in his great uncooked cake of a face; but while he was advising others those bright dark eyes seemed to be having a laughing colloquy with a spirit of irony that was hovering behind whatever Miss or Madame or Fräulein or Frau was consulting his omniscience. The clue to Ferdinando Zampone's character was that while he had inherited from Don Luigi cunning and cynicism and greed, his mother had mitigated those qualities with her own wisdom and benevolence. Donna Maria Zampone was indeed one of those classical figures of humanity that emerge from the shadowy profiles by which our memory is haunted, as a cartoon of Michelangelo would appear above a box of faded photographs. She sat in Zampone's Café as the sublime Demeter must once have sat in Cnidos. Her lineaments were not less noble, and if she was fat, as to be matter of fact she certainly was, it did not somehow convey the impression of superfluous flesh, but of draperies hammered out of Parian or Pentelican. Deep-voiced the Pythia of Delphi sounded in her chasm, and the voice of Donna Maria was deep and heavy and solemn, so that her simplest affirmative held the gravity of ancient wisdom, of elemental truth. And to receive from her hands a glass of vermouth was to drink deep from the prodigious breasts of Mother Earth.

Into Zampone's on this Sunday afternoon came Mr. Herbert Bookham the churchwarden, somewhat out of humour. He had just heard that this rich French count wanted to build a villa in Sirene, and owning as he did a most eligible site, he was wishing that he had not quarrelled with those two old harridans below. They would prejudice the stranger against him, and he might miss the chance of doing an excellent stroke of business. He pondered some way of effecting a reconciliation. He might, of course, as trustee of the Protestant cemetery, sell the plot Major Natt had bought for his grave to the Nortons. After all he had really only let Natt have it so cheap to annoy them. He could pretend to Natt that he had made a mistake, and give him the plot which the Macadams had chosen and not yet paid for. It might mean quarrelling both with Natt and the Macadams; but he should quarrel in any case with Natt, who would be sure to try to sell the Villa Capo di Monte to this Frenchman, and if he succeeded over Natt's head in selling him his land Natt would be jealous. He looked at the clock in Zampone's. Six. That damned chaplain would be wondering if he was coming to read the Lessons. He'd *give* him a lesson instead. The churchwarden was so pleased with his joke that he guffawed aloud, and Donna Maria who was nodding over the counter at the back of the shop woke up with a start and enquired "*Sis-signore?*"

"Niente, grartsi," Bookham hastily replied. One must draw the line somewhere on Sunday, and his boundary was buying himself a drink. He looked round for a paper, pen and ink, and began to sketch the draft of a letter:

Dear Miss Pepworth-Norton,
  I fear that our recent unfortunate misunderstanding left the question of your plot in the cemetery in abeyance. However, I am glad to be able to tell you that you can have the plot you originally chose for . . .

Bookham paused and laid down his pen. Perhaps it was the grey ink and the thinness of the paper that gave his unusually bold and confident handwriting this wambling, tremulous look. The old ladies were quite capable of taking his pacific overtures in the wrong spirit. He wished he could think of something more comfortable to bring himself and the Nortons together again than the site of their last resting-place and the price they were to pay for it. One did not want to offer a cypress-bough as an olive-branch. And here, puzzling over a road back to the Nortons' hearts, we may leave him for the present and return to the Villa Amabile where Marsac has just offered Follett a lift back in his carriage.

Michele, who had been denied the pleasure of expatiating to the Count on Sirenian objects of interest during the drive down, was determined to make up for it on the drive up. He much enjoyed airing his English, which the residents would never allow him to do, because they enjoyed even more airing their own Italian. Moreover, Michele was a reasonable man, and he would not have considered it reasonable to point out Vesuvius to people who had been living for twenty years in Sirene. He was a little hurt to find that his three passengers, all undoubtedly newcomers, were too much interested in their own conversation to pay proper attention to his information.

"Your quest in search of evil enchants me, Monsieur Follett," declared Marsac earnestly.

"I wouldn't have you misunderstand me, Count," the philosopher replied. "I am not actually searching for concrete instances of evil. My interest in it is purely metaphysical. I am engaged on a thesis with which I hope . . ."

"Surely here if anywhere," Marsac went on, paying no more attention to Follett's explanation of his interest in evil than to Michele's appeal to look at the island of Nepenthe rising like a great bronze on the other side of the Bay. "Surely here in this flowery island . . ."

"Apollonius Rhodius does call it Anthemoessa, you remember," Follett put in hastily.

Marsac brushed away Apollonius like a fly.

"Surely here where even now the *sirènes* chant their songs to those fortunate unfortunates who can hear them, surely here we may find anything. Myself I intend to make excavations in searching for the lost books of Elephantis. What villainy that these books into which the most poetic courtezan who has ever lived inserted all which she knew of her profession will be no longer at our service! I adore to think of the venerable Tiberius studying them in the seclusion of this *île enchantée* . . ." and so on till suddenly Michele swung round from the box as they were passing a rose-hung gateway and shouted:

"Anglish chimetery."

"Fine," acknowledged the Harvard philosopher, who was beginning to think Marsac a bore.

"Many Anglish and American deads inside," Michele commented, cracking his whip with a macabre relish. Then he added nonchalantly, pointing across the gilded azure of the Bay: "Vesuvio. Very nice."

"Bully," Follett agreed again, hoping that the diver would talk for the rest of the way and check Marsac's rhetorical egoism.

"What I demand for myself," the Count was beginning again, when Michele, who had been hesitating between the huge bulk of Monte Ventoso, the sheer precipices of which towered athwart the westering sun with a bloom on them like grapes, and the relatively commensurate bulk of Sirene's mayor who was walking meditatively down the road, chose the latter as an object of interest.

"The *sindaco* of Sirene," he informed his fares. "*Molto preoccupato*," he added when his salute had been ignored by the four chins resting upon their shirt-front. "Very thinkful. He must be elected again too much soon, and many peoples do not want of him."

"Why, how is that?" Follett asked.

Michele pulled in his horse, stood up, looked to right and left of him in the gardens on either side of the road, perceived nobody within earshot, leaned over and whispered hoarsely:

"Because he have eat all the money for making the roads."

"*Mais alors, assez!*" Marsàc exclaimed in irritation. "*Ah, mon dieu, que cet homme me rase!*"

His young secretary, who had been sitting in silence all the way, turned round and said something sharply in Italian to the driver, whereupon Michele slashed his Abruzzese cob across the crupper, so that in defiance of the ascent it leaped forward at a gallop. Notwithstanding the posterior discomfort that Follett experienced from the jolting he could endure the phrenetic shrieks of Michele urging his horse to greater exertion more easily than the verbosity of the Count. Still, the last lap along the level over the cobbles of the Strada Nuova, in spite of the radiant view of the two gulfs, was really excruciating. No wonder the Sirenesi were doubtful of re-electing the man responsible for this torture.

But when they all alighted in the Piazza, Marsac, leaving Carlo to settle with the driver, resumed inexorably:

"What I demand for myself and what even my *poésie* has not satisfyingly responded is the *but* of life. There are moments, I assure you, when I have demanded for myself the *courage* to find in death the answer to the eternal enema of life. You are a *philosophe*, Mr. Follett, and I envy your *point de vue*. Myself, I, alas, must deny myself the serenity which is for you. I toss upon a *ténébreuse* ocean of doubt. In the profondities of my being I have sometimes thought that I had founded the response to your quest. But the *illusion* passes, and once more I find myself gazing at life with the rictus of a deserted clown. *Enfin*, we shall be good friends, I hope, and I shall have extreme pleasure in uncovering for you the intimities of my temperament. . . ."

"I wonder if you'll excuse me, Count?" said Follett pausing outside the door of Zampone's. "I have to deliver a note in here."

But Marsac entered with him, and the philosopher, looking desperately round for help, rushed up to Herbert Bookham to whom luckily he had been introduced the day before.

"Mr. Bookham, I want you to meet Count Marsac, who is . . ."

The churchwarden asked for no testimonials. Crumpling up the half-written letter to the Nortons, he warmly shook Marsac's proffered hand.

"By Jove, I'm awfully glad you've looked in here. I've heard about you from everybody. Unfortunately I couldn't get down to the Nortons this afternoon."

His wavering eyes looked beyond the Count as he paused.

"Enchanted to make your acquaintance, monsieur. . . ."

Bookham breathed heavy relief. He was in time.

"Look here, do sit down and have a drink or something."

"You are very kind, monsieur. Permit me to present my friend and secretary Signor Carlo di Fiore."

"How d'ye do?" said Bookham with blusterous cordiality. "You're not a native of these parts?"

"My friend is a Roman," said Marsac haughtily.

"Oh, you come from Rome, do you? Jolly fine city, I always say. Now what's yours, Count? They give you a very decent glass of vermouth here. Hullo, where's our American friend gone?"

But Follett, deciding that he would try the effect of Duncan Maxwell's letter on Ferdinando Zampone some other time, had slipped away.

"I'm awfully glad I ran into you," Bookham declared, when the glasses were set out. "I always like to meet newcomers in Sirene as soon as possible, because I can generally help them a bit. Well, I've lived here now over fifteen years." Just then Bookham, with one of his mobile eyes, noticed that other guests from the Nortons were coming along to have their gossip before dinner.

"I say, let's have our drinks over into that corner, shall we? I think it's cooler over there."

He manœuvred his prey from the entrance to the furthest corner of the Café.

"Mustn't make ourselves too conspicuous," he explained jovially. "Don't mind telling you that I ought to be in church. Haw-haw! But you're a Roman Catholic, of course?"

"No, no, I am a Protestant," said Marsac.

"By Jove, are you? I say, I hope you'll look in sometimes at one of our little services. We get a chaplain here from November to the end of May. I'm afraid he's a dull dog this year, but I do my best to pull the thing through. But the collections have been shocking this Spring. I've been trying to raise the money to build a porch."

Marsac, who had been finding Bookham as tiresome as Follett had found him and as Nigel Dawson had found Follett, pricked up his ears. It occurred to him that it might create a good impression on Sirene society if he offered a porch to the English church as his first of many *beaux gestes*.

" I shall be most happy to offer you a perch, monsieur."

" No, not a perch, Count. Excuse my correcting you. A porch. Sort of thing with pillars you stick over a door."

" Yes, yes, I have understood that, monsieur. And I repeat that I shall be happy to offer you this porch."

" Oh, I say, that's much too good of you. Do you really mean that ? "

When Bookham had accepted what he called Marsac's princely gift he regretted that he had not mentioned the eligible building site before he began to talk about the porch. After all, the porch could easily have waited a few more years. What a fool he had been not to take advantage of the Count's impulse to please everybody by doing a little business on his own account. Of course, he would get a commission from Maestro Supino the builder, but that was a wretched trifle.

" You're thinking of building a villa, I hear, Count ? " he began.

" That is my ambition."

" I'd like to show you a beautiful piece of land with a magnificent view that I believe you might get fairly cheap."

" You are very gentle. Is it anywhere near to the ruins of the Villa of Tiberius ? "

" No, it's on San Giorgio, the other hill on that side of the island. I've lived up that way for ten years now, and I wouldn't change my view for anybody's in Sirene."

" I have an ambition to live near the Villa of Tiberius," Marsac insisted.

" Well, if you take my advice you won't," said Bookham earnestly. " There are more mosquitoes in that part of Sirene than anywhere. Now on San Giorgio, which, mark you, isn't half a mile away, you won't see a mosquito from one end of the year to the other. You won't see one and you won't hear one and you won't feel one. However, don't let me try to persuade you. I merely wanted you to know that there was this little piece of land on San Giorgio and that I could probably get it for you fairly cheap."

"You are excessively obliging, monsieur."

"Not at all. My chief pleasure nowadays is helping other people. All sorts of people come and ask my advice. 'Ask Bookham' has become quite a by-word in Sirene."

Marsac yawned.

"You're looking tired," said Bookham anxiously. "You mustn't overdo it. The Sirene air is horribly stimulating till you get used to it."

"I think I shall go to my hotel," said Marsac, rising.

"Let's see. You're staying at the Augusto, aren't you? Well, I think it's the best on the whole if you don't mind being disgracefully overcharged."

"But I have an intention to take a furnished villa as soon as I can fit myself with one."

"Oh, you are, are you?" said Bookham, trying to remember which of his friends was likely to pay the highest commission before he recommended his villa. A pity that the Major was so mean, because the Capo di Monte would have been just the place. "Well, now, don't commit yourself over any villa before you've consulted me. I can tell you the weak points of every villa in Sirene. I have made a particular point of going into the sanitation of them all."

"*Alors, au revoir, monsieur,*" said Marsac. "Many thanks for your gentleness."

"Not at all, Count. Not at all. Only too happy to be of any little assistance to you in any way. And about the church porch . . ."

"Ah, yes, the *portico*."

"Do you really mean your munificent offer?"

"Assuredly I mean it. I shall make my *dessein* and invite a fabricator to say his price."

"Oh, you'll design it yourself?" said Bookham a little

doubtfully. "I say, isn't that giving you rather a lot of trouble?"

"*Au contraire*, it will please me."

"Well, perhaps you'll let me send you round the design that we had already adopted. It was to cost two thousand liras—perhaps that is more than you were thinking of . . ."

"If my *dessein* pleases me I shall pay five, six, ten thousand francs," Marsac haughtily proclaimed.

"But you won't employ a mason without consulting me first?" said Bookham anxiously.

"*Ah, ça, c'est entendu*," Marsac replied.

"I shall send round our humble little design to you at your hotel this evening."

And as the Count, followed by his secretary, marched out of Zampone's Bookham began to dream of much more than a trifling commission from Maestro Supino.

In the end it was Zygmunt Konczynski, the Polish painter, who succeeded in letting the Villa Decamerone to the rich newcomer. The Decamerone had originally been built by a Dutch misogynist who had sold it to a female American misanthropist who in her turn had sold it to the painter. He bought it partly because it was the only villa in the South of Europe with rooms lofty enough to contain the immense unsaleable canvases he had painted to illustrate the Odyssey, partly because Miss Matcham, the misanthropist, accepted half the purchase money in kind, or, in other words, by letting Konczynski paint her as Sappho surrounded by four voluptuous maidens whom he enlarged and Hellenized from carte-de-visites of college friends at Vassar. The reason why Marsac took the villa was not entirely on account of its position halfway along the fashionable Via Caprera, or its suitability for the entertainments with which he proposed to astonish and captivate Sirene. He had no sooner met Konczynski than he made up his mind that the painter must leave the island. People were prepared to go to any lengths when they heard Konczynski's voice approaching; they had even been known to leap walls and conceal themselves in thickets of prickly pears until he had passed. He was a large creature of over sixty with bright, bulging, greedy eyes, perfectly bald except for one thick tuft of grey hair above the middle of his forehead, which he combed up into a point and never allowed to be flattened by a hat. In the tails of a voluminous coat he carried packets of postcards, on the backs of which were sunset-coloured reproductions of his illustrations to the Odyssey. These he would insist on showing you without mercy, offering them mercilessly one at a time for your admiration with the largest and dirtiest forefinger and thumb ever seen. And that voice relentlessly booming French with a metallic Polish accent! Ah, that voice, that voice, that hideous Niagara of egoism and shoddy rhetoric, that spate of nonsense, that maëlstrom of gaudy riff-raff!

"*Moi, moi, moi, moi, Zygmunt Konczynski . . . moi, moi.*"

One morning when Marsac had been walking along the Caprera dilating to Carlo on his own over-decorated dreams he had paused outside the arched doorway of the Villa Decamerone and read chiselled on a marble tablet this inscription: *MUSÉE DE L'ART MODERNE. ENTRÉE LIBRE.*

The door opened and out rushed Konczynski with the fearful rapacity of an ogre in a fairy-tale.

"*Entrez, monsieur. Entrez, je vous prie. Il faut absolument que je vous montre mon grand tableau des Sirènes. Superbe! Magnifique! Et il y a des autres encore plus merveilleux!*"

Marsac was so much taken aback by the irruption of this bald-headed giant that he lost his presence of mind and before he knew what he was doing he had allowed himself to be dragged inside the villa where he had to listen for an hour while the painter extolled the sublime beauty of one fourteen-foot nudity after another.

"*Et maintenant, monsieur, maintenant nous nous trouvons en face de mon chef d'œuvre. Celle-ci est la belle Nausicée. Regardez, monsieur, comme j'ai su depeindre sa forme idéale. Regardez ses seins, mon ami! Regardez ses cuisses! Regardez sa croupe ondoyante! Voulez-vous savoir mon inspiration, l'inspiration de Zygmunt Konczynski? Écoutez, donc.*"

It may have been the actual appearance of the undraped Nausicaa or it may have been the suggestive assonance in her name: whichever it was Marsac begged for a little fresh air and a glass of water.

"*Ah, vous êtes artiste vous-même, monsieur. Vous avez été accablé par toute cette magnificence de la génie. Je vous félicite, monsieur. Vous êtes heureux. Moi, Zygmunt Konczynski, je vous félicite.*"

"*De l'eau,*" the Count muttered feebly.

"*Vous êtes resté pendant toute une heure, mon cher, dans le monde enchanté du grand Omère. Et c'est, moi, moi, moi, Zygmunt Konczynski qui . . .*"

This was how Marsac came to rent the Villa Decamerone, and no slain dragon could have gained a knight-errant as much gratitude from the afflicted neighbourhood as the Count earned by ridding Sirene of Zygmunt Konczynski for eighteen months. The pictures were covered with Oriental stuffs which he had collected during his voyage round the world, and the Villa Decamerone, with its large Pompeian atrium, its portico modelled after the Erechtheum on the Acropolis, and its rocky garden blazing with the orange and vermilion spikes of many succulents and the magenta stars of mesembrianthemums, was the very place for Marsac to entertain Sirene until his own villa was built. Nor was the building of that villa likely to be postponed much longer, because Alberto and Enrico Jones were interesting themselves in the matter. While Bookham and Neave and the Major and a dozen were talking, Alberto and Enrico Jones were acting.

Some fifty years before this date a young man in Bradford, depressed by the prospect of entering the family woollen business, surrendered all his future interest in the firm to his younger brother for a cash payment and wandered away to the South. He was under the impression that he could paint, and if the occasional hanging of one's pictures in the Exhibition of the Royal Academy can be held to justify such a belief Henry Jones was justified. In due course he reached Sirene, bought a tumbledown old barrack of a house among the lemon-groves below the Strada Nuova, which had been called the Palazzo Inglese ever since it had served for a time as the headquarters of an incompetent English general during the Napoleonic wars. Within a few months of settling in Sirene the painter married the lovely daughter of old Cangiani, a peasant who owned large olive groves on the slopes of the Caprera. Cangiani cut down most of his olives to plant vines, supposing them to be more profitable. When Henry succeeded to the control of the property on his father-in-law's death, he dug up the vines and built villas, which were much more profitable than either. He was bitten by the gadfly of land-owning and ceased to paint pictures. His sons, Alberto and Enrico, never wasted much of their time over pictures; from their youth they were devoted almost entirely to land. When Marsac arrived in Sirene their mother had long been dead; but in one of the great untidy rooms of the Palazzo Inglese their father still survived and still spoke both English and Italian with a recognizable Yorkshire accent. He was little better than a mummy now, he who had been credited in his day with begetting half the population of Sirene. He sat up in his frowsy faded peacock-blue dressing-gown blinking with rheumy eyes at bundles of deeds relating to the sale of land and cursing the slatternly women that fluttered about the crumbling corridors of the Palazzo like dusty moths, when they did not answer his cracked bell quickly enough. And who had a better right to curse his servants than he who was the father of them all?

"*Futuit ancillas
domumque et agros implet equitibus vernis,
pater familiae verus est Quirinalis,*"

Scudamore used to quote from his beloved Martial.

Most of the *forestieri* in Sirene took no interest in old Henry Jones. But Duncan Maxwell cultivated him, and Duncan Maxwell knew what was worth while.

"Wonderful, wonderful," he used to say. "And so wicked! He's outlived all his concubines. Oh, yes, my dee-aw fellow, they're all food for worms—and he really does understand how ridiculous women are. A sublime old Turk. You don't find them so easily nowadays. He's had more children than Augustus the Strong of Saxony. And he had over seven hundred."

But Maxwell was always eccentric. He simply could not stand Alberto and Enrico, whereas everybody else thought them so amusing except to deal with in a matter of business. There was only a year between the two brothers; after that their father had tired of his wife. While aware of the material advantage that it was for them to act always as a dual alliance Alberto and Enrico were genuinely devoted to each other. Their mutual admiration was Latin in its respect for the ties of family. In fact, their point of view over everything was Latin. Silk had almost entirely displaced wool. The English in them merely existed to strengthen with another modern instance the wise old saw:

*L'inglese italianato
'È il diavolo incarnato.*

Outwardly Alberto and Enrico resembled figures on the stage of the Renaissance. Both stood well over six feet, broad and burly with a suave manner that should not have left the least observant creature in even a minute's doubt of the brutality it cloaked. Both were dark with black moustaches and imperials *à la mode*. Alberto, who was always hoping to find himself a rich wife among the visitors, dressed with an exaggerated neatness. Enrico, who took a great pride in possessing a normal and masculine appetite, was inclined to feel that by seducing peasant-girls he was setting a good example on Sirene. At the same time, he wished to be recognized as an unusual personality, to achieve which he dressed, if the comparison may convey anything, like something between Colline, the bass philosopher in *La Vie de Bohème*, and a Hampshire gamekeeper. Although the two brothers spoke correct English with but the slightest trace of an Italian accent, it was really to both of them a foreign language. Yet when they were together they always spoke it, translating their subtle and exact Italian thoughts into what seemed a disguise (for they were never really frank even with each other) that would always leave their utterances in a kind of fog, through which they could escape if necessary from what they had said and hide what they were really thinking.

" Are you proposing to buy any land on Timberio, Alberto ? " his brother asked him three or four days after Marsac's arrival.

Alberto looked much surprised by such a question; and Enrico, taking out a huge bandanna handkerchief, mopped his forehead.

" It's very hot," he murmured.

Alberto agreed and waited for the next remark. He knew by the way Enrico was sweating and the way his scalp was twitching that his brain must be hard at work.

" I was thinking that if I had not just bought that land below the Strada Nuova I would have bought 'O Gobbetto's land on Timberio."

" Is it good land ? "

Enrico shrugged his shoulders.

" There are about a dozen large carob-trees on it . . . but the wine is not good," he added hastily.

"Is the view good?" Alberto asked.

"The view is magnificent," said Enrico. "It would be a splendid site for a villa if there was anybody here with enough money to build on such an out-of-the-way point."

"One ought to be able to buy the land quite reasonably," Alberto murmured, "if the wine is not good. Carobs are not profitable."

"They would be useful if anybody thought of planning a garden. So many people like old trees. And we ought to do what we can, Alberto, to preserve the old carobs of Sirene."

"You are right. Yes, you are right," said Alberto meditatively. "But, of course, the land would be no use to me."

"No use at all," Enrico agreed. "But I think you might soon sell it again at a profit. I believe you could buy it from 'O Gobbetto for three thousand."

"And sell it again?"

"Oh, for ten thousand—or perhaps even fifteen thousand if one moved carefully."

"Naturally, if I managed to make that profit I would want you to share with me half and half, Enrico."

"I believe I can find somebody," said the younger brother, dabbing his forehead.

"Of course, we'll have to buy the land on either side of 'O Gobbetto," said Alberto quickly. He knew that Enrico was quite capable of buying this on his own account, and not giving him a penny of the profit when Marsac had to buy it at a high figure to preserve his view.

"Mere rocks," said Enrico remotely. "Five hundred on either side would buy all we wanted." He smiled. He did not bear Alberto any grudge for remembering the land on either side, and he knew that Alberto did not bear him any grudge for hoping that he might forget it.

That very afternoon Enrico Jones walked up the Via Timberio. On his way he passed old Zampone gloating over the immense foundations of the Hotel Grandioso. They saluted one another all the more cordially because they hated one another so bitterly. But each knew the other was too powerful to merit anything except the greatest politeness. Don Luigi observed that Enrico was choosing a steep road for so hot an afternoon. Enrico said that the clerk of the municipality had asked him to go into the question of the common land that some of the *contadini* on Timberio had been appropriating. Don Luigi smiled sardonically and replied that 'O Gobbetto had passed ten minutes ago. Enrico bit his lips in anger at the tell-tale flush of which he had been trying to cure himself for thirty years. He retorted on Don Luigi with a remark about the slowness of his workmen.

"*Piano, piano, signore mio,*" said the old man sententiously. "*Chi va piano va sano e va lontano.*"

Enrico walked on. The Via Timberio became a narrow paved *viale* ascending gradually between high walls until it reached the head of the plateau between the hill of San Giorgio with its girdle of orange groves sheltered against the wind by straw mats, and the hill of Timberio, beside the huddled ruins on the top of which a gilded madonna gleamed in the May sunlight. The *viale* went on and on with many windings; but though Enrico was wearing corduroy breeches and a large felt hat and was in consequence dripping with the heat, the prospect of acquiring more land took him up at a buoyant pace. At last he reached his destination—a grove of carob-trees and a level vineyard by the edge of a seven hundred feet cliff, which immediately to the right of this ascended in a rapid slope another three hundred feet to the summit of the famous hill of Tiberius. Enrico mopped his forehead and looked at the dark skyline of Sirene against the sun, and the valleys and precipices bloomed with shadow. He turned to gaze where, on the other side of the island, the pale blue Salernian gulf glittered in the south and back to where before him and beneath him was spread the deep blue (indigo deep where the cliffs dropped into the water) of the Bay of Naples. He looked up at the arid slope strewn with limestone boulders and misted with rosemary to the yawning ruins of the mighty Villa Jovis. He wondered with a shoot of jealousy why he could not have been Tiberius. And this young puppy of a Frenchman who could afford to come and do what he would have liked to do himself! The blood flowed duskily through Enrico's brain. How good to pick up that chatterbox, break his neck, and fling him over the cliffs like a dead parrot! He took off his broad-brimmed hat, wiped with his orange and red handkerchief his dripping hair, twitched his scalp once or twice, and shouted for the owner of the land to show himself.

At the sound of a voice there emerged from a shelter of straw that resembled a large bee-skip in the shade of one of the gnarled carob-trees what anybody would have been justified in fancying to be an authentic gnome. 'O Gobbetto was more dwarf than hunchback, although he had enough of a hump to merit his nickname. He was under four feet in height with powerful hairy arms that nearly touched the ground, and his bare feet caked and grimed with a lifetime's soilure had the eloquent toes of an orangoutang. His shirt open in front showed a chest covered with hair, and his trousers were not so much like trousers as a slough of which he would presently rid himself. At the moment, in view of the fact that he was going to do business with Enrico Jones, he was sober, and this was such an unusual condition that it gave him the dazed look of a nocturnal animal which has been chased out into sunlight. When he was drunk he was often to be seen on this part of the island haunting the corners of the little paved *viali* in extraordinary poses. He would stand for an hour with his long arms flung up behind him, his nose almost touching the ground, like a bewitched fowl. He would stand for an hour on one leg with the other outthrust at right angles;

he would even stand on his head with his legs in a V. Sometimes tourists sweltering up the exhausting road to view the ruins of the Villa Jovis would perceive in the midway of the path a face looking at them upside down between a pair of legs, and their memory would reach back nervously to childhood's tales of brigands in Italy. When the municipal authorities heard of such behaviour, they would order the arrest of 'O Gobbetto, because they did not think it was of advantage to the traffic in tourists that visitors to Sirene should be frightened. Then 'O Gobbetto would go to prison for a week, and when he came out he would sing all night long and go to prison again for making a public nuisance of himself. Yes, he was a queer figure, as queer as some of the foreign residents.

It took Enrico several of those long hot walks before he persuaded 'O Gobbetto to part with his land, and in the end he had to pay three thousand five hundred liras for it. He ascribed the owner's obstinacy to the machinations of old Zampone. However, he managed the purchase at last, and he obtained the land on either side for two hundred liras less than he expected to pay. So, it was not such a bad bargain. When the deeds were safe in Alberto's big desk at the Palazzo Inglese Alberto dressed himself with unusual care even for him and called on Marsac. Alberto flattered him beautifully, and was presented with a volume of his poems. On his return home he sat down and wrote the following letter:

> PALAZZO INGLESE,
> ISOLA SIRENE,
> *May 25th.*

My dear Count,
Please permit me to write to you in my own language which you speak so marvellously. I assure you I would be honestly ashamed to air my villainous French to a master of eloquence like yourself. I have been luxuriating in your poems. May

I without impertinence say that you have a great and wonderful genius? I have never been very fond of modern French poetry, to be candid. Perhaps I have lived too long out of the world which you adorn with such distinction. But your poems! Really, my dear Count, I hardly know how to express the rapture into which they have plunged me. I dread your leaving us! This afternoon you mentioned that you would like to build a villa somewhere in the neighbourhood of the Villa Jovis. A happy choice for one who is the heir of the golden age of poesy. I hesitate to suggest your taking the trouble to look at a little piece of land in that direction which belongs to me, and yet I sincerely believe it might be worth your while to give it a moment's glance—that is if your intention of building a villa here is serious and not merely a poetic but passing fancy. Please forgive me if I have impertinently intruded. I would not have dreamed of writing to you if I had not set my heart on your living here amongst us, and inspiring us with your wit and intelligence.

Yours most truly,
Alberto Jones

There are few expressions of hospitality that so much annoy newcomers as the warnings of old residents. When people heard that the Count was contemplating the purchase of land from Alberto Jones and begged him to be most careful of doing business with either him or his brother, Marsac looked down his shapely nose with an annoyance that but for his wealth might have made him unpopular. He listened with a superior smile to the most horrifying tales of the Jones's duplicity in the matter of cisterns, of their unscrupulous abuse of sanitation, and of the sly little clauses they were wont to insert in the leases of their villas. No sooner had Marsac surveyed the site Alberto suggested for his villa than he was determined that there and there only would he build it. In vain did Bookham thunder of the Tiberian mosquitoes; in vain did Major Natt point out the expense of building so far away; in vain did everybody urge the objectionable presence of something or the equally objectionable absence of something else. At the beginning of June Marsac paid Alberto Jones 12,000 liras for the site, and early in October the workmen began to excavate the ground for the cisterns of the Villa Hylas.

"Do be sure you have plenty of water," everybody entreated the Count.

"Whatever you do, don't save money over the cisterns. Don't stint yourself over *them*."

"I assure you that I have not the intention to stint myself over anything, *cher monsieur* (or *chère madame*)," he would answer loftily.

Nor did he.

"*Sit cisterna mihi quam vinea malo Ravennae*," Scudamore quoted. "And if the 'I' in Sirene hadn't been long it would have served just as happily to end that well-informed hexameter. Certainly Natt makes a good deal more out of selling his water than his grapes"

Chapter 5

Mercuri . . . alta via.

PROPERTIUS

Sed iam pompa venit . . .
tempus adest plausus—aurea pompa venit.

OVID

THE eruption of Joseph Neave from his afternoon nap and his volcanic flow over the Villa Amabile, set a sociable fashion among the old men of Sirene. When the Count issued invitations for a *thé japonais* at the Villa Decamerone, not merely did Christopher Goldfinch accept (that was to be expected) and Joseph himself (that was no longer the shock it would have been), but old Simon Pears and old Dr. Mewburn also accepted, and this in spite of a footnote on the card of invitation to say that Japanese costume was indispensable.

"No, granpa, you certainly can't have my kimono," Angela told the rugged old American poet firmly. "And I don't think you even ought to go."

"Shucks!" Simon retorted gruffly. "Then I'll see if Chris Goldfinch won't help me."

Christopher and Simon had been friends for fifty years. Simon had written a sonnet to Christopher on his seventieth birthday which began:

> *We twain set out to climb Parnassus steep,*
> *Thou with thy brush for staff, myself with pen;*
> *Comes now th' allotted threescore years and ten;*
> *So rest, old friend, till that long dreamless sleep.*

And Christopher had drawn a splendid head of Simon for his seventy-fourth birthday, which was inscribed in his own decorative handwriting: *The Old Poet Rests from his Labor*.

Actually, Christopher was as busy as ever turning out pastels of Vesuvius, and Simon was still writing at least one sonnet a day.

In response to his old friend's appeal Goldfinch wrote back to say that he only possessed a complete equipment for one Samurai in his collection of costumes and that he intended to wear this himself. However, friendship was friendship, and he was prepared to divide it with Simon. As a matter of fact, the painter would not have parted with one link of the costume if he had not discovered that the weight of it was insupportable. The three pretty little girls who looked after him at the Villa Adonis had spent an hour trying to hoist the metal curtains on to the Signore's shoulders; but when at last with the help of two of their sweethearts they managed the feat Christopher had simply collapsed under the weight.

"By gad," he sighed regretfully from the floor. "I'm just beginning to feel my age a trifle."

When Christopher and Simon were dressed, the problem arose of getting them to the Villa Decamerone, which was halfway down the Via Caprera and along which wheeled traffic was absolutely forbidden. In the end Simon was carried in the Sirene sedan and Christopher on the *portantina* which was a kind of stretcher on which an armchair was bound. Sitting up there in his Samurai armour Christopher looked remarkably like San Mercurio, the patron saint of Sirene, whose silver image was borne thus in solemn procession on his annual *festa* at the end of May. When Christopher and Simon arrived at the Villa Decamerone, they found it was also indispensable at a Japanese tea to sit on the floor. So down they sat, and there they both remained chinking for the rest of the afternoon, too proud to ask of youth a helpful hand.

"What tractable asses we do make of ourselves pro bono publico," Major Natt observed to Mrs. Neave. "I feel the most ostentatious buffoon in this pink bath-gown, squatting down here and sipping this preposterous liquor—saki or whatever it's called. My figure is utterly remote from the Japanese ideal. Good gracious, Mrs. Neave, here comes Mewburn too! Upon my word I believe he appears a bigger pantaloon than I do myself. He looks as if he were on his way to the operating-theatre. I really think his daughter should have kept him at home. She should have fastened him up with one of the chains they use for those ravening bloodhounds of theirs. He's utterly out of place trying to emulate the Mikado. Good lord, there's Neave too!"

"Don't I know it?" the distracted wife exclaimed. "He just would come, Major Natt. And he's eating and drinking everything Count Marsac's giving him. I know I'll be up all night with him after this. He's already so excited, Major Natt, and he's waxed his moustache and dyed it black, and I know it'll disagree with him. You can't play tricks with yourself like that at Joseph's age. And he's grazed the back of his head with one of my combs, and he was so cross with me. He said I didn't even know how to buy a reliable comb. Joseph! Joseph!" she called across to her husband pleadingly. "Don't drink any more of this saki. Please! Please!"

It was a habit of Joseph's before saying something sarcastic to his wife in public to suck his moustache with preliminary relish. Forgetting about the dye, he did so now, and made a face even more hideous than the Oriental mask through which Bookham, just arrived, was bellowing his first courtesies. Mrs. Neave was saved by the arrival of the Norton girls, who at that moment came through the gates of the Villa Decamerone seated on white donkeys, dressed in flowery silk kimonos, and carrying scarlet Japanese umbrellas. As the old ladies entered, Marsac produced his *pièce de résistance*, which was a beautiful and genuine Cingalese boy who salaamed before Miss Virginia and Miss Maimie with a sinuosity that no European could expect to achieve.

"Oh, isn't he too marvellous?" exclaimed Nigel Dawson. "*Do* you think *I* could bow like that?"

This ecstatic question was addressed to Austin Follett, who adjusted his pince-nez gravely.

"Why, I don't know," he replied. "But if you're not habituated to that kind of motion, Mr. Dawson, you might run a serious risk of dislocation if you tried it too abruptly."

"How frightfully prosaic you are! And I wish you wouldn't call me Mr. Dawson. *Every*body calls me Nigel. When people call me Mr. Dawson, it gives me quite an eerie feeling as they were talking to my dead father."

Follett seemed to shy at the intimacy and fell backward over the seated form of Simon Pears.

"Oh, pardon me, pardon me, Mr. Pears," he entreated, horrified by his clumsy treatment of a poet for whom he had such a sincere veneration.

"Quite all right," said Simon genially. "Sit down here on the floor and have a crack."

Soon they were deep in the discussion of prosody, or rather Follett was listening to the poet as attentively as he could in the intervals of being stepped over.

"Well, Mrs. Dawson, how are you?" Miss Virginia asked. "Don't you love our dear Count Bob?"

"Why, I think he's one of the most fascinating men I've ever met," said Mrs. Dawson. "Though I can't persuade him to give me one tiny little soft glance. I'm terribly discouraged."

Miss Virginia's eyes flashed. One felt that Mrs. Dawson had only to be a trifle more arch to get her cheeks soundly smacked with Miss Virginia's fan.

"He's a very intellectual man, Mrs. Dawson. I hope

the ladies of Sirene don't think he's come here to flirt," she said severely.

"Now, Miss Virginia, don't be cross with me," said the other good-humouredly. "I was only having my little joke."

"Yes, but I don't care much for jokes like that, Mrs. Dawson. Maimie and I don't intend to have our dear Count laughed at."

"But I'm not laughing at him at all, Miss Virginia. Not at all."

And Mrs. Dawson observed to several people that afternoon how lucky it was that Count Marsac really was so attractive as it made the poor dear old Nortons' admiration of him not too perfectly foolish.

Several minor entertainments followed the Japanese tea, but naturally it was the Villa Amabile that gave the first worthy response. This was a large party to watch the procession of San Mercurio, stay on to dinner, and dance by moonlight afterwards.

On the thirty-first of May in the year of grace 1173 a silver image representing life-size the upper half of a genial bishop in the act of episcopal benediction swam ashore one night at the Grande Marina of Sirene, walked up the hill to a little basilica which had just been completed, and took possession of a suitable niche behind the altar. That same night the Bishop of Sirene was aroused by a loud voice calling him by name "Innocente!", whereupon Bishop Innocente opening his eyes saw standing by his bed in a nimbus of celestial brightness a majestic episcopal form.

"I am San Mercurio," said the vision. "I was cut in half by the scimitar of an unbelieving Saracen, who was attempting to circumcise me against my conscience. My mutilated form has swum to Sirene from Ephesus in twenty-four hours. Henceforth I shall be the protector of this island. Appeal to me in times of difficulty, and be sure that my prayers for you shall not be unavailing."

With the progress of time a number of fantastic and incredible legends gathered round this miraculous arrival of San Mercurio, some of which are still believed by the more ignorant Sirenesi. Thus it was said that the church in which the blessed newcomer established himself was about to be dedicated to Santa Viva and Santa Voce, and that San Mercurio transformed the images of the holy virgins and martyrs already set up into the two big limestone stalactites that droop from one of the caves in the sheer face of Monte Ventoso. These anti-feminine legends have always been given too much currency in Sirene. Another story went that it was the actual body of the martyr which had swum ashore and that it was the Sirene priests who turned it into silver. This seems improbable. What may be true is that the image was originally of solid silver instead of being the silver shell it is now.

San Mercurio made a speciality of subduing earthquakes, and sceptics have to account for the indubitable fact that since his arrival Sirene has never felt a tremor during the worst excesses of Vesuvius, whereas before he came the island was in almost perpetual convulsions, the proof of which can be seen in its present distorted shape. San Mercurio did not confine his influence to earthquakes. It extended over everything, particularly the weather, and the Sirenesi did not allow him to forget it. They kept him up to the mark. They had no intention of allowing the pleasures of Paradise to make him lazy. If there was a drought and San Mercurio did not remove it at once, he was apt to find himself turned to the wall in disgrace. He had had his silver beard tweaked more than once, and had often been taunted in the rudest fashion by disappointed clients.

Up at Anasirene on the other side of Monte Ventoso they were protected by San Bonzo, who was in every way inferior to San Mercurio. He was neither a bishop nor a martyr, but a poor goatherd, about whose saintliness nothing was known until miracles were wrought at his tomb. There was indeed a grave doubt if he was ever canonized at all, and he was regarded by the Sirenesi as a ridiculous example of Anasirenese assertiveness. His festival in the middle of May was held this year in a storm of rain, for which the whole island had been praying to replenish their cisterns. The Sirenesi naturally gave all the credit for the downpour to San Mercurio, who had had his face turned to the wall for a week previously. They pointed out that, if San Bonzo had brought the rain, he would hardly have chosen his own feast day, at the end of which not a single firework would go off. Moreover, his image being merely of painted wood, the paint had run during the procession, and poor San Bonzo had looked a pretty sight before it was over. It had really been a lamentable fiasco, and the Sirene priests who had taken part in the procession out of courtesy to their humbler brethren could hardly hide their smiles of compassionate scorn.

But San Bonzo had his revenge on the thirty-first of May.

The azure serenity of the morning was interrupted at five o'clock by a series of explosions all over Sirene. First the line of mortars along the Grande Marina gave three dozen bangs. A minute later the mortars outside San Mercurio's own little basilica responded with four dozen bangs. Bangs in the Piazza, bangs beyond the Strada Nuova, bangs on the top of the Torrione, bangs on the top of San Giorgio, bangs on the top of Timberio, bangs on the top of the Caprera, bangs down on the Piccola Marina. As little Americans wake up with a fourth of July feeling, as little French boys wake up with a fourteenth of July feeling, as little Greeks wake up with a twenty-fifth of March (old style) and seventh of April (new style) feeling, but not as little English boys wake up with a fifth of November feeling, because all the bangs in the world could not put any champagne into an English fifth of November, so now all the little Sirenesi woke up with a thirty-first of

May feeling. They thought of the clean shirts they would be given for love of their Father and Protector, of the sweets they would suck, of the meat they would eat, of the music they would hear, of the squeakers they would blow, of the ticklers they would wave, of the fireworks they would see, all in honour of their Patron. At nine o'clock there was Mass in the Church of San Mercurio, with more bangs. Then came the solemn translation of the silver image from the saint's self-chosen niche in the little basilica by the sea to a throne in the Duomo, where his jovial countenance under a gorgeous canopy would beam a welcome to his clients all through the heat of the day. At five o'clock he would be translated back to his own basilica to the accompaniment of deafening bangs, cheers, and invocations. The Piazza would be given over to the fair, the Sirene band would play Verdi for a couple of hours, and at ten o'clock a grand display of fireworks would bring the day to a thrilling conclusion.

Of course everybody was in the Piazza that morning, and everybody was saying what a wonderful day it was even for San Mercurio, who with his influence over the weather usually took jolly good care to provide himself with a fine day. The terrace of Zampone's was crowded with foreigners waiting for the procession to pass through. Thanks to their educational advantages they were all inclined to patronize the patron of Sirene. When they scattered their own handfuls of rose-petals and genista blossom on the venerable silver saint they did so self-consciously, as if they really must do something to encourage the children; but they were careful to make it clear that their homage had nothing indolatrous about it. Æsthetics and good manners dictated their action, not superstition.

"Well," said Bookham in the deep superior voice of one who as a churchwarden might claim to know what genuine religion was, "I see you've come down, Major. You're in good time. The god hasn't arrived yet."

"I like these old ceremonies," the Major barked sentimentally. "It's great rubbish, of course; but there's something rather attractive about it all. I usually add my own little tribute of rose-leaves. I collected a small packet from my flowers before I came out. It's all tommy rot, but I am grossly swayed by popular excitement of any kind. I suppose you're going down to the Nortons this afternoon?"

"No, I'm not going down this afternoon," said Bookham remotely.

"Ah, no, I forgot your little rift, eh? Hullo, here's Goldfinch. Good morning," he called down over the railings of the terrace. "Aren't you coming up here to watch the procession?"

Christopher Goldfinch shook his head.

"Never come into Zampone's," he reminded the Major.

"Oh, of course, how stupid of me! I forgot your vow."

Thirty years before this Don Luigi had sent in his bill to Christopher with a demand for immediate payment and a threat of legal proceedings. Whereupon Christopher had paid the bill and told Don Luigi that he would never enter his café again as long as the owner of it was alive. This vow nothing would induce him to break. Duncan Maxwell had begged Don Luigi to try the effect of peremptory bills on some of the other residents in the hope that they too would make solemn vows never to darken his doors again. But Don Luigi had always regretted too much his treatment of the painter to oblige Maxwell. So, Zampone's remained a refuge only from Goldfinch.

The painter had declined Major Natt's invitation a little wistfully. He was so beautifully dressed this morning, and his cloth of silver waistcoat was creating some confusion in the minds of the youngest Sirenesi between himself and San Mercurio, so that wherever he went he was being followed by a gaping crowd of five-year-olds wiping their noses against his white piqué trousers.

Archie Macadam was melancholy on the greater festivals,

because his wife expecting him to drink even more than usual kept at his elbow all day and every time he raised it at once applied pressure to bring it down on the table again. This being San Mercurio's day he had not yet managed to drink a drop of brandy, although it was drawing near to eleven o'clock.

"Hate all this mumbo-jumbo," he said sourly to Madame Sarbécoff. "Reminds me of the kind of thing we used to see in Pekin."

Madame Sarbécoff was a delightful Russian woman who was all things except one to all men. She might have been compared to one of those mole-grey Russian cats if she had not had such a fine hooked nose. She purred her appreciation all the time a friend was talking, and there was nobody of either sex in Sirene who did not consider her a remarkably intelligent woman. According to the company in which she found herself she diffused an atmosphere of drugs and strange sins or of virginal innocence. She had even been known to sit for an hour and listen apparently in a rapture to Zygmunt Konczynski, her great blue eyes deep as the Mediterranean while he bellowed forth adulation of himself. She had allowed Joseph Neave to read her not merely the whole of his translation, but the various alternative versions as well. She had prepared to impress the new English chaplain by gushing over the beauties of *The Pilgrim's Progress* when she first met him at tea, but divining his tastes within ten minutes she had transformed *The Pilgrim's Progress* into *The Picture of Dorian Grey* so swiftly that before the visit was over Mr. Acott was confiding to her what difficulty he had to make his altar-boys see life steadily and see it whole. She would, without doubt, presently play Egeria to Austin Follett and fill him with fresh enthusiasm for his pursuit of the origin of evil by tales of her own naughty girlhood. She had very little money, but a number of precious stones, on the gradual sale of which she lived; and of course she spoke equally well half a dozen languages.

"In Pekin!" Madame Sarbécoff murmured ecstatically in a voice that would have been like a purring dove's, did doves ever purr or cats coo. "How wonnderful! How wonnderful!" she continued in that low dreamy voice of hers. "How wonnderful to have lived in Pekin! In a pagoda! I find that so wonnderful. Do tell me about Pekin, Mr. Macadam. It must be so wonnderful in China."

But Archie was much too sober to want to talk about Pekin, and at that moment Mrs. de Feltre, who always liked to do the talking herself, drifted along. She was a plump and handsome young American woman who either because she had been trained by a French husband or because she was just an exception to her countrywomen's supremacy was one of men's natural slaves, and it was strange that with all her devotion she had never learned not to talk ceaselessly about herself. Much to the relief of Sirene she had just got rid of Monsieur de Feltre who was a quarrelsome and drunken bully with a passion for upsetting the friendliest dinner-parties by suddenly calling his host a *sale cochon* and hitting him on the head with a decanter. The relief was tempered by some alarm among the Sirene men who were not protected by wives or mistresses, because poor Marian de Feltre was quite definitely on the look-out for somebody to whom she could devote herself again, and nobody was ever able to feel coldly secure in the Sirene moonlight. It seemed so rude to a woman not to make love to her in it, as if one had not noticed that she was wearing a new and becoming dress.

"Now, Archie, don't fly from me in that cruel way," she drawled.

"I'm looking for my wife," he muttered hastily.

"Don't be silly, Archie. She's sitting behind you. Morning, Effie."

Mrs. Macadam gave her a glum greeting. She was a pretty little woman, but she always seemed so dull and respectable. Even the most charitable could never help saying that she was the one person that was quite out of place in Sirene. Marian de Feltre turned to greet Madame Sarbécoff.

"Why, I never saw you, dear Madame Sarbécoff."

"How charming you are looking, Madame de Feltre. Quite charming. I have never seen you look more charming."

"Why, isn't that nice of you, Madame Sarbécoff! Do you know what I was thinking as I came across the Piazza? I was thinking what a splendid martyr I would have made."

"What wonnderful thoughts you have!"

"Well, I don't know how it is, but I just can't help them. Of course, I ought to have been a poet."

Madame Sarbécoff purred agreement.

"Of course, I've never written a line of poetry in my life, but what does that matter? I believe the greatest poets of all never do write poetry."

"I'm sure they donn't," Madame Sarbécoff purred.

"But what a martyr I would have made! I was reading all about San Mercurio, and I kept saying to myself, 'if that isn't exactly like you, Marian'. And you know the strange thing is I *was* a marvellous swimmer."

"I'm sure you were."

"Oh, I was some swimmer. And then I went and gave it up for the ban-jo."

"But don't you still bathe every Summer?"

"Oh yes, I bathe," she drawled. "And of course I splash around and all that. But when I was a girl I used to swim ten miles out at a stretch. And then I pitched it all up for the ban-jo. Certainly I could play the ban-jo, but I don't know. . . . I let that slide like everything else when I married René. Then there was my riding . . ."

"Riding is so wonnderful. I find there is nothing so wonnderful as riding," said Madame Sarbécoff. "When I was a girl I was always asking my father to take me out among our Cossacks. You know, the Cossacks are so wonnderful...."

"Oh yes, I know the Cossacks are wonderful," Mrs. de Feltre interrupted impatiently. "But you ought to have seen *me* ride. Why, my dear, I could...."

But the band leading the pageant of San Mercurio crashed into Marian de Feltre's reminiscences, and all the blasé foreigners of Sirene craned their necks over the railings of Zampone's terrace to see the head of the procession coiling like a great gaudy dragon round the corner by the Hotel Augusto. The genista blossom poured down from the balconies on either side in a golden torrent. The petals of pink and red roses turned the cobbles to velvet. First Beccafico the *guardia*, clanking his sword and very nearly as sober as Archie Macadam. Then two *carabinieri* displaying that marvellous coolness on a hot day in spite of their uniforms which is perhaps the most admirable quality of the many admirable qualities of *carabinieri*. Then the Sirene band blowing away like billy-oh at a jolly Southern march. Then various confraternities. Then the *frati di misericordia* in their white hoods with slits for the eyes, looking like familiars of the Inquisition. Then the wickedest boys in Sirene trying to look as pure as their patron San Luigi on his white silk banner. Then the young *figlie di Maria* in white muslin veils, singing in their shrill treble a holy song. Then the old *figlie di Maria* in black with black veils and pale blue ribbons, singing in the cracked treble of elderly virgins another holy song. Then about thirty-six fat belaced priests all carrying lighted candles. Then the Bishop of Sirene, with purple cassock and purple face, blessing everybody at nineteen to the dozen and spitting genista petals out of his mouth every few words. And then high on the shoulders of the six least blasphemous of the Sirene *facchini* under a huge red umbrella carried by two more of them San Mercurio himself.

"*Ecco il nostro padre San Mercurio!*" shrieked the crowd

in an ecstasy. "*Viva San Mercurio! Com' è bello! Com' è caro! Come sta bene, il nostro caro vecchio! Viva il protettore di Sirene!*"

"I love my dear old saint," cried Mrs. Ambrogio, who, it may be remembered, was a devout Catholic. She was leaning over the railings of the terrace, her face as crimson with enthusiasm as San Mercurio's umbrella, and flinging rose-leaves and genista blossom at everybody except the saint. "Isn't he an old darling? I love him! I love him! Answers all my prayers. Let my villa for me last Summer. Keeps Peter faithful. Bless his heart! I love him! I love him!"

She dashed back to snatch a last handful of petals, and in her excitement she hurled the whole basket into the middle of the crowd of black-garbed leading citizens of Sirene who were bringing up the rear of the procession.

"Most extraordinary thing," said Major Natt. "All tommy rot, of course. But I feel assailed by a kind of phrenzy on these occasions. Did you notice me, Mrs. Neave? There I was shouting and applauding and flinging rose-leaves—what is it Ovid says—I never can remember the appropriate classical quotation like Scudamore. The Army rots one's brains, you know. I'm in a state of mental decay. Starved of Ovid and Horace and Tibullus et hoc genus omne. Well, I suppose we all meet at the Nortons' this afternoon and repeat our primitive animism and fetichism and all that kind of thing, don't you know."

At the bottom of the garden of the Villa Amabile a long terrace ran above the wall from which one looked down on the road to the Grande Marina. For two days in preparation for the return of San Mercurio to his own home Peppino and Costanzo and fat Agostino had been gathering genista blossom and rose-petals for the guests of the *signorine* to shower upon the patron of Sirene. There were twelve great baskets full to the brim. The excitement of the celebration made Miss Virginia and Miss Maimie flutter round like two pearl-grey pigeons all day. The vaulted kitchen echoed with shrill preparations. A battalion of bottles was stacked in close formation on the table of the pantry.

"Oh, Maimie, I do love to have so many dear folks coming to enjoy themselves with us," Miss Virginia sighed.

"And our dear Count Bob," added Miss Maimie, kissing her.

"You know, Maimie, there's times when I just long for it all to be true—all the dear funny old tales about these funny old saints. I just don't want everything to stop short at the end."

The old lady shivered.

"Phew! It's turned kind of cold, Maimie."

"There's a cloud over the sun," said Miss Maimie.

"Why, isn't that too bad? I hope it isn't going to rain. Hark, there are the carriages!"

Presently Miss Virginia forgot the bleakness of eternity in welcoming her guests, in seeing that each was stuffing himself on the Amabile cream cakes, and in moving from one group to another who sat at the flimsy little white tables beside which there was always an empty chair for her.

The sound of the approaching band drew near.

"Come along now, everybody," Miss Virginia cried. "Come along and shower the golden broom on our dear old silver saint with a real hearty cheer. We'll come back for our whisky when the dear old boy's gone by."

When the company reached the terrace an inky cloud was overhanging Sirene, and just as the procession came round the corner there was a flash of lightning, a peal of thunder, a whirlwind, and a deluge. It put out the candles. It put out the music. The leading citizens tried to get under San Mercurio's umbrella. How it rained! The procession became faster and faster. How it rained and roared!

"Just throw the broom over them quickly," cried Miss Virginia. "And then we must run ourselves."

Twelve basketfuls of sodden flowers simultaneously emptied over it from the terrace of the Villa Amabile was too much for the procession. It broke into a run, and as the guests turned to fly up toward the house they had a glimpse of San Mercurio streaming with moisture, rollicking and wobbling along with a lack of dignity that he had never displayed before. San Bonzo was avenged. And if sceptics doubt the influence of San Bonzo, let them explain how it was that not a drop of rain fell in Anasirene that afternoon.

"Ah," said a wet but satisfied Anasirenese. "*Il nostro padre Bonzo ha dato una bella pugnalata a quello porco di San Mercurio, grazie a Dio. Mi ha fatto un gran piacere, vi giuro.*"

Nor were the Anasirenesi the only people who were pleased about the rebuff to San Mercurio. Marsac, who had been dull all day, became his voluble self again after witnessing the saint's discomfiture. San Mercurio had been monopolizing everybody's attention far too much to please the Count.

Chapter 6

crescit multa damnosa papyro;
sic ingens rerum numerus iubet atque operum lex.
quae tamen inde seges? terrae quis fructus apertae?
quis dabit historico quantum daret acta legenti?

JUVENAL

ALL through that Summer the Count became more and more popular among the *forestieri* of Sirene. At first there had been several people much inclined to doubt the genuineness of his wealth and in consequence to decry his accomplishments. After his purchase of Alberto Jones's land, for which he paid twelve thousand liras as if he were buying a packet of Macedonia cigarettes, the faintest breath of criticism was hushed; and those who had doubted were now inclined to declare that he was even more accomplished than anybody had imagined. Maestro Supino the builder added to his patron's renown by the accounts he gave of the palace that before another eighteen months had passed would shimmer at the high cliff's edge across the Bay.

"A marvel," he affirmed. "And the cost! *Mamma mia!* The cost of it!"

In fact Maestro Supino was going to make such a heavy profit out of the Count that he hardly grumbled at the swingeing commission which Alberto and Enrico exacted from him. He might have protested that it was Signor Bookham who was more responsible than anybody for getting him the job, since it was Signor Bookham who had put him in the way of building the portico of the English church.

However, he was not anxious to pay a second commission to Bookham, who was likely to net at least five hundred liras over the portico; and when the churchwarden hinted at something of the kind Maestro Supino insisted that the only people who had a right to expect a commission out of him were the *signorine dell' Amabile*, for whom he had done a great deal of building. The *signorine*, however, were much too *signorili* to suggest anything of the kind.

The unveiling of the new porch was to take place on the eighth of September, and greatly to Bookham's annoyance Mr. Acott the chaplain had announced his intention of remaining at Sirene all through the Summer in order to preside at the ceremony.

"Your stipend finishes at the end of May," the churchwarden had growled. "And the church is then closed until November."

Mr. Acott replied that he had written to the Bishop of Europe and offered his voluntary ministrations throughout the Summer, of which the Bishop had been only too glad to avail himself.

"My doctor recommends me to complete my cure by a course of sea-bathing," the chaplain said. "And by October I hope to be fit enough to resume my duties in the East End of London. Oh, and by the way, Mr. Bookham, I have obtained permission from the Bishop to appoint my own warden, who will, of course, take charge of the collections during the Summer."

Bookham gasped.

"And who may I enquire is going to be this excretion, I mean to say excrescence?" he bellowed.

"I have appointed Mr. Nigel Dawson."

"Nigel Dawson? Nigel Dawson?" he repeated aghast. "But look here, I say, you can't! Good lord, why, his reputation is appalling!"

"I do not pay the slightest heed to Sirene gossip," said Mr. Acott. "I judge a man by his actions, Mr. Bookham.

And I have no cause to complain of any of Mr. Dawson's actions that have come within my personal observation."

"Well, you're a clergyman and I'm not," Bookham retorted. "So I can't tell you the facts about young Dawson. The only point I wish to make about him is that he is an effeminate and corrupt young decadent. And I protest. I shall write and tell the Bishop what I know about him."

"The Bishop is also a clergyman," Mr. Acott reminded him tartly.

"Yes, but he's an older man than you and perhaps a wiser one."

And with this the senior churchwarden had gone off to consult Mrs. Onslow, Mrs. Gibbs, and Mrs. Rosebotham about what was to be done.

Mrs. Onslow, Mrs. Gibbs, and Mrs. Rosebotham were three sisters, all of whose husbands had found them impossible to live with. So they imported their old mother, Mrs. Kafka, to come out and form with them a thoroughly nice English household on the southern slope of San Giorgio. There in the Villa Minerva they protected themselves against the scorching rays of scandal which might have made hay of their grass-widowhood by making hay of other people's reputations first. There was nothing of which Mrs. Onslow, Mrs. Gibbs, and Mrs. Rosebotham were not ready to accuse the rest of Sirene. They thought it a great pity that a lovely place like Sirene should have such a bad reputation, and they decided that it was due to the presence of so many cosmopolitans. The best cure for the morals of Sirene would be a steady injection of well-to-do English residents—nice people with families who played golf. The island would soon acquire quite a different tone. They were so glad when the tennis-club was formed, because they hoped that it would link the English people together in good healthy sport and be the prelude to golf-links. Mrs. Rosebotham was sure that it was the absence of golf, more than anything else, which made Sirene so bad for people's morals. She was the most aggressive of the sisters. Not even the *scirocco* could defeat her.

"All stuff and nonsense," she barked. "Weak-mindedness, that's all it is. Do I give way to the *scirocco*? Of course not. Look at me now. As fit as be blowed."

Mrs. Onslow was the least aggressive.

"Poor Enid was worn out by her husband," her sisters used to sigh. "She put up with him too long. She tried her best; but he was continuously and steadily unfaithful to her."

Mrs. Rosebotham's husband had escaped from her by taking a post in some unhealthy part of the tropics which was guaranteed to kill any white woman in two months; and it was generally believed on the island that Mr. Gibbs had become a professional criminal so that he could always put a prison wall between himself and his wife should it prove necessary as a final resource. Mrs. Gibbs managed her sister Mrs. Onslow and her mother Mrs. Kafka. Mrs. Rosebotham tried to manage everything else on Sirene. Mr. Bookham was not a favourite in the Villa Minerva; but he had hopes of securing some support there against the pretensions of the chaplain, because Mrs. Rosebotham had quarrelled with him over the hymns on the third Sunday in March, since when she had not entered the church. Mrs. Rosebotham had chosen *Pleasant are Thy Courts Above*. She had put the number on the board: 240. Mr. Acott had come in and substituted 215 for 240. Mrs. Rosebotham was not going to stand that. She played the harmonium, and she jolly well intended to have the hymns she wanted. She played the harmonium, and if the chaplain announced *The Church's One Foundation* she jolly well intended to play and to sing *Pleasant are Thy Courts Above*. She did, and the harmony of the little English congregation was shattered. Of course Mrs. Rosebotham resigned from the harmonium itself and refused to come to church any more. Nor would she have allowed the two Miss Coopers to play except out of a ladylike consideration for the Almighty. The Miss Coopers were a pair of massive old maids, with hips that swung to and fro like immense satchels, who wandered round Sirene grunting at the bright colours worn by presumably respectable women, grunting and routing about in olive-groves for suitable views to paint, like a couple of pigs nosing for acorns. When one passed the open windows of their little villa in the Via Caprera, one heard them grunting away inside to one another, either that or playing Beethoven—a surprising alternative. And once they wore bright colours themselves, walking about all a fine May day in what looked like cerise and purple bed-jackets. But they never did this again, probably owing to the remonstrances of Mrs. Rosebotham.

"I'll jolly well write to the Bishop myself," Mrs. Rosebotham vowed when she heard Bookham's news.

"I wish you would, my dear lady."

"Have you got proof of any definite piece of immorality which I can put before him?" she demanded.

"I suspect him of the worst," Bookham replied. "But I haven't got any concrete facts—yet," he added significantly.

"Well, can I say 'Mr. Bookham, the churchwarden, assures me that his private life is flagrant'? That doesn't commit us to anything definite."

"But it commits me rather, doesn't it, Mrs. Rosebotham? I mean to say, I'd rather you didn't bring my name into it at all. I mean to say, dog doesn't eat dog and all that. I don't think the churchwarden ought to accuse the chaplain."

"The trouble with Bookham," Mrs. Rosebotham said to her sisters that evening, "is that he is a coward and that he is unfortunately not a gentleman. I do wish we could get a gentleman to come and live here and be churchwarden. I think it's so immensely important to set the Roman Catholics a good example. The whole point of the English Church is that it's managed by gentlemen. Imagine that little whippersnapper of an Acott having the jolly impudence to make that unhealthy young Dawson his churchwarden. An American too! And then he's a friend of that filthy Duncan Maxwell. I'm told that the orgies in the Villa Partenope last Winter were unspeakable. Unspeakable, my dear! Are we living in the time of Tiberius, or are we living in the time of Edward VII? I ask you. I simply ask that."

In justice to Mrs. Rosebotham it must be allowed that the behaviour of the Reverend Cyril Acott, since he came last Autumn as chaplain to Sirene, had grown increasingly odd for an English clergyman. Ten years before, as an undergraduate, he had been a prominent figure in the more tropical coteries of Oxford decadence. He had belonged to a club called the Pea Green Corruptibles. He had had two poems rejected by *The Spirit Lamp* as too daring, and a sonnet accepted by *Southernwood: An Interior Review* (*Quarterly*, £1 1s.), which was in the Shakespearian mode and ended:

> *And I would burn for evermore in Hell,*
> *Might I but swing there in thy thurible.*

Soon after this Cyril Acott entered a theological college, whence he passed out to an East End curacy in Popney. There he had worked hard ever since, and his appointment to a winter chaplaincy in Sirene was a thoroughly well-deserved rest. But gradually the island laid her spell upon him. He became faintly pea-green again, slightly corruptible once more. He found himself liking his congregation less and less, and the people against whom Bookham and Mrs. Rosebotham and the Miss Coopers had warned him when he arrived more and more. He longed to make friends with Duncan Maxwell; but Maxwell, who for ever had a faint dread of Divine Grace at the back of his mind, would have nothing to say to him.

"Why are you so unkind to poor little Acott?" Nigel Dawson asked him. "He's so nice."

"I won't have these blasted parsons in my house," said Maxwell, really furious. "If you dare bring him to the Partenope I'll go to Sicily for the rest of the Winter. Damned cringing miserable little brute. He stinks of incense and wax. He makes me perfectly ill. I've reached the age, my dear boy, when I don't intend to be bothered any more with people I can't stand. No fee-aw!"

So Nigel Dawson took Acott to see John Scudamore at the Villa Parnasso instead.

John Scudamore was an American scholar who had come to Italy to buy antiquities for his university and had remained there to study them on his own account. For the last two hundred years at regular intervals, perhaps for longer, foreigners had been coming to Sirene and there been seized with a passion to prove that Suetonius and Tacitus had monstrously slandered Tiberius. They had remained on the island for years some of them, working away with fanatical industry at his whitewashing. When Scudamore arrived the time was ripe for another coat. That was over ten years ago. By now he was a recluse—a tall thin man with a long fine beard and a skin unnaturally white and seeming tralucent as the rim of a sperm-oil candle. He possessed as a writer a slow, laborious, and Teutonic style, though he was a ready enough and at times even a diverting talker. No sooner had he set to work on what was to be the final and grand rehabilitation of the slandered Emperor than he decided that his task would be but superficially accomplished unless it were preceded by a vast history of Roman morals. So he set to work on this magnum opus, accumulating more and more books, collating more and more notes, finding it every year more and more presumptuous to make a beginning until he had acquired more knowledge and still more. Everybody vowed that he was ruining his health by sitting up all night and sleeping all day. At this date he had not been outside one of the seven gates of the Villa Parnasso for two years. Yet this withdrawal was not entirely due to his studies. When he came to Sirene he brought with him a gypsy-faced young woman as housekeeper, and it was as much her jealousy as his own books that kept him at home, as much her appalling middle-west American cooking as his own late hours that made him look so wan and thin. She loved him as women like her so often love with as much exasperation as passion. She could not endure to have Scudamore's 'lady' friends treat her as a servant; and she made his life such a misery with her tantrums that for the sake of peace in which to work he gave way to her by inviting no woman, whatever her station, inside his house. Then she tried to keep away his men friends; and she made herself so objectionable with her insolence that fewer and fewer even of them used to visit the scholar.

"The only way with Nita," Duncan Maxwell told Nigel Dawson, "is to catch hold of her and tickle her as soon as she opens the door. Oh yes, that's what I always do, and she becomes most amenable—and really rather charming."

"What a disgusting idea!" Nigel exclaimed with a shudder. "I wouldn't tickle that horrible hussy for anything. Ugh! I couldn't!"

"It doesn't matter where you tickle her," said Maxwell earnestly. "Oh no, my dear boy. I've tickled her in the most extraordinary places, and she always brings *me* tea. I should shay sho!" And he concluded with one of his earth-shaking guffaws.

Nita had a habit of refusing to serve Scudamore's guests with tea when he rang for it. And the reason why Joseph Neave never visited his old friend nowadays to ask his advice about the translation of a phrase in the *Inferno* was because

Nita had banged him three times on the head with the tray the last time he was at the Parnasso.

It was a large villa in the middle of the oldest part of Sirene and close to Goldfinch's Villa Adonis. One reached it by a *sotto portici* in which the dim shops on either side had an oriental look. So, too, had the patio and the Moorish windows of the Villa Parnasso, still more its long garden with the fountain and immense cypresses and half a dozen barred and bolted doors in the high wall all round it. Within, all the rooms small and large were lined with books. Books stood in heaps on the floor. Books with tabs of paper sticking out of them lay on every table. Scudamore worked in whichever of the numerous rooms his references of the moment were to be found, and sometimes when you called to see him and when Nita was in a good mood she would be ten minutes before she found him in a remote corner of the villa, and he would come blinking and shuffling along to greet you in his grey dressing-gown that swept the ground like a wizard's robe.

Scudamore's humour was a mixture of American pawkiness and international pedantry. An elfin ponderousness is the paradox that describes it best. But he had an honest mind, which was what endeared him to Maxwell, that and his earnest patient scepticism and mass of unassorted information which Maxwell's swifter intelligence knew so much better than himself how to use. The little pink-faced chaplain found his scholarly conversation absorbing; and presently he began to feel as strongly as Scudamore himself about the injustice done to Tiberius. He had felt the same kind of indignation when an undergraduate about the treatment of Oscar Wilde.

"Let me persuade you to read through these chapters of Suetonius once more, Mr. Acott, remembering that Tiberius at this date was considerably over seventy. These are not the amusements of a septuagenarian. We have on Sirene at this moment three distinguished septuagenarians in my old friends Christopher Goldfinch, Dr. Mewburn, and Simon Pears. Can we imagine any of them capable of the performances which Suetonius attributes to Tiberius? I say 'No.' Could Joseph Rutger Neave, who is still in his sixties, with the best will in the world compete with the alleged efforts of Tiberius? Again I say 'No.' Suppose that Chris Goldfinch painted a picture of Meleager and Atalanta such as that which Tiberius is alleged to have hung in his bedroom? And suppose further that Chris like Parrhasius bequeathed it to Joseph? Would it ever disturb Joseph's dreams during his afternoon nap? Once more I say 'No.' But read up the alleged facts, Mr. Acott."

So, Cyril Acott read his Suetonius; and the next time he visited Scudamore he borrowed one or two other books which might have a bearing on the matter.

"Oh, and—er—have you by any chance got a spare copy of that dictionary of Greek and Latin—er—I believe it's called—er—er . . ."

"You mean my Erotic Dictionary translated from the German of Hiffelsbaumer?"

"Yes, I believe that is it. I gather it is a very accurate work. I'm anxious to get at the facts. I'm sure you will agree with me that it is the only way to read history. And I really owe it to my penitents. Moral Theology is not enough; I've often argued that. Even at Popney I sometimes get the most complicated sexual aberrations with which I ought to know how to deal. A priest is so dependent on theory. One of the greatest benefits of my holiday will be that I shall return to Popney with such a much more practical—I mean a much wider point of view."

"My library is at your service," Scudamore told him.

"I shouldn't disturb you if I came and browsed here?"

"Not at all. I sleep till three o'clock every afternoon. I'll tell Nita to give you the run of the Villa any morning you care to come around."

Occasionally, of course, Nita refused to admit the browser,

because she felt out of humour; but he was able to chew quite enough of Scudamore's rich cud. All through that Winter the little chaplain became more and more classical, less and less gothic. Then he conceived a romantic passion for Nigel Dawson whom he compared to Lysis. Finally Marsac arrived with his secretary and his Cingalese; and the Church Lads' Brigade began to seem rather dingy, the Popney Boy Scouts not even Bœotian.

"Give me your advice, Nigel," he begged. "Do you think that I am justified in not returning to my job in Popney this Summer in order to complete my cure here? I feel a tremendous need of the sun. The Sirene sun has already done me an enormous amount of good. I was undoubtedly on the verge of a nervous breakdown through excess of parochial work in uncongenial surroundings."

"I think you ought to do exactly what you want," said Nigel. "I think everybody ought to do what he wants. Hedonism is the only . . ."

"Yes, but, Nigel, would *you* be bored if I stayed?" the little chaplain asked, blinking sentimentally.

"My dear, of course I wouldn't. I'd adore to have you stay."

"Well, if I stay, and I think you ought to know that if I stay I shall be staying here more to enjoy the pleasure of your company than anything else, will you do me a favour?"

"I'll be having a lot of friends here this Summer," said Nigel quickly. Like many other hedonists he had a horror of sentimental responsibility.

"Oh, please don't think I'm going to be a bore," Acott pleaded. "If I can come and sit on the beach with you occasionally I shall be quite happy. But I want you to do something for me. I want you to be my churchwarden. You see, I'm in need of moral support over the collections. And I think it would please your mother."

"Sure!"

"And it would irritate Bookham—indeed it would infuriate Bookham."

"It certainly would," Nigel agreed.

"And then there's that portico that Marsac is going to give us. I shall want your help to make the opening ceremony something rather interior and subtle."

"Wouldn't it age me a good deal to become a churchwarden?" Nigel suggested anxiously. "It sounds so frightfully old. Oh, but wait a minute, couldn't I wear a white wig?"

"What, to make yourself look old?"

"No, no, oh, no! But I remember now seeing a churchwarden in Seville Cathedral with a perfectly adorable white wig and a silver wand and silk knee-breeches. He was in charge of the dance of the altar-boys. Oh, my dear Cyril, couldn't we have a dance of boys here, and I'll telephone to Naples to send me over a white wig at once?"

"But really, Nigel, I'm perfectly serious about your being my churchwarden."

"Oh, but I couldn't be somebody else's churchwarden. I could only be my own ultimately."

"No, please stop making fun, because I really do require your support over the collections."

So Nigel agreed to be the chaplain's warden, and for two or three days after his nomination he kept running up to people on the Piazza and saying:

"Oh, isn't it too marvellous? Have you heard that I've become a churchwarden? I feel as old as God, and I'm quite prostrated by my duties. They're absolutely œcumenical. My head's in a perfect whirl of collects, and I'm writing a sequel to the Song of Solomon."

A week later Mrs. Dawson invited the chaplain to dinner.

"Mr. Acott, I want to have you know how perfectly sweet I think it was of you to make Nigel your churchwarden. I can't just say what courage it has given me. I've wondered and wondered sometimes if I was doing right in letting him play around in Sirene the way he's doing. . . . You'd like a dash of absinthe in your cocktail ? That's right, so do I . . . but he's very delicate. He looks so strong and healthy, but he is very, very delicate, and sometimes I've just racked my brains to know whether I oughtn't to take him away to Switzerland. Oh yes, his father died in consumption. But life in one of those Swiss mountain resorts is no kind of life at all for a young man, and I feel that if Nigel had a serious interest in Sirene I wouldn't bother so much about Switzerland. You know what I mean ? . . . Just a little drop more ? Let me fill your glass. . . . Now, I've always thought that religion was the finest interest a young man could have. I've never been very religious myself. I don't know why. I've always had very deep feelings about everything, but I never seem to have had the time somehow to take it up as I'd have liked. I had a very dear friend in America whose religion was Beauty. You may have heard of her—Mrs. Arkwright-Hughes. She belonged to one of the best families in Louisiana. She wrote several books which we think very highly of in America. Of course we take writers more seriously over there than you do. Yes, her religion was Beauty. She studied all those funny old Greek vases and things. You know what I mean ? And she evolved for herself a new religion which certainly was terribly striking. She said that, if one practised putting oneself into the positions you see on those old Greek vases and things, not only did it improve and preserve the figure and considerably assist the digestive organs, but it also produced the very deepest religious feelings in the mentality of those who were putting themselves in those positions. She made out a list of exercises which certainly was very remarkable. I remember there was one in which you put your arms one way and your legs another and felt all kind of twisted up and all wrong somehow till you saw how cute it looked in the glass. And then while you were standing like this, preferably nood, but I never practised entirely nood, because if there's one thing I hate it's people knocking at my door and having to shout 'Come.' So I had a special costume designed which Mrs. Arkwright-Hughes paid me the great compliment of recommending in her next book. Well, where was I? Oh yes, well, when you were standing in this particular position you were given certain thoughts to accompany every motion, just the same as if it was music. That was a great point in her religion. I remember she called one of her books *Thought Melodies*. In fact she was a very exceptionally gifted woman and had a great following all over America. The first thing you had to do when you were standing like this was to establish a domination over your stomach. That was one of Mrs. Arkwright-Hughes' fundamental points. She said we let ourselves be dominated too much by our stomachs. And she wouldn't have anything to do with diet. Oh, no! Mrs. Arkwright-Hughes said we had to teach our stomachs to take what we gave them and not allow them to rebel against us. And then when you felt you'd dominated your stomach sufficiently, you had to go on and think about the beginning of the world and how it all came about. And she had a most beautiful method for teaching little girls and boys how they all came about. She said the proper instruction for children in sexual matters was so important. And she used to lecture to them in the sweetest way you can imagine with the most cunning little diagrams. She just couldn't understand how any mother could be so wicked as to let her children find out for themselves by reading the Bible and getting hold of medical dictionaries. She said it spoilt all the beauty of what she called the creative act. Mrs. Arkwright-Hughes just worshipped Beauty. Oh, she was perfectly mad about Beauty. And she had a very great influence over me, Mr. Acott, and that is why I'm so glad about Nigel being a church-warden. Of course, I wouldn't want him to be a clergyman or a minister or a priest. Oh, no, I think that would be just a terrible mistake. But a churchwarden, that's different. And especially here in Sirene where a young man ought to have a serious hobby. He really ought, Mr. Acott. I felt that myself, and as you know I come to church regularly all through the season. Oh, is dinner servito, Maria ? Come along, Mr. Acott. Nigel's dining out somewhere. And I thought you wouldn't mind keeping me company this evening."

The chaplain did not give his churchwarden a great deal of work that Summer. He was enjoying too much the sun and the moonlight and the salt water, the picnics on Monte Ventoso, the exploration of curious grottos, and the parties at the Villa Decamerone. Miss Virginia vowed that he was the only minister she had ever met with as much spunk as a June-bug, and he became a feature of those gay nights at the Villa Amabile, he and the Temple of Vesta which was now finished. Marsac's patronage of him was quite enough to allay most of the criticism, for even Mrs. Rosebotham took to playing the harmonium again when she heard that the Count was spending seven thousand francs on the porch, which was probably a good deal more than the rest of the little white church cost originally. It was understood that a frieze of mosaic was to be a feature of the gift ; but the subject of this decoration was kept a secret, and special workmen had been imported from the mainland to carry out the donor's design. Marsac did not accept an invitation to the Villa Minerva, because Miss Virginia disapproved of that household, and she made it quite clear that she should resent extremely even dear Count Bob's having any truck with it.

On the seventh of September being the eve of the Nativity of the B.V.M. it was the custom of the Sirenesi to spend the whole night on the top of Timberio and to hear Mass at dawn in the little church beside the great gilded Madonna, who to John Scudamore's mortification now dominated the ruins of the imperial villa. It was a night of fireworks and feasting, of drinking and dancing and music and love. If it had not been for the lamentably pietistic conclusion to the revelry Scudamore would have given it his wholehearted approval as the nearest approach to the Bacchanalia now left. But he felt a deep bitterness against the gilded Madonna, whose image in his opinion occupied exactly the spot where a statue to the Emperor Tiberius should have been erected to commemorate his martyrdom by gossip. Sirene knew that the appropriation of Timberio by the priests was a perpetual grief to the scholar, so that, when it was announced that he had accepted an invitation to dine at the Villa Decamerone on the evening of September 7th, and take part with Marsac in his organized revel on Timberio afterward, the island felt that the Count's charm had marked its ultimate triumph.

The ladies of Sirene were inclined to be hurt when they found that they were not going to be invited to this party.

"I am sorry, madame," said Marsac to every woman who protested in turn. "But we have the intention to celebrate at dawn a mystic rite of strange significance from which I feel compelled to exclude *toutes les dames*. Oh, yes, I am afraid that I must do so. But I hope you will pardon me by coming to lunch with me at the Villa Decamerone after the unveilment of my new portico."

And with this the ladies had to be content.

"Well, I think Count Bob's right," said Miss Virginia to Mrs. Neave. "Let the men enjoy themselves without us for once. My! they don't always want us butting in and spoiling their fun."

"But, dear Miss Virginia, I can't possibly let Joseph go without I'm there to look after him," said Mrs. Neave. "He gets so excited, and he might drink too much, and his heart just won't stand it."

Mrs. Neave was remembering with some resentment for so good-natured a woman the numerous parties to which she and Joseph had both been invited and which she had had to forgo, because Joseph thought they might be bad for his heart.

However, Mrs. Neave's protests were no more successful than were the protests of Beatrice Mewburn against such an adventure for her father.

"I've done my best to dissuade him," she bemoaned. "But he won't listen to a word from me. There's no doubt he'll catch pneumonia and die. It's most distressing, and poor little Dorothy's Summer will be spoilt after all, just when I was really beginning to hope that she might get through without falling ill herself. Poor child, she has the tenderest heart and the notion of her grandfather's spending the whole night out on Timberio has quite prostrated her. I've left her lying down in her room with the most racking headache. I wish you could have heard the beautiful resignation in her voice when I asked her if there was anything I could do for her. 'Nothing, thank you, auntie dear.' It was really heartrending."

Angela Pears too was extremely indignant with Simon.

"Well, I think it's just derned silliness, granpa. What do you guess you're going to do anyway? You can't run about blowing a horn all night at your age, you old peanut."

"Where's my tuxedo?" the poet demanded obstinately.

"Well, just hark at that! My dear granpa, you gave your tuxedo to Antonio four years ago." Antonio was the domestic tyrant of the Villa Rienzi.

"Blast Antonio!" the poet swore. "I'll send around and borrow a suit from Chris Goldfinch."

"Granpa, don't *be* so foolish. You couldn't wear one of C. G.'s suits. You're three times his size around."

But Simon Pears intended to go to the Count's dinner-party in evening-dress, and in the end he borrowed a suit from Ferdinando Zampone, which was so big for him that he felt as comfortable in it as if he was in his own scarlet dressing-gown.

Mrs. Ambrogio was perhaps the only woman except the Norton girls who was not jealous of the Count's party.

"So glad Peter's going. So good for him. Trust him anywhere without women. Nobody to pinch. Nobody to pinch."

"He'll find plenty of girls to pinch on Timberio, Maud," said Mrs. de Feltre, who had not yet succeeded in being invited to the Villa Decamerone for any kind of party.

"No, he won't. Oh, no! He's too good a Catholic for that. Loves his Church. Won't pinch anybody with the Madonna looking on. Trust him anywhere in church."

"But he won't be in church before six o'clock in the morning, you silly thing," Mrs. de Feltre retorted pettishly.

"Don't care. Don't care. Peter's going. So pleased about it. Snubbed by some of the people here. Such a sell. Dear Count. Don't care what he does. Love him. Hear all about it from Peter."

Marsac had invited both Alberto and Enrico Jones; and it was typical of the Jones system that one should accept and the other should decline. The Jones system was never to commit yourself unequivocally to anything or anybody. Suppose that the party created a scandal? Alberto and Enrico had their own ideas about Marsac. A scandal was possible. In that case the presence of Enrico would be forgotten in the more conspicuous absence of Alberto. And if all went well yet awhile with Marsac, as seemed probable, the presence of Enrico would be more conspicuous than the unavoidable and greatly regretted absence of Alberto. The brothers had their own ideas about the newcomer; but of course neither of them had admitted to the other that he had any of these ideas.

"I don't believe that I will be able to go to our friend's party to-night, Enrico. I seem to have a disturbed stomach," Alberto announced.

"*Meglio riposare*," Enrico murmured, twitching his scalp sympathetically.

"It is nothing, but I think it would be wise," Alberto agreed. "I will write my excuses now."

Enrico politely pushed the inkhorn toward his brother, and it was strange to see him mopping his forehead like that, because there was a chill in the air of the Palazzo Inglese that evening—the first touch of Autumn perhaps.

Chapter 7

non tu, Pomponi, cena diserta tua est.

MARTIAL

SIRENIAN tradition has played as many tricks with Marsac as it has played with Tiberius. All sorts of people living on the island at this moment are credited with the most fantastic behaviour on the night of that dinner-party. Many of these tales can definitely be traced to Duncan Maxwell, who was chasing snakes in Bavaria when it took place and so must deliberately have invented them all when he came home. However, he was probably not responsible for the legend that immediately after the dessert was cleared away Major Natt, wearing nothing but a red rose, danced an erotic Persian dance on the table. Maxwell would have been too nice about his botany to give him a large enough rose in a Sirenian September. Madame Sarbécoff is supposed to have gone to the party disguised as a Georgian prince and made love to the Cingalese servant in the pantry. This, of course, is absurd. Equally absurd is the story that Mrs. Ambrogio bribed the Count's chef to serve her up in a large pie. Neither lady was present. Nor was Bookham present, and the stories about his having stolen all Marsac's silver spoons can certainly be attributed to Maxwell. Bookham was invited, and he had every intention of going. Unfortunately he had talked so loudly of what he intended to do with the chaplain on the first suitable occasion that Mrs. Bookham, who never went out of the Villa San Giorgio, and pictured Herbert dealing with the ill-behaved foreigners of Sirene like a berserker, locked him in his room to prevent his murdering Acott. Indeed to this day she will assure you that it was only she who kept Herbert from murdering everybody present at dinner that night.

"Herbert hates vice, and Herbert is such an Englishman that if he had seen Major Natt dancing that disgusting dance he'd have been bound to kill him for the honour of his country," she still assures strangers who put half-crowns in the collection and are therefore invited to tea at the Villa San Giorgio. And the strangers are only too eager to believe such stories, because the more credulous a tourist the better value he feels he is getting out of his trip.

Actually there were present at this dinner Marsac and his secretary, Christopher Goldfinch, Simon Pears, Dr. Mewburn, Joseph Neave, Nigel Dawson, Peter Ambrogio, Svend Ibsen, Francis Cartright, Enrico Jones, John Scudamore, Austin Follett, Cyril Acott, Archie Macadam, Major Natt, an ebullient Belgian hunchback called Martel, who was trying to grow rich intellectually as quickly as his father had grown rich materially out of cheap glass, a decayed French symbolist poet whose name is forgotten, and four or five others whose personalities have left no mark on Sirene.

Marsac had spared neither his ingenuity nor his pocket to make the dinner-party remarkable. There was a moment when success trembled in the balance, and this was at the very beginning while the host was reciting an ode to Dionysus of Pindaric complexity and, to his guests it seemed, of epic length. The only people who could follow Marsac's swift and florid French were Martel, who did not understand what the poem was about, and the decayed symbolist who thought he could have written a much better one himself. Luckily a tray of superb green and golden cocktails arrived as the host declaimed the last half-dozen 'Evoes.' With these buzzing in their heads the twenty-four guests sat down cheerfully to unhook the fat pink prawns from their finger-bowls.

"I have had the fancy, gentlemen," the host proclaimed, "to make this dinner *couleur de rose*. Everything will be rose to-night."

"*Bien, bien*," Martel yapped. "*Couleur de rose*, that is good. I like that much. The idea is clever, I think. Original. Yes?"

"Except *naturellement* the wine," added Marsac. "Rose wine would not be very amusing, I think."

"Drink hearty, Count," cried Goldfinch, raising his glass of amber Sirenian.

"*Couleur de rose*," the Count repeated complacently. "I flatter myself that I shall have some pretty *surprises* to show you."

"I hope to goodness he doesn't mean to give us underdone meat," Macadam muttered to Cartright his neighbour.

"Oh, I don't think so, Macadam," said Cartright in that queer awed voice he always used when he was dining out.

"Because if there's one thing I cannot stand, it's underdone meat," Macadam continued sternly.

The prawns were succeeded by bortch, the bortch by crayfish, the crayfish by red mullet.

"Alas, I am afraid I cannot offer you *saumon* as I would like," said Marsac. "Monsieur Ibsen, to whom I applied for some of his Norwayian *saumon*, would not provide us with that extreme delicacy."

The ladylike Norwegian wriggled on his chair, not unlike a landed salmon himself.

"Oh, Comte Marsac, how cruel of you to taunt me! Most cruel, I declare."

He went on wriggling so much that the Major, who was sitting on one side of him, put out an arm to prevent his wriggling off his chair under the table, at which the Norwegian giggled shrilly:

"Oh, Major Natt, Major Natt! You're tickling me!"

"Most embarrassing," said the Major, relating this incident afterwards. "Sort of thing that happens to a clergyman in a railway-carriage. I suppose it'll be all over Sirene now that I was tickling that epicene Scandinavian at Marsac's dinner. My almost brutally normal appetite shrinks from such an aspersion. I hope you'll bear me out, Cartright, that my impulse was purely humanitarian without the least tincture of philandrogyny."

"Waste no regrets on salmon, Count. The red mullet is the more classic fish," said old Dr. Mewburn. "It was a mullet with which a Sirenese fisherman greeted Tiberius."

"But to be strictly in the manner," Scudamore added, "our host should have had them boiled alive before us in glass bowls, and so, as Seneca says, fed our eyes before our throats with the spectacle of their changing hues in death reputed to rival the dolphin's."

The Count was evidently vexed by the suggestion that he had missed a picturesque opportunity.

"I have always found Sénèque an excessively annoysome writer," he said, frowning. "But I sincerely regret the unimagination of my cook."

Everybody made haste to reassure him with praise of the dish as it had been served.

"By gad," Christopher Goldfinch hastily exclaimed, "these red mullet are great. Count, drink hearty!" He raised his glass again to the host. "And this Sirene wine is stunning. I've never tasted better in all the years I've lived here."

"I regret that I cannot offer to Mr. Scudamore antique Falernian or Opimian," said Marsac, who was still feeling a little huffed over the mullet.

"Don't apologize," Scudamore replied imperturbably. "Anyway, this is not the Sorrentine that Tiberius called a generous vinegar. And it is the best Sirenian. I doubt if Caecuban or Mamertine or Nomentan were better. By the way, Opimian was not a distinct wine. It was a vintage of Caecuban; but the mistake is a common one."

The host frowned at this second correction; but the red mullet were succeeded by cockscombs *à la financière*, and with them luckily appeared the champagne.

"By gad," said Christopher, "I don't know when I've enjoyed a Sirene dinner so much. Simon, old friend, drink hearty."

"Fifty years, Chris, my dear old friend," responded the poet.

"Oh, hell, I can't believe it," the painter groaned.

The cockscombs were succeeded by braised tongue.

"Monsieur Scudamore, I regret excessively to see that you are eating nothing," said the Count with a mixture of arrogance and solicitude. "I fear this dish offends against your classic taste."

"Why, I'm eating a whole banquet," the scholar affirmed, interrupting with evident reluctance the lecture he was giving his neighbour on the wines of ancient Rome to toy with the food on his plate.

"Scudamore, old friend! Drink hearty," Goldfinch adjured him. "Wine and women! Women and wine! What more do we want?"

"Permit me not to agree with you entirely, my dear Monsieur Goldfinch," said Marsac. "Personally I find that women partake too much of the dish which we now see before us."

"What's he saying?" murmured Goldfinch to his neighbour. "I'm damned if I can understand what he's talking about. He talks so blasted quick."

"Women frighten me to death," Ibsen announced with a shudder.

"No woman ever frightened me," said Goldfinch. "No, sir!"

"You were frightened by your wife, Chris," his old friend Simon reminded him.

"Never!" the painter maintained. "Gad, if it had to be, I wouldn't be frightened by Mrs. Rosebotham."

And here we may trace the origin of the Sirene fable that soon after the date of this dinner-party Christopher Goldfinch followed Mrs. Rosebotham into her bathing-hut and begged her to elope with him to Naples by the afternoon boat, giving as his reason that she was the only woman on the island to whom he had never tried to make love.

"I think women are monsters," Nigel Dawson cried. "They say the Sirens had claws and fishes' tails. What woman hasn't?"

"Gad, I can't stand this," said Christopher, rising unsteadily to his feet. "Where's the son of a bitch who said women were monsters? Where is he? I don't want to break up a good dinner, but I won't eat another drop until the man who said women were monsters apologizes."

But just then the braised tongue was removed, and the babble of excited chatter in the ante-room suggested that the next dish was likely to be something unusual.

"Gentlemen," Marsac shouted, "I implore your attention for my *couleur de rose*. Gentlemen, I have procured roast flamingos."

"The authentic phœnicopter," exclaimed Scudamore, genuine admiration in his voice. "Count, I congratulate you. If, like the Spartan with the sea-urchin of whom Athenæus tells us, I never eat another I'll eat this!"

"*Moi aussi*," Martel yapped. "Before last year I have the kidney who floats; but last year I have the operation and he floats no longer. I eat and drink all I see, yes! For which I rejoice, yes!"

And as the birds in full rosy plumage were carried solemnly in on silver dishes Nigel Dawson shrieked:

"Oh, my dear, how too marvellous! I've longed all my life to eat a flamingo."

"My god, I hope he doesn't give me the drumstick,"

Archie Macadam muttered. "Either I'm a bit more drunk than usual, or else those ruddy birds are pink."

"Scudamore," old Dr. Mewburn boomed, "this is Trimalchio's banquet laid anew. Do you remember . . ." And in his sonorous voice he began to quote from the *Satyricon*. Scudamore responded from Martial:

"*Dat mihi pinna rubens nomen, sed lingua gulosis
   nostra sapit. Quid si garrula lingua foret?*"

Whereupon Joseph Neave started to reel off the stanzas about gluttons from the *Inferno*.

"I do not altogether agree with you that my dinner is à la Trimalchio," said Marsac haughtily. "I would prefer to suppose that it resembled more the divine Symposium of Plato."

"Plato. That is good. I like that much," Martel yapped. "The god of averse love, I think. Yes?"

Simon Pears snatched a handful of feathers from the flamingos, stuck them in his hair, and began to declaim the opening lines of his notorious epic about Red Indians.

"It's uncommonly like eating an expensive hat," said the Major, looking dubiously at his portion. "I wonder if it would be good manners to suck the plumes. What is your opinion, Macadam?"

"My opinion is that if I'd seen these sanguinary birds by myself I'd have been told I was drunk."

The rest of the dishes were actually as rosy as those that had preceded them; but if they had been bright blue the guests would still have thought them rosy, so richly incarnadined did they themselves become.

Now, when the host stood up on his chair to recite another ode to Dionysus even more Pindarically complicated than the first, they applauded loudly almost every line, though they probably understood even less of it than they had understood of the other.

"Brother, I salute you," Simon Pears proclaimed with

internal noises like a bass trombone. "You are a true poet."

"Corking," Christopher Goldfinch agreed.

"I'll dance the hula-hula," Nigel Dawson offered with a shriek of enthusiasm.

"I'll try to remember a sonnet I once wrote," cried the chaplain. "Oh, how does it begin? How does it begin? I know. I know. I know.

> *"I saw the acolytes about the chancel sway*
> *Like dim red roses in the moonlit dusk."*

"Like dam red noses in a Putney bus," Archie Macadam shouted. "What did I tell you, Cartright? What did I tell you half-way through the course before the course before last?"

"You were talking about a good many things, Macadam."

"No, I wasn't, you liar."

"I say, steady, Macadam. Don't let's get unpleasant with each other," Cartright protested.

"The origin of evil is buried in the mists of antiquity," Follett proclaimed in his high nasal treble; and then, overcome by the humour of this discovery, he slid from his chair to the floor, and spinning round on his bony posteriors declared he was a teetotal teetotum, at which joke he continued to laugh to himself for ten minutes without stopping.

"Gentlemen," Marsac cried, "I must beg you now if you please to wreathe your brows and hang yourselves with garlands."

> *"Quis udo*
> *deproperare apio coronas*
> *curatve myrto?"*

Scudamore asked.

No doubt the sober onlooker would have decided that the revellers thus bedecked with parsley and myrtle resembled more a company of people who had reached the stage of pulling crackers and dressing themselves up with their contents than the authentic conviviality of imperial Rome. Luckily, except Enrico Jones, who was pretending to be as drunk as everybody else, there was no sober onlooker to chill them with prosaic eyes.

"Gentlemen, I regret extremely," said the host, "that I cannot provide you with flute-girls from Lesbos. For music we must content ourselves with the mandolins and guitars of Sirene."

Doors opened. Six of the Sirene barbers, most of whom were musical, entered and marched round the room playing Neapolitan airs.

"Oh gad, I feel twenty-five again," Christopher Goldfinch groaned in a senile rapture.

"They are waiting to escort us to Timberio," the host announced, "and I can promise you that we will divert ourselves exceedingly on the way.'

A huge honey-coloured moon hung over the Salernian gulf, the placid waters of which sparkled with the torches and lamps of two or three hundred boats fishing for some delicacy of the season. There were lights, too, twinkling on the topmost slopes of Monte Ventoso where the Ana-sirenesi were dancing and drinking and feasting like their cousins on Timberio, from the direction of which came the distant confused noise of trumpets and squeakers being blown. The mandolin escort led the way up. The guests followed, dancing and singing. Every half mile of the road Marsac had provided tables loaded with fruit and wine where the players refreshed themselves; and if they were drunk when they started from the Villa Decamerone they were not less drunk when they arrived at the ruins of the Emperor's villa. The cavernous cellars, all that remained of that imperial grandeur, were illuminated with candles and lanterns, and inside most of them the Sirenesi were dancing tarantellas to the accompaniment of bands, hand-organs, and stringed instruments. Everybody seemed to be drinking red wine or eating sausages. The night reeked of garlic, and from the vineyards the heady perfume of crushed grapes filled the air. The natives were delighted to welcome the foreigners, especially when word went round that the *signor conte* had provided twelve barrels of red Sirenian for the refreshment of the populace.

Simon Pears was greeted by an old woman with whom he fancied vaguely that he had an idyll some forty or fifty years ago.

"*Io sono la bella Concettina*," she assured him.

"*Io remember bene*," he vowed. "*Abbiamo baciato molto, molto, molto.*"

"*Sì, signore, e chiù ancora*," she shrilled to the intense delight of the onlookers. "'*O signor faceva bene l'amore quando era giovanotto. Bel lavoro! Evvero, signorino?*"

The venerable American poet nodded his head in solemn agreement.

"*Balliamo la tarantella*," he suggested with grave courtesy to the old lady.

"*Con piacere, signorino*," she enthusiastically agreed, setting her arms akimbo in readiness, and let it be remembered that '*signorino*' means 'young sir.'

The guitars and mandolins were reinforced by an orchestra that seemed to consist chiefly of wooden clappers played by the local youth.

Simon Pears had been a notable exponent of the tarantella long ago when the foreign society of Sirene was exclusively bohemian. And even to-night he gave a remarkable performance for so old a man, in spite of the fact that Ferdinando Zampone's suit hung round him in folds. Simon was heavily built himself. So was the ancient Concettina. And the thud of their *culate* would not have disgraced a big drum. The applause of the onlookers made Christopher Goldfinch, Joseph Neave, and dear old Dr. Mewburn a little jealous, and they presently got themselves partners too; but the comely young wenches they so carefully selected would giggle all the time, and the performance entirely lacked the *brio* of the original pair.

"I can no longer hold my own with Venus Callipyge," Mewburn sighed ruefully to Scudamore as he withdrew from the arena.

"*Intermissa, Venus, diu rursus bella moves,*" Scudamore warned him.

"You're right, ah yes, you're right," the doctor sighed. "*Non sum qualis eram bonae sub regno Cinarae.*"

The defender of Tiberius consoled him with some graceful lines of resignation from elsewhere in Horace; and soon afterward Marsac was calling on his guests to follow him down through the dishevelled vineyards to the site of the Villa Hylas. Here they found that a large marquee had been erected in which they could rest and refresh themselves. The Count retired into a smaller tent alongside whence he emerged again dressed in an orange tunic and pale yellow chlamys stencilled with gold, on his fair wavy hair a scarlet Phrygian cap.

"Gentlemen, I hope you will do me the honour of aiding me to insert some trees I have designed to insert here in honour of the gods."

Gardeners appeared; and the guests planted very crookedly, owing as they said to the wavering light thrown by the torches, myrtles and roses for Aphrodite, for Artemis a plane, for Hera pomegranates, for Pallas Athene olives; and for Demeter they sprinkled the fine seeds of poppies. Then for Apollo they planted bays and palms, for Dionysus vines and ivy, for Heracles white poplars, for Hermes whispering reeds, for Hades cypresses and the bulbs of narcissus, for Poseidon Aleppo pines, and oaks for Zeus, the father of gods and men.

"And if we want to avoid the most merciless jag," Scudamore suggested, "I would recommend the sacrifice of a cock to Aesculapius as well."

Marsac, in spite of the gardeners' protests, was now

sousing all the newly planted trees with wine, after which he recited a dedicatory poem in French nebulous with invoked abstractions.

"And now, gentlemen, there remains to be celebrated the most mystic and solemn rite of all. You have perceived my costume?"

They had. They were not yet too drunk not to have perceived that.

"Instead of greeting the dawn with the bourgeois celebrations of an *épuisé* Christianism, I invite you to greet it in the spirit with which in the time of the admirable Tiberius it was greeted by sailors."

"My hat," muttered Archie Macadam, "if he thinks I'm going out in a boat after all this wine he's made a very big mistake."

But Marsac was planning a visit to an ancient grotto of Mithras which lay at the head of a narrow gorge above the sea and which must often have been visited by sailors landing from the corn ships that brought the grain to Rome from Alexandria.

"I have ventured to vest myself in the costume of that charming young god," he observed, "and, though I regret that I cannot offer you the spectacle of the sacrificed bull, I think that we shall prepare ourselves very well for the ceremony of the unveilment of my portico to-morrow by spending an hour or two in the sacred grotto, where I have commanded breakfast to be prepared for us."

The grotto of Mithras at Sirene is given but a single star by Baedeker. Had he seen the procession which corkscrewed down the cliff path below the future site of the Villa Hylas at three o'clock of this September morning he would have added another and accorded it the highest decoration he confers. But it proved the final effort of the guests. When they reached the grotto in the chilly hour before dawn and found it full of fur rugs and cushions they sank down exhausted.

"Gentlemen," said their host, "permit me to offer to you something which will make you pleasant dreams."

Some vowed he had put opium in the punch; others declared that it was cocaine; a few held out for hashish. Whatever it was, the guests were overcome by an inextricable drowsiness, and while Marsac spoke to them of the necessary Mithraic initiation that they ought to undergo and of the eighty trials that they must suffer they began to nod. He spoke of the courageous spirit they must keep up in fire and in water, in hunger and in thirst. He spoke of scourging and solitude and heaven knows what; but they only nodded more profoundly. He babbled of the seven degrees of the initiation; of the Ravens, the Secret, the Fighters, the Lions, the Persians, the Sun-runners, and the Fathers; but they began to snore. He proclaimed himself to be the Lord and Creator of all things and the Father and Source of all life; but they heeded him not, and the cave was filled with the rich breath of vinous sleep. Soon Marsac himself followed the example of his guests. The candles stuck on the ledges of rock wavered and guttered in the sharp air of dawn, which was stealing up from the gorge below from a sea that was like grey satin. Quails on their way to Africa sank weak-winged in the dewy *macchia*, calling to one another with sweet notes. The horns and squeakers on the slopes of Timberio far above were silent now. The revellers must have been shivering and yawning and wishing it was already six o'clock with the lemon sunlight warming the stones against which they would loll while Mass went cheerfully forward.

Enrico Jones rose quickly and, leaving his companions fast asleep in the cave, walked home by a path cut in the cliffs. On his way he met several sportsmen after quail, their lean red or black dogs ranging the thickets of myrtle and heather for their game. The nearer he drew to the town the more superior he felt himself to those snoring pigs he had left behind in the grotto. And most of them at some time or another had been inclined to patronize him. Enrico scowled. The indignation of a reformer burned within him. Were he Tiberius he would have the whole lot of these degenerates flung headlong from the *salto* into the dark sea a thousand feet below there to be clubbed to death by the oars of waiting mariners. He would purge Sirene of this corrupt society. Let this French pervert build his villa, and then let him live in it. He would learn that he could not buy the real Sirenians. Enrico dreamed like a Collot d'Herbois of aristocratic affronts, and of his vengeance for them one day. It was a queer mood for a man to bring away with him from what had been such a jolly evening; but the Joneses were a queer family. You could always prophesy easily enough what they would do; but you never knew what they were thinking or what they would think. Enrico's mind was like his room in the Palazzo Inglese, unimaginable, and instead of a bee he had a very alert spider in his bonnet.

The door of Alberto's equally unimaginable room was ajar when the returned reveller passed it, and heard his brother's voice call from within:

"My stomach is better."

Enrico nodded.

"Did you have a pleasant night?" Alberto asked.

Enrico shrugged his shoulders, and pulled the lobe of his right ear with a significant gesture.

"I've left them all drunk in the grotto of Mithras."

Alberto clicked his tongue and, turning over with a sigh of relief, wished his brother *buon riposo*. He always had a dread when he refused an invitation that he might miss the rich bride of his dreams. He could now sleep in peace.

The unveiling of the new portico was scheduled, as Bookham put it, for ten-thirty that morning; but long before that hour the anxious womankind of Marsac's guests were calling upon each other for news. When it was established

that not one of them had been heard of since they were
seen dancing in the cellars of the Villa Jovis, some of the
anxiety was allayed. They could not all have had accidents
or eloped or died of heart failure. A theory gradually
gathered ground that the whole party had invaded the
Villa Amabile for breakfast. But at ten o'clock the old
ladies arrived on the Piazza on their white donkeys, and
were as much astonished as everybody else at the absence
of the revellers.

"I guess dear Count Bob is preparing some surprise for
us at the church," said Miss Virginia. "Let's go right
along. He'll surely be there."

But dear Count Bob was not there, nor any of his guests.

"Has anybody been down to the Decamerone?" Miss
Maimie asked. She was beginning to feel a little anxious
herself now.

The Villa Decamerone was visited; but all the servants
declared volubly that they were without news of the *signor
conte*.

"I don't see how we can very well postpone the unveiling
of the porch," said Bookham. "After all, it *is* a sacred
matter."

The feud between the Pepworth-Nortons and Bookham
had until now prevented any acknowledgment of one
another; but this was too much for Miss Virginia.

"I'd be mighty glad to know who is going to unveil the
porch if it isn't the Count?" she snapped.

"I shall unveil it myself, Miss Pepworth-Norton," the
churchwarden proclaimed majestically.

"Turn your donkey's head right around, Maimie," she
commanded. "We'll go back to the Decamerone and wait
there for dear Bob."

Bookham had no desire at all to flout the donor; but he
was extremely anxious to flout and also to humiliate the
chaplain, and that was the reason why he was bent on holding
the ceremony at the advertised hour. To the ladies of the

congregation (and those old harridans were not that) he implied that any delay would be disrespectful to Heaven. Mrs. Rosebotham was as anxious as he was to score off the chaplain, and with her support it was idle for the rest of the congregation to object. So it was Bookham who with a tremendous gesture tore down the covering; and it was Bookham who had to explain why it was that the angular figure of a Saint Sebastian wearing nothing but four arrows should be considered an appropriate decoration for a place of worship dedicated to St. Simon and St. Jude.

"Did you pass this disgusting design?" Mrs. Rosebotham demanded.

Bookham was in a difficult position. He could not disown a porch for which he had accepted a commission from the builder of five hundred liras.

"My dear lady, you can hardly call the representation of a saint disgusting," Bookham parried. "I think that's going too far."

"I shall telegraph to the Bishop and ask him to come down here at once and reconsecrate the church," said Mrs. Rosebotham. "And I shall have Mr. Acott unfrocked."

Bookham attempted a heavy joke:

"I say, don't let's have any more unfrocking. Haw-haw!"

Mrs. Rosebotham, Mrs. Gibbs, Mrs. Onslow, Mrs. Kafka, and the Miss Coopers blasted him with a look.

"It may be a little modern, Mrs. Rosebotham," the churchwarden argued. "But Count Marsac *is* very modern, and after all he has spent a large sum of money on our little church. I can't help thinking that the Bishop will appreciate that. Personally I think that if we look at this design in the right spirit it's going to be very helpful."

"*Molto bello, evvero?*" interposed Maestro Supino, admiring his work. "*Naturale assai.*"

But further expressions of admiration or disgust were interrupted by the rumour of an excited crowd approaching;

and the horror inspired by that decadent mosaic on the frieze of the portico was nothing compared with the horror with which so many of the ladies of Sirene beheld their nearest and dearest being led along the Via Timberio by four *carabinieri*.

"Joseph, Joseph," cried Mrs. Neave rushing forward. "What has happened, what has happened?"

"Don't get so excited, Elsie," he snapped. "The whole thing is a misunderstanding."

The ladies looked at one another in dismay. What should they do? Their menfolk were apparently under arrest, and yet their menfolk presented such an astonishing spectacle that they hesitated to join the crowd of small boys that brought up the rear of the disreputable procession.

To see Mr. Pears in a dress-suit that hung round him in folds and with a laurel wreath round his neck, to see the Count in bright orange and yellow attire with a scarlet cap of liberty on his head, to see Nigel Dawson with the blurred appearance of one swimming under water, to see Mr. Goldfinch leaning in a state of bedragglement on the arm of a Cingalese, to see Mr. Macadam being carried by Mr. Ambrogio and Mr. Follett, to see in fact the whole of that party in the cruel light of the morning being led like felons along the public street was beyond anything that even Sirene had performed in the way of caricaturing respectability.

"Take courage, ladies," the Count besought them with a cheerful wave of his arm. "These excellent *carabinieri* are only acting under orders. I hope excessively to have the pleasure of seeing you all at lunch."

"I think we'd better stay quiet right where we are," said Mrs. Dawson. "I don't know what they've been doing, but in case it's anything just a little bit . . ." She coughed discreetly. . . . "I'm sure you agree with me, Mrs. Neave, and you too, Miss Mewburn, we'd better stay right here."

Naturally, as soon as the *maresciallo* saw who the prisoners were, he released them with many apologies. What had happened was that an enthusiastic tourist led by the star in Baedeker had visited the grotto of Mithras. He had entered the cave just as the Cingalese was massaging away the effects of the riotous night from his master. Startled by this Mithraic vision and the presence of a number of shadowy forms apparently clothed in leopard skins, the tourist had hurried as fast as he could to the *municipio* to relate his ghost-story and obtain witnesses for his credibility. The city fathers of Sirene did not care a button about ghosts, but they were jealous of their caves' reputation. They did not want a recrudescence of that undressing in public places which had given the island such a bad name. So the *sindaco* went off to the *maresciallo* and begged him to send his *carabinieri* at once to the grotto of Mithras and arrest everybody inside for an outrage against pudor. When the *carabinieri* arrived and found some two dozen of the leading foreign residents of Sirene yawning themselves out of a heavy sleep they were most unwilling to incommode the *signori*, but orders were orders. Nobody who has lived for any length of time in Italy ever argues with a *carabiniere*. Hence the procession that so much shocked the ladies of Sirene. It was some time before the party could get home and change, because the *maresciallo* (with many apologies for the delay) had had to enter the names of all the prisoners together with their ages, the places of their birth, their occupations, and the names of their fathers and mothers in one book when they were brought in under arrest, and then enter all these autobiographical details over again in another book when they were set free again. This occupied over an hour because not only did the *maresciallo's* pen and ink behave like the pen and ink of all Italian officials, but also the names being foreign were most difficult to transcribe. However, the documentation was accomplished at last, and they parted with much cordiality, the *maresciallo* assuring his captives that he should lose no time now in effecting the arrest of the tourist who had laid the false information. This was done, and the tourist spent three days in the Sirene gaol, after which he was expelled from the island as a dangerous pest.

In most places the arrest of so many prominent foreigners would have been a topic of conversation for weeks. In Sirene it was forgotten the next day. It is only to the sentimentalist over some tame midland prospect that man appears vile. In Sirene he holds his own with the sublime eccentricity of the natural scene. In Sirene he lives.

Chapter 8

*Decembri mense, quo volant mappae
gracilesque ligulae cereique chartaeque
et acuta senibus testa cum Damascenis.*

MARTIAL

THAT extravagant party at the Villa Decamerone brought the Summer to an end. Rain fell for ten days afterward, after which Sirene settled down to the tranquil enjoyment of its benign blue and white Autumn. The Reverend Cyril Acott went back to the East End; and if the Bishop of Europe paid any attention to the numerous letters of protest that Mrs. Rosebotham sent him, the only sign of it was the appointment of the Reverend William Wills as chaplain for the following season. Mr. Wills was the oldest-looking clergyman ever seen on the island, indeed probably the oldest-looking clergyman ever seen anywhere. Had you been told that he was the favourite preacher of the Prince Regent when he stayed at Brighton, or even of George III when he visited Weymouth, you would hardly have said more than ' was he indeed ? ' He had a beard so long and so thick that he was never upset by the hoops of the little Sirenesi being driven between his legs, for it served as a sort of cow-catcher, and it was generally believed that he used it as a most efficacious mosquito-net. Scudamore had a theory that he had already been dead for some years and that it was only his beard and nails which were still alive, it being a well-known fact that the beard and nails continue to grow long after death. In addition to being excessively old Mr. Wills was married, and his wife accompanied him to Sirene. She was very old too, shrivelling up inside her stays like a stranded winkle in its shell. Mrs. Rosebotham felt hopeful of avoiding any ecclesiastical scandal this year; but she never met the chaplain and his wife without taking care to warn them of the danger of accepting invitations to what might sound like quiet parties, but were really orgies. Poor Cyril Acott wrote several letters to Nigel Dawson from St. Aidan's Clergy House, Popney; but Nigel forgot to answer them, and all too soon the late chaplain became a Sirene legend. At this moment he is the vicar of a parish in the North of England, and Sirene to him is now no more than a sunny snapshot turning a little browner every year in the album of his memory. Bookham began by being very friendly with Mr. and Mrs. Wills; but soon after Christmas he was quarrelling with the new chaplain over the collections. The old gentleman finally took to counting the money under his beard, which irritated the churchwarden so much that by early Spring they were not on speaking terms except during the responses at Morning Prayer.

Up at Timberio the foundations of the Villa Hylas were being dug, and the most pessimistic adviser had to admit that the Count was making sufficient preparations against the longest drought, so immense were his cisterns. None of the trees planted on the night of the party in honour of the gods lived more than a fortnight. Somebody had told Marsac that the Sirene gardeners were too fond of the pruning-knife, and he got it into his head that it was that which was to be blamed for the death of his trees. He sent for Gigi Gasparri and commanded him never to touch with a knife anything he planted in the gardens of the Villa Hylas.

"Not a twig. Not a sprout. I will not have a bud or a flower picked. I wish to protect the trees of Sirene. If you ever touch them after they are planted I dismiss you from my service."

Gigi bowed his comprehension. He was inured to the eccentric horticultural views of foreigners.

"And now plant all those trees again. Three times as many next time."

Gigi, who did not take the gods too seriously, pointed out that some of the trees were ill-chosen for the soil and situation.

"*Cioè il platano, signor conte. Il platano,*" he said, speaking in the slow voice he used for foreigners. "*Il platano ama l'acqua; desidera l'acqua; tiene proprio una passione per l'acqua. È inamoratissimo dell' acqua. Allora è ermeticamente inutile piantare il platano qui sopra dove la terra è asciutta, arida, bruciata.*"

Marsac waved his arms with the frenzy of a spoilt child. He *would* have plane-trees. Was he not building enough cisterns to water all the plane-trees in Europe? Let the plane-tree love water. Let it desire water. Let it have a genuine passion for water. Let it be utterly enamoured of water. Let the ground be dry, arid, and parched. Where would Artemis be without her grove of planes?

"*Ma chi è questa signora? Non la conosco. Sarebbe un' americana?*"

A goddess, he was informed.

"*Allora, uno scherzo.*" It would be a pity for the Count to waste his money on a joke.

"It is not a joke," Marsac fumed. "I insist on having a grove of plane-trees."

"*Ma scusi, signor conte. Le assicuro che il platano è ermeticamente impossibile qui sopra.*"

You will notice the grand adverb. Gigi had once read on a tinned tongue that it was hermetically sealed, and he had spent so much time trying to open that tin that thenceforward *ermeticamente* became his adverb of extreme degree. For a thing to be hermetically impossible implied something beyond even the omnipotence of the Almighty. Yet in spite of that the Count insisted on his plane-trees. With a shrug Gigi surrendered; but luckily for his credit as a gardener Marsac discovered in conversation with Scudamore that he had been wrong in ascribing the plane-tree to Artemis. It should have been the stone-pine. He read the Horatian ode dedicating a pine to Diana which begins: *Montium custos nemorumque, Virgo.* And then for Gigi's benefit he translated it into what was not quite the Italian verse of Carducci. The gardener listened politely. It helped him to listen politely when he knew he could charge for it in the bill.

One of the minor amusements of Sirene tea-parties that Autumn was finding a wife for the Count. Women even in Sirene will scale the most forbidding obstacles of temperament to make a match, and in spite of the men's theory that Marsac was a confirmed bachelor, as in deference to his wealth they put it, the women were sure that he would very soon propose to Angela Pears. There had been a group which for a while had favoured the chances of Dorothy Daynton, but Dorothy had gone back to England until next Spring.

"Well, I don't see who else he can marry except Angela," said Mrs. Dawson to Mrs. Neave. "That's one thing where I must say Sirene does fail. We do want a few nice marriageable girls."

"I don't know so much about that, Mrs. Dawson," said Mrs. Neave, who had a genuine simplicity which was rather charming, and completely disarming. "I think it's so nice not to have a lot of young girls always around."

And when at the Nortons' Christmas party the Count led the cakewalk with Angela Pears—you may nearly date the beginning of this tale by that dance—the engagement was expected by some before Twelfth Night.

Christmas parties at Sirene were very much like Christmas parties anywhere else except that the average age was a little higher and the average behaviour not lower, but a little younger. This Christmas party not merely marked the culmination of Marsac's popularity; it marked also the end of a Sirenian epoch, being as it was the last occasion on which all the foreign residents on the island met with goodwill to enjoy themselves together. To be sure, none of the Rosebotham set was there, nor was Bookham; but their absence did not constitute anything like a rift in the harmonious lute of that small and gay society. What a jolly night it was! Everybody was happy. Marsac had commissioned Goldfinch to paint a portrait of Hylas (for which Carlo was to sit) being raped by the fountain nymphs; and the old painter had been so pleased with the twenty thousand francs he was to get for it that he had presented his patron with a fine column of *giallo antico*; and the old ladies had been so delighted with Goldfinch's present to dear Count Bob that they had commissioned him to paint for another four thousand dollars a portrait of themselves sitting together in their Temple of Vesta. Christopher was beginning to wonder if after all he should not be able to build for himself that Arabian Nights palace on the site he had failed to sell to Marsac, and his eyes were glittering in the candlelight of the parties he was dreaming of giving there down an endless vista of hospitable old age. Mrs. Ambrogio was beaming because she had received no less than half a dozen Christmas cards of snowy scenes in England and the Count had given Peter entire charge of his legal affairs in Italy. Mrs. Neave was happy because Joseph had not grumbled at her annual Christmas tree for the youthful poor of Sirene. She did so love to play Lady Bountiful and feel like somebody in dear Washington Irving. Not only had Joseph not grumbled, but he had actually hinted that with a little persuasion he might appear himself as Santa Claus. Since Marsac's parties everybody wanted to dress up. Marian de Feltre was happy merely because she had been invited to the Villa Amabile to-night. She had had to walk so carefully on crumbling soil round some very difficult corners of Sirene society lately, and for the first time since her divorce she felt that she was once more on a comfortable high road. Cartright was enjoying himself in his own awed deferential way. He, too, had received a commission to paint a picture for the old ladies. But indeed everybody was happy, and the happiest of all were the Norton girls themselves sitting one at either end of a linked-up series of tables that stretched from the dining-room to the other end of the big *salone*, Miss Maimie in dove-grey silk and Miss Virginia wearing all her lace.

" Empty your glasses, you lazy folks. My sakes, you're none of you drinking anything at all," Miss Virginia vowed, dipping her hand into the basket of carnation petals that stood on the table before her and showering them upon those of her guests she could reach. She had put Marsac by Miss Maimie to-night at the other end of the tables, because she knew how much Miss Maimie would love to have him by her, and it seems hard to have to spoil the atmosphere by saying that Marsac had been a little bit piqued by this for the moment, supposing in his vanity that his precedence had been slighted in favour of Goldfinch and Simon Pears. The guests, too, all had baskets of carnation petals with which they showered a response upon Miss Virginia until she looked like a bride, her ivory cheeks flushed to the same hue of creamy rose as the falling petals. And then in the middle of a toast nearly everybody felt happier and jollier than ever, because there was a loud knock on the door and who should walk in but Duncan Maxwell.

" Can I join the party, Miss Virginia ? " he asked. " I'd have let you know before, but that damned train was late in Naples and I missed the boat. So I had to hire a sailing-boat from Sorrento. And what do you think they tried to charge me ? Seventy liras because it was Christmas. Yes, it takes a good Christian to rob you in honour of his beastly religion." He paused and stood smiling his rich smile on the company.

"Why, if it isn't our dear Mr. Maxwell!" Miss Virginia cried in delight. "Well, isn't that just fine? Maimie, do you see who it is, honey?" She might well ask, so far away was Miss Maimie at the other end of that long table. "But why didn't you come back to us earlier this Fall?"

"My dear woman, I couldn't come back till that horrible bore left Sirene. I was furious. I've been wandering about all over Italy with thirty-two bottles of snakes in spirits of wine. I tell you it was damnable."

"What bore do you mean anyway?" Miss Virginia asked. "Why, I don't believe we have any bores in Sirene except that old rascal Bookham."

"I mean that beastly philosopher with a face like a squashed orange. I had the greatest difficulty to get him out of Bavaria, and he's been waiting for me ever since in Sirene. I had to stay away till he sailed back to America. I couldn't have stood any more of him No fee-aw!"

"Oh, you mean Mr. Follett."

"I don't know what his blasted name is. Writing me his infernal postcards every day!"

"Well, sit right down and forget it," said Miss Virginia. "And I want you to know our dear friend Count Marsac."

Marsac, resenting the excitement caused by Maxwell's arrival, greeted him with what he imagined to be his most aristocratic hauteur.

"Ah, you're the Frenchman who's building a villa on 'O Gobbetto's land," Maxwell chuckled. "The worst place you could have chosen, my dear fellow. You'll get no sun in Winter. You'll have the most dreadful rheumatism. I know what it is. Oh, don't I? I should say so. Before you know where you are it gets your heart. It's no joke I can assure you. And these damned Italian doctors can't even keep a rich man like you alive. Oh yes, if you stay on up there, they'll kill you in the end."

"I regret that I did not have the advantage of your counsel earlier, monsieur," said Marsac coldly.

"Yes, and you'll regret it still more after your first Winter up there. All your fires will smoke when the wind's in the south which it always is in Sirene. And probably when it's in the east as well. And I shouldn't be surprised if they smoked when it was in the west. They won't smoke when it's in the north, but you'll be so damned cold then that the fire won't make any difference, however well it burns."

"Now, Mr. Maxwell, don't be so discouraging," said Miss Maimie sharply.

"I'm not being discouraging. But I only wish that beastly philosopher had asked me where to build a villa. I can tell you that Marsac has chosen for himself the very place I would have recommended to *him*."

We have become accustomed to think of Silenus as a little bald pot-bellied old man riding on an ass; but ancient sculptors loved to present him quite differently as the instructor of the youthful Dionysus, and that is the Silenus which Duncan Maxwell resembled as he sat at the Nortons' table that Christmas night, pouring out for himself glass after glass of wine to catch up with the rest of the company. Laughter enveloped him in a cloud through which his small deep-set eyes came glittering like two stars. He was of a florid complexion with a long tip-tilted sliced-off pragmatical nose such as you may see in any number of portraits of eighteenth-century Lowland lairds; but his magnificent vitality instead of exhausting itself in a struggle with agriculture, and his subtle mind instead of wasting itself on the split straws and dusty chaff of Presbyterian theology, had been allowed to swell and ripen in the sun. When he came into a room, one had the impression that an enormous creature had come in, a prodigal and overwhelming Pantagruel of a man, and it was always a surprise to find that actually he possessed no more than a reasonable burliness of stature and that his hands were white and soft with long taper fingers. He had lived on and off in Sirene for many years now and in many habitations; but he had recently built himself a villa in a cleft of the Torrione only attainable by a long narrow causeway constructed against and following the slope of the hill in a long diagonal. There, some eight hundred feet above the Salernian, shaded against the noontide sun by a grove of aboriginal Aleppo pines (for until Maxwell built his causeway the cleft was inaccessible), he set down on paper the observations of a passionately empirical life, many of which were published in brochures and given away to friends. There, sitting in the moon's eye when the white walls of his villa were a filigree of ebony shadows cast by the trees, he would drink much wine and instruct the youthful Dionysus until the hooting of an owl among the crags might remind him that there was an owl in Austria or Tunis whose habits he had not studied. And the next day he would be gone. Mellow as a pear, stringent as *nespole*, sweet and sun-dyed as an apricot, bitter as an almond, bitter-sweet and poisonous sometimes as the berries of nightshade, crisp as a pippin, ruddy and comfortable as a plum, juicy as an orange, taut as a grape, spicy as a peach, shameless as a fig, assertive as a pineapple, all these he was in turn, for he was the fruit of the ages.

It was as a pineapple that Marsac beheld him to-night, and it was so like Marsac to complain to several people in the course of the evening that Maxwell had referred to him by his name without the prefix of his rank.

"I assure you I find that excessively impertinent," he told Mrs. Ambrogio.

"Wickedest man in Sirene," she babbled. "And such a dear! I love him so much. Never can understand what he's talking about. Much too clever for me. Love him just the same. Frightfully cynical. Love to hear him swear. *Can* understand that, thank goodness, and it always reminds me of dear old England. Hope so much I'll hear him swear to-night as it's Christmas. Went to midnight Mass. Cried all the time. Love Christmas. And Mr. Maxwell's such a dear too."

The Count turned away and tried Miss Virginia.

"I assure you I find that excessively impertinent," he told her.

"Now, my dear Bob, you mustn't mind what Mr. Maxwell says. All his friends put up with just anything from him."

"His friends may do that," said the Count. "But I must insist for you that I do not consider myself one of his friends. If I am presented to the Duc d' Orleans, I do not permit myself to speak to him as Orleans, and I attend that I am accorded the politeness I give to others."

"Oh well, you know, in America we don't give a darn for titles. We just think they mean nothing at all."

"But I must license myself to observate, mademoiselle, that I am not in America."

"But you're in a perfectly good American house," she insisted, tapping him with her fan. "And you'll just have to put up with our country manners."

Miss Maimie was more sympathetic than Miss Virginia, and she gave Maxwell several very severe looks, to every one of which he raised his glass and drank heartily in response.

Soon even Marsac's petulant vanity was swamped by the merriment of the party. He found that in spite of Duncan Maxwell's return to Sirene he was still able to hold the stage, and as he cakewalked round the room with Angela Pears his attitude seemed exactly what was wanted to express the admiration he felt for himself.

In a corner Duncan Maxwell and Scudamore sat drinking their wine and watching the dancers.

"If the black races ever conquer the white races it will be because the white women will have been corrupted by negro dances," Scudamore observed sardonically.

Maxwell yawned. He never encouraged Scudamore when he was in the mood for pretentious apophthegms. It was Scudamore's raw material that amused him, not the exiguous evidence of his laborious digestion.

"And yet I must admit," the American went on, "that

if it were not for our capering young friend over there I would not have taken to social peregrination once more."

"What does Nita say about that? I bet she raises hell, eh?" Maxwell laughed. "But you'd better be careful, my dear fellow. Don't let her get hold of any books on poisons, or she'll certainly poison you. She'll probably choose white lead. Oh yes, because nobody will ever know the difference between the effects of her cooking and slow poisoning by lead. The symptoms will be identical. Constriction of the throat, twisting pains round the umbilicus, rigidity of the abdominal muscles, and dragging pains at the loins. Now, I've never eaten one of Nita's meals without having all those symptoms. But if you ever see a blue line round your gums, you'd better look out, my boy. Women are devils. I wish I had strangled more than two in my life. Not enough, you know. It's not enough, my dee-aw fellow. You never ought to let a year go by without strangling at least one woman. I tell you we should all of us have been poisoned by lead long ago if the devils didn't know that it was a powerful anaphrodisiac. That's what has saved us. But Nita probably doesn't know that. I'll tell her if you like that white lead is as discouraging to the appetite as white water-lilies."

"Are water-lilies discouraging?"

"My dear fellow, their powdered roots are used in every Oriental harem. You don't suppose the Turks would be able to knock those blasted Armenians on the head the way they do if they didn't occasionally protect themselves against their wives with water-lily pills."

"Is that so? I don't believe I ever came across it in any of my authors."

"I daresay you didn't," Maxwell went on. "But in your history of Roman morals you ought to go very carefully into the question of anaphrodisiacs. Think of the effect tobacco has had . . . most lowering, my dear fellow. Its effects were not really felt before the Victorian era. That's when men really began to smoke, and it was the effect of nicotine, and nothing else, which made them feel the nobility of their own human nature. They really had no more sexual energy than was enough to supply themselves with children and their faces with hair."

"Heirs and hairs! That's not bad, eh?" laughed Scudamore, who relished a schoolmaster's joke.

"I think it is rather bad," said Maxwell gravely. "And it's nothing to joke about. The world will be a worse place than it is now when we lose all carnal desire."

"And now women are beginning to smoke hard quite extensively," said Scudamore.

"They've jolly well had to," Maxwell replied. "With the gradual lowering of the masculine temperature they've had to bring down their own temperatures proportionately. That's why fans have gone out of fashion. They used to be able to keep cool with them for half an hour; but fans weren't any use when men got saturated with nicotine and often kept them waiting a month. No, by Jove, they had to saturate themselves too. There's a strong movement in favour of prohibiting all tobacco in America. Oh yes, my dear fellow, the women of your country know jolly well what they're about, I can tell you. The Chinese would never have been allowed to smoke opium if they hadn't taken jolly good care to keep the upper hand of women by squeezing their feet and exposing all female babies at birth whenever it was thought advisable."

"Talking of opium, I hear our young French friend proclaims himself a devotee of opium," said Scudamore. "That's something new in Sirene."

"Not at all new," Maxwell contradicted. "I've known at least six confirmed opium smokers in Sirene during the last twenty years. I hope you're not going to suppose that ridiculous frog is original just because you've not been outside the Villa Parnasso for two years?"

"Oh, I don't suppose him to be original; but I think

he's added something to the gaiety of the island. I'm grateful to him for that."

"You'll be more grateful to him soon, because from what I can see he's going to add a great deal more."

But at that moment Miss Virginia came along and separated the gossips.

"We can't bear to see folks getting into corners and not joining in the fun," she said severely.

The party took its course with all the prodigal hospitality for which the Villa Amabile was renowned. There was a large Christmas tree hung with presents, and all the happiness of the season shone in Miss Maimie's eyes when Marsac drew the number that entitled him to receive at her hands an illuminated poem in a little gilded frame, which she could not resist reading aloud for the thrill it gave her to do so.

> BECAUSE YOU'RE YOU.
>
> Just Because
> Your Ways are Ways
> Of Sweetness
> Just Because of
> Everything You Do,
> Just Because
> Of Your Complete
> Completeness
> And Just Because
> You're You—
> JUST YOU.

"My! aren't the little birdies just as cunning as they can be?" Miss Virginia asked, looking over Miss Maimie's shoulder at the picture of two robins that faced each other on two sprays of foliage linked by a true lovers' knot in the shape of a heart. "Just as cunning and cute as they can be."

Marsac bowed in the most gallant fashion and kissed the hands of the two old ladies.

"I esteem the presage excessively fortunate," he exclaimed

in what he thought was the grand manner of courtesy, but which, alas, like a toy balloon popped under his inflation and evaporated in a puff of pomposity leaving behind nothing but a horrid little dribble of damp membrane.

There was more dancing after the Christmas tree, and after the dancing supper, and after supper more dancing, until at four o'clock of a starry winter morning, in spite of Miss Virginia's denunciations of time, the guests declared that they must really go.

"Oh my, I do hate to have folks go," she lamented. "Isn't it too bad we can't keep it up for ever? Well, anyway, you can't go till you've sung Old Acquaintance."

So all joined hands to sing *Auld Lang Syne*, or rather to repeat more or less in time 'Should Auld Acquaintance be forgot' and fill in the rest with humming. There was a rumour that Archie Macadam knew all the words; but Archie Macadam was petrifying fast in alcohol and looked between his two partners like a drowned man being pumped back into life. He had passed beyond the stage of coherent speech hours ago, and when the chorus came to an end he sat down in the bowl of hot soup which had arrived to fortify the parting guests. This accident would have annoyed an ordinary hostess; but it delighted Miss Virginia, because it gave her an excuse to detain her guests while a fresh bowl of soup was being heated, and thereby prolonged her pleasure.

However, the fresh soup came at last and, hot though it was, at last it was drunk. Then the guests set out for home, some driving, some walking up through the sharp air that was faintly perfumed by mandarins. And when they were all gone Miss Virginia stood in the south loggia and listened to their voices and to the slow crackle of wheels up the steep road, fanning herself in the winter starlight.

BOOK TWO

Corpora Vestales oculi meretricia cernunt,
  nec domini poenae res ea causa fuit.

                                            OVID

Nam Vesta . . .
  Culpam alit et plures condit in ossa faces.

                                       PROPERTIUS

Chapter 1

vae tibi, causidice!   MARTIAL
difficile est vero nubere, Galla, viro.
   MARTIAL

IT was early in the following Spring that for the first time a catspaw of rumour ruffled very faintly the surface of Sirene's foreign society. Yet to attribute this hardly perceptible malaise in the atmosphere to anything so definite as a rumour is really to exaggerate, because not behind the deafest walls nor in the most intimate and secure gatherings was it once hinted that there was anything even so much as odd about Count Marsac. Whatever might be learnt about him in circles where Spring visitors penetrated, he was rich enough to make the most reckless gossip hesitate before he pressed home an enquiry that might give him the right to raise a questioning eyebrow; still more before he committed himself in any gathering of real Sirenians to repeating the loose scandal of transient strangers. Yet in spite of the fact that the entertainments at the Villa Decamerone were as popular as ever, in spite of the outward jollity of parties at the Villa Amabile, in spite of the evidence of tremendous wealth that the building operations on the cliff's edge demonstrated, there was nobody except the dear old Nortons who had not been touched, was it never so lightly, by that sly uncomfortable catspaw.

The apprehension in the social mind was reflected in its attitude toward a ludicrous display of vanity on the occasion of Mrs. Pape's *contadino* party. Mrs. Pape had arrived in February and taken the Villa Eolia for the season, bringing with her as usual several protegés from America. Last year these had been three deaf and dumb girls. This year they were three young women who wanted to study singing in Italy and a young man from a New York drugstore who Mrs. Pape had been assured was likely under her patronage to eclipse Caruso himself. The Moorish arcades of the Villa Eolia echoed to the trills and cadenzas of these four aspirants, whenever they were not sitting in Zampone's chattering about themselves and their careers to anybody that would listen to them.

"I mean to say what I feel is I must get an engagement somewhere next Fall. You see, what I want is experience. I know my voice is quite all right. Only I just haven't had the experience. But when one knows it's all there, well, why not give it a chance? That's what I say. Of course, I don't want to step right into leading sopranno rôles. I could play Madame Butterfly right away in some dirty little provincial Italian town, don't you know. But what I feel is I'd rather sing a smaller part at San Carlo or La Scala. Don't you agree with me that I'm right?"

And the middle-aged Sirenian who had thought it would be rather pleasant to spend an idle half-hour over a glass of Zampone's vermouth instructing this bright-eyed young American in the sophisticated life of the island would always agree, with a weary and disillusioned politeness, that she was wise to aim at nothing lower than Milan itself, wondering the while to himself at the miracles of elimination that a good singing master could apparently work with the most ruthless New England accent.

Mrs. Pape had lost no time in giving a party to show off her four singers; and her kind heart had been so deeply touched by the responsive enthusiasm of her Sirenian friends that she felt they deserved another party without being interrupted by songs when they were all talking so happily and comfortably.

Said Nigel Dawson, made aware of her benevolent plans for further hospitality:

"Oh, Mrs. Pape, *do* give a fancy-dress dance. I'm *so* tired of wearing trousers." Then he bit his underlip like a schoolgirl who thinks she may have said too much. "You do know what I mean? They're the sign of our bondage. John Scudamore always says that when Prometheus gave men fire he gave them trousers at the same time. You do know what I mean, don't you, dear Mrs. Pape? And I know you sympathize, because you *are* so sympathetic."

Little Mrs. Pape, who was sitting perched up on her chair like a sagacious baby, was saved from having to reply to this by the interruption of Miss Openshaw, the brightest of her protegés.

"Why, I think a fancy-dress dance would be just too divine for words, Mrs. Pape. Oh, Nigel, aren't you an angel child to suggest it! But do let's have an unusual kind of a fancy-dress. Couldn't we have a Venetian masque? Wouldn't that be lots of fun?"

"I'm afraid that would be a little too elaborate for Sirene, my dear," said Mrs. Pape. "But what I do think would be very very pretty would be a *contadino* dance. Just everybody wearing those pretty peasant costumes. It will be like one of our own harvest dances at home. And that's so easy for everybody, my dear," she added to Miss Openshaw who was looking a bit disappointed. "You know, so many people can't afford to spend a great deal of money on costumes, and that means they'll be afraid of looking homely and won't want to come."

"Oh, Mrs. Pape, let's call it a *Cavalleria Rusticana* dance," cried Miss Openshaw, trilling out one of Santuzza's phrases.

"Oh, that would be too marvellous," Nigel gushed. "And I'll be a Sicilian bee-herd tending his swarms on Mount Hybla."

The invitations were sent out, and it showed how well Mrs. Pape had judged Sirene's capacity for fancy-dress when they were all accepted. To be sure, Mrs. Neave nearly had to refuse, because by now the novelty of appearing at parties had worn off again for Joseph, and he hummed and hawed a great deal at the idea of being left alone. His wife to whom Carmela had lent a most beautiful old *camicia*, a relic of her grandmother's trousseau, begged Duncan Maxwell to come in and spend the evening with Joseph.

" No, I won't do it, my dear woman," he declared. " No fee-aw! Joseph's getting a damned bore. He is really. I can't stand any more of his blasted Dante. I really can't. Besides, Joseph himself doesn't care a button about Dante. He simply takes a geographical interest in Hell because he thinks he'll go there one day. He just uses the *Divina Commedia* as a kind of Baedeker. No, I won't spend the evening with him."

" Oh, Mr. Maxwell," the wife expostulated, " how can you talk so? It's most unkind."

" People are a jolly sight too kind to Joseph. That's the trouble with him. He just lives on kindness and gruel and purgatives. No, you ask Scudamore to dine with him and keep him amused. And that'll be a kindness to poor old Scudamore, because every dinner he gets without Nita's cooking will keep him alive for a few days longer."

" Well, why don't you and Mr. Scudamore both dine with Joseph? And perhaps Mr. Pears would come too."

" I don't want old Pears. Damned old impostor. All he can talk about are Longfellow's filthy metres, and female behinds."

" Mr. Maxwell!"

" It's perfectly true, my dear woman. He spent the whole of last Summer with his telescope focussed on the diving-board at the Grande Marina. I wonder he didn't burn a hole in the bathing-dresses. I'd sooner listen to Joseph talking about Dante. No, by Jove, I won't be used as a male nurse for either of them."

However, in the end on consideration of being allowed

to order the dinner and the wine himself Duncan Maxwell agreed to dine with Joseph that night, and Mrs. Neave was able to appear at the fancy-dress dance in the milk-white *camicia* of Carmela's grandmother.

The guests were all assembled in the *salone* of the Villa Eolia, and the preliminary compliments upon one another's costumes had been uttered with a good deal more sincerity than is usual at fancy-dress parties, owing to the fact that there was really not a pin to choose between any of them. Angela Pears was tapping her trim foot impatiently, for although she had been very faintly stroked by that catspaw she was nowhere near to forgoing what by now was established as her prescriptive right to open any Sirene ball with the Count. But the Count had not yet arrived, and the mandolins were beginning to tune up.

"The Count's late," she said sharply to Miss Maimie.

"Why, Angela, I suppose the Count may be a minute or two late if he wishes. Don't you worry your little head about him, my dear child. You go find yourself a partner."

Miss Maimie spoke with a trace of asperity. She had been at some trouble to contradict the foolish talk about there being any attraction for Count Bob in that direction. Angela Pears was pretty enough in a peaky kind of a way, but not the bride for one whose great-great-grandfather had been the lover of a queen. Besides, what would Count Bob do with that ugly messy droning old Simon for a grandfather-in-law?

"I really do believe that poor Miss Maimie is jealous of me," said Angela, who had turned away with a petulant laugh to the guest behind her. This happened to be Mrs. Ambrogio.

"Most jealous woman in Sirene," avowed Mrs. Ambrogio, who looked in her peasant's dress something between a gypsy-woman running a coconut-shy and an allegorical figure of Southern Europe. "Love her madly. Dearest old pet in the world! But terribly jealous. She never got over being jilted by that cochary."

"*Cochiere*, Mrs. Ambrogio," corrected Angela, who having been born in Italy never had any qualms about adjusting the mispronunciations of her English and American friends.

"Can't help it. Tongue too large for my mouth. Can't pronounce any word more than three syllables. Never could. Know I'm a fool, but can't help it. Jump any five-barred gate. Jump anything. Poor Miss Maimie never got over it. Took all her money and married a fisherman's daughter in Naples. Jealous ever since. Old maids always run after coachmen. Look at old Miss Jamieson up at Anasirene. Drives up with a different coachman every night. Asks them in and gives them vermouth. Don't know what she does after that, but quite harmless otherwise. Weeds in her garden all the time. I've seen her myself hundreds of times driving up to Anasirene as red as a poppy and puffing with excitement. Only for goodness sake don't tell anybody what I've told you, because she's *such* an old dear and I love her so much."

"Well, I'm so peeved with Miss Maimie at the moment," said Angela, "that if I could I would believe you, but I don't just believe she's ever had a love-affair in her life with anybody."

"*Most* passionate. *Most* passionate," Mrs. Ambrogio burst out excitably. "Most passionate woman in Sirene. Not a bit passionate myself. Always laugh. Peter gets so angry. Can't help it."

"Well, I just don't believe you. And anyway, last time you told me it was Miss Virginia who loved the coachman."

"Always speak the truth. Must speak the truth. Tried hundreds of times to tell lies. Simply can't. Stick in my throat. Long words. Lies. Stick in my throat."

The players of Mrs. Pape's orchestra were just shaking their hands before they struck their mandolins and guitars in the chords proclaiming the first dance, when the shuffle of preparatory feet and the murmur of conversation were drowned by the blare of a brass band immediately outside the windows of the Villa Eolia playing with full volume a triumphal march. The mandolin players let their hands fall upon their laps in consternation. Several guests rushed to the window.

"It's the Sirene band," they cried, pulling back the curtains to reveal two dozen brass instruments gleaming in the fairy-lamps of the Villa Eolia's most Alhambrian courtyard.

Poor little Mrs. Pape, who had been lifted up and set on the highest chair out of reach of danger from the dancers, asked plaintively if it was the anniversary of anything. But nobody heard her question, and anyway she would never have heard the answer, because the band was much too loud. The guests stood about looking dazed. The blare stopped. A well-known voice outside was heard saying:

"*Les clairons, s'il vous plaît. Incominciate, prego.*"

Whereupon six of the smaller instruments sounded a shrill tucket. After the echoes had died away in the gorges of Monte Ventoso, the same voice cried:

"A knight-errant has the honour to demand shelter and entertainment from Mrs. Pape. May he enter?"

"Gracious me, what *is* happening?" cried the hostess all in a flutter and preparing to slide down off her chair to deal with the crisis.

And then through the Moorish portals of the big *salone* entered the six trumpeters scattering the guests before them and followed by the Count covered in silver armour, a white plume floating from his helmet, a pale blue cloak streaming in his wake. He was followed in their turns by Carlo dressed in, or rather wrapped scantily round with a leopard's skin, and by a painter friend, who was staying with Marsac at the Decamerone, disguised as Mephistopheles.

The trumpeters sounded another tucket, and then Marsac

held up the opening of the ball with a long speech in his most rapid French, which set before a bewildered company of people the claims of the Platonic theory of life. However, it would not have mattered what it was about, because nobody caught more than an occasional tense of the verb 'to be.' At the close of this declamation there was not the outburst of enthusiasm which had greeted so many of the Count's extravagant displays. The other guests all disguised as peasants plainly resented his ostentatious appearance; and when Miss Virginia exclaimed, "Doesn't our dear Count Bob look the very picture of romance?" there was not one whisper of assent. It seemed as if that infernal catspaw were slyly ruffling every woman's *camicia*, as if it were suggestively and maliciously rubbing up the wrong way the nap of the men's velvet sleeves. There was an embarrassment, almost a chill, over the feast, and for the first time even the most cautious snobs allowed themselves to criticize Marsac.

When a cosmopolitan and tolerant society like the foreign colony of Sirene allows itself to criticize a rich young count's manners, it is obvious that it will sooner or later have to criticize his morals in order to justify such presumption. Yet the fascination of Marsac's apparently boundless wealth was still so potent that everybody wanted to turn a blind eye toward certain uncomfortable indications of his point of view about life; and that catspaw might have ceased to worry people had not Bookham let the cat out of the bag.

Not that he could have done otherwise. The information he received from Mr. Hartopp was too definite; and Mr. Hartopp was a little dried-up American lawyer who had been practising for years now in Paris. This was not mere gossip. This was authoritative. A lawyer always spoke the truth outside a court of law. Tired of the monotony of putting through French divorces for his compatriots Mr. Hartopp had left the last few dozen clients of the season to his partner and wandered South for a holiday. He had declined any letters of introduction.

"No," he had told his friends, "I guess I'll just sit around and sip vermouth outside some sunny old café. The fact is I badly need a rest from confidential human nature."

Such a figure strolling up and down the Piazza and eyeing the vivacious crowd from a pair of wrinkled-up humorous grey eyes was marked down as the natural prey of the churchwarden. The courtliness of the little American led him to submit with a twinkling resignation to Bookham's gusty protectorship. Perhaps the habits of a lifetime were too strong for him. At any rate he found himself unable to refrain from asking questions about the various bright oddities of humanity that thronged the Piazza.

"Queer kind of a crowd," he observed. "After my Paris office I feel I'm looking at the gay little people you see running about in the background of a Crivelli picture. But I'm a lawyer, Mr. Bookham, and I get the ashes of all this," he added, indicating the crowd with a slim ebony stick.

Presently they adjourned to Zampone's and sat on the terrace, sipping their vermouth and quizzing the passers-by through the railings.

"Yes, I guess you lead a pretty good kind of life down here," said the dapper little lawyer. "There certainly is a mighty fine air of *dolce far niente* about this island. Look at that couple passing now." He pointed to a tall handsome young man wearing a red silk fisherman's cap over his curly fair hair, and to the pretty bare-legged girl hanging on his arm and laughing up at him over some lovers' intimate joke. "There they go, with the whole world before them," he added with a sigh.

"Well, as a matter of fact," said Bookham, deep and disapproving, "that's a young German and his sister, and I'm told, though of course I won't vouch for the truth of it, that the—er—well I mean to say it's all very degenerate and unpleasant."

"You can't shock me, Mr. Bookham," said the little lawyer. "Hullo, why talking of degeneracy there goes Lagerström!" He whistled his amazement. "Well, well, so this is where his voyage round the world ended!"

It was the Count who was striding past Zampone's terrace, his head held high, his light blue eyes radiating a slightly too self-conscious pride of birth.

"I beg your pardon," Bookham exclaimed. "But do you mean Count Marsac?"

"That's right. Marsac-Lagerström, to give it him in full. What does Sirene make of *him*?"

"Well, I think we all liked him very much at first," Bookham replied, "though I hear that one or two people have been a little inclined to give him the cold shoulder lately. I believe there has been some rumour about his having been mixed up in a rather unsavoury mess in Paris. But I keep myself as free as I can from gossip. You see, I'm the senior British resident here, and somebody's got to set an example, don't you know."

"Did you never hear of the Lagerström scandal?"

The little American leaned across the table and lowered his voice to remind Bookham what that had been.

"Miners?" the churchwarden bellowed. "Good lord, what a degenerate brute! Not coalminers surely?"

"Minors not miners," the little lawyer made haste to explain.

Bookham mopped his crimson brow with a purple handkerchief.

"Well, that's bad enough," he rumbled.

"The Napoleonic code, however, regards it, and rightly I cannot help feeling, as more reprehensible than the other. Anyway, our friend was sentenced to a year's imprisonment."

"In prison?" Bookham ejaculated. "You don't mean to tell me that Marsac was in prison? Why, it's far worse than anything I ever imagined from the comparatively mild rumours that were flying round."

"Yes, he went to prison," the lawyer continued. "But fortunately for him he could afford to pay a sufficient number of mental specialists to declare him temporarily insane."

"Do you mean to say he's been in an asylum too?" Bookham gasped.

"No, he was released from gaol on the condition that he took a voyage round the world to recover his health and absented himself from France for a year. And so he's ended up here."

"He's building an enormous villa here," Bookham added indignantly.

"Well, well, I think he's chosen the right place," the little lawyer commented. "Sirene has been a refuge and a consolation for sinners for a good many generations, has it not? At least that's what we always hear about it up north."

Bookham left the lawyer still surveying from his wrinkled-up humorous eyes the little world into which he had so carelessly dropped this bombshell, and hurried off to consult his wife about his own attitude. On the way back to the Villa San Giorgio he overtook Major Natt stalking up homeward. To him he confided the authoritative information.

"What a bewildering propensity," the Major panted. "The notion is really outside the imagination of simple creatures like you and me, Bookham, is it not?"

"I should hope it was," said the churchwarden grimly. "By Jove, I should jolly well hope it was! The question is what are we going to do about it?"

"Yes, exactly. However, there is a fortunate paucity of mineral deposits on Sirene, on which we may congratulate ourselves."

"Minors not miners!" Bookham shouted contemptuously.

"In what an embarrassing state of amphibology our language exists, Bookham. There was I on the verge of assigning to Marsac an unique predilection, and all the time he's a mere paragraph in any English Sunday newspaper you pick up."

It was all very well for the Major to make his pompous polysyllabic jokes about this horrible business, Bookham grumbled to himself as he puffed up toward the Villa San Giorgio. But the Major was not a churchwarden. He was not even a married man. What on earth was going to happen about the church porch? There had been that case when a convicted felon had presented a set of gold communion plate to an English cathedral which the Dean and Chapter returned as soon as they heard the verdict. But you couldn't return a porch, even if you felt you ought to return it. Of course, you might return the money for it, but if it had taken ten years to collect fourteen hundred liras to build one, how long was it going to take to collect nine or ten thousand to pull one down?

"I'm in a beastly quandary," said Bookham aloud. He had just remembered his own commission from Maestro Supino. Really, it was enough to make one tired of trying to do a bit of good in this world.

"There's one step you must take immediately, Herbert," said his wife, when she heard the horrid news. "You must warn Mr. Pears so that Angela can be protected."

"You'll pardon me, my dear, but I don't quite see where any danger to Angela comes in."

Mrs. Bookham uttered an hysterical little laugh, at the sound of which Herbert shivered as might a man who walking in the permanent way heard the whistle of an approaching express hard upon his heels. He often told people what an emotional and highly-strung woman Mrs. Bookham was. When he was away from her, sipping the tea of respectable households, he felt that the possession of a wife of such extreme sensibility lent him a touch of

Byronic mystery and romance. But at home this sensibility was merely a nuisance.

"Now, Herbert," she breathed excitably, "you know that I never go outside the house?"

"Yes, my dear, I know that. I sometimes wish that you would."

"But thanks to my friends—and thank God, I have several dear dear friends in Sirene—thanks to them I know a great deal of what is going on."

"I believe you know everything," said Herbert, hoping to flatter her into tranquillity.

"And I know that Angela Pears is expecting Count Marsac ... Count indeed! Yes," she declaimed tragically, "there was a time when rank *meant* something, when nobility was not a mere empty expression. But now! Ugh, how I hate this soulless time! Angela is expecting Count Marsac to propose to her, Herbert."

"That may be only Sirene talk."

"Let me for once know better than you, Herbert."

"Certainly, my dear."

"This marriage must be prevented. You will go down immediately after lunch to the Villa Rienzi and warn Mr. Pears. Now, don't argue with me. Don't argue, I say. Thank heaven, even if I have forgotten what the world looks like outside the Villa San Giorgio, thank heaven my woman's heart still beats."

"Well, don't work yourself up, Carrie. Let's have lunch quietly."

"Lunch!" she moaned. "Lunch! Herbert, has Sirene so utterly blasted the finer side of your nature that when a young girl's innocence is in deadly peril you can talk about lunch? What has happened to you, Herbert? Have you forgotten that you were once my knight?"

"My dear, it was you who suggested going after lunch. I never mentioned the word till you did. Oh, now for goodness sake don't start screaming! The last time you had a screaming fit it was all over Sirene that you had been beating the maid with a frying-pan. I don't think you realize how far away your screams can be heard."

"Are you going down to the Villa Rienzi?" Mrs. Bookham demanded, clutching her breast with one hand and twisting up a handkerchief with the other.

"I'll go at once, my love," said Herbert desperately.

"No," said Mrs. Bookham, becoming abruptly calm: "you must have your lunch first. Herbert, forgive my emotion and kiss me. I suffer so terribly when I hear of evil. Sometimes I think I ought never to have been born. Oh, Herbert, when I hear of brutes like Count Marsac I'm so thankful that we have no children."

Simon Pears swore by Hick and by Heck when Bookham uttered his warning. What really enraged him was the notion that his granddaughter should be contemplating marriage at all, not so much that she should be contemplating marriage with the Count in particular.

"Never mind whether the fellow's been in gaol or not, Booky. That's not the point. The point is what the blazes does Angela mean by getting engaged without saying a word to her grandfather? Blast it all, I am her grandfather, I suppose?"

"Of course, of course, why, of course you are. I say, don't let this infernal business make you cynical about women. And I don't want you to misunderstand me, Pears. I am not aware of there being anything in the nature of an open engagement or even of a secret understanding between them. The point is . . ."

"No, by Hick, it derned well isn't the point. The point is that she's been flirting around with this dago while her grandfather . . ."

"Look here, my dear man, I really must insist that Angela is entirely blameless in this matter. The point is that some of us have fancied that this rascally Frenchman might propose to her; and Mrs. Bookham, who loves Angela like her own daughter, insisted that you ought to be warned so that you could interfere."

Simon Pears grunted; and just then Angela herself came into the room, whereupon to Bookham's acute embarrassment her grandfather lowered his head and charged into the situation.

"Angela, this must derned well stop!"

Angela raised her eyebrows. Never, the churchwarden thought, had he seen a young woman so entirely capable of looking after herself without the vicarious maternity of Mrs. Bookham.

"Oh, indeed? And may I ask what it is that must derned well stop?" she enquired from a lofty altitude.

"I don't often put my foot down firmly," Simon began.

"No, my dear granpa, you're much too gouty," she interrupted sharply.

"But I won't have your name mixed up with this ruffian of a French Count."

"Who did mix that cocktail, anyway?" Angela asked.

"Pears, as you've dragged me into this," said Bookham, "please let me explain my own position in the matter. I'm awfully sorry, Angela, to seem interfering and all that, don't you know, but I've just received definite information that this Count Marsac, under the name of Count Marsac-Lagerström, is a convicted felon, and I thought your grandfather ought to know it. We all have eyes, and we can't help noticing that the scoundrel is very much attracted by you. Not unnaturally—I mean to say quite naturally—I mean to say it's what one might expect. And Carrie insisted that you ought to be warned."

"What did he go to gaol for?" Angela demanded.

"That's hardly here or there, is it?" Bookham suggested. "I mean to say if a man's been in gaol, what he went there for becomes rather a secondary matter."

"And you wouldn't understand if we told you," Simon added.

The maiden in distress screwed up her eyes and, as the churchwarden told his wife later, looked as hard and bright as a diamond.

"Now, see here, granpa, I don't intend to be treated like a British girl."

It should be borne in mind that these were pre-Stopesian and proteropsychoanalytic days. Travelled and sophisticated Englishmen still returned from America amazed at the worldly wisdom of American girls; American girls still thought of their English sisters as drooping roses in a vast vicarage garden.

The two men looked at each other apprehensively.

"Oh well, as you can't either of you say out what it was, I suppose I can guess," she declared. "What did you say his other name was, Mr. Bookham?"

The churchwarden sighed with relief. One could always hope that she had guessed wrong.

"Lagerström."

"I'll write to Saidie Carthew in Paris and have her find out all the details and send them to me right away," she announced. "And if it's what I think it is I'll tell the Nortons myself," she added viciously.

So Angela wrote to her friend in Paris, and in about ten days' time, armed with a wad of newspaper cuttings, she set out to the Villa Amabile. There was in the set of her tight mouth a determination to make Miss Maimie in particular feel mighty small. Rather to Angela's disappointment the old ladies were alone that afternoon. She would have welcomed an audience to witness her triumph.

It was a sparkling May afternoon, and Miss Virginia and Miss Maimie were taking tea inside the Temple of Vesta. Angela was invited to admire the wonderful growth of the stripling cypresses planted a year ago.

"It seems kind of foolish for me to be watching trees at

my age," said Miss Virginia. "But if they grow as fast as this every year, maybe I'll live long enough to see them peeping over the top of our little Temple."

"Why, surely you will, Miss Virginia," said Angela.

"I guess I'll have a mighty good try," the old lady declared.

Miss Maimie was pouring out the tea, and Angela fidgeted resentfully under the silence of her brooding gaze. Miss Virginia chattered on.

"Isn't it a glorious health-giving day! I thought we were in for a spell of that nasty old scirocco this morning. The clouds were quite thick all around Monte Ventoso. But they've all blown away, and our beloved summer breeze has begun. Look at the fishing-boats like little white butterflies. My, my! I do just pity the poor folks who've never been able to sit like us and see this lovely, lovely view."

"Where every prospect pleases," said Angela sententiously. "And only man is vile."

"Well, I don't think poor old man's so vile as all that," the old lady replied with a toss of the head. "And anyway you're years too young to be talking so, my dear."

Angela looked down her nose.

"One grows up rather rapidly in Sirene, Miss Virginia."

"Why, you aren't even married yet," Miss Maimie put in contemptuously.

For a moment or two while Miss Virginia was chattering Angela had half decided to leave the old ladies in ignorance of their favourite's disgrace; but Miss Maimie's malice hardened her heart.

"Did you know that Count Marsac's name was really Lagerström?" she asked.

"We certainly did," said Miss Virginia. "But he's dropped the Danish name and taken his mother's, because he's a French subject."

"Oh no, that wasn't the reason," said Angela. "He

dropped his Danish name because it became too notorious after he went to prison as Count Lagerström."

"Went to prison?" Miss Virginia echoed.

"Oh, then you didn't know he had been to prison?"

"No, we did not, you lying little hussy," Miss Maimie flashed, her face white as Miss Virginia's fichu with anger.

"I dare say it does sound rather improbable," said Angela. "Unfortunately, however, it happens to be true. And if you'll look through this packet of newspaper clippings you'll see for yourselves that it's true."

"Angela Pears," said Miss Virginia, grasping her fan as if it were a scimitar, "go out of our house, and never let you or your grubby, dusty, fusty old grandfather ever dare come through our door again. I can abide most mean things in this world, but oh, dear heaven, I can't abide liars."

"Before you're so ready to abuse me, you might at least take the trouble to find out if what I say is true. After all, newspapers don't lie."

"Newspapers don't lie?" Miss Virginia echoed, turning her head with a shrill laugh that sounded not unlike the scream of a falcon.

"Not when they're reporting criminal proceedings."

"Criminal proceedings for what?" Miss Maimie asked in a low voice.

"Why, anybody who's been such friends with Count Marsac-Lagerström as you are, Miss Maimie, oughtn't to have to ask for what," Angela sneered. "Not in Sirene anyway."

Miss Virginia seized a bell and rang it as if for a fire, until fat Rosina came hurrying out to see what was the matter.

"Rosina, mettere questa signorina—oh, hell, Maimie, I wish I knew the Italian for a mean ordinary little sneak—mettere questa signorina chi è niente signorina fuori. Subito! Subito! Subito! E non entrare in nostra casa again. What's never, Maimie?"

"Mai."

VESTAL FIRE

"Mai, mai, mai. Have you capitoed what I'm telling you, Rosina?"

The maid assented vigorously, and Angela, feeling rather glad now that the old ladies had been alone this afternoon, followed her to the door of the Villa Amabile, through which she never passed again.

The Nortons let it be known that they would receive nobody who was suspected even of criticizing their friend Count Marsac. They did not believe the disgusting gossip about him, and friends of theirs who paid the least heed to it could be friends of theirs no longer. Such was the hold those parties at the Villa Amabile possessed over Sirene that for awhile there were few defections, and most people consoled themselves with the opinions of the mental specialists. Of course, the Bookhams, who had already been excommunicated by the old ladies, and Mrs. Rosebotham, who had never been invited to their house, were very fierce against the Count. Indeed there was a moment when it looked as if Mrs. Rosebotham was going to make an attempt to pull down with her own hands the porch he had presented. As for the poor Bishop of Europe he began to wish that he was the Bishop of Polynesia, so many letters did Mrs. Rosebotham write him on the subject of Count Marsac. Then there were one or two particular friends of Angela Pears and her grandfather who found the situation becoming awkward.

"What are we going to do about this Count Marsac business?" Mrs. Neave asked plaintively of Major Natt.

"Well, really, it is deuced awkward, is it not? I haven't actually cut him yet, but I find my nod getting colder and colder every time I meet him," said the Major. "What does Neave feel about it?"

"Why, I think he feels just as you feel, Major Natt. Not that he's said anything at all to me yet. But he's been complaining a great deal lately of his glasses. He says he's continually not recognizing people. You see, Joseph is so soft-hearted. He'd always find a way out of hurting anybody if he could."

It was Christopher Goldfinch, however, who found his position most awkward. He had been a lifelong friend of Simon Pears, and he was devoted to Angela. In fact Mrs. Ambrogio asserted positively that he was her father, having once heard somebody say that he treated her like a father. On the other hand, the Nortons had commissioned him to paint a picture, for which they had paid him four thousand dollars. Christopher had much enjoyed taking rich American tourists down to the Villa Amabile and pointing out this picture hanging in the *salone*.

"That's my latest work," he had been able to say. "In fact I only finished it in March. I rather like the composition. I'm old enough to be able to say that now,'"he would add with an apologetic smile. Considering that for thirty years he had been painting the same group of Greek-nosed females lolling about in heavy draperies on a marble terrace with the Bay of Naples in the background and a flautist in the foreground he certainly was entitled to say that he rather liked the composition. To be sure, in this case he had substituted for the marble terrace the Temple of Vesta, but he had given to Miss Virginia and Miss Maimie the Grecian noses and draperies he had been designing for so many years, and the difference was hardly noticeable.

"Wonderful old boy," the tourists would comment. "Fought for the Union, and still able to ask four thousand dollars for a picture. Some painter!"

Moreover, besides the advertisement that his latest canvas gave him, there was always the chance that the Nortons might order another next Christmas.

"Too bad," muttered Christopher to himself, as he sat in his panelled and gilded study surrounded by the glory that was Greece, the grandeur that was Rome, the flotsam of the Middle Ages, and the jetsam of the Renaissance, and looking himself like a genre study of an old curiosity dealer.

"Too bad that this swine should try to break up our little society like this. By gad, I wish I were twenty years younger. I'd call the blackguard out."

He turned again to the letter from Angela Pears which had provoked this outburst.

*Villa Rienzi,
Isola Sirene.*

Dear Uncle Chris,

I hate to say what I'm going to say, but Grandfather and I both agree that we can't do otherwise than take it as a sign that you're tired of our friendship if you continue to visit the Pepworth-Nortons. Quite apart from the abominable way they behaved to me you can't afford even at your age to be mixed up with people like Marsac.

Christopher laid the letter down for a moment to recover from the shock of the innuendo and passed a slim white hand across his splendid brow.

"My gad, what are girls coming to nowadays?" he groaned in an anguished amazement. In spite of the large number of women with whom he had had love-affairs Christopher still regarded Woman as the incarnation of an angelic purity. If a cynic had pinned him down to defend his own relations with them, he would have argued that in every case he had been the only man each one had ever loved and that not excluding those of them who were already married. "They know everything," he groaned again, as he turned back painfully to Angela's letter.

However, if new friends are to count for more than old ones, and you intend to have it so, why, so be it. Neither Grandfather nor I would wish to influence you either way. The only thing is I'm afraid we'll have to tell Antonio to say 'not at home' when 'il signore' taps on the door of the Villa Rienzi next time.

*Your affectionate
Angela*

Christopher sat as far back as it was possible to sit in a *seicento* Paduan chair, and meditated on his course of action. At last he decided that he could say more to Miss Virginia and Miss Maimie than even a modern girl and that it was his duty to point out to them the impropriety of constituting themselves the champions of a reprobate like this fellow Marsac.

" By gad, I'll go down and have it out with them this afternoon," he declared, and he went upstairs to choose his costume for the argument. After an hour or so of experiments he chose a light biscuit-coloured cashmere suit, a waistcoat of beautifully faded lavender grosgrain, a mauve tie passed through a large amethyst ring, a lawn shirt, and a broad-brimmed hat of white hare's fur.

Like Angela, Christopher found the old ladies alone; but they did not suggest tea in the Temple for him. No doubt Miss Virginia enjoyed saying:

"Maimie, I don't believe Mr. Goldfinch will want to take tea outside with this breeze blowing. We'd better have it in the *salone*. All old folks aren't as hardy as us."

So they sat in the big *salone* among the chairs that were so like bird-legged little girls tied up with pink sashes, and looked out at the sunlight through the Gothic windows that were so surprisingly draped with curtains of Nottingham lace. Dear Miss Nortons! They would have made the Parthenon resemble the inside of a work-basket. By the rich and sombre interiors of the Villa Adonis the picturesque foppery of Christopher's appearance was somehow enhanced; but in the *salone* of the Villa Amabile he appeared to be a part of the decorations, or a large doll that the old ladies had dressed up to amuse themselves and their visitors.

" I've been so very much upset to hear of this misunderstanding between you and the Pearses," he began. " Awfully sorry, I've been."

The wind from Miss Virginia's fan swept across the table

and wrinkled the creamy surface of the tea in Christopher's cup.

"There's been no kind of a misunderstanding at all, Mr. Goldfinch. Angela Pears took it upon herself to bring us some of the filthy Sirene gossip about our friend Count Marsac, and we told her that neither she or her boring old grandfather would be welcomed again in the Amabile."

"But old friends, Miss Virginia," Christopher protested, shaking his venerable head. "Old friends and American citizens. We ought to hold together. Yes, ma'am, by gad, we ought to hold together."

"That's punk," Miss Virginia snapped.

"Poppycock," Miss Maimie growled.

"We don't give a dime for any old friendship if that old friendship tries to break up new friendships with low-down mean ordinary lies," said Miss Virginia.

"Now, that's not fair to Simon or Angela," Christopher argued. "What they told you about this Frenchman was true."

"My sister and I choose to think otherwise," said Miss Maimie. "If Count Marsac went to prison he went to prison unjustly."

"But he went to prison," the old painter insisted. "That's the point. And the scandal was an atrocious one."

"You're not the man to talk about scandal, Christopher Goldfinch," Miss Virginia shrilled. "Look what your own life has been. One damned great scandal after another. And look what it is now, living up at the Villa Adonis with those three young hussies. You've no right to talk. Gemini! You with one foot in the grave and an arm around every young girl's waist you meet. Maybe you think we have old-fashioned notions about young girls. Maybe we have."

"I've never pretended to be a saint," said Christopher. "But I'm not a degenerate brute like this fellow Marsac."

"We know you're a wicked old man," Miss Virginia cried. "And that's enough for us."

"It certainly is," Miss Maimie added scornfully.

"Your infatuation for this Frenchman will end in your losing all your real friends," the painter warned them; and no living man could have looked more like a major prophet than he at that moment.

"Well, we'll make sure of ridding ourselves of one so-called friend as quickly as possible," cried Miss Virginia. Whereupon snatching a knife from the tea-table she swept across the room to where hung the four-thousand-dollar picture of herself and Miss Maimie in vestal contemplation of the Bay and fiercely slashed the canvas through and through. "And I'll have Costanzo take back the frame to you this evening," she added, standing back to survey in grim exultation the effect of her onslaught.

Christopher passed that slim white hand across his brow and sat for a moment dazed, his lower jaw dropping. Then he pulled himself up from his chair, bowed ceremoniously to the two old ladies in turn and, such an old man himself, walked very slowly and a little unsteadily over the pale blue porcelain tiles of that big *salone* for the last time. As he opened the door, Miss Virginia flung wide the windows, and in the *maestrale* the ribbons of the ruined canvas fluttered to and fro.

Chapter 2

*verum a te metuo . . .
infesto pueris bonis malisque.*

CATULLUS

THE knowledge that Marsac had been sent to prison as a martyr to temperament filled Nigel Dawson with an enthusiastic respect for him, and the thought that twelve mental specialists should have certified him not to be responsible for his actions at the time added, perhaps a little paradoxically, an almost devotional reverence. To have been compromised, to have been arrested, to have been found guilty, to have been carried off to gaol, to have been certified insane, to have been released, to have been banished, to have voyaged romantically round the world, and all the time to have been the centre of public attention, that was living indeed.

"My dear boy," said his mother, "I don't at all want to interfere with your friendships or pry into your amusements, but don't you think in view of what everybody is saying about Count Marsac you'd be wise not to *afficher* yourself too much with him?"

"Oh but, mother," Nigel protested ecstatically, "I must stand by him. He trusts me. And you don't know what he has suffered. It's been too awful. Oh, but simply frightful."

"Well look, Nigel, don't start smoking opium, that's all I ask."

"I can't!" Nigel declared, opening wide his lustrous

large eyes. "That's the tragedy of our friendship. One has the most marvellous yellow dreams if one can only get accustomed to it. But I can't. I'm sick! It's too humiliating. I simply writhe."

"That's a very great relief to me," said Mrs. Dawson.

"And I've been translating some of Bob's poetry," Nigel continued. "Listen to this." He turned his eyes heavenward and began to declaim:

> *"Luca della Robbia, tell me he was fair*
> *And that you might have modelled him in glaze . . .*
> *I see him singing on the blue of your cymaise*
> *Above a tomb, with cold ecstatic air.*
>
> *Child of the heavenly choir or infant saint,*
> *He has the same voluptuous virgin eyes;*
> *Holds high a candle in the same prim guise*
> *With open mouth that seems, perfumèd faint."*

"But I thought cimaise meant a bug. Oh, no, I am muddling up my French and Italian," said Mrs. Dawson. "Cimice and punaise. But who is this conceited little choirboy? Some relation of the Count?"

"Oh no, no, no! It's an ideal love in the key of blue. That's the whole point of the comparison with della Robbia."

"My dear Nigel, you're getting me all muddled up. Now what in the world is the key of blue?"

"John Addington Symonds, of course."

"I seem to have heard that name; but see here, Nigel, if you'll take my advice you won't begin translating anything or anybody. Look at poor Joseph Neave. He started in on old Dante back along in the early 'nineties, and he's nowhere near the end of the *Inferno* yet. He's been living with poor tortured sinners and medicine bottles for nearly twenty years. And that's no life at all for anybody. However, so long as you don't become a dope-victim I don't so much mind your friendship with Count Marsac. Still, don't forget that these excitable kind of friendships usually come to an excitable kind of an end."

So Nigel frequented the company of Marsac more than ever, which did neither his reputation nor Marsac's any benefit. All went well, apart from Nigel's reputation, so long as he was content with translating the Count's verses or listening to his unending rhetoric on a divan in the opium-den he had fitted up in one of the few small rooms at the Villa Decamerone. For a time he enjoyed Marsac's apostrophes addressed to the Goddess Kouan Yin who was apparently in the habit of appearing to him in the sacred mist along the margin of the lake of Longevities and teaching him love as Çakya Mouni learned love. He was pleasantly thrilled to imagine Marsac caressing the ivory of a pipe of tâo taï in the green gardens of Chang-Hai walled in with black and red lacquer, to follow with him the exquisite way rosy with peonies that led to the porcelain pagoda where Li Han Ko was smoking and there to stretch himself on a bed of jade encrusted with amber, while through the geranium evening a flock of ibis passed overhead and the poet's soul evaporated in the perfume of opium. The moony summer nights of Sirene went by most pleasantly in such exotic idleness.

Then one day there arrived on the island an undergraduate from Oxford, younger than Nigel and better looking. And Cecil Upjohn was able to smoke pipe for pipe of opium with Marsac without turning as green as one of those jade thrones the poet was always apostrophizing. This might have been borne; but when Marsac wrote a sonnet to Cecil Upjohn on his golden beauty as he lay drying in the sun after a bathe, and asked Nigel to translate it into English verse, that was too much. He refused with such evident pique that Marsac declared himself affronted and made it clear that he was growing bored by Nigel's visits to the Villa Decamerone. This turned Nigel into just as much of a fury as any woman scorned. He perceived that Carlo was inclined to resent the favour shown to this ridiculous undergraduate, and he proposed to Carlo a trip to the mainland. At the last minute, however, Carlo grew frightened and gave away the plot to Marsac. Nigel whistled beneath Carlo's window and heard the answering signal; but while he waited for him in the shadow of the palm-tree that overhung the gate of the Decamerone it was Marsac himself who emerged, not Carlo, Marsac dressed in the robes of a mandarin and armed with a scimitar, with which he made a slash at Nigel, who had to run for it. And Marsac ran after him, shouting in French terrific denunciations of his conduct. It was really rather too much like the Arabian Nights to be pleasant. Nigel looking back over his shoulder saw the scimitar glittering in the moonlight, and ran faster. So did Marsac, as he pursued what was now his worst enemy down the Via Caprera. He chased Nigel as far as the Piazza. He chased him three times round the Piazza. He chased him into the entrance of the funicular and out again the other side. He chased him up the steps past the Duomo, and through a maze of alleys, and down the steps into the Piazza again. And then, luckily for Nigel, Ferdinando Zampone appeared on the scene, and as the clock in the Piazza tower struck one he was able to shelter behind his bulk.

Late though the hour, there were quite enough people about to exaggerate the incident into fifty different versions and turn it into as bloodthirsty a piece of bashi-bazoukery as had ever thrilled Sirene. There the arrival of the midday boat with letters and newspapers was as nothing compared with the arrival of one's cook in the morning as heavily loaded with piazza gossip as was the basket of the porter who accompanied him or her with the day's provisions. Next morning every housewife on the island heard that Count Marsac had severely wounded with a knife—the weapon was the only thing that shrank in the narrative—

Ferdinando Zampone and the *signorino* of the Villa Florida. Many were told that Beccafico the *guardia*, the *maresciallo*, and the *sindaco* himself had also been wounded. When the cooks of Sirene had glutted their *padroni* with horrors, the *padroni* on going out obtained for themselves a version that while still much exaggerated was nearer the truth. And this habit of exaggeration in Sirene was really beneficial. Scandals always began with such atrocious dimensions and details that when the facts finally transpired they seemed so tame in comparison with the first account as to seem nothing at all really. So now, when it transpired that nobody had been wounded and that indeed nothing more untoward had happened than the pursuit of Nigel Dawson through Sirene by Count Marsac dressed as a mandarin and armed with a scimitar, everybody agreed that it was nothing after all. It had been the news of Ferdinando's serious injury which had really alarmed the *forestieri* of Sirene, and not unnaturally, for it was hard to imagine how a foreigner was going to continue to live comfortably on the island without him. But there he was as usual in the darkest corner of Zampone's, hatching out his bills, able to cover with his corpulent acreage a sitting of twelve or more large ledgers.

"Oh, Ferdinando, then you weren't hurt in the battle last night," cried one relieved housewife after another.

And Ferdinando would look up from his task, those bright little dark eyes of his twinkling in and out of the cumulus of fat that wreathed his face, and say:

"Why must I be damitched, *signora*? Two chentlemans wishes to fight. *Mi son messo in mezzo*, and it is finish. *Pardon, signora, venti tre cinquanta . . . sette quaranta cinque . . . trenta novanta cinque . . .*" And he was away mumbling to himself again over his additions and entering with spidery figures in grey ink on a page webbed with blue lines the indebtedness of his clients.

In this case, however, although the picturesque externals

of the quarrel between the Count and Nigel, which set down in print must seem so farcically improbable, were forgotten by lunch-time, once it was evident that as usual the casualties had been much exaggerated, the results of that absurd scene affected profoundly the attitude of society toward Marsac.

Until now people had been able to excuse their toleration of the Count, in spite of his having been to prison for a scandalous offence against morals, by arguing that whatever he had done in the past he had paid for it, and that after all twelve mental specialists had certified him to be irresponsible at the time. But the quarrel with Nigel Dawson changed this. It was no longer so much a question of what he had done in the past as of what he was doing now. Nigel's body had escaped Marsac's scimitar, but the wound to his vanity was fatal. The friendship turned to a fierce hatred. The thought of the ridiculous figure he had cut, fleeing along the Via Caprera and scuttling round the Piazza and finally hiding behind Ferdinando Zampone, was an agony to that young man. He could not believe that the suicide of a Russian exile, who having been arguing incessantly for a year about the merits of Dostoievski as a writer and the advantage of the Muzio gambit as a chess opening, had been able to stand the irreconcilable variety of human opinion no longer and had hanged himself the following afternoon, should have obliterated the memory of his adventure as rapidly as the memory of the Russian was obliterated in its turn a day or two later by the news that an Austrian baron, who had kept tongues wagging all last Summer over his intrigue with a charming Italian girl in Sirene, had committed suicide with a Dutch woman in an Amalfi hotel. Nigel felt sure that everybody must still be laughing at him, and he was determined to justify himself. The Oxford undergraduate, who was the original cause of the strain in his relations with Marsac, had blown on his way like a dusty rose-leaf, and such jealousy as still existed in the situation was Marsac's rather than Nigel's. Yet even in Marsac's case it was as much vanity as jealousy. His vanity had been outraged by the thought that Carlo could even contemplate for an instant a midnight elopement with Nigel to the mainland. To his fantastic egoism that made him as ludicrous in the eyes of Sirene as Nigel felt himself. In the accusations that he and Nigel flung at each other the Count was at a disadvantage. Whatever his reputation, Nigel Dawson could not be accused of having been to prison. So, when he assured Sirene that he had had to give up visiting the Villa Decamerone on account of the life its inmates led, a great many people decided that the time had come to follow the leaders of the anti-Marsac party into ostracism by the Villa Amabile rather than run the risk of ostracism by the rest of Europe. And how the old ladies revelled in handing out the fatal potsherds! The defection of Nigel Dawson filled them with a savage joy, and time after time did Miss Virginia shrill exultantly:

"Well, whatever anybody may have the wickedness to think about Count Bob, everybody knows for sure what Nigel Dawson is."

There was an attempt by the anti-Marsac party to suggest that all who continued to visit the Villa Amabile exposed themselves to an imputation that their morals were as much widdershins as those of the Count.

"Well, I'd just like to know what they'll have the impudence to invent about our dear Beatrice Mewburn?" demanded Miss Virginia.

And even Mrs. Ambrogio, to whom the question was put, could not think of anything. She herself was protected against the other side by being the wife of the Count's legal adviser, of which she talked loudly.

"If I hear anyone has said one word against me I'll have a cowzer against them," she hurried round proclaiming. "First atom of scandal I hear, Peter will have them arrested. Heard last week in Naples I gave an orgy at the Villa Botticelli with six naked boys to wait at table. Peter furious with anger. I know who invented that, and if she invents it again, I'll have her put in prison for slander. Won't stand it. Dear Count Marsac innocent as a lamb. Hate all this filthy gossip. Darling old Nortons. Love them so much. Don't care if the Count is one of those. Every man in Sirene one of those except Peter. Peter can't understand it. Makes him laugh."

The first outward token of an united society to smash was the tennis-club, because Marsac would go there and not only go there himself but take his Cingalese servant there to pick up the balls. Bookham wanted to call a meeting and expel him from membership, but being advised that an action at law might lie against him he resigned instead. Major Natt, who succeeded to the presidency, decided on the advice of Alberto Jones that the safest thing to do was to dissolve the club and sell the site, which was done. Alberto Jones bought it, and a Jones villa rose like a white phœnix from its ashes. The next thing to smash was the Sirene Club for Residents and Visitors, to the committee of which in the first flush of welcome to his riches the Count had been unanimously elected a fortnight after his arrival. It returned to what it originally was—a greengrocer's shop.

Naturally, there were some people in Sirene whose position was so powerful and whose toleration was so wide that they were under no necessity to take sides. Amongst these was Scudamore, who had retired from society again to the seclusion of the Villa Parnasso, but who derived the greatest pleasure from discussing with members of both parties the niceties of the moral problems involved. It was his chief recreation, before he settled down to a laborious night with his thousands of annotated slips, to hold forth upon the situation with solemn humour and classical allusions and obscure pedantic wit. For everybody he could find something appropriate to the fortunes of the war in Tacitus or Martial, in Juvenal or Propertius. He even penned a copy of heavy-footed sapphics supposed to be addressed by Miss Virginia to Mr. Bookham and an answer from him in the Second Asclepiadean metre.

"This Marsac business is doing Scudamore a great deal of good, you know," Duncan Maxwell declared. "Even the bawdiest passages in his authors were getting dusty, and one by one they're turning as fresh and rosy as the day they were written."

If Scudamore stirred everybody up in the academic shades of his study, Maxwell himself was peripatetic in his incitements. He would go to Christopher Goldfinch and relate the most appalling scenes of debauchery alleged to have taken place at the Villa Amabile.

"My gad, it's incredible," Christopher would gasp, his jaw dropping. "Those poor old women must be mad!"

And then chuckling all the way to himself Maxwell would hurry down to the Amabile and regale the old ladies with an outrageous account of what went on daily at the Villa Adonis.

"And that damnable old hypocrite dares to talk against poor Count Bob!" Miss Virginia shrilled. Neither she nor Miss Maimie had the least difficulty in believing all that Maxwell told them about the painter.

"I'm not at all surprised at what you tell us," said Miss Maimie. "I've thought it all along, the humbugging old goat!"

"Of course, of course, my dee-aw Miss Maimie! No man wears a beard like that unless he has a great deal to hide," Maxwell gravely urged. "That's why the patriarchs all had beards. You remember the way Noah behaved, and Lot? They're all alike these old men, my dee-aw Miss Virginia. Just a little wine, and they'll do anything. Or try to. And it needn't be a vintage wine either. No fee-aw!"

It may be asked what the Sirenesi themselves thought of this war among the foreign residents. The Sirenesi thought that Count Marsac was building a magnificent villa and that he was spending a large amount of money in the island. The Sirenesi thought that for the present at any rate there was no reason to be anything but extremely polite to Count Marsac. As for Alberto and Enrico Jones, while Alberto made a point of avoiding him, Enrico was always cordial. At the same time, Alberto invariably took his part in discussing him behind his back and Enrico as steadily abused him.

Chapter 3

quid dignum tanto feret hic promissor hiatu ?
                                                    HORACE

THAT Winter Zygmunt Konczynski returned to Sirene and made the Via Caprera once more unsafe for sunny meditations. Marsac decided not to take another villa, but to live at the Hotel Augusto until his own house was finished. This was welcome news to Don Cesare Rocco the proprietor, who had been feeling much depressed by the sight of Zampone's big new hotel rising magnificent upon the hillside above his own. Old Don Luigi had chosen his site so well that though Don Cesare had been racking his brains for two years to think of some way of making the new hotel uninhabitable he had discovered none. The nearest land obtainable in front would have involved his building a sky-scraper if he wished to shut off the view from the Hotel Grandioso. To the right and left of him Don Luigi had carefully protected himself against any jealous nuisance from his neighbours. To be sure, immediately above the spacious flat roof of the Grandioso the top of Monte San Giorgio was covered with immense Roman cisterns; but the owner of the Hotel Augusto had not been able to devise any method of letting loose a flood of water on the Hotel Grandioso that would not inundate his own hotel a few minutes later. And so week in week out for two years now Don Cesare had had the mortification of watching the walls of the Grandioso rising higher and higher all the time. On Sirene a jumble of arches and the windowless shells of buildings were often to be seen in the proximity of many of the famous belvederes. These were not, as enthusiastic tourists liked to imagine, the relics of Roman villas and gardens. They were all that were left of several attempts to build a rival hotel to the Augusto, attempts which had been defeated either by Don Cesare's purchase of a vital approach or by securing a site to block out the interloper's view with high walls. Now toward the close of a long and successful career, which had begun as a scullion, he was seeing himself outbuilt for the first time. The Count's decision to make the Hotel Augusto his headquarters sprayed with a delicious antiseptic the mortification of Don Cesare's mind, and the prospect of being able to overcharge his rich guest for months to come swept away like a change of air most of his depression.

"*Je pince que vous voudrez avoir la meilleure suite, monsieur le comte?*" Don Cesare suggested, rubbing his hands and bowing low.

"*Mais sicuro!*" Marsac agreed loftily.

"*Come parla benissimo italiano il signor conte! Ella l'avrebbe studiato a Siena?*"

Sienna is the Hanover or Tours of Italy.

"*Non; l'ho studiato ici à Sirene*," Marsac admitted.

"*È un miracolo!*" Don Cesare vowed, holding up his plump hands in amazement at Marsac's throaty Franco-Sirenese Italian. "*Ma forse il signor segretario del signor conte L'avrebbe insegnato lingua toscana in bocca romana, come diciamo noi altri italiani. Allora, ecco la suite!*" he proclaimed, flinging open the door and revealing splendours of rose du barry curtains and upholstery. "*Salone, salotto, due stanze di letto, entrata privata, e un bagno che funziona sempre!*" he enumerated proudly.

Don Cesare had the right to open his eyes and look astonished. Such a claim could not have been made for any other bath in Sirene. Every villa on the island possessed if not a bathroom at any rate a bath. But most of them did not function at all, and not one of them functioned always. They were chiefly used for storing things that might suffer from damp.

Some of the anti-Marsac section tried to make Don Cesare's flesh creep over the effect on the other guests of sheltering such a notorious character as the Count under his roof. He shrugged his shoulders. He could afford to shrug them. The Hotel Grandioso was many months away from opening, and the Augusto was still the only hotel of luxury in Sirene, the only one that could be patronized by those who travelled in the Pullmans of the great European expresses.

However, the anti-Marsac faction received a very strong reinforcement that Winter from America, which was most heartening to Christopher Goldfinch. The fact that the Miss Pepworth-Nortons were as American as himself had been a great grief to him. He would have liked to point a finger of scorn at the Marsac party as a mix-up of Dagos, Swedes, and Britishers. He wanted people to understand that, whatever Europe might be, America was still morally sound.

There were moments when, after hearing some 'fierce' new story about the behaviour of the Nortons, he reminded one of the Federal soldier wrapped round with the Union flag, his brow bloody but unbowed, defying the Confederates to take him alive. It was true that he had Simon Pears and Joseph Neave on his side, to which the rather doubtful advantage of Nigel Dawson's support had now been added; but Scudamore corrupted by his researches into Roman morals had failed entirely to give eloquence to the disgust that every American ought to feel at the presence of a scoundrel like Marsac. It was Mrs. de Feltre of his compatriots in Sirene who had expressed most nearly what he felt about this toleration of the Count. She had made up her mind quickly which side she should take, and after the trouble she had had to get into the Villa Amabile it was sad that she should have had to get out of it again so soon. However, it was not much use hoping to find an unprotected male in that circle, and while she was looking round for an object to swathe with the rich and soft shawl of her affection she attached herself to Christopher Goldfinch, to whom as a woman of the world who had divorced her husband he could talk more freely than to Angela Pears.

"My gad, I've had good news by this morning's mail, Marian," he told her one afternoon. "There's a bunch of good fellows have taken the Villa Eolia for the Winter. Claude Wilmer the painter, Chester Harrison the sculptor, John Steed Canning and his wife . . ."

"Isn't that stunning!" she exclaimed.

"Yes, but the best of the bunch is still to come. Who do you think is with them?"

She shook her head.

"Why, Sheila Macleod! Say, isn't that corking news?"

Marian de Feltre tried to look blissfully corked. The presence of Sheila Macleod was not from her point of view a desirable addition to the game of love on Sirene. Sheila Macleod had visited the island three years ago and swept the board clear of men in a week.

"Gad, to think that perfectly lovely woman is coming here again," Christopher sighed. "I tell you, Marian, it makes me feel forty years younger. I'd like to have you see what I've gotten for her."

He rose and went to fumble through the drawers of a carved cedar-wood cabinet until he found a necklace of aquamarines.

"That ought to please her, eh?" asked the old man fondly.

"It certainly ought," Mrs. de Feltre answered with a touch of indignation in her tone.

"What a woman," he sighed, kissing his hand to the air

so soon now to flash with the numberless facets of Sheila Macleod.

"May Marian try it on, Uncle Chris?" she asked, hoping that in the tone of her voice there might be an echo of those baby accents of Sheila's which had enthralled the old man.

"Very fine," said Christopher coldly, regarding with anxious disapproval the necklace quivering upon Mrs. de Feltre's emotion. "But amber would suit you better, Marian," he added, as he received back the necklace with some eagerness and replaced it in the cabinet. Then he looked up at the portrait of a young woman whom Rubens would have painted with pleasure.

"What a radiant spirit, eh? To think of any woman being as beautiful as that and just as witty as she's beautiful. Yes, by gad, and with the delicate imagination of a fairy. What can't she do? Nothing that I know of. Come in here a minute." He led the way through several small rooms crowded with carved wood and hung thick with brocades to another small room opening to a view of the salmon-brown precipices of Monte Ventoso and to right of them the azure Bay. It was filled with workmen.

"Last time Sheila was here she said to me I ought to gild this ceiling and panel these walls, and I told her that if she ever came back to Sirene I'd have it ready for her. Quannto tempa finire?" he enquired anxiously of the chief decorator.

"*Non abbia paura, signor Goldafeench. Tutto sarà pronto fra una quindicina di giorni.*"

"All finished in a fortnight," explained Marian de Feltre, who loved translating the simplest sentence of Italian for her friends.

"Capital!" the old painter croaked. And for the benefit of the foreman he courteously added, "Capitale."

"Oh my, don't you spoil your friends?" Marian sighed.

"But you couldn't ever spoil a woman like that," the old man rhapsodized. "You can't spoil perfection, my dear girl."

"Well, I guess we'll have a little bridge anyway," said Marian with a hopeful sigh. "And now I must run along, Uncle Chris. Good-bye, you dear sentimental old darling."

She pecked at his magnificent forehead and went on her way.

The American reinforcements arrived. The Moorish arcades of the Villa Eolia which all the Summer had echoed to the trills and cadenzas of Mrs. Pape's aspirants now echoed to the chink and clink of glasses.

"Well, they may be painters and the devil knows what," said Miss Virginia, fanning herself furiously. "But they behave more like a bunch of down-town bar-tenders."

"I don't know what our poor old country's coming to," said Miss Maimie. "We never used to get such low-class American tourists once on a time."

"They'll be just the right company for that miserable old Goldfinch," Miss Virginia avowed. "Mrs. Ambrogio tells me that this Sheila Macleod creature was hugging and kissing the old sinner in a carriage all the way up to Anasirene, until Domenico the driver turned around in his seat and said, 'Excuse me, but signori don't behave like that except in their own houses.'"

"Next time we drive up to Anasirene we'll drive up with Domenico," Miss Maimie vowed. "He looks after his horses so well, and we haven't driven up with him for a long time."

And up at the Villa Adonis Christopher Goldfinch's pretty little girls, all decked out with sequins and bright kerchiefs, were handing round the cocktails before another uproarious dinner. Sheila Macleod was saying:

"What *do* those two poor old dears down there get out of their friendship with this naughty young Frenchman? Chris, my darling, tell Sheila what they get out of it?"

"Gad, my dear girl, don't ask me! It's fierce. Come, drink hearty. Gelsomina, porta an altra cocktail to the signorina," he commanded with a courtly wave.

Every electric lamp in the Villa Adonis masked in rose

silk was burning just as down below at the Villa Amabile every electric lamp masked in amber silk used to burn for a party. The enemies had at least in common a lavish hospitality and a profusion of electricity. A fire was crackling in the dining-room, for the crispness of November was in the air to-night. The walls were lined with richly-carved panelling. The gilded ceiling lent an added richness to the laden oak table beneath, where the decanters of wine brooded like immense rubies and topazes. There was a recess in the overmantel rose-lighted from behind, from which the host had removed the cinquecento saint in painted wood that usually occupied it and had put in its place the portrait of Sheila Macleod. Himself, in a dinner-jacket of damson velvet and instead of a waistcoat a crimson pleated sash buckled over his slim hips, sat in a great Venetian arm-chair at the head of the table, appearing genuinely magnificent.

"Chris, you look an angel," cried Sheila. "My dears, and doesn't he?" she demanded of the company in that crooning voice which made her host feel that he had not lived nearly long enough. "My, what a perfectly wonderful time we're all going to have in Sirene this Fall."

"I wish we could have gotten rid of that scoundrelly degenerate," said the old man gloomily. "Hell, my dear girl, I tell you he sticks in my gizzard. It's fierce. And you know before I found out what this swine was I gave him my best column of giallo antico and I'm darned if he hasn't set it up in his garden."

He croaked a laugh at his own folly.

"Oh, Chris, my darling, I must kiss you. You're so sweet." She jumped up from her place and put her arms round him, the while he gaped a fond grin and patted her shoulder. "And, Chris, my honey, you haven't said if you like Sheila's dress? Don't you see I've put on a sea-green dress to wear with your dear necklace?"

Christopher clutched her hand and wrung it emotionally.

"Fine! Fine!" he gulped. "Gad, what a relief it is to look round at a bunch of men again," he went on. "Drink hearty! Drink hearty! I don't know what Sirene's coming to. Why, if we had an effeminate brute like this fellow Marsac in America he'd be lynched."

"See here, Mr. Goldfinch," said a wild-eyed heavy-weight called Duplock at the other end of the table, "can't we do something that way ourselves?"

Nobody knew quite what Duplock was. In spite of his blatancy and commonness he had managed to make friends with the rest of the Eolia party in the steamer, though not one of them would have spoken to him at home, and he was now staying at the Hotel Augusto. He appeared to be one of those virile primitives who even as long ago as this made a practice of visiting Europe for a six months' bat. He talked incessantly whether drunk or sober about the moral grandeur of the United States, talked like a Hercules whose task in life was to cleanse the Augean stables of Europe. People put up with his manners because he tried to knock them down if they showed the least sign of trying to avoid his company. Intercourse with him was conducted on the principle of anything for a quiet life.

The other Americans talked a great deal about the scandal of Marsac's being allowed to remain on the island; but none of them seemed inclined to support the measures of violence advocated by Aston Duplock, who deplored the inertia of his countrymen.

"You don't see him all the time," he grumbled. "He's gotten me so as I can't eat the food on my plate with watching his blasted antics."

It is true that the sight of Marsac sitting at dinner with Carlo in the dining-room of the Augusto, particularly the presence at his elbow of the Cingalese servant, exasperated Duplock to such a degree that he did hardly eat anything at all. However, the less he ate the more he drank, and his bill had by now mounted up to a figure that was beginning to worry Don Cesare. With many apologies he suggested that something on account of it would be welcome.

Duplock referred him to his friend Mr. Goldfinch.

"See here, Goldfinch, I want you to talk to this hotel guy at the Augusto," he blustered in the Villa Adonis. "He's had the noive to bother me about my bill. Can't you come right around and tell him that's no way at all to treat a man like me, especially when he's keeping this pink-faced Cissie under his roof?"

The painter demurred to this.

"Now, see here, Goldfinch," said the heavy-weight, "that's as good as saying you think my money's bad. Now, I'm not going to stand that from any man. No, Sir! I've fought good and plenty for less than that. But I'm not going to fight you. No, Sir! And I'm not going to start hitting your household gods about," he went on, looking menacingly at a marble Diana whose broken nose suggested that she had already been in the ring. "No, Sir! I'm just going to drink your health and say I'm sorry. I repeat . . . and say I'm sorry, derned sorry that the leading American citizen on this sunnavabitch of an island should refuse to come forward and testify to the financial stability of one of his own countrymen." He gulped down a glass of Goldfinch's best brandy, and poured himself out another. Then he pulled out of his pocket a wad of twenty-dollar bills. "Paint me a goddam picture," he hiccupped. "How much is there there?" He licked his thumb and counted over the bills. "Four hundred dollars," he announced. "Paint me what you like so long as it's a woman. Nood or draped. I don't give a nickel. I don't want a big picture. No, Sir! I want a picture I can stick up on my table at the Augusto and look at while I'm eating, so as I can remember there is such a thing as a real woman left. Something with coives an honest-to-god man could cuddle."

Poor old Goldfinch was in a quandary. If he refused this commission his visitor, who had just swallowed a third glass of brandy on top of all he must have been drinking already to-day, might not be able to restrain himself; but the idea of painting a picture for him to put on his dining-table offended the old romantic's sense of fitness. Perhaps the simplest way, now that he had evidence of Duplock's possession of some money, was to do as he had been asked and speak for his stability to Don Cesare. He pushed away the wad of bills.

"By gad, I wish I *could* paint a picture for you," he croaked with all his courtliness, "but I've too much work on hand already this Winter. Anno Domini, you know," he went on, waving lightly his beautiful hand. "But if you'll wait a moment—and—er—help yourself," he indicated the brandy, "I'll put on my hat and walk along with you to the Augusto right away."

Aston Duplock rose to his feet and proffered a huge fist.

"Goldfinch, you're white. And now, I'm going to do something for you in return. Don't worry, old man. I'm going to clear this fairy out of Sirene. There won't be any Marsac after I've done with him. Count, does he call himself? I tell you, boy, the only count he'll ever get from me is the count out." And he sealed his promise with a hiccup like the clap of castanets, the mightiest hiccup ever heard in the Villa Adonis through the bacchanalia of forty years.

When Christopher had remonstrated suitably with Don Cesare for doubting the substance of a man like Aston Duplock, and when Don Cesare had assured Christopher Goldfinch that his recommendation was good enough to secure any guest from even the sight of his account were it displeasing to him, the great simple-hearted, prairie-souled, heavy-weight American sat in the vestibule of the hotel and pondered the elimination of Marsac. Sitting thus in a wicker arm-chair near the main entrance, he saw his abomination coming down, and it occurred to him that to put out his leg as Marsac was passing might trip him up into a pretty quarrel. So he put out his leg, and Marsac did trip over it. However, instead of protesting he raised his hat and begged pardon so politely that even Duplock was unable to find a pretext for using his fists.

"If that sweet-scented stiff does it again, I'll say he did it on poipose, and hit him," he muttered to himself.

But the next time that Marsac passed the out-thrust leg he perceived it in time to walk round the obstacle. Duplock tried once more. On this occasion Marsac paused and frowned at the limb, and the owner of it could almost feel his sleeves rolling themselves up of their own accord in anticipation of the fun, as his victim drew near the table by his chair. He glared at him from a pair of eyes that bulged like plums. He fancied that Marsac was going to ask him if it was his leg, upon which he was planning to reply as he rose like the Statue of Liberty:

"Yes, ladybird, and it's my boot too," proving the statement on Marsac's posterior.

The Count, however, instead of addressing himself to the American, struck the bell on the table.

"Somebody has left a leg here," he told the head-porter who came hurrying up to see what the chief source of his present income required. "I have already had the inconvenience of falling over it once or twice. Please have it put somewhere out of the way."

With this the Count passed quickly on, and Duplock was left to argue or fight with the head-porter. Now, head-porters have been trained from infancy to deal with people like Duplock. There was no fight, and he won the argument. The corn-fed husky child of nature retired downstairs in a dudgeon to the Augusto bar.

"Hell, Tony," he observed to the barman who had worked for ten years in New York and was really the only being in all Sirene with whom Duplock felt at home. "Gimme a treble brandy. My mouth's like a powder puff. If I can't wash the stink of scent out of it good and quick, I'll sure vomit."

The next day Duplock walking past the door into the lobby of the private suite occupied by Marsac, noticed that the next room to it was vacant. He was seized with an idea.

"See here, Mr. Cheesery, I don't like my room a bit. I'd rather be on the first floor. Can't you let me change into Number 12? I see that's empty."

Don Cesare was willing to oblige, though he hoped that Signor Duplock would not misunderstand him when he ventured to point out that the charge for Room 12 was four liras a day more than for Room 121 now occupied by the signor.

"It don't matter to me if it's forty liras," said Duplock.

A week or so later there was another of those uproarious dinners at the Villa Adonis which so much scandalized Miss Virginia and Miss Maimie. Everybody was astonished when about eleven o'clock Duplock announced that he was going back to his hotel.

"And if two of the bunch will come right along with me I'll be glad. What I want are witnesses."

In spite of the protests of her host Sheila Macleod vowed she was ready to go anywhere with Aston.

"No, Sheila, this isn't a job for a woman. I want a coupla fellows."

He turned to the bachelors of the party.

"Claude and Chester, are you coming?"

"Sure, we're coming, Aston."

In vain did the host protest strongly against the breaking up of his dinner-party. Duplock was mysterious, but firm.

"We'll be back before eggnog time," he said. "Don't worry."

When he and his companions left the Villa Adonis Duplock explained the plot.

"See here, fellows, I've got our friend the Count fixed.

I couldn't say too much in front of the women. You've hoid of what they call flagrant delight in France?"

"They don't call it quite that," Chester Harrison murmured. "But I know what you mean."

"Well, we're going to have some flagrant delight with Cecilia Marsac," Duplock announced. "And I guess after that even Sirene will be too hot for him."

"Or the other way round," suggested Wilmer.

Duplock produced from his pocket a tool.

"See what that is?"

"Looks like a gimlet."

"Sure, it's a gimlet, and that's what's going to put the Countess off this island. But say, you wouldn't believe what a trouble I had to make these wops comprenny what I wanted. Hell, you stick an 'o' on most English words and you've put 'em wise to what you want. But not with gimlet. No, Sir! Then I tried to show 'em in action, and I was offered everything from a toothpick to a watch-key."

"But what's the gimlet for anyway?" asked one of his companions.

"Oh, boy!" Duplock gurgled in an ecstasy of anticipation; and he would say nothing more until they reached Room 12 in the Hotel Augusto. Then he explained his plan.

"I'm going to bore a hole through the wall between the two rooms, so as we can say we know all about his orgies and opium and all the rest of it."

"Bore away," laughed Claude Wilmer.

So Duplock set to work. Presently he stopped and looked up.

"Say, did either of you hear something like a squeal?"

They shook their heads, and Duplock resumed his boring, after which he blew heavily through the hole. And this time from the other side of the partition there did come the distinct sound of a scream.

A minute or two later there was a loud knock on the door of Room 12.

"Come!" cried Duplock.

And in came Don Cesare himself.

"What you doing? What you doing with my wife's room?" he demanded angrily. Behind him were two waiters, the night-porter, and the cashier.

"Your wife?" repeated Duplock. "Why, I understood that Count Marsac had the suite next door to me."

"On the other side, yes, sare! But on this side is my wife! Why you make holes in my hotel?"

"Well, I guess I can make holes in a room for which I pay twenty goddam liras a day?" demanded Duplock.

"No, sare, you cannot make holes in my hotel."

"Can't I? I'll make your derned old hotel look like a blasted pepper-pot if I like," said Duplock truculently. "See here, Mr. Cheesery, you quit from here, or I'll make holes in you."

There were twenty different versions in the Piazza next morning of what happened at the Augusto after this, from which two positive facts at last emerged. They were the departure of Aston Duplock from Sirene by the afternoon boat, and the settlement of his bill by Christopher Goldfinch and his American friends at the Villa Eolia.

The general feeling in Sirene was that this time the pro-Marsac faction had scored.

Chapter 4

*sed quae mutatis inducitur atque fovetur
tot medicaminibus coctaeque siliginis offas
accipit et madidae, facies dicetur an ulcus?*

JUVENAL

THE next person to play a part in the Marsac affair was Mrs. Edwardes, who arrived in early Spring, just when the greyness of the terraced slopes was turning to a rosy mist of peach-blossom, when the purple anemones were starring the windy hillsides and when in all the *pensions* the toothglasses of English old maids touring Italy were full of fly-orchises. Mrs. Edwardes was reputed to be as old as Miss Virginia, but she had caulked all her wrinkles so carefully and painted her face so cleverly that at fifteen and even ten yards away men involuntarily straightened their ties when they saw her coming. Mrs. Edwardes had known Miss Virginia and Miss Maimie for years—long before they ever arrived in Sirene. Those who had regretfully come under the Amabile ban hoped that Mrs. Edwardes might be able to convince her old friends that in championing thus ardently the cause of a creature like Marsac they were exposing themselves to a terrible disillusionment in the future. Mrs. Edwardes was the very person to open their eyes. For one thing she was extremely rich. This was important, because the Nortons could not taunt her, as they had taunted some of their friends, with being jealous of Marsac because they dreaded losing whatever they might have been left by Miss Virginia in her will. It was a habit of Miss Virginia's when she took a great fancy to people to incorporate that affection practically in a codicil. Some people said she only did this for the pleasure of cutting them out of her will when they would no longer allow her to tyrannize over them. But that was unjust. It was never anything but the purest benevolence that led Miss Virginia to mention people in her will. It was indeed a kind of post-mortem hospitality, and if there was in her impulse a touch of self-interest it was certainly no more than a desire to be remembered warmly when she herself was for ever cold. Besides being extremely rich Mrs. Edwardes was not in the least likely to covet Marsac for herself. She was extremely fond of young men (it might be said that she was scandalously fond of them) and she spent a great deal of her large income on them; but, as she so often insisted, she liked men to be men. In old days, when people had gossiped about Mrs. Edwardes, Miss Virginia had always taken her part with characteristic vigour and fierceness. In fact she had excommunicated one or two of her acquaintances who had allowed themselves in her presence to suggest that Mrs. Edwardes's habit of presenting the handsome young mariners of Sirene with gold watches was not entirely due to her anxiety that they should know the right time.

So, as soon as Mrs. Edwardes was installed in the Villa Mortadella with her French maid and her English butler, Christopher Goldfinch, Joseph Neave, Mrs. Dawson, and one old friend after another came and begged her to do what she could to save Miss Virginia and Miss Maimie from making fools of themselves over Count Marsac any longer.

Raddled and powdered and corseted she sat up in a straight-backed chair, swinging her still shapely legs enclosed in very long kid boots with very high heels, and listening with the greatest relish to the tales of Marsac's behaviour. When she had accumulated enough evidence she dressed herself in her brightest satins and longest plumes to pay her visit of remonstrance.

It happened that on the afternoon Mrs. Edwardes went

down to the Villa Amabile to visit her old friends Miss Maimie was up at the Villa Hylas with Marsac himself, admiring the progress of the building and listening in an enchantment to the Count's florid account of the way he intended to decorate it inside. Miss Virginia would have been there too, had not the March wind been blowing so shrewdly and she with a slight cold. Miss Maimie had been perfectly sincere in dissuading her from the long ride up on a donkey's back to the Villa Hylas; but Miss Maimie could not help enjoying perhaps a little more than usual this visit when she could have dear Count Bob entirely to herself. They sat regardless of the wind in the columned portico that looked down over Sirene to the Grande Marina, and Miss Maimie was thrilled by Marsac's saying:

"As soon as I shall be installed in my house, Miss Maimie, I shall arrange signals with the Villa Amabile. Do not doubt that. Oh yes, I shall have flags of diverse bright colours which I shall elevate, inviting you to lunch or to tea or perhaps asking your permission to come myself to tea or to lunch or to dine with you. I am convinced that it will be excessively amusing."

"Why, it'll be perfect, my dear boy."

"Maestro Supino assures me that all will be ready next Autumn."

"Isn't it all just wonderful?" she sighed. "But, Bob, you won't live in it the first Winter?" she continued anxiously. "You know, it's hardly safe to live in a Sirene house for the first six months after it's finished building."

"*Ah, c'est entendu*, my dear Miss Maimie. I shall occupy myself during the winter with the transportation of my tapestries, my pictures, my bric-à-brac, everything I have in Paris."

"I think it's all just wonderful," she repeated. "After these long months of waiting, here you'll be at last in your own beautiful home with your own beautiful possessions all around you." Her eyes clouded, her mouth tightened to a thin line. "And to think that these vile hypocrites here would like to keep you out of your beautiful home for ever."

"Pray do not regard them, my dear Miss Maimie," he begged with lofty disdain. "I assure you that I have been compelled to learn to mock myself at the world. Ah yes, when one has suffered as I have suffered, that is a necessity."

"I know you've suffered, my dear boy," she said, putting out a hand in impulsive sympathy to pat his arm. "But at least you will have two friends who will never be anything but the truest friends, always and against everybody and everything."

He picked up the old maid's hand and bent over to touch it lightly with his lips.

"You have no obligation to tell me that, *très chère mademoiselle*, for I must assure you that it is already written very profoundly upon my heart."

And then they put emotion aside to talk of the hard tennis-court that Marsac was laying down and of how it was to be surrounded by borders of white marguerites and a grove of mimosas; and from that they went on to a denunciation of the way Sirene gardeners would mutilate all the trees so iniquitously.

Thus it fell that the fortune of war gave Mrs. Edwardes an opportunity to find Miss Virginia alone, and not merely alone but in rather a bad temper with everybody on account of her cold.

There might never be a moment more propitious to prejudice Miss Virginia against Count Marsac, and Mrs. Edwardes opened firmly:

"Now it's not a bit of good your sitting up and abusing me, Virginia Pepworth," she declared. "I can give you back as good as I get. I'm not Christopher Goldfinch, and I'm not Angela Pears. I'm a friend of a great number of years, so don't you flash your eyes at me, Virginia, but listen awhile to what I'm going to tell you."

Whereupon Mrs. Edwardes explained at great length

and with much frankness of detail the kind of life that Count Marsac-Lagerström was now living on Sirene.

Miss Virginia fanned herself and bit her lips and rocked back and forth in her rocking-chair; but she listened. Had Miss Maimie been present Mrs. Edwardes would have been bundled out of the Villa within two minutes; but Miss Maimie was up on Timberio, and without her a kind of weak reasonableness overcame poor Miss Virginia. For the first time since that meeting by the Temple of Vesta in Rome her opinion of the Count wavered.

"Well, maybe, poor boy, he did something wrong once," she allowed. "But he has paid for it."

"I'm not talking of what he did. I'm talking of what he's doing now."

"Sirene gossip," said Virginia, her mouth working.

"Virginia Pepworth, I've satisfied myself that it is not just Sirene gossip," Mrs. Edwardes declared solemnly. "I tell you, that man's life is an open scandal, and for you and Maimie to talk about him as if he was a martyr is just making fools of yourselves."

With this Mrs. Edwardes retired and left Miss Virginia to meditate upon the situation. No doubt her cold made her irritable and pessimistic. Miss Maimie was later in coming home than she expected; and when at last she did arrive, escorted by the Count, Miss Virginia fired off at him all the tales of his behaviour she had heard from Mrs. Edwardes.

"Now, is all this true?" she demanded. "Dear knows I don't give a cent what anybody does. If you tell us you can't help it, I guess Maimie and I will just have to pretend we haven't noticed anything peculiar. We aren't going to turn our backs on you. But we can't turn on everybody else the way we have if it's all true. Some folks feel pretty bad about things like this. We may think them funny and old-fashioned, but maybe they can't help feeling like that. So if it's all true, we'd rather you told us."

"Speak for yourself, Virginia," said Miss Maimie glowering. "I'll never believe it is true."

"And I won't believe it's true, if Bob says that it's all a pack of lies," Miss Virginia answered.

Why Marsac lied to those old ladies is idle to speculate, as idle as it is for an outsider to speculate what it was in him that led them to abandon everybody for him, to sacrifice every friendship for his, and ultimately to suffer for him all that they did suffer in their pride and their affection. There were some who said that the infatuation was all Miss Maimie's for a handsome young man.

"My dear Miss Virginia, I swear to you by the memory of my dead father that all you have heard this afternoon is a web of lies."

And this he swore not haughtily, but emotionally, bursting into tears and falling on his knees beside Miss Virginia to weep into her lacy lap.

"There, there, honey," she murmured as she petted him like a child. "We don't believe a word of it. We never will believe a word of it."

"I never did believe a word of it," Miss Maimie added in her low passionate voice.

The next morning Mrs. Edwardes received one of those letters that Miss Virginia and Miss Maimie wrote when they intended to make a quarrel perpetual.

> VILLA AMABILE,
>   GRANDE MARINA,
>   ISOLA DI SIRENE,
>   ITALIA.

Adelaide Edwardes,

After what you had the impudence to come and say this afternoon please understand that we do not wish to see your painted face inside our house again—instead of slandering innocent people you would do better to look in your glass and ask yourself what right you have to slander anybody—we are sorry to hear the dreadful things we have heard about the way you behave at your age—but we suppose that your friend Mr. Goldfinch appreciates your manner of life filling up people with wine and lies as he always is—we do not know Miss Sheila Mcleod but from what we hear about her we would be ashamed to know her—we hope you will receive this notice that our friendship is terminated with as little regret as we feel being as we are so happy about it all.

Virginia and Maimie Pepworth-Norton

Mrs. Edwardes was so angry about this letter that she showed it to everybody including her butler. Now, Mossop was thoroughly bored with life on Sirene. He heard from his mistress, who was talkative and indiscreet, a great deal about the foreign residents, and what he did not hear from her he heard from Marguerite her maid. But there were no other English butlers in Sirene with whom he could gossip, and even if he had been able to talk enough Italian he would have scorned an intimacy with the Italian men-servants on the island. Italians for him represented a class of human beings that were hardly removed from the monkeys with which he had all his life associated them.

"I really don't know why you go about looking so bad-tempered, Mossop," his mistress expostulated.

"It's the leck of society here, meddam," he replied gloomily.

"Well, I hope you'll cheer up presently, because I've rented this villa right along through the Summer."

"The Summer, meddam? But I always understood that Italy was so uncommonly hot in the Summer."

"So it is. That's just why I intend to stay on here. I want the sun."

"Quate so, meddam," he said, inclining his head and, after a supercilious glance round the room, retiring.

"The old beauty wants the sun now," he observed

sardonically to Marguerite later. "Nothing else is hot enough for her."

"*Comme t'es méchant, t' sais!*"

"Yes, and I'm going to be a bloody sight more mayshong in a moment."

"*Ferme-la!*" she adjured, putting her hand over his mouth. "*Pourtant je t' adore, sale gosse,*" she added with a wicked kiss.

One might have supposed that even a wilderness like Sirene with Marguerite beside him would have been enough for Mossop. Unfortunately he had carried matters so far with Marguerite in Mrs. Edwardes's New York apartment that the Sirenian moonlight was superfluous. Mossop pondered a way of compelling his mistress to abandon her plan of spending the Summer on this benighted island, and in order to work off his feeling he sent her an anonymous postcard written in red ink:

You painted and padded old bundle of peppermint!!! Look out, or this island won't hold you much longer.
Bill Bailey.

"There's only one place where that could have come from," Mrs. Edwardes shrilled when the postcard was brought in with her mid-day mail. "And that's Maimie Norton."

The ascription of his postcard to the Villa Amabile amused Mossop, and it struck him that it would be equally amusing to send an anonymous postcard to the Villa Amabile. So he wrote one in green ink:

Everybody knows what you were doing with Count Marsac the other day. But if you can't be good be careful.
(signed) W. G. Grace.

Miss Maimie was convinced that only Adelaide Edwardes would have sent her such a postcard, and without a moment's hesitation she replied with this:

You abominable woman, I know quite well what you're doing.

Maimie Pepworth-Norton.

By the same post Mossop sent his mistress a picture postcard of the Naples Narcissus on which he wrote:

> *This is how you like it, eh?*
> *For shame.*
> (signed) *The Archbishop of Canterbury.*

After this he let himself go, and the postcards he sent to the Villa Mortadella and the Villa Amabile became so outrageous that the recipients were no longer able to read them out to their supporters, and they had to be handed round with the bread and butter to be read in silence and passed on. Those that were supposed to come from the Villa Amabile were naturally more deadly than those that were attributed to the Villa Mortadella, because the writer was able between what he knew and what Marguerite told him to get very hard home at his mistress. And then there arrived in Sirene another French maid. The silver of the moon was useful currency again. Under the spell of prospering love Sirene became more than tolerable, and Mossop ceased to derive any amusement from writing letters and postcards signed by famous statesmen, murderers, divines, and athletes. But Marguerite grew jealous, and when he ignored her protests she gave him away to her mistress, who sacked him immediately. The Nortons, however, refused to believe that it was Mossop who had been writing to them. They said that the real reason Mrs. Edwardes got rid of her butler was because he had caught her out in an affair too disgracefully shameless even for her to brazen out. As for Mrs. Edwardes, though she had to acquit the Nortons of the deed, she could not acquit them of the intention. So, even when Mossop had been pushed off the island, they did not hate one another any less.

When Mrs. Edwardes was thrown out of the Sirene sedan and broke her leg, thereby causing the *municipio* to pass a law making it a criminal offence to use that sedan, the Nortons vowed she had done it on purpose when drunk to have an excuse for employing the services of a young Swedish masseur who happened to be on the island; and when in the Fall she returned to America with the masseur and married him as her fourth husband, they declared that it served both of them right.

Observers of human nature like Maxwell and Scudamore had the best fun of the war between the factions, the bitterness of which was increasing every day. Maxwell as a matter of fact went off to Crete early in the Summer in pursuit of a Praying Mantis he had not yet encountered. Scudamore, however, sat in the shades of the Villa Parnasso and continued to stir everybody up. It was he who did the Marsac cause the greatest disservice of all by putting into the Count's head the idea of erecting a gilded statue of Tiberius that would at once outshine and overshadow the great Madonna who now sanctified the accursed ruins of his infamous palace. There was not the least malice in this. Scudamore genuinely felt a profound compassion for the slandered emperor, and he was perfectly serious when he urged Marsac to spend some money in doing him tardy justice. Marsac enjoyed the notion of taking an emperor under his wing and entered into the scheme with enthusiasm. He prepared a florid manifesto in French, which Scudamore translated into his own ponderous Latin, and this was sent round to the classical savants of Europe asking for their support. This many of them, finding that the whole expense of the memorial would be defrayed by Marsac, willingly gave. Armed with the approval of their learned names Marsac approached the *municipio* for a site. And then the priests felt that it was time to interfere. The individual members of the *municipio* were many of them bad Catholics and most of them anticlerical; but the municipal elections were due in the

Autumn, and the councillors were all making too much out of office not to be very anxious to be re-elected. It was no time to quarrel with the priests. Marsac's offer was declined, and when in the Autumn the *sindaco* and all his associates were rejected by an indignant community chiefly in revenge for the way they had furnished their homes out of the money that should have been spent on mending the Sirene roads, they blamed Marsac and his proposed statue for their discomfiture. The new *sindaco* and the new *municipio* were strongly clerical. So, the Count had enemies on both sides. On top of that he offended the new *pretore*, as a local police-magistrate is pompously called, by reading him a long lecture on the superiority of French administration over Italian, which his own legal adviser Peter Ambrogio warned him had been most impolitic. Finally he had a row with the Jones brothers, which was even more impolitic.

One afternoon, when the Count went up to see the progress of his villa, he found workmen digging on the rocky land beyond his own boundaries, and on enquiring what they were at he was told that the signori Jones were going to build a villa on this site. Furious at the threat to his lordly seclusion Marsac wrote an indignant letter to Alberto asking why, when he sold him the land for the Villa Hylas, he had not mentioned that he still retained some of the adjacent property. To this he received the following reply from Enrico:

Palazzo Inglese.

Dear Count Marsac,

I would be immensely grieved if the slightest misunderstanding could arise about the poor little plot of land which my brother Alberto sold to me at the same time that he sold to you his property on Timberio. He had not any idea that you would be interested in such a barren and stony piece of cliff. You are right in surmising that I am intending to erect upon it a

small hermitage—quite a humble little cell where I can get away from the noise and glitter of Sirene and take up my palette again and paint in peace. At the same time if I felt that my neighbourhood could possibly annoy you in any way I would be most distressed, and rather than have that happen I would be most willing to part with my interest to a man who appreciates as you do the solitude that even in these days those who search for it can still find on our island. I need hardly say that I can only accept a purely nominal price for the land. I dare say you will think me sentimental when I say that I would not care to treat this little transaction as a commercial proposition. The fact of the matter is I am too fond of this stretch of primitive cliff to make an affair out of it. Provided that I can recoup myself for the little expense to which I have already been put over the beginning of my little hermitage, for which I must now find another site, that is really all I want.
                            Yours very sincerely,
                              Enrico Jones

Whereupon Marsac wrote to ask exactly how much he did want. To this Enrico replied:

My dear Count Marsac,
 I will be happy to accept 5500 liras for the land you want, and I dare say you will prefer to pay the legal costs connected with the transfer of the property.
                            Yours very sincerely,
                              Enrico Jones

Now, Alberto had paid three hundred liras for those few hundred square metres, so that the profit for two idealists was not bad.

However, Marsac accepted his offer, and having accepted it he was foolish enough to write and tell Enrico that he considered he had been swindled by him and his brother.

Enrico flushed darkly.

"Do you care for the style of Marsac's new villa?" he asked Alberto.

"Oh yes, I think it is handsome," the brother replied.

"It ought to be for sale fairly cheap one of these days," said Enrico. "I don't feel myself that this *orecchione* will stay in Sirene much longer."

Chapter 5

> *nam prodiga corruptoris
> improbitas ipsos audet temptare parentes.*
>
> . . . .
>
> *i nunc et iuvenis specie laetare tui, quem
> maiora expectant discrimina.*
>
> JUVENAL

BY the end of October the Villa Hylas was finished, or at any rate as much finished as any building ever is on Sirene; and as soon as the first consignment of his furniture arrived from Paris the owner could not resist the temptation to instal himself partially in his new house. It was chiefly his own natural impatience to be quit of hotel life which was responsible for what everybody warned him was a most premature occupation. But what actually decided him to move up to his villa was the opening of the Hotel Grandioso and the hints thrown out at Zampone's that it was his duty to leave the Hotel Augusto and occupy the best suite at the Grandioso. Don Cesare had treated Marsac very well, and he was anxious not to hurt his feelings by deserting him for his rivals. He was equally unwilling to offend the Zampones, and the easiest way out of the difficulty was to stay in neither hotel and give a great order for household stores to Ferdinando Zampone. He pointed out to the old ladies at the Amabile, who were much worried by the notion of his spending the Winter in a damp house, that he should be away much of the time in France. When they protested on behalf of Carlo, he argued that Carlo was used to damp and reminded them that he had taken Carlo as a boy of fourteen from the dampest corner of the Trastevere to make a secretary of him. The seal was set on his determination to move up to his villa by the discovery of a wonderful housekeeper. This was Madame Protopopesco, a Roumanian who had run away from Bucharest with a young violinist and had been deserted by him in Sirene a few months later. She was a handsome parched hungry-lipped creature of the dangerous age, whose looks would have told against her with Marsac, had he not had from every quarter the most fervid testimonials to her good behaviour. Overcome by grief at the loss of her violinist she had twice attempted to drown herself from the outlying rocks of the Piccola Marina; but, when her suicide had been twice frustrated by the mariners on that side of the island, who were naturally anxious not to give their strand a bad name just before the opening of the bathing season, she had pulled herself together, and donning a native costume of her country, which was either the only heirloom she remembered to bring with her on her elopement or the only one left her by the violinist, she had earned a living all through the Summer by serving delicious Roumanian meals to the bathers. The Marsac faction always bathed from the Piccola Marina much to the distress of the old ladies, who could see from their own loggia the Grande Marina abandoned to the enemy. However, they had to admit that their friends were wise to take refuge on the other side of the island, because by now the anti-Marsac faction was considerably stronger and there had been one or two unpleasant incidents caused by Neapolitan visitors, such as pushing the Count's Cingalese off the wooden stage when he was waiting there to receive with a rose-coloured bath-towel his master's emersion from the water. Marsac found Madame Protopopesco's cooking so much to his taste and the general opinion of her behaviour, once she had got over the habit of trying to drown herself, so favourable, that he engaged her to superintend his own household.

The Villa Hylas certainly occupied what house-agents

call a unique position, and the most phlegmatic observer could not have found fault with Marsac's salutation of it as a pearl when he celebrated in verse his return from the raw fogs and confusion of Paris to the warmth and tranquillity of Sirene. The poet might have added that his villa was nearly as cold and uncomfortable as a pearl. In the first place, as Maxwell had warned him, the low winter sun only reached it for an hour after rising and an hour before setting. The rest of the day it was hidden by the steep and stony slopes of Timberio. He had planned a terrace, over the balustrade of which one could stare down into the peacock-blue sea hundreds of feet below. This was to be a pleasantly cool spot in Summer. So it was, but in Winter it was like the top of an ice-box, and when the northeast *grecale* blew, it was like the cold circle of Hell. The great portico on the other side of the house with its glorious view was miserable in Winter when the *libeccio* and the *ponente* drove sheets of rain through it, and savagely cold when the north-west *maestrale d' inverno* made a *tempo d' inferno*; and on summer afternoons it was intolerable when the dawdling sun blazed through a golden fume of mosquitoes, which found in a lily-pool Marsac had contrived at great expense just the breeding-place they required. The gardens were full of statuary and since, apart from 'O Gobbetto's ancient carobs, the trees were still nurserymen's striplings, these statues gave a restless look to the landscape, seeming to be hanging about like people with nothing to do. The life-size bronze of Carlo as a nude Hylas pondering the mosquito-grubs in the lily-pool would no doubt in another decade look attractive, half-veiled as it would be by a thicket of mimosas. At present it suggested a youth about to defy the municipal authorities by bathing in a public park. Even inside the villa, in spite of the many really beautiful pieces of furniture and objets d' art that Marsac had collected, the whole effect was uncomfortable, not with the discomfort of a museum, but with the discomfort of an overstressed femininity of arrangement. The marble staircase that took up so much space in the middle of the house looked all wrong with its Aubusson carpet; and on the walls the immense pictures of sunburnt naked young men riding enormous percheron horses across terracotta deserts swore at the carpet and embarrassed the visitor. The most comfortable room in the house was a subterranean opium-den full of magnificent Eastern fabrics and containing part of a collection of pipes that was reputed to be the finest in the world. Yet it seemed hardly worth while to spend a fortune on building oneself a house in a remote corner of Sirene for the sake of the view and then try to justify one's extravagance by pointing to the perfection of a subterranean opium-den. Really the best thing about the Villa Hylas was the view of it from the loggia of the Villa Amabile. Beheld from there its white shape gleaming in the sunlight upon the edge of the dizzy cliff appeared the crystallization of a dream. Oh, to live there, one sighed, swung between azure sky and peacock sea! Oh, to live in that cloud-cuckoo palace which might charm Arethusa from her couch in the snows of the Acroceraunian mountains!

To the old ladies gazing at it from their favourite loggia the Villa Hylas looked at once exquisitely attainable and sublimely unattainable.

"So near and yet so far," Miss Virginia used to sigh.

"But just the dreamy location where a poet like dear Bob ought to live," Miss Maimie would add fondly.

And in the fine November weather the Norton girls would ride up twice a week on their donkeys to admire the furniture and pictures that used to arrive almost every day, passing on the road their excommunicated friends like two indifferent sultanas.

At the beginning of December Marsac went again to Paris to superintend the packing of his wonderful Chinese vases and the final and most precious consignment of his three hundred and sixty-five opium pipes. Brittle may have been the jade from which many of those pipes were carved, but it was not more brittle than the affections of his establishment, and he would have done better to risk some of them being broken than to leave his secretary exposed to the guile of Eve. No sooner was Marsac dreaming in the key of blue on the Naples boat than Madame Protopopesco set out to seduce Carlo from the key of blue with the scarlet discords of Woman. Incidentally she seduced the Cingalese as well and with even less difficulty than Carlo. Finally she told as many people in Sirene as she could, boasting of the merit of her deed.

Marsac travelled back from Paris, longing for a sight of his villa after the foggy North. All the way he was writing odes to Sirene and lyrics to Carlo. To quote from one of these which was translated by an English sympathizer when it appeared in print some months later:

> *Carlo, thy name is*
> *An azure sky,*
> *A beam of the sun*
> *Behind the eye . . .*
>
> *The bittersweet scent*
> *Of a flower's smart,*
> *Of a flower that lives*
> *But in my heart. . . .*
>
> *The echo of some ancient lay*
> *That shepherds sing,*
> *Who in the Roman weather play*
> *Upon their pipes the livelong day,*
> *And my soul wring!*

And there were several other verses much more explicit.

Even a rough crossing from Naples did nothing to spoil the author's pastoral mood. *Formosum pastor Corydon ardebat Alexim.* As with Carlo beside him Marsac walked up to the Villa Hylas through the gusty darkness of the December evening, he would pause from time to time to listen with him to the distant droning of *zampognieri* who every year at Christmastide came from the mountains to play upon their pipes before the little roadside shrines of Sirene. And every time he paused he would repeat to Carlo a verse from one of the lyrics he had been writing to him ever since he went away.

"You are very silent, my Carlo," he said to him at last in French. "*Qu'est-ce que tu as, mon beau berger?* Do you not like the verses I have written to you?"

Carlo replied that he liked them excessively; but his conscience haunted by Madame Protopopesco distracted him so much that he could not express the sincerity, still more the emotion and enthusiasm of praise for which the poet was hungry.

"It would seem that you are not quite so overjoyed by my return as I am," Marsac grumbled.

Carlo protested; but it was a half-hearted protest, and it had the effect of throwing his patron into a gloom of jealousy. The droning of the distant pipers which he had been finding so attractive he now cursed for its monotony. He could not understand why the *municipio* allowed them to irritate people with such a detestable noise.

"You have not spoken to Nigel Dawson while I have been away?" he asked sharply.

Carlo welcomed an opportunity to assert his innocence in that direction, and he was so effusive in his denials that Marsac suspected him of lying.

"Listen, Carlo. If I discover that you have even acknowledged his salute, I have finished with you for ever."

Carlo shivered. Five years of luxury with Marsac had not been long enough in which to forget the misery of his childhood in that swarming Trastevere alley. To whatever there was abnormal in his relations with Marsac he had become easily habituated in that strange bisexual pause in the growth of a normal adolescence. He had the capacity for facing facts which is the birthright of every young

Italian male or female, and though there might be moments when the temptation to be normal was irresistible (of which the Roumanian had taken advantage) he recognized that his life with Marsac was a career. The long Latin civilization has had time to incorporate so much of masculine experience, so much of feminine wisdom that the sentimentality of a semi-barbaric culture like the American or English is obnoxious to a Latin. The Latin individual is capable of what seems to the Anglo-Saxon a cynicism in sexual relations utterly beyond his comprehension. A decent Englishman would have despised Carlo; but a decent Italian would not have despised him, however much he might abominate his detestable situation. A decent Italian would have blamed Marsac's wealth and would have deplored the outraged dignity of his nation in the abuse of a humble compatriot, would have felt precisely that emotion of resentful pride at the way the world treats his whole country like a *fille de joie* to which Mussolini has known how to give practical and rhetorical expression.

Carlo shivered. He was so horribly aware that if Marsac did disown him he might as well cease to have any ambitions above being a waiter. That was the utmost he could expect from life. It never entered his head that he might profit for awhile yet from his good looks and find another Marsac. Indeed he would have been sincerely shocked by such a proposal. He was now a perfectly healthy, perfectly normal young man of nineteen condemned to smoke opium and listen to Marsac's exotic rhapsodies for the sake of his career, a career which it must be remembered had been chosen for him by his poverty-stricken parents in that Trastevere slum, when they allowed Marsac to take him to Paris as a boy. Carlo's jealousy of the Oxford undergraduate, which had nearly involved him in a ruinous escapade with Nigel Dawson, had been jealousy for his career. Marsac's jealousy sprang from a passionate obsession in the clutch of an overmastering vanity. Propertius did not torture himself more savagely with the imagination of golden Cynthia's infidelities than now Marsac over Carlo's. And when Propertius wrote:

> *Hostis si quis erit nobis, amet ille puellas :*
> *gaudeat in puero, si quis amicus erit.*
> *tranquillo tuta descendis flumine cumba :*
> *quid tibi tam parvi litoris unda nocet ?*
> *alter saepe uno mutat praecordia verbo,*
> *altera vix ipso sanguine mollis erit,*

he could scarcely have numbered a Marsac among his Roman friends.

"You must not suspect me of that, Robert," Carlo entreated, abandoning French for his own language and acquiring with the change a warmth of sincerity for his denials to which fear of the waiter's tail-coat lent the final touch. Marsac seemed convinced; and nothing more might have been heard of his suspicions had there not turned out to be an absence of paprika when they sat down to dinner. Marsac sent for the housekeeper and demanded why when she knew how much he liked paprika she had dusted everything with the black pepper he so much disliked.

Madame Protopopesco told him curtly, almost insolently, that Zampone's had been out of paprika, whereupon Marsac nettled by her manner retorted that he paid her not to allow Zampone's to run out of the condiments he preferred and that it was precisely the judicious use of paprika in her own cooking which more than anything else had led him to engage her as his housekeeper.

"Pepper!" the Roumanian shrilled in her tinny East-European French. "As if in a house like this it was of the least importance what pepper a woman uses. Red, black, or white, it is all the same in this disgusting house."

"I do not wish for your vulgar insolence, madame," Marsac replied, himself unbearably insolent as always when he was angry.

His manner was too much for the Roumanian, whose fever of concupiscence had been exasperated by the Count's return. She went up to him and shaking her fist in his face taunted him with the way she had known how to abuse his pride while he was away in Paris superintending the despatch of those brittle jade pipes.

"*Du reste*," she added, standing with arms akimbo on her hips and divining, with a woman's diabolical instinct for the way to feed the oily flames of jealousy, that the pose she had adopted was the very one of an aggressive femininity that would most madden her adversary. "*Du reste*, there is a big leak in the largest cistern."

Marsac stared at Carlo in pallid horror. That this vile creature had spoken the truth was evident in the quivering lips and frightened eyes of the miserable young man.

"*C'est bien*," he groaned to himself, plunging his face into his hands to shut out the picture of that black-moustached whore in the triumph of her hideous possession. "*C'est bien*," he groaned to himself. "*Alors, ma passion n'a pas d'échos en lui. Pour lui mon tragique amour n'est rien qu'un blasphème anormal. Oh, mon Carlo, mon Carlo, et toi, tu étais mon sang, ma chair! Comme je souffre! Grand dieu, comme je souffre!*" He let flow for awhile the tears of an ineffable humiliation, the Roumanian still triumphing over him, her arms akimbo, and Carlo quaking miserably on his chair. Then leaping to his feet he shrieked in a crisis of hysteria. "*Alors, Carlo, puisque rien ne paraît te valoir cette femme, cette vache, pars avec elle! Tu m'entends? Va-t-en bien loin de moi! Va renifler sa jupe. Va-t-en! Oublie-moi. Ah si, je le veux! Va te barbouiller le corps aux baisers de cette putain-là. Tu es libre, libre, libre cette fois. Tu es libre, tu m'entends, libre à la fin!*"

But Carlo, who could feel the greasy coat-tails of that waiter flapping round him in the draughts of a third-rate café, had no desire at all to be free. He flung himself on his knees and implored his protector to forgive him, turning from time to time to abuse Madame Protopopesco over his shoulder for taking advantage of his weakness. Hippolytus and Joseph, being innocent, probably defended themselves feebly. Carlo, being guilty, had somehow to convince his enraged patron of the Roumanian's unscrupulous wiles, and he was so unsparing of detail that at last he managed to direct most of Marsac's rage to her.

"*Fripeuse de möelles*," the Count now shrieked. "*Vous souillez d' un vil rut un enfant, vous engloutez même son âme . . . et puis, puis vous me parlez d'une citerne! Une citerne, mon dieu, une citerne que ne fonctionne pas! C'est risible! Vous arrachez l'espoir à mes mains, vous brisez ma statue, vous semez entre nous la misère, vous prenez tout en ne nous laissant rien que des remords et des sanglots, vous volez mon amour, vous faites mourir nos cœurs jusqu'à la fin, et puis vous me parlez d'une citerne. Allez-vous-en, immonde Ève-Vampire! Partez, vipère! Partez, partez, ou je vous étranglerai de mes propres mains.*"

With this he picked up from the table a porcelain bowl of pot-pourri and flung it at Madame Protopopesco's head; but she dodged the missile and withdrew from the room that her parched and hungry femininity so monstrously outraged.

Marsac's eye caught the big picture he had commissioned from Christopher Goldfinch, when they were still on friendly terms. It was a representation, it may be remembered, of young Hylas being dragged down by the fountain-nymphs to live with them in their crystal world where the voice of the disconsolate Heracles would never more reach his ears. He remembered Madame Protopopesco's remark about the cistern, and a dreadful analogy invaded his fancy. He snatched a knife with the intention of ripping up the canvas; but the Count lacked the old ladies' ruthlessness when it concerned something for which he had paid as much as he had paid for that picture. Just as he had hesitated before he sent back the column of *giallo antico* and finally decided to put it up in his garden, so now he decided that it would sufficiently punish the offending picture to take it down from the walls of the dining-room and hang it in the second-best spare bedroom.

"But I cannot sleep under the same roof as that vampire," he told Carlo. "We will go and stay at Zampone's hotel until that infectious squaw has ceased to poison my house with her presence."

So down into Sirene marched the Count and his secretary, and during that long walk Marsac's rhetoric flowed without a single interruption from the penitent sinner. He painted for the young man the appalling prospect of further intercourse with women. The consumption of Herod by worms was, it would seem, a pleasant death compared with what Carlo's promised to be. Then he returned to the effect on himself of Carlo's treachery, and drew a picture of their old age together alone when Carlo's hair should be white and his eyes dim, his sunburnt face all wrinkled, his classic profile blurred.

"That is the time you will be grateful for my affection, Carlo," he warned him. "That is the time you will realize how much more precious than the love of women is a faithful and lasting affection such as mine. Alas, the beautiful serenity of our old age together will now be tainted by that foul vampire of a Roumanian, because her loathsome shadow will even then come between us, and her memory will blast the most sacred moments of our lifelong friendship."

And as he delivered this mournful prophecy to Carlo, who was thinking that he could stand even baldness quite stoically provided that he was wearing a well-cut suit and not a waiter's greasy tail-coat, the light in a wayside shrine of St. Anthony cast a pale beam upon the form of 'O Gobbetto standing cataleptically on his head in the path before them. Comic though the vision really was, it presented itself to Marsac like some macabre wood-cut of the Durër school.

"There," he cried, pointing dramatically to the old gnome upside down before them. "There is what by your behaviour you have made of our old age! There it stands before you!"

As he spoke 'O Gobbetto slowly changed his posture. He stood now on one leg, the other at right angles to his squat form, a soil-grimed finger pressed to his nose.

"*Buona festa, eccellenze*," he wished them in a voice that seemed to come gurgling up from the depths of a cask of wine.

"He wishes us a merry Christmas! He does not comprehend the agony of my spirit," said Marsac sadly; and they swept on their way downhill toward the Hotel Grandioso.

Chapter 6

aut ubi non mors est, si iugulatis, aquae?
                                         MARTIAL

THE arrival of the Count to spend the Christmas festival at the Hotel Grandioso gave great pleasure to the Zampones, not so much on account of the custom it meant for them as for the chagrin it would cause Don Cesare at the Hotel Augusto. The Villa Hylas was abandoned until it should be purified of the corruption bred in it by Madame Protopopesco. She had departed immediately for the mainland, taking with her the money for the household books, a certain amount of Marsac's silver, and the Cingalese. When it was suggested that he should put the police on her track he dismissed the idea with a fine gesture; and the two old ladies of the Amabile, though they disapproved of letting the thief go free, could not help displaying a good deal of sentimental raptute over dear Count Bob's generosity. As a matter of fact Marsac was so glad to be rid of the Cingalese that he counted his abduction cheap at the price of a few spoons.

There was the usual Christmas dinner at the Amabile, and as usual it was a very jolly affair, though not so many tables had to be linked together in these days to accommodate the guests. The old ladies were going to America in the first week of January. Last year in their desire to stand by Marsac in his fight with society they had postponed their visit; but now that he was safely installed in his villa, even though temporarily a thieving housekeeper kept him out of it, Miss Virginia felt that the claims of her country must be honoured again. At her suggestion Costanzo, the eldest son of Micheluccio, the *colono* from whom they had bought the original cottage, was to enter the Count's service. Fat Agostino the youngest brother was getting older and becoming more useful every day, and it would be such a splendid reward to Costanzo's devoted service if he joined the Count's household.

" But, Bob, my dear boy, if I was you I wouldn't go back to the Villa Hylas before Spring," Miss Maimie advised. " I'm sorry about that vile woman who stole all your pretty things and I know how you must feel about losing them, but with our trusty Costanzo up there now to give an eye to everything you needn't be afraid of anything more, and I know you ought to let the place dry out for another month or two. And look, don't you think you'd be wise to have Supino put that old cistern in order right away ? "

Carlo, who took his duties as secretary much more seriously than anybody supposed, had been fretting over the cistern ever since the Count and he had left the Villa that night. But he had had to endure so much of Marsac's jealous pangs, so many rages and recriminations, such dramas at the least excuse he gave him for drama, that he had dreaded referring to the cistern, lest Marsac should accuse him of pining for the Protopopesco woman, since so very unfortunately it had been she who in the middle of that emotional crisis had first drawn his attention to the cistern's misbehaviour. Even now, when Miss Maimie pressed Marsac to do something about it, Carlo did not dare to urge the wisdom of her advice. However, when they returned to the island from seeing Miss Virginia and Miss Maimie off to America in the *Transylvania*, Marsac of his own accord and without any reference to the past bade Carlo summon Maestro Supino.

Both old ladies had made it their final charge to the Count before he took leave of them and went down the side of the great Cunarder not to neglect the cistern any longer, and not to dream of spending the rest of the Winter at the Villa Hylas. And when he stood up in the prow of that small boat, which he had filled with mandolin players to strike up *Torna a Surriento* as the screws of the steamer began to churn the waters of the harbour, he shouted a reiteration of his promise through the still air of the January dusk. Then he flung carnation blossoms toward the shape that now loomed so dark against the lucent green and orange of the wintry sky and the lights of Naples twinkling out one by one, until suddenly the great ship was chequered with a blaze of gold from all her ports and she began to move very slowly out toward the open sea that shimmered like a pearl in the windless evening air.

"*Bon voyage*," Marsac cried.

"And a quicka come backs," Carlo shouted.

Two handkerchiefs were fluttering from the promenade deck; the opening chords of the *mandolinata* twanged farewell.

Maestro Supino was most apologetic over the leak. He could not understand it, and he hinted at foul play.

"Who knows? There are many evil subjects in Sirene among the lesser *muratori*." He made the gesture that signifies jealousy, involving all the rivals of a successful builder like himself in an implied accusation.

After the inspection Maestro Supino presented himself at the Grandioso to make his report.

"*Mi dispiace, signor conte*, but I hold the impression that an earthquake has shaken one of the supporting piers in such fashion that there is a large crack right up one of the sides."

"An earthquake?" Marsac scoffed. "But I thought San Mercurio did not permit earthquakes on Sirene."

The fat builder shrugged his shoulders.

"It cannot be my building, *signor conte*. Therefore, it

must be an earthquake. If you would have the goodness to accompany me down into the cistern, I can demonstrate to you how some earthquake has ruined my beautiful work."

So the Count and his secretary marched up to the Villa Hylas and descended into the dark damp empty vaulted cistern, where by the light of a lantern Maestro Supino showed that one of the piers was out of the perpendicular and in shifting had not only torn away the *intonico* from the walls, but had made a great fissure in the masonry.

"How am I to know that it wasn't your bad building that was responsible?" Marsac demanded.

"It pleases the *signor conte* to joke," said the builder, with a humble recognition of the privileges of rank and fortune.

Carlo who was anxious that his protector should not involve himself in a dispute, which as a rich stranger he would certainly lose, plucked Marsac's sleeve to urge discretion. Finally it was arranged that Maestro Supino should set to work immediately on strengthening the weak pier, for which labour he was only to charge the Count half the cost, thus sharing in the loss. Maestro Supino looked very sad over his weakness in agreeing to such an arrangement; but, though he could feel confident of winning any lawsuit the Count might bring against him, he was not anxious for such publicity and he considered that he should in the long run lose less by making a compromise.

The following day he sent four of his masons up to the Villa Hylas to set to work immediately on the strengthening of the pier and the repairing of the crack; and a day or so later he decided to walk up to the villa himself and see what progress had been made. When he had covered about half the distance from the Piazza he met three of the workmen much agitated hurrying back.

"*Ma che?*" he expostulated, opposing his burly form to their further progress down the narrow walled *viale*, and opening wide his arms in most indignant astonishment.

"There has been a great disaster, Maestro Supino," they wailed in explanation of their flight. "The roof of the cistern has fallen in upon the poor Alfonso."

"And where is Alfonso?" demanded the employer.

"The poor Alfonso is dead."

"*Sacramento di California!*" the employer swore, even in his horror and emotion taking care to guard himself against blasphemy by a geographical euphemism. "*Mamma mia!* I am ruined," he groaned.

"We must inform the *maresciallo*," the workmen reminded him.

"Certainly, we must inform the *maresciallo*," the builder agreed. "But first it would be better to inform Alfonso's wife. One must not leave her in ignorance of this misfortune."

Maestro Supino begged his workmen to take upon themselves the sad task and to meet him in half an hour's time *dal maresciallo*. So, the workmen turned aside at the next cross-road to break the news to the widow, and Maestro Supino hurried as fast as he could to the Piazza. One or two acquaintances whom he passed on the road called out to ask where he was off to in such a hurry, and he muttered something about having left his rule at home, as he hurried on.

"*Menaggio!*" he swore when on arriving in the Piazza he found that he had just missed the half-hourly funicular to the Grande Marina, and that he should have to hurry downhill for another mile. However, he thanked his good fortune when he saw that the sea was calm, because it was his intention to get on board a boat and escape to the mainland.

This may seem strange behaviour for a prosperous builder after one of his men has been killed in an accident. But the law in Italy when it worked at all worked with extreme rigour, and Maestro Supino knew that the only way to avoid arrest and imprisonment was to take refuge in a neighbouring commune and there remain until the preliminary enquiry was over, and the civil action, if civil action there was, began.

By the time the three uninjured workmen had managed to get away from the widow of Alfonso and leave her with dishevelled hair to moan and shriek and beat her breast surrounded by a moaning and shrieking crowd of female friends and relations Maestro Supino was on board a fishing-boat; and by the time the three uninjured workmen reached the office of the *maresciallo* he was half-way to Sorrento, terribly sea-sick in spite of the placid sea, but mentally much relieved.

When the *maresciallo* had taken down the statements of the survivors he buckled on his sword, despatched two *carabinieri* to the scene of the accident, and accompanied by two others visited the new magistrate at the *Pretoria*. Signor Numa Fogolare was a thin sandy-haired shrivelled creature with red-rimmed eyes and a limp. He was a product of Italian officialdom at its worst, one of those beings that the *scirocco* seems to possess like an evil spirit, a withered foxy man with bad breath and teeth the colour of parsley sauce, which he picked with the nail of his little finger that for a mark of gentility was allowed to protrude a good inch beyond the finger-tip.

On hearing of Alfonso's death Fogolare gave orders to arrest *il Supino*, and when the *maresciallo* came back with the news of the builder's escape he was extremely angry.

"Somebody must be held responsible," he snarled.

The *maresciallo* saluted his recognition of such a reasonable demand.

"You had better arrest *il Marsac*," said the judge, clearing his throat and spitting on the stone floor of the *Pretoria*. He was remembering the Count's criticisms of Italian administration.

The *maresciallo* saluted and preceded by his two *carabin-*

ieri marched at the slow gait with which *carabinieri* convey an impression of the slow grinding of the Divine mills toward the Hotel Grandioso. The incarnate vengeance of the law reached the hotel when Marsac was actually in the vestibule discoursing in his voluble incorrect English to a pair of old maids who had arrived that morning from Roehampton to spend the Winter in Sirene.

"Oh dear," one of them was saying, "but I had always understood that Tiberius was a monster of cruelty."

"Ah, my dear madame," the Count laughed complacently, "I am afraid you are excessively old-fashioned in your ideas. I must take the liberty to inform you that Tiberius was one of the noblest men who ever adorned this abominable universe in which we . . ."

But the two old maids never had the advantage of hearing the eulogy completed, because at that moment the two *carabinieri* at a signal tapped the orator's shoulders, and the *maresciallo* informed him that he was under arrest.

The two old maids were so much upset to hear, as they understood with their Ollendorfian ears, that the man who had seemed quite a gentleman was really a murderer that they decided to spend their Winter abroad in Sorrento instead of Sirene and departed from that dangerous island on the morning boat.

There are moments when even those of us who are most infatuated with the Latin culture have horrid doubts about it, and when domination by the Nordic races seems really after all the only possible solution of life's problems, moments when our admiration of Napoleon wilts and when we ask ourselves if the Pax Romana was quite such an admirable nurse of civilization as we should like to believe, moments when we are inclined to say that Bishop Stubbs was right and Fustel de Coulanges wrong, even moments when Mr. H. G. Wells appears to knock the wind completely out of Mr. Hilaire Belloc, so that the champion of Rome reels against the ropes of controversy in a gasping unwonted silence. The arrest of Count Marsac because a badly constructed cistern, for which he had certainly paid the price of the best constructed cistern obtainable, had collapsed and killed a workman was one of these moments.

It was all very well for Christopher Goldfinch on hearing the news to rattle his teeth fiercely and croak:

"By gad, I'm delighted to hear it. Serve the fellow right! I only hope they'll keep him in prison till the poor old Nortons get back from America. Prison is the right place for degenerate brutes like him."

"That may or may not be true, Goldfinch," said Scudamore, to whom it was that the painter had just delivered this sentiment. "But that's not the point. He has not been arrested for a breach of the Lex Scantinia."

"Eh?" Christopher gaped.

"And we ought to do our best to get him out of prison," Scudamore went on. "I will go around and talk to this comic judge myself. It's a darned nuisance, because I'm right on the track of an interesting theft from Martial by Ausonius. You never read Ausonius?"

"Can't say I ever heard of him. Who was he, anyway?"

It was all Scudamore could do not to instruct the old painter with a brief biography of the poet, interpersed with some heavy sarcasm at the expense of his courtier's Christianity; but he resisted the temptation and went off to look for a suit in which he could sally out of the Villa Parnasso to the rescue of the Count.

To Numa Fogolare he addressed himself in what may be called Ciceronian Italian. The red-headed judge listened with a sneering politeness to Scudamore's helical rotundities of phrase, and at the end of the protest he shrugged his shoulders.

"*Mi dispiace, signor Scu d'Amore*, but, what can I do? The law is the law."

"*Si, si, si,*" the moralist affirmed three times in most earnest agreement. "But in Italy there are always ways of . . ." He could not find a sufficiently impressive word in Italian to indicate circumvention, and in his anxiety to express his meaning he tried to do so with a gesture.

"*No, signor, no!*" the judge declared, raising his scabby eyebrows in horror at the suggestion implied by Scudamore's gesture. "*Della legge italiana nessuno non si . . .*" He paused and substituted for the grosser action innocently implied by Scudamore's gesture, "*infischia.*"

With this he indicated that the interview was closed.

"My dee-aw fellow," Duncan Maxwell told the suitor afterwards, "you went entirely the wrong way to work. It's no use talking to an Italian judge with your pompous and elaborate reasonableness. You ought to have found out something against him first. For instance, if he was known to have made immodest proposals to an old woman of ninety-two on her death-bed, you ought to have said to him, 'Oh yes, I perfectly understand what you say about the law and I quite agree with it, but after all our friend Count Marsac did not make immodest proposals to an old woman,' etc., etc. That would have made the brute squirm, and this poor frog would have been back in his hotel by now. And it's jolly decent of me to give you such good advice, Scudamore, because Marsac is a most horrible bore and prison is much the best place for him. He's been pestering me to death with his blasted theories about Tiberius. Still, if you insist on setting him at large the only way is to blackmail that pink-eyed judge."

"Yes, but I haven't anything up my sleeve against him."

"Nor have I as yet," said Maxwell. "But I shall have. Oh yes, my dear fellow," he chuckled, "I make a point of that. I can assure you I have a list of crimes committed by Italian officials which would make your hair stand on end and your beard bristle. I should say so! You don't think *I'm* going to take any risks? No fee-aw! I daresay you'd be surprised to hear that the new *sindaco* used to make love to his sister before she married. But he did, and don't I know it! Oh yes, and that's why he's always so jolly polite to me, though he's as black as the parroco's toe-nails."

"Yes, but I haven't anything against this darned judge except his breath," Scudamore insisted a little irritably, for he was genuinely concerned about Marsac's position.

"I know, I know! The stale *maccherone* of a lifetime. Dreadful, my dear fellow, dreadful. And now with this damned Italian government you can't even get a good *napoletano* to keep off the stinking breath of their officials. I tell you I had to pinch twenty-two at the tobacconist's this morning before I could get one fit to smoke. Half of them as hard as a brandy drinker's liver and the other half as soft as a High Church curate's brains. I tell you, our civilization is crumbling."

With this Maxwell took a case of cigars from his pocket and, after sternly eyeing and pondering the collection, chose one at last, cut off the end, and lit up.

"This is a beauty, Scudamore. There's no smoke like a really good *napoletano*." He waved the incense of it under Scudamore's nose. "Beautiful, eh? That makes you a bit jealous, eh? If I could find another as good I'd offer you one, but I don't think I can."

And lest there should be any doubt on this point he put on his hat and declared he must hurry away because he had an appointment on the top of Monte Ventoso with an old *contadino* who "knows a place *I* don't know where you can find flint arrow-heads."

"A wonderful old man," he continued. "Most interesting. Full of wisdom. Ripening slowly, you know. That's the way. Oh yes, slowly and surely in the sun. None of this damned hot-house forcing. No fee-aw!"

"Yes, but see here, Maxwell, what about our friend Marsac? We must do something to help him. The poor devil will die of rheumatism in the Sirene gaol."

"I tell you I can't do anything now. I've got to see

about those arrow-heads. But when I get back I'll make some enquiries about the judge. He's only been here a short time, but *aria di Sirene* . . ."

And a few minutes later he was hurrying along up the Anasirene road, his bright eyes noting in turn crocuses growing where he had not yet seen them in some freshly cleared *macchia* on the slopes of Monte Ventoso, a new kind of charm against the evil eye on a jingling team of mules, and finally a good-looking boy of about thirteen who asked him for a cigarette.

"No, I won't give you a cigarette," he replied, speaking in rapid dialect with a marvellous accent. "What do you want to smoke cigarettes for?"

The boy was cast down by this rebuff and replied that he did not know.

"Then if you don't know why you want to smoke them, why do you ask *me* for them? Do you know old Porco Maiale up at Anasirene?"

The boy shook his head.

"*Chi è?*"

"He's a very wise old man who's going to show me some flint arrow-heads on the top of Monte Ventoso, and I daresay if you ask me I might take you up there with me, and perhaps old Porco Maiale will show them to you as well. Do you know what flint arrow-heads are?"

The boy shook his head.

"Of course you don't. Yet here you are asking *signori* for cigarettes, and you don't know that! You come along with me, young man. Do you like walking?"

"*Così, così*," said the boy.

"Well, you've got to learn to like it more than *così, così*, if you want to be friends with me. Would you like to be a friend of mine?"

"*Sì*," and his affirmative sounded not unlike the answering cheep of a bird charmed by one who knew how to make the wildest birds of the air perch upon his finger.

"Well, you jolly well step out, because I'm late, and we don't want to keep Porco Maiale waiting."

The boy trotted along happily beside him; and all the way up that dizzy road, all the way up that long climb to the top of Monte Ventoso, where beside the boulder-strewn path the lentisks were brown from the wintry blasts, Maxwell poured out for him the wisdom on which boys will feed if they are given it in the right way by the right person. Thus may Silenus have trod such a path with the youthful Dionysus beside him.

Incarcerated in a miserable cell, the plaster walls of which were scrabbled with the obscenities of earlier prisoners, with nothing to sit upon except a wooden bench, with a high barred window looking out on a depressing notice to say that bill-sticking was prohibited, though why anybody should ever be tempted to stick bills on such a wall was hard to understand, poor Marsac found his position the reverse of pastoral. In vain had he stormed at the *maresciallo*. In vain had he threatened diplomatic action ending in the degradation of the red-headed judge. To all his protests the *maresciallo* had replied with a shrug of his burly shoulders and another laborious entry in his big book.

"But how long am I to be shut up in this pest-house?" the Count demanded.

"I am not in a position to say," the *maresciallo* informed him. "If the *perquisizione* shows that you were not to blame for the death of this man you will no doubt be released; but if the *perquisizione* shows that you were responsible . . ."

Another shrug indicated unknown and terrible possibilities—a subterranean dungeon perhaps on the savage Ponza Islands.

"I demand to see Signor Ambrogio, my legal adviser," the prisoner shouted.

"You can see nobody until the *signor giudice* authorizes me."

"*O, mon dieu, ces sales italiens!*" Marsac apostrophized in a frenzy of Gallic superiority.

It happened that Peter Ambrogio was over in Naples at the time of his client's arrest, so that even had the *maresciallo* been corruptible he would not have been at hand to corrupt him. However, Mrs. Ambrogio rushed about Sirene in her new dress of spinach-green face-cloth denouncing the persecution.

"Oh, have you heard the disgraceful news?" she cried. "That damned judge has had poor Count Marsac put in prison. Oh, I'm so annoyed I can hardly speak. Peter will be absolutely furious. Tried to telephone over to him. So furious, couldn't do anything but spit into the thinguma-bob you hold up to your ear. Hope to goodness this beastly judge gets sacked and they make my dear old Peter pratora. Only honest lawyer in Italy. Thanks to me. Wouldn't marry him till he promised to be honest. Hate dishonesty. Hate everybody who's trying to persecute the poor Count. Wish the dear Miss Nortons were here. Everybody against the poor Count because he's one of those. Can't heip it. Doctors tell you it's all a disease. Such hypocrisy. Hate hypocrisy. Can't stand hypocrisy. Shan't sleep a wink to-night thinking of the poor Count. Sospit-able, dear thing! Poor Carlo cried like a baby. Had to kiss him to console him. Couldn't help it. Don't believe the dear Count would mind a bit. Don't believe a word they say about him. Not a bit the same as that filthy Ammenian Procesco. Dear old England! Best country in the world. People say I'm an Italian subject. Dam nonsense. I won't be an Italian subject. English as you make 'em. Never felt so proud of being English as when they told me poor Count Marsac had been taken off to prison. Even if he did push the man down the cistern, I'm sure he deserved it. The farmalarmy (thus *falegname*: carpenter) came to mend my wardrobe last week. Worse than before. Could *shut* the dam door. Can't *open* it now.

Went down to his shop and shook a hammer in his face. Only wish *I'd* had a cistern to push him in. Let them try and put me in prison. Must do something for the poor Count. Think I'll send Concetta round to the marryshawl's with a hot-water-bottle."

But when Mrs. Ambrogio's maid arrived with the hot-water-bottle, the *maresciallo* refused to allow it to enter the prison. Indeed it would have gone very hard with Marsac's comfort if Ferdinando Zampone had not taken it upon himself to procure him the necessities of a tolerably civilized existence. And even Ferdinando had some difficulty, such was the animus of the judge, in persuading the *maresciallo* to close his eyes while he and one of the waiters at the Grandioso smuggled a bed and bedding into the prisoner's cell and provided him every day with decent food. It was this difficulty that Ferdinando found in getting round the representatives of the law which ought to have warned the Count's supporters that there was now among the Sirenesi themselves a powerful faction against him. The law in Italy is as much an ass as it is anywhere else; but in Italy that ass is particularly susceptible to carrots offered it round the corner. The refusal of such delicacies on this occasion was ominous.

"I sink zere was many peoples in Sirene *molto contro* Count Marsac," Ferdinando told Scudamore when at the end of five days the Count was still in prison and Peter Ambrogio was hoarse from his unending legal arguments with the judge. It was Scudamore who had continued to exert himself above everybody on Marsac's behalf, partly out of a genuine kindliness, but perhaps a little from an unwillingness to lose such a perfect piece from his museum of classical immorality. He used to say that a talk with Marsac always sent him back in a kind of spiritual excitement to probe the corpus of Latin poetry for fresh examples of his type in ancient Rome. When Duncan Maxwell talked of some new orchis he had found to supplement the *Hortus*

Siccus Sirenum of Don Pasquale Buongiorno Degli Angeli written in the year of grace 1679, Scudamore would smile and say that in Marsac he possessed a grass-green blossom far more interesting than any habenaria or ophrys in Maxwell's collection.

"You're one of those damned ingenuous Yankees," Maxwell would tell him. "Always just thirty years behind England, which is ten years behind France. Always teaching your grandmother to suck eggs. Good god, I tell you, my dear fellow, that for me Marsac has been dead and buried since 1898. He stinks like an unwrapped mummy of stale spice. I've no patience with these soulful pederasts. Everything must be turned into a blasted religion, that's what makes me so furious. If we hear a tom-cat howling on the tiles we jolly well throw a boot at him, but when these blasted lovesick poets and pederasts start howling we sit round and admire them. And when it comes down to it, my boy, there's precious little to choose between a tom-cat's howling and Shakespeare's sonnets."

But to return to the conversation between Ferdinando and Scudamore.

"Sure, there are lots of people against him ever since they heard he'd been mixed up in that Paris scandal."

Ferdinando nodded his head mandarin-fashion.

"I do not speak now of the chentlemans and ladies of Sirene, I speak of the Sirenesi themselves. They make now the *camorra* against him."

"Who's stirring them up?"

Ferdinando's lower lip protruded Buddha-wise, and his mandarin's nod slowed down to the grave and regular pace of a grandfather-clock's pendulum.

"Perhaps I have my own sinks for this. Perhaps I have not no sinks at all. *Ma, acqua in bocca!* It is better for me to say nossings. If I say it was Don Cesare Rocco it is *la gelosia*. If I say it is *i signori Jones è sempre la gelosia*. If I say it was *i preti, allora non sono cristiano!*"

He gave a curious little grunt which is the conventional way a Southern Italian expresses his apology for being the victim of circumstance, simultaneously bringing together the fingers of his fat hands in the conventional gesture that begs forgiveness for a weak humanity. " The priests carry petticoats like the womans. Excuse to me, but I do not wish to fight myself wiss the womans."

" But what is the idea behind it all ? Do they want to drive him out of Sirene ? " Scudamore persisted.

" You aska to me the idea, *signore*," said Ferdinando, beaming with good-natured mockery. " I sink if I tells to you *lo scopo* I tells to you who was the peoples *contro lui*. The best *consiglio* you give to Count Marsac when he will come out from the prison is to say nossings. He must to treata this bad business *come se fosse nulla*. *Meno se ne parla meglio è*. The less he speak the better is."

And when four days later Marsac was released this was the advice that Scudamore gave him, and not merely Scudamore but Ferdinando himself. So, too, did Peter Ambrogio, who had had a hard task in trying to expound to his client the rigours of the Italian law and justify his own inability to mitigate those rigours in the face of a judge that chose to worship *au pied de la lettre*. Then there was Gigi the gardener who put a finger to his nose and assuming a dark Cumean wisdom spoke of ' *qualchecosa per aria* ' which the Count would be prudent to treat with respect.

" What is in the wind ? " Marsac asked furiously.

But Gigi would not be more definite.

" *Soltanto, io Le consiglio di stare zitto, zitto, zitto*." To illustrate this imperative need of silence he took his forefinger from his nose and squeezed between it and the thumb his two lips.

The Count demanded of his secretary what all these mysterious warnings were intended to convey ; and when Carlo himself began to shrug his shoulders and shake his head the Count was driven into an exasperation beyond everything.

"Listen, Carlo," he shouted in French. "I forbid you to make those hideous Italian grimaces at me. I have always had as you know an immense affection for your country, and in my affection for you I have tried to express the poetry of my emotion for classic soil. But I cannot suffer this *bourgeois* mediæval priest-ridden Italy. I find it insupportable. I assure you that I am inclined to leave Sirene and install myself again in Paris. Yes, I am inclined to give the Sirenesi a lesson in good manners. Perhaps they will understand when I am gone that a crowd of vulgar Americans and seedy English people do not represent a very high degree of civilization. Finally, since you betrayed me for that corrupt mass of female flesh the prospect is disenchanted."

"*Ah, n'en parle plus,*" Carlo begged him. "*J'étais fou.*"

"What I have suffered in that horrible cell," Marsac groaned. "My dreams haunted all the time by vampire Eves who were stealing you from me while I was powerless."

"Better we go away for awhile," said Carlo. He was beginning to feel the strain of these recurring scenes of retrospective jealousy. Moreover, he was young, and the prospect of Paris attracted his youth a great deal more than to sit perched on a Sirenian cliff, was his pose there never so classical, listening to Marsac's eternal descant. Yet it is only fair to point out that the advice he gave was what he would have given, had there been no emotional complications between himself and Marsac; and there is no doubt that in the circumstances it was the best and most practical advice he could have given.

The absence of the old ladies in America was in Carlo's favour, and without them to spur him on to defiance Marsac decided to leave the Villa Hylas in the charge of the Nortons'

Costanzo and Gigi the gardener, and for awhile to abandon the island.

Perhaps if Marsac had contented himself with staying away for a few months, returning inconspicuously, and then living quietly for a few months, the curtain would have fallen on this strange mixture of farce and drama. Unfortunately he had no sooner arrived in Paris than a nostalgia for the South seized him, and he began to write about it.

Chapter 7

Di magni, horribilem . . . librum!
                                    CATULLUS

PERHAPS a temporary abstention from the fatal poppy was responsible for Marsac's fecundity during these months of voluntary exile from the island. At any rate, besides writing a novel he founded and produced a monthly critical review called *Symposion* and, having made a point of celebrating with a poem every scene of retrospective jealousy over Madame Protopopesco, he collected these *cris de cœur* in a volume entitled *La Victime Ravie*, which was saluted as a masterpiece in the first and only number of *Symposion*. The introduction of the review was typical of Marsac when he was under the impression that his soul was storming the empyrean, but when in reality it was bobbing against the ceiling of a room like a toy pink balloon filled with gas.

We come, he wrote, *from that clear, that luminous and tranquil country where Plato once walked, where Virgil once sang.*

It was in the silence and freshness of this Attic and virginal setting, not far indeed from mighty Greece, and looking out on Cape Misenum, upon the strand visited long ago by Ulysses, that we heard a cry for help from Beauty—Beauty maltreated and enslaved, a statue mutilated by the Barbarians—but who, incarnate by Pan, the eternal and manifold God, has never been able in spite of everything to die.

She who is Simplicity and Calm, befouled by the pretentious obviousness of our epoch, stunned by the vulgarity of our noises, the horrors of automobiles, the hysteria of the telephone, the vertigo of railway-trains, the hoot of departing steamers, all the sad rabble of a uniform humanity, She will presently no longer have even the stars left with which to purify Herself.

And an echo of immortal speech has told us:

> *'The Sirens still sing their song beside the blue Tyrrhenian, and there Daphnis doth defy thee. The nakedness of Phryne blinds her judges, and the smile of Antinous compels Cæsar himself to bow the knee...'*

Come, all ye who feel the inspiration of Athens, come and with your fervour liberate our Latin France from Russian decadence, from German ponderousness, from Anglo-Saxon vulgarity, and above all from that narrow-minded mob half Jew half Christian which corrupts Human Thought and the Natural Paganism of Man.

From ancient marbles and forgotten poems restore to the artist the Simple Idea, the pure and free Line. Nothing that touches Beauty is criminal, and any kind of expression is beautiful if truly inspired. Obscurity, hypocrisy, and ugliness alone corrupt. Come then, all ye who feel the inspiration of Athens; and let your work make sweet the air of contemporary existence as spontaneously and as naturally as the perfume that rises from a garden.

A number of well-known writers cordially promised to contribute to future numbers of *Symposion* because they felt reasonably sure that the first number would also be the last. In the list of pledged contributors was the name of John Scudamore, to whom Marsac had been anxious to extend some courtesy as a sign that he appreciated the trouble Scudamore had been put to over the matter of the cistern. And to invite him—an American—to contribute to this distinguished French review struck the editor as an almost exaggerated compliment with which to repay his friendly offices.

"I must certainly confess it is indeed a little ridiculous," he declared. "But, poor fellow, he deserves all my thanks, and I am happy to be able to give him the elation of reading his name in such company."

The first number of *Symposion*, which was not so much an imitation as a perversion of the *Mercure de France* and ought to have been called the *Ganymède de France*, appeared in April. Naturally, a number of complimentary copies were sent to Sirene. One of the features of this original number was a photogravure of the portrait of a most extraordinary young man in what was apparently a skin-tight bathing dress over a pair of skin-tight trousers and wearing his thick dark hair in a fringe, the middle of which was cut out in such a way as to expose a piece of white forehead the shape of a heart, cusp uppermost. Add to this a large hooked nose, slanting lascivious eyes, and a long-fingered vicious hand resting upon his hip, and it will not be astonishing to hear that the picture was labelled *Unquiet Youth*. The person in Sirene on whom this portrait made the greatest impression was Nigel Dawson, who rushed round showing it to everybody and exclaiming, "Isn't his figure too perfectly marvellous? My dear, he thrills me to death!"

"Why, Nigel, I don't think I care a great lot for this picture," Mrs. Neave objected. "I daresay you'll call me old-fashioned, but frankly I find it just a little unhealthy, not to say unpleasant. Anyway, I wouldn't want to have him come to Sirene."

"I wonder how long it would take me to grow my hair in that style," Nigel exclaimed, pondering the mode in an ecstasy of aspiring imitation. "Oh, Mrs. Neave, if I had a suit like that, *do* you think I could persuade somebody to paint me chained to a stalagmite?"

"Chained to a stalactite?"

"No, *no*, Mrs. Neave, a stalagmite. I don't want to be chained to a stalactite yet, thanks very much."

"You just fuddle me all up," said poor Mrs. Neave. "I don't see what you want to be chained to anything for. I know I just long sometimes not to have any chains at all."

But Nigel did not want to hear about Mrs. Neave's longings. He rushed away from her across the Piazza to show Mrs. Ambrogio the portrait.

"Sat down on the steps up to the church and burst out laughing," Mrs. Ambrogio proclaimed when she was relating the incident afterwards. "Couldn't help it. Purple in the face. Thought I should have choked with laughing. See everything! How I laughed! Couldn't stop myself. Everybody staring at me. Sure they all thought I was drunk. Most extraordinary young man you ever saw. Peter came along. 'What is this, Mauda, are you illa?' Couldn't speak. Couldn't explain. Rolled about laughing. Dear Nigel. So simple. Heart of a child. Nothing but a jersey and hair like a clown. Count's magazine. Dear Count. Love him so much. Treated abominably. Nothing but a jersey! Hair like a clown!"

The more Nigel Dawson pondered this portrait the more he desired to meet the original of it. Then he ordered a copy of Marsac's latest book of poems of which he had read the notice in *Symposion*.

"You know he really *is* rather wonderful," he declared to Duncan Maxwell. "He's put it all in here."

"All what?" Maxwell asked, guffawing like a satyr.

"The whole of his agony over Carlo and that appalling Roumanian female creature with a black moustache. He leaves nothing unsaid. It's quite amazing. Do let me read you . . ."

"No, by Jove, you don't," said Maxwell hastily. "If you think I'm going to sit here and listen to Marsac's infernal miaows, my boy, you're jolly well mistaken, I can tell you. No fee-aw! I've looked at all that blasted twaddle of his about Greece. If he'd been eaten alive by fleas and bugs as I've been in Greece and had drunk that filthy mixture of eucalyptus and red ink which they have the damned impudence to call wine, he wouldn't write like that about Greece."

"But this isn't about Greece. This is all about Carlo."

"Well, I don't want to hear about Carlo. When the old *guardia* before Beccafico came round the corner of the Piazza and caught Burlingham out, he tapped him on the shoulder and said, '*Scusate, signore mio, ma queste cose non si fanno sulla strada. Queste cose si fanno a casa sua.*' I don't care what this frog does, but let him hop about at home and not go croaking about his inside all over Europe."

"Duncan, I wish you wouldn't be so cynical."

The cynic roared with laughter, looked at his watch, said he had an important appointment at the Piccola Marina to show somebody the only place where the lesser asphodel grew on Sirene, and hurried on his way still laughing.

The more Nigel read of *La Victime Ravie* and the oftener he turned the page to gaze at the portrait of that young man in *Symposion*, the more he regretted his quarrel with Marsac. At last he could stand it no longer and wrote off to Paris:

> VILLA FLORIDA,
> ISOLA SIRENE,
> ITALIA.
> *May* 22.

My dearest Bob,

Can you forgive me? That is the question I have been asking myself ever since I read 'La Victime Ravie.' Your marvellous poems have caused me an absolute torment of self-reproach! If I tell you that I now feel I was horribly to blame, will you be reconciled? I cannot help looking back to those wonderful days at the Villa Decamerone, alas, already so terribly long ago. In those days you used to be glad to have me translate your poetry into English verse. That poem about you and Carlo in your old age still haunted by the spectre of that disgusting woman! My dear, I wept. I wept! Of course I will never be able to do justice to it in a translation, but may I try? Nobody has ever quite so marvellously interpreted what you and I and others feel about life. If I could even faintly reproduce that marvellous poem I would feel that I had expressed myself. While taking all the blame for our unhappy quarrel, you must realize that I have never for a moment ceased to regret it. You have every reason to hate Sirene, but reading your introduction to 'Symposion' I felt that you had forgiven the island even as you have forgiven Carlo. Can you not forgive me? And when are you coming back? I've had such an appallingly dull winter and spring. Nobody here at all interesting. By the way, who is the original of that portrait in 'Symposion'? I can't believe it's just an imaginary person. It's so 'done,' isn't it? No more till I hear from you.

As ever,
Nigel

Marsac, who was correcting the proofs of the novel he had been writing even while he was overlooking the production of his review, read through this letter, his upper lip curling in a consciously aristocratic sneer.

"Listen, Carlo," he ordered; and he translated the letter into French for his benefit. "You may consider yourself fortunate," he said when he had finished. "Because you are the only person who has done me an injury whom I have pardoned. In fact, you are the only one I ever shall pardon."

Carlo, whose visit to Paris had been marked by several new suits of clothes, looked as uncomfortable for a moment in the one he was wearing as Nessus in his shirt. He was watching Marsac tear Nigel Dawson's letter into small pieces, and he was thinking with a shudder by how little he himself had escaped being torn up like that into small pieces.

Marsac put the torn letter into an envelope and addressed it to the sender. Then he exercised the privilege of a rich amateur to insert a long paragraph in the chapter he was correcting. And that paragraph was a malicious addition to his already malicious portrait of Nigel Dawson.

"*Phui!* How this nib scratches," the author exclaimed petulantly. And indeed one might easily have supposed after reading the added paragraph that it had actually been written with a claw.

When Nigel opened the letter and shook out the fragments of his rejected address he said:

"Beast!"

Miss Virginia and Miss Maimie returned from America at the end of May, and both of them wrote urgently to beg dear Count Bob to come back to the 'enchanted isle' at once. They wrote of the pleasures of their terrace and their loggia. They wrote, Miss Virginia of the 'pounding', Miss Maimie of the 'sounding' sea they were sitting by and listening to in the cool of the summer *maestrale*. They wrote of tea in the Temple of Vesta and of how dull it was without their dear Count Bob and their dear Carlo to amuse them with tales of all 'the tiresome Sirene contingent'. And as the Summer went on they wrote of the scarcity of water and how that 'dull old Joseph Neave had been cussing because he couldn't get his bath and vowing to leave Sirene' and how 'some folks mightn't think that altogether a disadvantage'.

And then one morning there arrived at the Villa Amabile a copy of Marsac's novel entitled *La Statue Mutilée*, on the cover of which was printed *Dédié respectueusement à Mesdemoiselles Pepworth-Norton*. As usual with Marsac's literary efforts *La Statue Mutilée* began with one of those rhetorical rhapsodies to the mouthing of which the French and Italian languages lend themselves too easily. After invoking Sirene as the Island of Clarity he proceeded to wrap it up in a nebulosity of abstract nouns, even as in scirocco weather the outline of it is only visible here and there above the damp cotton-wool in which it seems packed.

When the book arrived, the old ladies sent for one of the multilingual Russians of whom there were never less than fifty on the island, political exiles mostly, all anxious to earn a lira or two somehow. A farouche young doctoress, banished from her country since 1905, who in spite of spectacles and an unsolved chess-problem expression had been the mistress of two leading revolutionaries at once, arrived at the Villa Amabile to read aloud—and read aloud remarkably well if a little too literally—Count Marsac's novel to Miss Virginia and Miss Maimie.

"*Thou art the isle of the Clarity, of the Languor and of the Calmness, O Sirene! Thy pink rocks, thy gardens in flower, thy . . .*" the doctoress paused, and the chess-problem expression deepened. "*Treilles?*" she murmured, "I fear I am not knowing the English word for *treille*."

"What comes next?" Miss Virginia asked encouragingly.

"*With grapes of violet and gilded,*" the doctoress read on.

"Oh," said Miss Maimie. "That would be 'trays'. The same word, my dear, almost."

"Thank you, mademoiselle. *Thy trays of grapes violet or gilded, thy atmosphere of phosphos seems from far to let train on the limpid gulf as a long cloak of stoneries.*"

"Long cloak of stoneries? I don't quite get that Maimie."

"No more do I. Never mind, I guess it's some of the dear boy's poetry."

The doctoress resumed.

"*And those who love the Light go towards Thee. Thou art also the Siren whom they have chanted on the lyre Virgilian and flutes of Pan. The soft caress of the waves upon thy shores, the homesickness of thy smells, the freshness rustling of thy shadows, the blood Latin who palpits in the heart of thy young girls."*

"Girls?" Miss Maimie echoed in a sharp voice.

"Yes, mademoiselle," the doctoress insisted firmly. "Must I continue?"

"Sure," Miss Virginia urged.

"*Render thee parallel to some voluptuous vessel deriving full of ecstasy. . . .*"

"My, my, that certainly does sound mighty good, but I'm not there," said Miss Virginia. "Never mind, I guess it's poetry. And poetry goes a bit lame sometimes in another language. Read right on, Miss Ratibórsky."

"*And those who love the kisses go toward Thee.*" The doctoress paused and frowned. "But I think," she explained, "that there is another word for the kisses which I am not knowing in English."

"No, that's the very word, my dear," said Miss Virginia.

"Yes, but when they make more than the kisses," the doctoress insisted with the conscientiousness that comes from a medical training, "I think here the writer wishes to make more."

"Well, I guess kisses is just about as far as two old ladies like us want to hear about, my dear," said Miss Virginia. "Read right on."

"*But thou art, O Sirene,*" the doctoress resumed, "*above all by the majesty of thy altitudes, by the bronze blue of thy profile, by the haunting melancholy of thy legends, by thy stones, by thy sky, by the cruel grandness of thy Past, the sphinx, the decapitated sphinx, crouched in the solitude of the centuries at the entry of the Tyrrhenian, the androgynous and mute sphinx who is still regarding the route by where parted Cæsar . . .*

And those who love the Silence and the Life come towards Thee . . . thou Statue mutilated by the Barbarians who swarm at the foot of thy serene Indifference."

The doctoress paused for a moment to allow this exordium

to affect her audience suitably before she embarked on the story itself.

"And all that beautiful page is dedicated to we two!" Miss Virginia sighed. "Why, Maimie, isn't he just the dearest boy that ever was?"

There were tears in Miss Maimie's eyes, and she could but nod her assent.

"Read right along, Miss Ratibórsky," Miss Virginia commanded, fanning herself and rocking slowly back and forth in that wicker chair in which perhaps she had rocked herself as a girl, away out in Idaho.

So the doctoress set off with the tale and finished it in four successive afternoons, enjoying very much the enormous tea with which the old ladies rewarded her labours and embarrassingly grateful for the hundred-lira note they pressed upon her at the end of the reading, because such a sum would keep her in comparative comfort for six weeks as Russian exiles lived on Sirene in those days.

The story of *La Statue Mutilée* was about a young Frenchman who cut himself off from his family and came to live on Sirene as a sculptor. There he met a young American girl who had also cut herself off from her family. After a perfectly innocent companionship which the evil tongues of Sirene turned into a shameful intimacy he discovered that he was in love with her, and they were married. Then a Hungarian count arrived with whom the wife eloped, after which the young Frenchman discovered that she had been a well-known cocotte on the Riviera before he married her. On hearing this he mutilated a statue he had made of her and in pushing it over the cliff into the sea pushed himself over on top of it. The final page following upon a tornado of invective against the falsity and lust of Woman consisted chiefly of dots.

Then one heard the heavy sound of a falling body . . . . sudden . . . . . voiceless . . . a dull thud.

. . . . . . *There was a long silence.* . . . . . .
So be it. . . . .
. . . .

It was not even a moderately good novel, and in justice to Marsac it should be said that he could write a good deal better than this when he expressed himself in verse. The poems in *La Victime Ravie*, however embarrassing as an exhibition of hysteria, had at least a directness which, granted that one could stand directness on such a topic, occasionally achieved a kind of tortured beauty. *La Statue Mutilée* had all the hysteria without any of the sincerity of the poems, and the tawdry prose with which it was bedizened made that insincerity nauseating. Anybody who knew the story of Madame Protopopesco would recognize that she was really the Hungarian count. As for the wicked young American girl, she was Carlo dressed up in the petticoats of Angela Pears. And Marsac like so many writers of his temperament attributed to two young people supposed to be normal the characteristics of an abnormal passion. It is remarkable how nearly always fatal prose is to the pretentiously styled Uranian temperament, which time after time shirks honest self-revelation in such a medium, but continually seeks by an endogenous understanding of women, an almost uterine intelligence, to atone for its inability to create men. One day a novelist with that temperament will have the courage to write about himself as he is, not as he would be were he actually Jane or Gladys or Aunt Maria. And that will be a novel worth reading, not an obstetrical feat. However, for this story the importance of *La Statue Mutilée* did not lie in the quality of its literary style or of its psychological fancy-dress, but in the bitterness of the personal attacks, so thinly disguised as hardly to be disguised at all, upon various residents interspersed with abuse of Christianity, eulogies of paganism, and florid apostrophes menacing the island itself with destruction. In spite of that flattering exordium, by the time the author came to the end of his book he had worked himself up into such a phrenzy of rage over the thought of Carlo's seduction, the affair of the cistern, and the opposition to his statue of Tiberius, that he was making his hero address the island in these terms:

'*Land of murder, of vice and luxury, listen to the voice of one who will conquer thee at last. One day despite thy scents and sound of joy, despite thy perfumed slopes and gleaming white terraces, despite* (a page of overloaded description), *thou shalt disappear, O Sirene, because thou art no more thyself, because thou hast denied that which made thee great.*'

This was followed by a denunciation of Woman, and a particular word of warning to the young men of Sirene who by persisting in kneeling before that shameless Mother of Calamities would end by destroying all that made them Virgin Kings.

But it is idle to quote any more. There was hardly a person or a profession, a nationality or an individual on Sirene that did not find something to insult him in Marsac's book.

A hive of bees robbed of their honey could not have buzzed more furiously than the people of Sirene thus robbed of their reputations. Everybody was walking about the Piazza reading to one another the insulting descriptions of his neighbour. We may agree with La Rochefoucauld that nothing gives us greater pleasure than to hear of the misfortunes of our friends, but the aphorist would have to admit that nothing makes us more indignant than to read about their misfortunes in a novel, whether we read about our own at the same time or not.

"I can forgive his calling me a threadbare John Bull with the eyes of a dishonest billiard-marker," said Bookham to Major Natt. "Well, I mean to say, damme, I can afford to laugh at such a description. But to call poor old Goldfinch a goat with nothing left but his hair, I say, that's a bit thick. What?"

"Astonishingly thick when I remember my own last sad red hairs," the Major agreed.

"Yes, but wait a minute, that's not all. I've made a note of it somewhere. Oh yes, here we are. I'll read it in English."

"That's most considerate of you, Bookham."

"'Constantine Sparrow like a bankrupt Doge of Venus—I suppose he intends some kind of a joke there—Doge of Venus turned pavement-artist to elicit charity for his crapulous senility.' I say that's pretty infernal, eh? I only hope the poor old chap hasn't read it. I think I'll toddle up to the Villa Adonis and warn him not to let anybody else translate it for him."

With a whistling sound the Major drew in the necessary breath to overwhelm Bookham with the sesquipedalian style he so much disliked.

"This is an occasion when one laments one's pitiable lack of scholarship," the Major replied. "If I could command the Muses, you'd find me up at sunrise, Bookham, pinning gross pasquinades to the tablet of Umberto Primo in the Piazza. I should retaliate upon this debauched chatterbox in hendecasyllabics of the most ferocious obscenity. But alas, my martial cloak is not the mantle of Martial. Forgive the tenesmus with which I void my coprolites of wit, Bookham, and let poor Goldfinch remain in his happy ignorance of the French language."

"Aren't you going to Switzerland this year, Major?" Bookham asked.

"No, I didn't manage to let my villa."

"I'm sorry to hear that," said Bookham, feeling that he had scored rather neatly over the Major's more elaborate humour.

Mrs. Ambrogio complicated matters by borrowing from three different people their copies of *La Statue Mutilée* and lending them to other people, who of course allowed other people to pick them up from their tables and carry them home, so that the original owners soon lost sight of them for good. On top of these misdeeds she kept asking the people from whom she had borrowed their copies if they had noticed this, that, or the other about themselves, supplementing from her own memory of what Marsac had written so much that he had not written that the legend of the book's iniquity grew rapidly with every hour of its existence.

"Have you read the Count's book? I've read it three times already. Know it by heart. Some people treated him disgracefully, but don't think he ought to have said Mr. Bookham made love to his wife in a bathing-machine before he married her. No doubt whatever it's true, but I don't believe it. Too bad to start a story like that. Poor old Bookham. Can't stand the sight of him, but I do think that's going a little too far. And I don't believe old Goldfinch began life as a pavement-artist, but if he did he deserves a lot of credit for what he is now. And he never ought to have said that Angela Pears used to be a cocotte at Nice before she came to live with her grandfather on Sirene. Especially as she isn't married yet. So glad he's a friend of mine. Don't know what he might have said about me otherwise. And Peter would have been so angry. Fought a duel once and shot one of the seconds by accident. Never fought another. Changed man ever since. So glad he hasn't got to fight with the dear Count. But most insulting of all about Alberto and Enrico Jones. Don't know what they'll do about it. Why, there they are. Must ask them what they're going to do."

And though Marsac had neither said nor even implied half of the things about other people attributed to him by Mrs. Ambrogio, he really had amused himself at the expense of the two brothers. Malice with the pen could have gone no further. For them and Nigel Dawson he had kept his choicest venom.

And now as one looked at the brothers striding like a

couple of *condottieri* across the Piazza, one asked oneself how Marsac had dared challenge those two swarthy giants who twisted with so superb a swagger their black moustachios and flashed such brilliant dark eyes at the women they coveted as they coveted plots of land, Alberto chiefly for the profit that might accrue from them, Enrico more for the amenities of the situation, provided always that such amenities cost next to nothing.

"How d'ye do? How d'ye do?" Mrs. Ambrogio cried effusively. "We're all so anxious to know what you're going to do about the Count and what he says about you in his book?"

Alberto raised his eyebrows in surprise.

"What book, my dear Mrs. Ambrogio?"

"Count Marsac's book." Then as Alberto still looked blank, she dug him jovially in the ribs. "Oh, go on, you silly man, you must have read what he says about you in the Statue Mutely."

"Ah," said Alberto, "I understand. I did not read it yet, Mrs. Ambrogio. But Enrico has read it. You read it, Enrico?"

Enrico nodded.

"And what does he say about us?"

Enrico looked helplessly puzzled.

"I don't think I read anything about us," he murmured.

"Oh, go on!" Mrs. Ambrogio exclaimed, prodding Enrico in his turn.

Enrico smiled with no doubt what he imagined to be a courtly irony; but owing to the whiteness of the teeth that suddenly appeared between jet-black moustache and jet-black imperial his sudden smiles often gave the effect of sudden snarls.

"Not us in particular," he insisted suavely. "I don't think that my brother and I were singled out in the general bombardment directed against our poor island."

"Even if there had been a personal attack on us," Alberto

added, "my brother and I would have paid no attention to it. We wouldn't have felt that it was of sufficient importance. But from what Enrico had told me about this book I do feel that the *municipio* has reason to feel a little aggrieved. In fact I believe you were going to speak to the *sindaco* about it this morning, were you not?" he turned and asked his brother.

Enrico twitched his scalp.

"It seems all wrong," he growled, "that a comparative newcomer, however rich, should be able to give such a wrong impression of the essential Sirene. We don't want this exaggerated idea of our vice and luxury to be spread all over Europe."

"I have been sadly disappointed in Count Marsac," Alberto continued with a suavity that seemed to rebuke his brother's sullen accents. "I thought at first he would be a real addition to our intellectual life. Had I known what his morals were, I would never have parted with that building site to him."

At this moment Enrico looking at his brother suddenly realized that in what must have been the emotion of hearing himself described in Marsac's novel as 'Francisco Brown, a half-bred Englishman, a shark with a mackerel's tail' he had neglected to finish off the fastening of his trousers this morning, two buttons of which, seeming to the shocked eyes of Enrico as large as pewter plates, were now winking in the sunlight.

"Come along, Alberto," he said hurriedly, "we won't catch the *sindaco* before lunch unless you come along now."

"*Un momento, caro*," said Alberto, turning again to Mrs. Ambrogio. "As regards this novel, perhaps those who have found in it references to themselves may feel a little aggrieved. But to me the publication of that volume of poems in which nothing is left to the imagination and in which . . ."

"Alberto, *andiamo*," Enrico begged, dabbing his forehead with his big silk handkerchief in an agony of hot confusion.

"Whatever any of us may have thought about Count Marsac's inclinations," Alberto continued, "it has been left to himself to accuse himself openly and brazenly of behaviour that . . ."

Enrico, who like so many rakes suffered from a most uncomfortable, an almost morbid pudicity, grabbed his brother's arm which was now waving to and fro in graceful accompaniment of his still suave but severe condemnation of the Count.

"We are keeping Mrs. Ambrogio," he choked, and this time he succeeded in conveying to Alberto that there was something seriously the matter. One could see Alberto's expression of anxious arched interrogation as his brother duskily blushing guided him through the crowd on the Piazza to a safe seclusion.

Enrico had hoped that Mrs. Ambrogio might not have noticed his brother's unadjustment. Alas, for his self-consciousness, within twenty seconds of his escape with Alberto she was telling Madame Sarbécoff that Alberto Jones had been so much upset by what the dear Count had written about him in his novel that he had been talking to her in the Piazza with his trousers unbuttoned from farthest North to farthest South.

"How wonnderful!" Madame Sarbécoff purred. "I find that so wonnderful, dear Mrs. Ambrogio. Quite undonn! Women have not such a wonnderful way of showing their emotion, I think. I was feeling so upset last week over some news I had from Russia, and I would have so loved to express my emotion like that. And do tell me about Count Marsac's book. Is it very naughty?"

"Read it three times. Found it worse every time I read it."

"How charming! I find that so charming," Madame Sarbécoff sighed. "I have ordered a copy of it. Perhaps it may arrive with this post."

"Expect you'll find more in it than me. No brains.

Wish I had. You're a clever woman. How I envy you. My god, how I envy you!"

"*La Statue Mutilée*," Madame Sarbécoff purred to herself meditatively. "Where was it mutilated, Mrs. Ambrogio? Do tell me. I am so curious."

"Knocked off her nose with a hammer. Poor Angela Pears, I do feel so sorry for her. Such a hit at her nose which was always much too large. Men like that are always cats. Love him just the same. The dear old parroco's furious with the poor boy for running down Our Lady. Wish he'd become a Catholic. Love my Church. Only thing for men like him. Knew a man just like the Count once. Spent pounds every day sending himself telegrams. Became a Catholic. Never sent another telegram as long as he lived. Wouldn't even go inside a post-office. Dead now. Went to his funeral and cried my eyes out. Can't remember his name." Mrs. Ambrogio crossed herself rapidly and rushed away to the other side of the Piazza to tell Mrs. de Feltre about Alberto. This time she added East and West to farthest North and farthest South.

"Well, I'm not surprised, my dear," Marian de Feltre drawled, "I'm not at all surprised. Thank goodness, that beastly Count didn't ever really get to know me. So I've escaped."

"Yes, but don't you think it's dam funny about Alberto's trousers?" Mrs. Ambrogio spluttered.

"No, Maud, I don't think it's one little bit funny. I'm just so sorry for poor Alberto I could cry. And dear old Uncle Christopher! I know it'll break his heart if he reads this filthy book."

"Stupidest woman in Sirene," said Mrs. Ambrogio, relating this encounter to others. "No sense of humour. Told her Alberto's trousers came down in the Piazza while he was talking to me, and she wagged her head at me like a cow over a hedge. The woman's a damned fool."

It was close on noon when Mrs. Ambrogio met the Jones brothers. By half-past twelve Sirene believed that in a crisis of rage over Marsac's attack Alberto had rushed out of the Palazzo Inglese and along the Strada Nuova clad in only a vest and pants. By lunch time the pants had vanished. By three o'clock even the vest no longer existed.

"And then," Scudamore said, "we're invited to believe all this poppycock about Tiberius. If Sirene can strip a man of his clothes in three hours, what can't it do with his reputation in nineteen hundred years?"

While the Piazza buzzed with rumour and counter-rumour of what was going to be done about Marsac's disgraceful book, down at the Villa Amabile Miss Virginia was in her favourite loggia swept cool by the *maestrale* and, with Miss Maimie seated at her sewing beside her, was writing to Marsac about that disgraceful book:

>   VILLA AMABILE,
>   GRANDE MARINA,
>   ISOLA DI SIRENE,
>   ITALIA.
>   *August* 20.

My dear Bob,

We were so pleased to receive your lovely book and read that sweet and dear dedication to our two selves that I must sharpen my quill at once to tell you of our pleasure! We had a nice little Russian woman come and read it to us from beginning to end and how we have enjoyed all the beautiful poetry of your descriptions and all the hits at the beastly folks who have lied and slandered you and made your life on this 'Dream Island' of 'sweet do-nothingness' into a regular 'inferno' and general damnation of vile gossip.

Ah, well—" There's a bad side—'tis the sad side. Never mind it! There's a bright side, 'tis the right side—Try and find it:—"

We are glad to think that you are going to wait till after the first rain before you tackle our 'Isola Bella' again. We have missed you, but the summer has never been too hot for us, and always our dear sea breeze at the Amabile! Perhaps we have gotten so much of Italy 'in our blood' that we do not feel the heat any more. We just love the everlasting sunshine —even if we have no rain, night or day for weeks and weeks, and we do have a dusty road! We always have our blessed little temple and our vine-covered terrace and the music of the pounding sea and the smoky old mountain to gaze at and distant Naples town. But perhaps you will find it too dusty after the North and when the rain has freshened up our wee island you will see it again at its best and come back to your lovely Villa Hylas and the blessed Sirene air like a 'giant refreshed'. I hope you give me credit for being a nice, quiet, old lady and not bothering you too much with my twaddle when you were busy with all those wonderful books. Old ladies is so tiresome! Still, my dear boy, you know full well how much my sister and I joy in you and in your cleverness and poetry and romance. We hope so much now that all your troubles are over and that you have taught that beastly old Goldfinch and his crew of 'merry (?)' men a good lesson. Give our love to dear Carlo and tell him that his 'Bella Italia' is longing to see him again.

And with all most loving greetings from my sister and myself.

  I remain,
    Yours affectionately,
      Virginia Pepworth-Norton

To which Miss Maimie added a postscript in her round and upright and black handwriting:

Here's hoping that we shall soon be sitting all together on our Amabile terrace and drinking 'King Charles and who'll do him right now?'

Loving greetings from

      Maimie Pepworth-Norton

Chapter 8

perdiderint cum me duo crimina, carmen et error.

OVID

IF Marsac had confined his revenge to individuals and left vested interests alone, he might have escaped the consequences of his book; but owing to the comprehensiveness of his attack the wounded individuals were able to command the sympathy of the whole community in their counter-attack. He had insulted the Church and made a mock of the Christian religion. He had denounced the tradesmen of Sirene as a pack of voracious wolves. He had called the hotel-keepers brigands, the doctors assassins, accused the law of blackmail, and the civic authority of corruption. He had suggested that the youth of the island both male and female existed on vice. He had even declared that the bathing in Summer was bad and the climate in Winter much exaggerated. His book was a weapon in the hands of rivals like Sorrento and Amalfi and Nepenthe, and if he were allowed to come back and reside on the island his presence would be a perpetual menace not merely to its good name, but also to its material prosperity. Even Ferdinando Zampone bowed before the storm and entrenched behind his ledgers declined to discuss the crisis with anybody.

" I will not to speak no more. This ploody damned affair makes me too much nervous," he avowed. " Please to leaf me in peace, signore. All comes to me and says ' Ferdinando, what you sink about Count Marsac ? ' And I sinks nothing,

I occupy myself wiss my own businesses and I will not hear nossings. *Per me, il conte è stato sempre gentile, sempre signore.* Excuse to me please, why must I to make the *camorra* against him? If the *signori Jones* are wishing *cacciarlo via dell' isola*, let them to make their own hunts. *Io non mi metto in mezzo. E basta!*"

This answer was provoked by Herbert Bookham's suggestion that Ferdinando should form one of a deputation representing the finer elements of Sirenian society which was being convened to visit the Prefect of Stabia and petition him to sign a decree banishing Count Marsac-Lagerström from the island of Sirene on the ground of his moral obliquity and the risk of corrupting the natural virtue of the inhabitants by such moral obliquity.

This deputation, after a protracted babble of discussion, had been decided upon as the most practical move; and in view of the particular threat to the now purified hill of Timberio that was involved in his residence upon it, the clerical party had managed to arrange that the deputation should proceed to Stabia on the seventh of September, being the eve of the Nativity of the B.V.M. and the annual Timberian *festa* on which three years ago so many of Marsac's present enemies had partaken of that *couleur de rose* dinner.

Scudamore grunted contemptuously when Goldfinch came round to the Villa Parnasso, chuckling over the project and expecting that this would be the end of the degenerate scoundrel.

"*Multo me turpior es tu hercule,*" he quoted from Petronius. "*Qui ut foris cenares, poetam laudasti.*"

"Sorry, old man, I didn't quite get all that," said the painter. "I'm no hand at Greek, you know."

"It means, 'By gad, the man who used to flatter a poet to get asked out to dinner has nothing on me.'"

"I wouldn't have put a foot in his house," Goldfinch protested, "if I'd known what the skunk was."

"Wouldn't it be nearer the mark to say if you'd known he'd been found out for what he was? I'm sorry, Goldfinch, but I can't go this blasted hypocrisy. Say you're trying to out the man for laughing at you all in a book, but for the love of Mike don't be moral over it."

"I don't know what's come over poor old Jack Scudamore," Christopher wandered about lamenting. "I think all this cursed Latin and Greek has turned his head. And he used to be a regular fellow. Hell, it's fierce to see a great old boy like him going under."

It must not be supposed that because the deputation sailed for Stabia under the protection of Our Lady it was entirely composed of devout Catholics. On the contrary there was only one devout Catholic upon it, and that was the *parroco* himself. It is pleasant not to have to impute to him any motive that was not perfectly sincere. He had been genuinely horrified by the proposal to erect a statue to Tiberius, and then moved by Mrs. Ambrogio's account of Marsac's soul he had been inclined to wonder whether an attempt to convert him from his errors of morals and belief might not be worth while. A penitent as rich as Marsac would have such wonderful opportunities of giving practical demonstrations of his changed spirit. There were so many penurious charities that would benefit from the good will of a wealthy soul at peace with God. The Bishop, however, thought differently. Even were such a conversion brought about, it would lie under the gravest suspicion of expediency. Furthermore the Bishop was beginning to get a little tired of a parish priest whose personality was in danger of overshadowing his own. Don Pruno had for some time now been inclined to assume an excess of pastoral authority and, though of course he had never transgressed obedience or flouted episcopal discipline, he had more than once managed to convey that he expected to be a bishop himself one day and with it the most irritating suggestion that he would make a much better bishop than his Lordship of Sirene.

Therefore to Don Pruno's hint of a possible salvation for Count Marsac Monsignore shook his head.

"This is an occasion when the Church must take the lead in getting rid of an abuse. The least hint that we were protecting this notorious evil-liver would go far to destroy the moral effect of our recent victory in the municipal elections."

"You are aware, Monsignore, that one of the members of the deputation is Alessandro Cacace who with his own hands cast down the embroidered banner *Ubbedienza al Papa* which we caused to be suspended across the Via Partenope on the morning of the elections?"

"So much the better," the Bishop replied. "People will think that he regrets his insolence."

Don Pruno saw that it was idle to argue further with his superior and, being as jealous as anybody of the authority of the Church, when it was once decided that he should lead the deputation, he played his part with fervour. It was he of course who planned that the visit to the Prefect of Stabia should be made under the direct protection of Our Lady, and he chuckled drily to himself when he saw this band of heretics and rationalists striking a blow for morality under her ægis. Bigot though he was and the possessor of a childlike faith that made him seem ingenuous, even simple, Don Pruno had few illusions about human nature, always excepting the human nature of his own converts, about which he was inclined to be unduly optimistic. He certainly had no illusions about the members of the deputation he was to lead over the water to Stabia, and he took a great many large pinches of snuff while he waited for them at half-past four a.m. to join him at the entrance of the funicular.

The boat had just outraged with warning hoots of departure the placid sea and pale blue airs of that September morning, when the first member of the deputation arrived. This was Herbert Bookham as befitted one whose national punctuality has given a colloquialism to Italian, so that when an appointment is made for two o'clock *ora inglese* it means two o'clock and not a quarter to four. Bookham represented the foreign colony's protest against the presence of Marsac on the island. He was chosen in preference to Goldfinch, partly because he was determined to go and partly because the only phrase in Italian that Goldfinch after over fifty years in the country had really mastered was a command to fill his guests' glasses. There was a doubt too in some people's minds whether the exquisite costume which the painter would certainly don for this moral jaunt might be quite the thing to impress the Prefect of Stabia with the disgust that a man of Marsac's character inspired in the Nordic breast. There being at the moment nobody like Duplock to represent the healthiness of sexual America, it seemed advisable to impress with the virile boisterousness of a typical British resident an Italian official who might be liable to suppose that all English, Americans, Germans, Dutch, and Scandinavians visiting Sirene did so for no other purpose than to indulge themselves cheaply and easily *nefanda venere*. The romantic dandyism of Goldfinch might prejudice the case of the foreign colony. In Bookham the Nordic race would have a worthy champion, and mightier than the Jovian bull he would convey not merely Europa on his back, but America as well. As Scudamore said, paraphrasing Martial and apologizing for the excess of ' ams ' :

"*Vexerat Europam fraterna per aequora taurus;
Nunc etiam Americam taurus in astra tulit.*"

Alessandro Cacace was the next member of the deputation to arrive. He was a rationalist barber bitterly anti-clerical; but he possessed such a reputation as an agitator and *imbroglione* that the Sirene tradesmen, whatever their religious opinions, had no hesitation in choosing him to be the representative of their outraged feelings. Cacace hated the

Count because he had never entered his shop, and not being musical he had never even had an opportunity to put some of the Count's money in his pocket by playing the mandolin at one of his entertainments. In youth he had been the favourite of a Bavarian nobleman to whom he owed his shop. This made him hate Marsac all the more, because he felt that if he had only been born fifteen years later he might have occupied the position now held by Carlo. Fifteen years ago the reward his youthful career brought him had seemed handsome enough; but now Alessandro after watching the careers of other young men had reached the bitter conclusion that he had made too little out of his own. Now there was nothing left for him but to spoil the future for as many as possible of these pampered juniors. The *parroco* had a long memory, and it took an extra large pinch of snuff to help him to stomach the company of Alessandro Cacace at this hour of the morning.

"*Buon giorno, Don Pruno,*" Alessandro muttered, his thick lips curling in a sneer, his oily pompadour glistening as he raised his hat.

"*Buon giorno, figlio mio.*"

"A calm sea," the barber observed, writhing at the *parroco's* contemptuously paternal form of address.

"Whether the sea be calm or agitated is of no importance if the conscience be calm," the priest answered.

"Let us hope that this affair will come out well," the barber sighed.

"The Madonna guides us," said the priest. He turned away from the oily little barber and gazed lovingly to where her gilded image blazed in the morning sunlight on the summit of Timberio.

Alessandro squirmed; but as he hated Marsac even more than he hated the Madonna he forbore to sneer.

Doctor Squillace and Maestro Perella came along at this moment. The doctor was a wolfish-looking man with a trim grizzled beard and an eager hungry stare in his eyes when he asked after the health of an ex-patient. In his hands a hypodermic syringe appeared as alarming as a stiletto, and he bade a patient prepare for an injection as a highwayman might demand his money or his life. But the comparison is unfair to highwaymen. Doctor Squillace did not always offer the alternative; he often took both. He was hostile to Marsac because Marsac on the advice of the Nortons had declined his medical services and preferred those of a newcomer to Sirene. His consent to serve on the deputation was considered a good omen for its success, because it was felt that he would know exactly how best to put before the Prefect the danger of Marsac's presence on the island to the public health. There was not a great deal against the doctor's private morality except the reputation he had for taking advantage of his poorer female patients, but on this occasion such a reputation told if anything in his favour. As a doctor he was of course a rationalist and an anti-clerical, the former because of the intellectual advantages conferred by a medical training, the latter because the priests were an obstacle in the way of an extension of medical tyranny.

Maestro Perella, the doctor's companion, was a teacher of languages, who had once been the master of an elementary school on the mainland. That he was not still one was due to some odd tales about his behaviour out of school, and the violence of his disciplinary methods in school, which being contrary to Clause I of Article II of the Law of January 9th, 1876 and March 1st, 1885 approved by Royal Decree of April 19th, 1885 Number 3099 (Series 3) and to Clauses A and B of Article 40 of the Regulation dated September 11th, 1885 Number 3946 (Series 3) had led to his dismissal by the municipal authorities. Since then he had been earning a livelihood by teaching Italian in Sirene to adult foreigners on whom he could not use violence. He too was a rationalist and an anti-clerical, for much the same reasons as Doctor Squillace, to which in his case was added a special animosity against religion on account of the part that the parish priest had played in getting him out of his schoolmaster's job. Maestro Perella hated the Count because he had refused his services as a teacher, and moreover had added contemptuously in his hearing at Zampone's Café, "I find it excessively droll that such a *crétin* considers himself entitled to teach anything except the language of apes." Maestro Perella gained a place on the deputation because he was outwardly a fine figure of a man, and was mixed up in all the petty intrigues of native society, and had played the jackal at some time or another to most of the local lions.

"*Que voulez-vous?*" he used to say to his pupils in the halting French that he used as the common medium of conversation. "*Un pauvre diable d'un mâitre d'école doit vivre. Alors, madame, si vous louez la villa de Monsieur Tale je vous prie d'insister auprès de lui que c'était moi qui vous l'a raccomandé.*"

"Why, we surely will, Signor Pereller," the American matron in search of a villa would assure him, feeling so sorry for the distinguished military-looking gentleman driven by poverty to teach her the verb 'to be.'

Last of all to join this party of suppliant moralists was Arturo Westall, the owner of the Anglo-American Stores. Naples is the gateway of the East, and it is in Naples that you first find members of the ruling Nordic race in the state of degeneration of which the Levantine serves as the type. As the tissues of the body fester and rot under X-rays, so under the sun fester and rot Anglo-Saxonism and Teutonism and Scandinavianism if left too long beneath its influence. Arturo Westall's father had been an English doctor who had settled early in life in Naples and raised there a large family of sons, most of whom had been apprenticed to various trades on which Nordic superiority would have looked down for the sons of a doctor. All that was left of England to Arturo was an ability to speak the language with a strong Italian accent. He was a shrivelled-up little man with a grey-green face the colour of the faded prints which visitors who took their snapshots to be developed by him found that most of them became a few months later. It was not so much that he was dishonest with his chemicals as that he lacked the energy to develop his negatives any better than he had developed himself. He was not actively malicious; but like the chameleon his appearance rather resembled he took on feeble shades of the bright passionate hues with which he came into contact. Able to gossip with equal facility in English and Italian he was the chief clearing-house of Sirene scandal. Respectable women like Mrs. Rosebotham did not feel that it was beneath their dignity to gossip with Mr. Westall. They felt that in social status he was something between a dentist and a shopkeeper of the old-fashioned type. In spite of the fact that he had a wife in Naples and was living with a handsome and intelligent Sorrentine, in spite of the fact that there had recently been a scandal over a little girl of fourteen, people like Mrs. Rosebotham did not forsake poor old Westall. They were always careful to call the pseudo Mrs. Westall by her name Fortunata, and when the natives alluded to Signora Westall they were always careful to ask if they meant Fortunata, and this they felt expressed the measure of their disapproval.

"After all," Mrs. Rosebotham said, "we're not to know that he's actually living with her. She may be living with him. The Sirenesi are such scandalmongers. And anyway poor old Westall *is* so useful."

So was Fortunata, whose lovers in Naples all had motor-cars in which she used to drive old Mrs. Kafka about when Mrs. Rosebotham sent her mother over in charge of Fortunata to buy her winter underwear. But of course Mrs. Rosebotham's implication was that Westall was useful in the way that an emporium is useful. And indeed Westall himself did dare to cherish an illusion of his shop's serviceableness. That Marsac should never have bought so much as a five-year-old bottle of vinegar from him had galled his vanity to an open sore. But it was as a chameleon that he was despatched upon the deputation, to reflect for the Prefect of Stabia with his own faded tints the many vivid aspects of public disapprobation. He too, of course, was a rationalist and an anti-clerical. He probably felt that these qualities were sturdy and English.

"*Allora siamo tutti*," said Don Pruno, as Arturo Westall with a coat-collar turned up against the chill of the morning air came shivering across the Piazza.

"*Mi sento un po' raffredato stamattina, Don Pruno*," he wheezed. "I have a cold, Mr. Bookham."

"*Andiamo giù*," said the priest, surveying the complete deputation for a moment as if he wanted to cross himself, and then taking the largest pinch of snuff he had taken yet.

The credit for the idea of this deputation belonged undoubtedly to Alberto and Enrico Jones, and it was more particularly owing to the tact of Alberto that the Bishop became such a strong supporter of it. Not that either brother was conspicuous for his devotion. Indeed they were as unwilling to make themselves conspicuous over that as over anything else. Their attitude was always one of a regrettable inability to believe in what they would have liked to believe. They were always congratulating other people on the possession of faith. The *parroco*, who in spite of his judgment of human nature was such an invincible optimist over people's susceptibility to salvation, used to talk enthusiastically of the brothers' genuine devotion to the Madonna in spite of their being Protestants and free-thinkers. He deduced this devotion from the photographs of *settecento* paintings he had seen in the Palazzo Inglese. It never struck him that the Madonna might figure impersonally in a work of art any more than Garibaldi or Umberto Primo. If he had seen a photograph of these on a parishioner's wall, he would have looked down his nose and sniffed brimstone. And in the Jones Madonnas he perceived not the luscious pietism of Guido Reni or Carlo Dolci but the proof of a sentimental loyalty which made him comment afterwards:

"Strange! The room of Alberto Jones is full of the Madonna. Certainly we may hope that one day he will become a good Catholic. *Che bella cosa!*"

And as if to support his faith in the Divine Grace that was hanging over the heads of the Jones brothers like a blessed cloud which at any moment might burst in a shower of life-giving rain, the Jones brothers had been insisting to the Bishop on the pain Our Lady of Monte Timberio must be suffering from gazing down at the roofs of the Villa Hylas. When Monsignore informed his parish priest with what warmth Alberto and Enrico had welcomed the suggestion that the deputation should sail on the seventh of September Don Pruno forgot all about his optimism over Marsac's conversion and said a Mass with special intention for the conversion of the Jones brothers. He had been most anxious that they should accompany the deputation in person; but this honourable conspicuousness the brothers gently declined. It was always possible that the Prefect of Stabia might refuse to sign a decree of expulsion against Marsac, which would place the members of the deputation in a ridiculous position, though that was not quite the excuse they made to Monsignore.

"There is always something a little invidious about a layman, particularly a layman who whatever his sympathies may be, alas, is not himself a Catholic, setting himself up to claim a moral superiority over his fellows."

Thus Alberto unctuously.

"Alberto is right," said Enrico, twitching his scalp. "Whatever we may feel privately about Marsac, we do not think that we ought to push ourselves forward in this matter."

"People might suppose that we had taken such a step

because we were annoyed at being caricatured in his book," Alberto pointed out.

"If we *have* been caricatured," Enrico added quickly.

"If, as my brother says, we *have* been caricatured."

"Oh, but of course, it was a caricature, a most malicious caricature," Monsignore assured them with a prelate's urbane bow.

This was not quite what the brothers had meant. They had wished to imply a doubt of the writer's intention not of his skill.

So the deputation sailed without the brothers Jones, and later on that very morning Alberto said to Enrico:

"I have been thinking, Enrico, that if the *prefetto* refuses to sign the decree Marsac will be arriving in Sirene this week."

Enrico nodded.

"You might read through this letter, will you, and let me know if there is anything you think I ought to add?"

> PALAZZO INGLESE,
> ISOLA SIRENE.
> *September* 7.

Dear Count Marsac,

I think it is only just to write and inform you that there has been a strong agitation on the island to obtain a decree from the Prefetto di Stabia forbidding you to land on Sirene and prohibiting you from residence there in future. I need hardly add that my brother and myself have done what we could to allay public indignation, but vox populi vox Dei and so we have unfortunately been unable to do very much. Plain-speaking is always best, and at the risk of offending you I must speak a little plainly. I would have been standing at your side all this time if it were not for one embarrassment. That embarrassment is the presence in your household of the young man Carlo di Fiore. Can I, my dear Count, persuade you to dismiss him from your service? I feel sure that if you could see your way to do this, it would be a great deal easier for me and my brother to come forward more openly as your champions. The unfortunate publication of your book of poems entitled 'La Victime Ravie' has greatly upset us all. No doubt, the expressions you use are highly poetical and must be read as such. But the average man does not make allowance for poetical licence, and what you write has been taken as direct evidence against you. I confess that the idea of your being debarred from further residence in your beautiful villa on that site which you persuaded me into letting you have does shock me painfully. Yet even if this decree should be signed, I believe that with a little diplomacy (involving perhaps a slight expenditure in the right quarter about which I would be happy to advise you) and with some evidence of your own desire to dispel the popular view of your character, such as dismissing Carlo di Fiore from your service, yes, I believe that we might get the decree rescinded.

Believe me that I would not have written to you on this matter had I not been most sincerely grieved by the thought of your difficulties, for I cannot help preserving a sentimental memory of our former friendship, which if I may venture to say so was only interrupted by your unworthy suspicions of our good intentions over that extra plot of land.

*Yours most truly,
Alberto Jones*

I have forgotten to mention that my brother and myself enjoyed so much your novel 'La Statue Mutilée,' for of course we are both sufficiently broadminded to appreciate the amusing portraits of some of the foreign colony.

"But what is the idea of getting the ruffian back as soon as we have managed to get rid of him?" Enrico asked angrily, when he had finished the letter.

"We are not sure that we have got rid of him," Alberto reminded his brother.

Enrico's scalp twitched viciously.

"*Sei troppo ansioso,*" he said in net Italian. "Even if we do lose the profit on that piece of land, it is worth while to be rid of that *orecchione.*"

"*Ma, scusa, Enrico, sono io chi l' ho comprata.*"

"I'll pay half. *Per Bacco*, I'll pay the whole of it," Enrico swore.

"*Va bene,*" Alberto agreed with a resigned air and tearing up the letter into small fragments. "*Allora tu mi devi trecento lire.*"

And it says much for Enrico's hatred of the Count that he was ready to forgo the profit on that other piece of land and, what is more, reimburse Alberto for the three hundred liras he had spent on it in order to drive him off the island.

There should have been no doubt in the mind of its promoters about the deputation's success. The Prefect of Stabia recognized immediately what a representative selection it was that waited upon him in his dusty little office that September morning. In spite of the calm sea both Alessandro Cacace and Arturo Westall had contrived to feel sick and even to be as sick as it is possible to be on a tiny cup of black coffee, which was all they had taken before the crossing. However, their arguments were not required. The testimony of the *parroco*, of Bookham, and of Doctor Squillace was enough for the official.

"And wasn't *il Marsac* involved in some affair of a cistern?" he asked. "I remember something of the kind, I fancy."

"*Scusi, signor prefetto,*" said Don Pruno. "We are less concerned for what happened in the past than for what may happen in the future. *Il nodo della questione* is that he is a danger to the morality of the youth of Sirene."

"*Facilis descensus Averni,*" added Bookham solemnly.

"Bravo, Signor Bookham," the priest exclaimed with a gratified smile. "*Proprio appunto.*" And afterwards he told several people of his astonishment at hearing '*quello*

Bookham' quoting from one of the Fathers of the Church. "È stato molto valente. Mi ha fatto un gran piacere."

"Also from the point of view of hygiene," Dr. Squillace added, " I "—he indicated himself with a gesture of mingled pride and humility—" I, speaking as a medical man, permit myself to observe that Count Marsac's further residence on Sirene may have a grave effect on the public health with the propaganda he is always making on behalf of opium-smoking."

"And then he has mocked at religion," said the *parroco* earnestly. "He has even advocated circumcision for all Christians, who, he says, are only Jews in white nightshirts."

"*Brutto! Brutto assai*," the Prefect declared, clicking his tongue. "He is very dangerous, this Frenchman."

Bookham joined in with a long speech about the resentment that the other foreigners in Sirene felt at the ingratitude Marsac had shown for the hospitality which he and they were privileged to enjoy at the expense of the noble Italian nation, during the delivery of which the Prefect fidgeted in the respectful way that people fidget during a protracted performance of the national anthem.

"Well, we have said what we came to say," Bookham wound up. "And we must leave the rest to you, *eccellenza*."

Not even a blind beggar showing his sores on the steps of a church had ever addressed the Prefect as Excellency, and if anything was still needed to confirm his determination to sign a decree of expulsion against Marsac, that happy little courtesy supplied it. The Prefect shook hands with every member of the deputation in turn. The deputation withdrew from his office with profound bows. A small typist looking like a piece of biscuit which a mouse had nibbled and left in a fluffy corner was summoned. The law was set in motion. The ghost of some dead Cæsar inhabited for a space the shrivelled form of Stabia's Prefect.

The decree banishing him from Italy met the Count at Rome on his way South. The *carabinieri* entrusted with the business of communicating to him the decision of the authorities arrived at the Grand Hotel Colosseo when he was taking a bath to get rid of the effects of the journey. It has already been pointed out that nobody dreams of arguing with *carabinieri*. As for attempting to stop them you might as well fancy trying to stop a glacier. Partly it is their awe-inspiring gemination which conveys such an impression of ineluctable fate in their advance. The Hydra, the Chimaera, the Sphinx, the Siren herself, these are familiar instances upon the human mind of a combination of two or several forms in a single organism. The two in oneness or one in twoness of a pair of *carabinieri* is not less dreadful in its suggestion of a preternatural power. The gendarme has become the butt of comic opera, because he was merely one man in a ridiculous uniform. The *carabinieri* in much the same kind of uniform have never been laughed at. And they never will be laughed at, for we may say without exaggeration that every pair of *carabinieri* are Romulus and Remus eternally founding the eternal city.

So while Marsac lay in his bath and listened in pleasant egotistical dreams to the noise of the multitudinous swifts gathering in the wine-gold morning air of Rome, the *carabinieri* reached the lobby of the hotel and demanded of the head porter his whereabouts. On being informed that he was in his bath they demanded to be taken to the bathroom. Now, a certain majesty clings to the head porters of great hotels, and if ever anybody might have been supposed capable of bandying arguments with a pair of *carabinieri* it was the head porter of the Grand Hotel Colosseo; yet without a moment's hesitation he dismissed half a dozen rich and noble clients waiting to consult him and led the way himself to the bathroom.

"*Ouvrez la porte, s'il vous plaît, monsieur le comte*," he begged.

"*Mais attendez*," the indignant voice of Marsac responded from within.

"*Ce sont les carabiniers, monsieur le comte, il faut absolument ouvrir la porte.*"

There was a sound of splashing, and then the door was opened to display Marsac standing haughtily indignant in a gown of salmon-pink *crêpe de Chine* which was rapidly becoming transparent from the wetness of his body.

One of the *carabinieri* read the decree of banishment, merely holding up an immense hand for silence when Marsac interrupted him with protestations.

"Leave Italy within twenty-four hours?" Marsac repeated. "Not permitted even to travel as far as Naples? I assure you that the French Embassy will have something to say in this matter, my friends."

The *carabinieri*, their task achieved, turned round and left the hotel in silence and at the same pace as they had entered it.

The Embassy speaking through the mouth of a Third Secretary had nothing to say except that it thought it was perhaps a matter for the Consulate-General. The Consulate-General speaking through the mouth of the Vice-Consul was convinced that it was nobody's business except Marsac's own. In any case the only thing for him was to return from Italy and see what could be done about the future when he was back in France.

Marsac retreated over the Alps, vowing vengeance upon Rome like a discomfited Gaul; but he left Carlo to continue south to Sirene and there find out who was responsible for the intrigue which had caused this fresh humiliation. The northward-bound train had hardly completed the circuit of Rome when Marsac began to worry over the new housekeeper who had been engaged to direct his comfort during the following Winter. She was not a Roumanian. She was not a Hungarian. She was Dutch. Could he have heard of an Esquimaux able to cook in the style of three kitchens, he would have engaged her. He had interviewed

Madame Thijm in Paris and finding that she had divorced her husband he felt safe, because for a woman of her appearance to divorce the only man she was ever likely to persuade into marriage seemed to argue a quite remarkable indifference to her carnal future. Yet now when her outward form recurred to his jealous fancy, it recurred with the seductiveness of a Carmen. To be sure, more preposterous females than Madame Thijm have ventured to dance the *seguidilla* on the operatic stage; but still it was going rather far to suppose this wooden-faced creature capable in real life of luring Carlo to a second fall. Before the train reached Civita Vecchia Marsac felt that in letting Carlo out of his sight he had consigned him to the Venusberg itself; and he took advantage of the brief wait to send off an *urgente* telegram ordering his secretary to follow him immediately to Paris without crossing from Naples to Sirene. And no sooner had he saved Carlo from the allurements of Madame Thijm than he began to torture himself over his behaviour at the Grand Hotel Eruzione in Naples this very night. At Grosseto he sent another telegram ordering Carlo to catch the midnight train to Rome. At Modane he decided to wait on the French side of the frontier until Carlo overtook him; and a night, or what was left of a night, tormented by jealousy and the fleas of Modane, which found in Marsac a dainty morsel after the hardy mountaineers they were accustomed to, was followed by a miserable day of platform-trudging in the Alpine blasts, a prey to jealous fantasies, the most persistent of which was Carlo's elopement with some rich and voluptuous widow with whom he would have fallen into fatal conversation over passing the cruet to her at lunch in the dining-car.

However, in the small hours of the morning Carlo was looking out of the window of the train to greet him, and Marsac was able to express some of his affectionate solicitude by extracting a piece of soft coal from Carlo's too rashly devoted eye.

"*Ah, ce que j'ai souffert!*" he groaned. "*Et les puces! Mon dieu, ces impitoyables puces de Modane!*"

And the soft coal produced in Carlo's lustrous brown eyes a very good imitation of the emotional sympathy for which Marsac craved.

Arrived in Paris the Count set about obtaining the revocation of the decree. It proved to be much more difficult than he had expected. The French Government found itself unable to take any action on his behalf. Considering that a few years before the French Government had itself been under the necessity of moving against Marsac, its unwillingness to employ diplomacy on his behalf now was not to be wondered at. In Italy Peter Ambrogio worked away as hard as he could, interviewing deputies, drawing up counter-petitions (which unfortunately had a much less impressive list of signatures than the petition for the Count's expulsion), and trying to persuade the clerical party that the persecution was a clever anti-clerical move in preparation for the next elections. But it was all to no purpose, and the exile turned to the Muses to see if they could achieve what Justice denied him. He sat down and wrote a long ode to Italy, reminding her of what France had done for her in the past and avowing what a Frenchman was ready to do for her in the future. This ode, though printed on hand-made paper and sent to every senator and deputy, evoked no response from the prosaic authorities. So he sat down again and wrote an even longer ode in the course of which he flattered the Prime Minister of the moment more abjectly than Ovid flattered the deified Augustus from wind-swept Tomis. The Prime Minister paid no more attention to him than the Emperor paid to the exiled Roman poet.

Then Madame Thijm who was beginning to despair of giving her employer a taste of her quality in the style of three kitchens and fretting perhaps, alone on that Tiberian cliff, for the dykes of home, took to drinking Marsac's orange curaçoa. No doubt she found a sentimental companionship in those stone bottles of Bols that were inscribed with her own language and that in shape so closely resembled the people of her own country. From Marsac's orange curaçoa she passed on to his green curaçoa and from his green curaçoa to the rest of his liqueurs. Her end was curiously like that of the mutilated statue in the offending book, for on a moonlit January evening, perplexed by the combination of Grand Marnier, Cento Erbe, Strega, and a quantity of Canadian Club whisky, she apparently mistook the moonbeams for the marble balustrade of the terrace and leaning back against them toppled over the edge of the seven-hundred-foot cliff.

The death of Madame Thijm was a great worry to the red-headed judge, because he was unable to arrest anybody for being indirectly responsible for it, and it was obviously impossible for the sake of the island's good name to arrest anybody for being directly responsible. The clerical party boldly claimed that the fatal accident to Madame Thijm was a Divine judgment upon the accursed villa. The anti-clericals, who ever since the deputation had been growing increasingly restless under the insufferable patronage to which the priests and their friends had been submitting them, resented extremely this fresh leg-up for superstition. They insisted so strongly that the housekeeper's death was caused by an injudicious mixture of drinks and nothing else that Peter Ambrogio was able to take advantage of this common-sense explanation and obtain from the authorities permission for Marsac to visit Sirene for twenty-four hours every month in order to look after his property and give an eye to his servants. Moreover, as even Italian bureaucracy perceived the unreasonableness of expecting a man to visit his property in the South of Italy for twenty-four hours once a month from France, clemency was extended so far as to rescind the decree of banishment from Italy. Thus it came about that for the rest of the Winter Marsac had the mixed pleasure of occupying a suite at the Grand Hotel Eruzione in Naples, from the windows of which he could actually see the Villa Hylas, like one of those little shimmering seed-pearls scattered round the great cabochon sapphire of Sirene eighteen miles away across the Bay.

The effect of these monthly visits on the old ladies of the Amabile may be imagined. Their beloved Count landed like a Prince Charlie come to his own kingdom and like a Prince Charlie he was driven forth again. And when he was on the Sirene boat, whether the *tramontano* blew cold across the dark blue bay or whether the *scirocco* came whipping down over the island through the lemon-groves to lash more fiercely the dirty grey and white sea, Miss Virginia and Miss Miamie were always outside in their loggia gazing through a verdigrised telescope for the first sight of him. And when they had discerned him striding up and down the deck so tall and handsome and so fair among the prostrate mob of seasick peasants, Miss Maimie would hurry away to the kitchen to make sure that the soup would be served piping hot at the very moment his *carrozza* pulled up at the gates of the villa, while Miss Virginia would stay pacing up and down the loggia until the boat dropped anchor off the island. No matter how hard the wind blew she would be fanning herself hard all the time, from time to time putting up a lean old hand to adjust her fichu or push a strand of white hair back from her bright eager countenance.

Those monthly visits continued through the Spring, and then one morning in April a small steam yacht arrived, from which Marsac disembarked to surprise the old ladies. This craft had been chartered by some pleasant Canadians with whom he had made friends to visit the Cyclades, and Marsac tired of the noise of Naples and the indignity of his position had accepted their invitation to join them for a two months' cruise. The old ladies were happy that he had found some people so nearly American who appreciated him; but they were grieved to think that they should be unable to offer such dear folk their most prodigal hospitality, since they were to sail for Greece to-morrow and there had been no time to prepare an adequate feast. However, as usual at the Villa Amabile, nobody except the hostesses themselves could have imagined any addition to the feast they did provide. Fat Agostino—twelve years old now and fatter than ever—was sent off with a bundle of notes to command the attendance of their still loyal friends and several of those 'strangers within their gates', meaning the transient foreigners who wanted to have a good time during their stay in Sirene and did not care a damn for the moral problem that vexed the residents.

It was a warm wonderful night scented with orange-blossom under a full moon so resplendent that the illuminated bunches of glass grapes hanging from the pergola seemed not much brighter than real fruit. There was dancing, and talking, and laughter, and shadows moving to and fro across the blazing windows of the villa, until the dawn was rosy above Minerva's cape.

Christopher Goldfinch had given a dinner-party in the Villa Adonis the same evening, and to his mortification, when he strolled out to speed his parting guests across the Piazza at the premature hour of half-past three, the feast down below at the Villa Amabile was evidently a long way from breaking up. The gardens glittered like a necklace of topazes, and looking down at them from the columned terrace of the funicular one could hear the sound of guitars and mandolins rising through the perfume of orange and lemon blossom and dewy geraniums and the prime of the year's roses.

"My gad," Christopher groaned, "if that isn't defiance what in hell is?"

Next morning Marsac said good-bye to the old ladies in the Temple of Vesta that had been the cause of their first growing close together in friendship. He bent over to kiss their hands.

"But, my dear boy," Miss Virginia exclaimed, "we can't say good-bye in such a ceremonious old way, sweet though all these dear old ceremonious ways are to my old-fashioned heart."

She drew her to him and kissed his cheek. So too did Miss Maimie, flushing like a schoolgirl.

"Happy times in Greece, and damnation to all our enemies," Miss Virginia cried fiercely. Then her shrill voice melted abruptly to a Southern tenderness, an echo it seemed of some black nanny's lullaby long ago. "Look after our dear boy, Carlo."

The *famiglia* pressed round to kiss the Count's hand in turn and wish him *buon viaggio* and a *presto ritorno*, while Miss Virginia stood by proud as a hawk to see that at any rate one *famiglia* in Sirene knew how to accord the respect that was owed him.

The *maresciallo* with two of his *carabinieri* was down at the quay of the little port to watch the Count safely off the island until his next twenty-four hours' leave arrived. It is not easy to make a *maresciallo* feel small, but Marsac did his best to express in a glance all the contempt he felt for him and what he represented.

Handkerchiefs fluttered from the loggia of the Amabile as the little yacht steamed out of the harbour and Marsac like a second Byron set sail for Greece.

"See how close under Timberio the cunning little ship is going," Miss Virginia cried, following her course through the telescope.

"Poor boy," Miss Maimie said, the tears in her eyes. "He surely wants to take a last look at his beautiful villa."

But the steersman in standing out to round the point of Timberio on which the lighthouse rose misjudged his course and piled the yacht on a jutting reef.

"*Accidente!*" the *maresciallo* swore when he saw the

wreck. "*Egli l' avrebbe fatto così con uno scopo. Che animale!*"

And he rushed off to telephone to the keeper of the lighthouse to prevent Marsac's landing at all costs, at the same time ordering the harbour-master to have him and his *carabinieri* rowed out immediately to the scene of what he was convinced was an attempted evasion of the law.

"*Mais, mon dieu*," Marsac expostulated from the deck of the yacht. "I cannot remain here for another month."

The *maresciallo* shook his head.

"And I cannot allow you to land on the island of Sirene in contravention of the permission accorded you to land once every month for twenty-four hours," he declared.

And for awhile it did look as if the *maresciallo* did seriously intend to keep Marsac on board the wrecked yacht for another month. However, at last after a fierce argument he agreed so far to violate the strict letter of his orders as to conduct the Count ashore under close arrest and keep him in that condition until the afternoon steamer for Naples sailed, when he was put on board and released.

This final blow to Marsac's pride was too much for him. The wreck of the yacht had postponed indefinitely the trip to Greece, and he was not prepared to remain any longer in Naples exposed to the insolence of officialdom. He made up his mind to go back to China and not return to Europe until he could live undisturbed in his own villa. This was the letter he wrote to the old ladies:

> Grand Hotel Eruzione,
> Napoli.
> *April* 20.

My dear Miss Virginia and Miss Maimie,

After the ultimate outrage which I have now suffered at the hands of these abominable Sirenesi I cannot tolerate to remain here like a clown. I part with Carlo for China where man is still civilized and where, in a palace of white marble surrounded by peacocks and the heavy perfume of the daturas, leaning against a porcelain dragon I can watch the sampans creeping through the fog that veils the river and dream that life is not an evil jest. I will never return to Sirene no more until I am free of this tyranny of bourgeois hate. I shall write to you again very soon to make your acquaintance of my motions. Adieu, très très chères mesdemoiselles. I wish you all the sympathy you have given to me.

Devotedly and affectionately,
Marsac

It was to Donna Maria Zampone that on a sudden impulse the old ladies first confided what had happened.

"*Coraggio, signorine,*" said that Demeter in her great deep earthy voice, more than ever a Demeter beside those two old Vestals. "*Il nostro Ferdinando farà tutto tutto per aiutare il signor conte. Povero figlio! L'hanno assassinato. Mi dispiace assai.*"

And two great teardrops rolled very slowly down those massive cheeks carved at Cnidos out of Parian or Pentelican.

BOOK THREE

probro Vesta pudenda meo.
                    PROPERTIUS

Chapter 1

aspice ut aura tamen fumos e ture coortos
in partes Italas et loca dextra ferat.

OVID

FOUR years passed away. In the course of them several little paper-bound volumes under the signature of Robert Marsac Lagerström were published in Paris at intervals of about six months, and what almost amounted to a diary in verse conveyed a clear impression that the exiled Count in his wanderings round the East had come to depend entirely on opium for the satisfaction of his intellect and his senses. An amorphous hedonism, which was as near as he attained to any kind of creed, extolled opium as the one inexhaustible fount of pleasure; and he was now apparently convinced that the dreams of an opium-smoker provided a solid background of reality to the unreality of the visible world. The fumes of his pipe had for Marsac as much significance as the fumes of Hegelian sentences for so many Oxford dons in the nineteenth century.

The friends of the Count, who never allowed much time to go by without agitating for the repeal of the decree of banishment, pointed to these poems as evidence of the exile's changed outlook on life. They reminded the hostile party of the play it had made with *La Victime Ravie* to procure his expulsion, and they demanded that equal attention should be accorded these later poems. The hostile party offered a compromise: if the Count would leave

Carlo permanently behind him they would withdraw all further opposition to his return.

From the ruins of Angkhor Marsac responded to this proposal with a ferocious ode in which he threatened to nail his enemies like owls to a fence, in which he compared them to vampires crawling about the dust of a cemetery too much gorged with stale blood to rise aloft, and in which he concluded by assuring them that even the toads waxing fat beside the foul corpse of Judas would be unable to survive contact with such carrion as they would make. Beneath all this macabre rhetoric a genuine indignation made itself felt, and his bitterest critics had to admit a kind of respect for the completeness of the lamentable obsession that dominated him. It was evident that if the decree should be rescinded it would have to be rescinded without conditions, and that if ever the exile should inhabit again his white villa on the cliff's edge he would be living there in a lofty and complacent insensibility to there having been that in his conduct which might have provoked anybody to emit even the most diminished cough of disapproval.

While Marsac roamed the East, addressing sonnets in turn to the black juice of the poppies of Benares, of Java, and of Yurmam, at home in Europe Peter Ambrogio was addressing appeals to Italian politicians to use their influence to remove the injustice under which his client was suffering. The arguments he employed would fill a volume, and they might have filled twelve volumes without this story ever getting written, had not Advocate Cerulli decided to seek the votes of the electoral college in which Sirene was included, and that at a moment when the Government was extremely anxious to retain the seat.

In those days, when Italy still relied upon the parliamentary system, it was the habit of candidates to flatter the constituencies they were courting with suggestions that the particular benefits which might accrue to these constituencies from their election were bound up with the general progress of humanity. This style of flattery is always employed with an extra lavishness at bye-elections. Advocate Cerulli after canvassing the island decided that the surest way of winning the Sirenian vote would be to promise the island a more commodious harbour. He became very eloquent on the subject of this harbour. At political meetings he would lash himself into a frenzy over this harbour, until his audiences began to suppose that the future of Italy, nay, the future of Europe itself, was somehow closely connected with the proposed enlargement of their own inadequate anchorage. Under present conditions the Naples steamer had to lie off the island and discharge its passengers into small boats; and who on Sirene was not aware of the heavy loss in tourist traffic that was caused by such a primitive and barbarous method of transportation? How could one gaze at the political horizon with any confidence while the harbour of Sirene was cramped for space? So strongly did the patriotic government (of which he hoped soon to become he would not say a conspicuous member, but at least not, where Sirenian interests were concerned, a silent one) feel on this matter, so acutely aware was it of the presumptuousness of its claim to be called a government at all so long as Sirene lacked a proper harbour, that he had no hesitation in declaring that the first step of the government, on receiving the assurance of Sirene that it enjoyed Sirene's confidence by the arrival of him Fabiano Cerulli in the corridors of Montecitorio as the elected representative of the island, would be to offer that enchanted spot a harbour which would compete in efficiency with the splendour of the natural scene and the salubrious purity of the air. Let the municipal authorities of Sirene vote a sum of 50,000 liras toward the expense of the work, and he undertook to say that the government was ready to spend another 200,000 liras at once.

Advocate Ambrogio, who was one of Advocate Cerulli's most enthusiastic supporters and who had occupied a place on the rostrum from which the candidate made this announcement, took the orator aside afterward.

"It is a pity," he said, "that you cannot make a personal contribution to the sum which the government expects the *municipio* of Sirene to provide."

Advocate Cerulli recoiled from the suggestion that he was capable of such a flagrant piece of bribery; and indeed the notion of putting his hands into his own pockets did shock him genuinely and profoundly. His brother advocate laid a hand upon his arm.

"But supposing I knew of a great admirer of the government who would offer a large sum—let us say for argument as much as 10,000 liras—to the *municipio* and thereby encourage them to vote the remainder? Figure to yourself that I do know of such a loyal and philanthropic person, my friend."

The candidate wrinkled his forehead in token that he was concentrating upon the feat of imagination that was being demanded of him.

"What," continued Advocate Ambrogio, "would be his reward?"

"*La Corona d'Italia*," the candidate replied without a moment's hesitation. "He would be nominated *cavaliere* at once."

Advocate Ambrogio shrugged his shoulders with a grimace that seemed to imply something like contempt for the fifth class of the Order of the Crown of Italy, the red and white ribbon used for which, it had been computed by a statistician, would have stretched from Turin to Taormina even at this date before the war.

"The person whom I have in mind," said Peter Ambrogio, "would not be impressed by the *Corona d'Italia*, even were he to be nominated *commendatore*. He would not be impressed by the *San Maurizio e San Lazaro*." The emerald ribbon of that order was rare as grass in August.

"Perhaps he would turn up his nose at the *Annunziata*,"

said Advocate Cerulli huffily. The blue ribbon of that order makes its wearer a cousin of the King of Italy.

"*Parliamo sul serio*," said Peter. "The person whom I have in mind does not require any decoration. He asks nothing more than a simple act of justice."

The candidate looked relieved. Justice was not such an expensive business for a lawyer who knew the way to handle her. Peter, seeing that his brother advocate was in the humour to listen, gave him a brief history of the Marsac affair.

"If the Count's offer is accepted by the *municipio*," he concluded, "you will not find them against the rescinding of the decree."

"*Si capisce*," the candidate assented.

"And I do not think you will have much difficulty with the Minister."

"None whatever if the Government holds this seat."

"I might add," said Peter, "that a judicious amount of money will also be spent on various charitable works throughout the island, should the inhabitants have the good sense to elect you as their representative."

The candidate nodded.

"A thousand thanks," he murmured. "It is always a pleasure to hear of foreigners who appreciate the privilege of living in our lovely country."

So Advocate Cerulli was elected, and the ministerial press wrote enthusiastically of the confidence that the Government enjoyed among all classes of patriots. And then one fine afternoon in March Peter Ambrogio and his wife drove down to the Villa Amabile to inform the old ladies that a telegram had arrived from the Honourable Cerulli announcing that the decree of banishment against Count Marsac had been rescinded. He was free to return at once to Sirene and to inhabit his white villa at the cliff's edge in perpetual peace.

"Dear old pets," said Mrs. Ambrogio, describing the

scene in that lace-hung *salone*. " Both of them cried for joy. We all cried for joy. Peter cried too. Most emotional man in Italy. Saw a little stray kitten the other day and brought it into the Villa Botticelli. Such a sweet little kitten with one eye. I gave it some milk and sent it round as a present for little Mrs. Neave. Love all animals so much. So does Peter. Both the old pets kissed him and said he was the saviour of Sirene's good name. Nearly burst out laughing, but cried my eyes out instead. Peter so proud, bless his heart! Dear old boy, so glad for his sake. Worked so hard for the dear Count all these years. Got his reward at last. They've started work on the new harbour. Everybody says when it's finished it'll be more inconvenient than ever. Quite useless. Naples boat will have to anchor further out than ever. Going to cost millions of liras. Peter won't get a penny of it. Throwing money away. Never mind. The dear Count's coming back, and I'm jolly glad! Give people a lesson. Going to have my beloved Villa Botticelli done up this summer. Red dining-room."

The news that Marsac was coming back to Sirene had not been in circulation for an hour before there were plenty of people to announce authoritatively the very day fixed for his return, though he would have required a magic carpet to transport himself from the Far East to arrive on any of the various dates fixed by rumour. When he failed to put in an appearance either in March or April, rumour declared on the most reliable sources of information that he was not coming back to Sirene at all; and no sooner had rumour obtained general credence for this than Miss Virginia and Miss Maimie announced at their tea-party on the first Sunday in May that dear Count Bob would be home in the course of the very next week and that they were giving a large dinner of welcome to which all their real friends were invited to come and greet him after his wanderings.

Four years had passed away; but Sunday afternoon at the Villa Amabile was as much a feature of Sirenian life as ever it was. There were changes in the guests, and the slim tops of the young cypresses were now quivering in the warm air above the Temple of Vesta; but Sunday afternoon at the Amabile would have seemed to Austin Follett, had he returned to the island this Spring, exactly the same as when he first made acquaintance with Sirenian society twice four years ago. Not that the old ladies had been reconciled to any of their enemies; but the gaps that their absence had caused for a time had been filled by newcomers to the island, who had arrived to spend a day, or at most a week, and who like so many predecessors had remained there ever since.

Of these newcomers undoubtedly the most conspicuous was Mrs. Hector Macdonnell. She was a rich Scots widow with all the faults and none of the fine qualities of her Lowland race. Her tongue was sharp, her accent broad. She was purse-proud, snobbish, odiously mean, and ineffably vain. She mistook pruriency for puritanism, and affected a ludicrous sensibility to the beauties of nature. She was the worst kind of scandalmonger, because her tongue, dressed with the vinegar of malice and the oil of self-righteousness, lacked the honest mustard of ribaldry or the salt of wit. She was so well pleased with herself that she was never lonely, and she would sit for hours with no other company except her own portrait, which occupied a large easel in the middle of her *salone* at the Villa Candida. That portrait, executed by one of the Sirene painters, who in the hope of gaining an extra hundred liras on his commission had striven hard to flatter his sitter, was as ugly and garish as the original. It represented a bouncing woman with a hard carmine face, who, dressed in an elaborate cerise gown, sat gazing out across the Bay of Naples. The effect was of an advertisement for some distemper or dye; and yet the colours were, if anything, toned down from the original. Mrs. Macdonnell rarely wore anything but some crude shade of pink for her trailing gowns of silk and satin, and her immense picture hats built up with gardens of sham flowers were always hung with coloured streamers that could have made a bridesmaid of 1896 feel ashamed of herself. She laid great stress on a long pedigree, and had adopted her late husband's family with such a romantic Highland devotion that she had by now entirely forgotten that her own maiden name was—but let no offence be given to the countless owners of that name by revealing it. Anyway, lest anybody should forget that she was Mrs. Hector Macdonnell, she had caused to be engraved on her cards her late husband's crest and motto. That motto happened to be *Always ready*, and the delight this gave to a ribald society may be imagined. Her nickname was ' Bonny Sarah ' owing to a Sirenian legend that when she first came to the island and was wished *buona sera* or good evening by passers-by she had supposed them to be commenting on her good looks. Mrs. Macdonnell (whom in spite of the crested card Mrs. Ambrogio would call Mrs. Macdonald) was at the Villa Amabile this afternoon, creating in the big *salone* as brilliant but not so beautiful an effect as the judas-tree on the Strada Nuova in full bloom of hot carmine against the azure velvet of the May sky. Miss Virginia and Miss Maimie loved this aggressive female, but why they did was a riddle that nobody on the island ever succeeded in solving. Perhaps it was that Mrs. Macdonnell's venomous propriety reassured them over the Count. Mrs. Macdonnell was determined to be one of his most fervid supporters, and she, who was even shocked by the light behaviour of a niece that was staying with her and who was always confiding in Miss Virginia and Miss Maimie how much the unbridled manners and morals of contemporary girlhood distressed her, did seem to lend a real weight of respectability to the Marsac cause.

Phyllis Allerton, the unsatisfactory niece, was one of the

numerous prototypes of the post-war girl, and the faithfulness with which she and her fellows resembled their successors proves that the post-war girl is not in the least the product of the war, but the natural development of young womanhood. Queen Victoria lived too long. King Edward died too soon. Hence the apparent rapidity of development for which the war has been given undeserved credit or blame. Mrs. Macdonnell did not realize that Queen Victoria was dead. Hence her objection to this niece whom she had invited to spend the Spring and Summer with her in Sirene, and who had repaid her kindness by being consistently late for every meal, by accepting invitations to go bathing with young men without asking her aunt's permission, by smoking in the public street, and worst of all by being obviously a much more welcome addition to any party than she was herself. In fact the one Villa on Sirene where Phyllis was not a great success was the Amabile. There she was tolerated only out of consideration for her disgracefully used aunt; and Miss Maimie was so much perturbed over her naughtiness that she used to take aside elderly gentlemen of grass-green propensities and solemnly warn them against the allurements of modern young women. These elderly gentlemen would have been virginally secure with Cleopatra, nay with Circe herself; but nevertheless Miss Maimie felt that it was her duty to protect them so far as she was able from what Miss Virginia called the redoubtable Phyllis. It was surprising to meet this young woman after hearing about her from the old ladies. One expected serpentine coils and lustrous almond eyes, full scarlet lips and perfumed enchantments. Instead, one met a slim clear-cut creature with sunburnt boy's hands and rose-browned cheeks; and though Miss Maimie vowed that she was neither so young nor so innocent as might be supposed, that, with all the bloom and charm of eighteen-year-old girlhood upon her, did not seem greatly to matter.

"Dear girl! I love her so much," Mrs. Ambrogio was

spluttering to some stranger that afternoon. "So natural. Love people to be natural. Thank heaven I'm natural myself. And if you hear that Phyllis spent the whole night with young Lorenzo Marolla on the top of Monte Ventoso, don't believe it. Lies. Lies. Filthy lies. Don't believe a word of it. All the fault of her beastly old aunt. Can't stand that awful woman. Cannot stand that disgusting woman. Stand anything, but cannot stand her lies. Only smile at her to please the dear old Nortons. Spit in her eye if I didn't know it would hurt their feelings."

While Mrs. Ambrogio was thus giving vent to her own feelings, Mrs. Macdonnell herself, in silk and satin and a huge basket of a hat filled with sham wistaria blossom, was sailing graciously round the *salone* and conferring her smiles upon everybody she met.

"Behold our sisterr island," she exclaimed in accents like a caricature of a Scottish comedian as she pointed to where the bronze of Nepenthe towered across the Bay. "The most beautiful loggia in all Sirene," she vowed. "Ye have the most beautiful loggia in all Sirene, Miss Virrginia, and I always say there's no view that can compare with the view of our glorious Bay."

"Damned old fool," Mrs. Ambrogio spluttered. "As if we wanted Mrs. Hector Macdonald's opinion of the view. The woman's a fool."

"I should think not indeed," said Mrs. Macadam, who joined Mrs. Ambrogio at that moment. "Do you know what that woman is, Maud? She's a damned idiot."

"Damned fool," Mrs. Ambrogio repeated.

"Damned idiot," Mrs. Macadam repeated.

And then for a moment they stood silently glowering at the preposterous cerise and carmine draperies of Mrs. Macdonnell, who moved and looked and spoke as if she were perpetually opening a bazaar.

There was one person on Sirene in whom this interval of four years had wrought a profound change. This was

Mrs. Macadam. Four years ago she would never have called even Mrs. Macdonnell a damned idiot. But four years ago her husband was still alive; and it was only after poor Archie's death that Effie became herself. Archie died of pneumonia in the Winter after the Count left Sirène; and on a bleak January day Mrs. Macadam, attended by mourning friends and supporters, went down to the cemetery, the same dull, pretty, and common-place little woman she had been ever since she and Archie came to live on the island. Owing to the fact that the Anglican chaplain had most inconveniently died himself about a fortnight earlier, the funeral had to be taken by Herbert Bookham, whose possible chairmanship at one's funeral added a terror to protestantism that with sensitive souls weighed far more heavily than the problem of ultimate salvation. It was computed that the prospect of being buried by Bookham had brought more people back to the Church than anything else. Bookham was boisterous even at a funeral. He could spoil even the exquisite cadences of the Burial Service with his taurine snorts; and he was so clumsy that when the moment came to fling the last handful of earth into the grave he was capable, as when he buried Archie Macadam, of flinging a large rock which thundered on the coffin and dismayed the mourners shivering at the edge in the raw north-east *grecale* with the prospect of waking the dead in earnest.

When the funeral was over, Effie Macadam astonished her friends by inviting them to come back with her to Zampone's and there ordering a round of hot rum.

"My poor darling old Archie," she said, sitting at the head of what was a kind of epilogical wake. "This is what he will like to see us all doing. Donna Mareer!"

"*Sissignora*," responded that Demeter gravely, crystal globes of tears rolling one by one down her marble cheeks.

"Portate altri rum. Tutto. Tutti."

Then she addressed the company whose presence she had just indicated with a comprehensive wave.

"Do you know what I think Bookham is?" she demanded. "I think Bookham's a blooming idiot."

The churchwarden had been the only mourner to decline her invitation to drink away the cold, pleading the necessity of getting back to his wife as quickly as possible.

"Here we are all of us alive. Aren't we? And my poor darling old boy is dead. Isn't he? And Bookham's neither. He's just a blooming idiot. Donna Mareer!"

"*Sissignora.*"

The widow waved her arm in another gesture of comprehensive hospitality.

"Portate altri rum. Tutto. Tutti."

And from the moment that she sat at the head of that long table in Zampone's and ordered three rounds of hot rum and lemon for her friends Effie Macadam became a Sirene personality. Those who dimly remembered her in old days as a tiresome little woman, always seated at her husband's elbow to nag him out of accepting or offering any more drinks, revisited the island and found that their social adventures were considered incomplete until they had seen Effie in one of her expansive moods. People were inclined to make their reminiscences of Effie the touchstone of their Sirenian experience. Just as mountaineers question one another about their ascents, so visitors returned from Sirene who met in the dullness of a London drawing-room used to ask one another not if they had explored such and such a grotto or bathed in such and such a cove, but if they had seen Effie Macadam, using her slippers as castanets or beating time with them on the bald heads of elderly grass-green gentlemen, dance a *pas seul* in a Sirene studio. They would boast to one another of the times they had escorted Effie home after parties, making competitive statements about the number of hours it had taken, and the whereabouts of walls on which she had rested and from which she had toppled backward into terraces of lupins or young wheat, and the height of the sun when at last they had reached Effie's *villino* on the slopes of San Giorgio, where she lived with six geese, two yellow cats, and a little maid with whom she carried on ceaseless gossip in a dialect as extraordinary as the French that Mrs. Ambrogio used with her husband.

As Effie's fame grew she became aware of being what is called a 'character'; and there is no doubt that what began as mere exuberance after three or four drinks developed into a deliberate comicality. She acquired a sense of responsibility for the success of a party, and one of her chief pleasures was to descend into the town the next day and listen to the accounts of her fantastic behaviour the night before. The other Sirene matrons were apt to be a little jealous of her success as an entertainer, and several of them criticized her rollicking performances as unbecoming, perhaps as definitely immodest.

Yet, even Effie had her moments of a rather tiresome respectability, and sometimes for several weeks at a stretch she would become excessively *per bene* and frequent dinner parties given by rich Americans followed by long evenings at bridge. It was fortunate that her zest for life always asserted itself again after one of these intervals, because Effie enjoying herself and playing the buffoon was worth a journey across Europe, but Effie on her best behaviour required no more than a bus ride to the suburbs to find innumerably, and even a twopenny bus ride would have been too much trouble to take for that. At her best, however, when the wine was flowing about two o'clock of a warm moonshiny night . . . but alas, she does not play an important part in this tale and, as one turns away from a view greatly loved in youth and revisited a little sadly in middle-age, one must turn away from Effie to meet what Miss Virginia and Miss Maimie called " our dear Bilton girls."

The Biltons were two Quaker sisters from Pennsylvania. Miss Rachel, the elder, must have been at least fifty and looked it, with her grey hair done in a pompadour, her pince-nez, and her elderly ample figure. She was pleasantly colourless and flabby, the sort of pasty old maid one sees by the dozen on steamers crossing the Atlantic, by the thousand when one lands in America. But Miss Hannah, the younger, was by no means ordinary. She was about thirty-three, thin almost to emaciation, with a plume of grey in her dark brown hair and a fine profile. Her complexion was of that lighted rose which suggests fever, and her vivid hot blue eyes were illuminated from behind, not by Quaker fires. Her appeal to a libertine was always immediate, because she had the charm of having evidently never experienced love with all its irksome implications of emotional standards, but of having been often at any rate half possessed, so that she could be approached in the spirit of perfect cynicism. Sentiment was wasted upon Miss Hannah. She was out to spend the accumulated purity of her Quaker ancestors, and there was no need to waste time over accepting from her the small change of sensuality. When a woman only draws near to men by the highroad of sex, it is not astonishing that she should become inured to heavy traffic. But what was astonishing was that Miss Hannah Bilton should have succeeded in impressing herself on the Nortons as what they did not hesitate to call their ideal of a young woman. They never tired of praising the two sisters, and it was understood that this time Miss Virginia had done more than remember them in the ultimate disposition of her property, that in fact she had forgotten everybody else.

"If only Phyllis could take a few lessons from our dear Hannah in how to behave," Miss Virginia would say. "It just makes me tired to see a young girl of her age flinging herself at the head of every man she meets."

It was true that Hannah did not appear to fling herself

at men. In public her behaviour was demure enough, and one of her most precious thrills was the way she could surprise a dancing partner who was supposing that he held in his arms a prim Quakeress with the realization that he held instead an accomplished wanton.

Although neither Miss Virginia nor Miss Maimie seemed outwardly a day older with the passage of these four years, something in the way that the Biltons were looking after the guests this afternoon produced an effect of age. Perhaps it was merely the sense of possession that emanated from the solicitude of the Biltons, this and the unexpectedness of hearing Miss Maimie dispense some of her hospitality through the medium of another, which seemed to indicate a subtle change in the atmosphere of the Villa Amabile. Coupled with this the obvious influence of Mrs. Macdonnell over Miss Virginia suggested that the old lady really was becoming a little bit dependent upon others. You heard people murmuring that after all she must be quite eighty now, and you felt that this comment was the unexpressed thought that at last she was beginning to break up.

But such apprehension was premature, and it was not long before Sirene was to have proof that Miss Virginia's passion was as fierce as ever, her hold upon life as firm, her energy as inexhaustible, her courage as grim.

The proclamation of a dinner to welcome the Count home affected with uneasiness only one of the guests at the Villa Amabile that Sunday afternoon. This was Harry Menteith, a young American painter who had settled in Sirene three years before, flying from the sorrow of losing his beautiful young wife in Florence and bringing with him twin baby girls. Celia and Evadne, now aged five, were a great joy to Miss Virginia. They used to drive down with their nurse three times a week to play in the Amabile garden, where in their short smocked tabards over boys' knickerbockers and with their dark hair bobbed they looked exactly like the two cunning little Jacks of Clubs that Miss

Virginia called them. She had recently commissioned their father to paint her a portrait of them on one of the sunny Amabile terraces, and this picture of youth and dappled sunlight now hung in the big *salone*.

Harry Menteith was on good terms with everybody on the island, and though the old ladies used to refer sarcastically to his friend Mr. Goldfinch they had never suggested that he should make any kind of final choice between the Villa Adonis and the Villa Amabile. But the young painter's weak good-looking face was perplexed as he drove back to the Piazza that Sunday afternoon between his two little girls, who sat solemnly on either side of him, their laps heaped with the little presents that Miss Virginia and Miss Maimie were wont to shower upon them. It was bad enough that this fellow Marsac should be coming back to Sirene, but why the deuce couldn't the Nortons keep quiet about it and let his company at parties be tacitly accepted or avoided. Why must they give this fool dinner as if they were welcoming home a hero? Everybody who went to such an affair would by going express an open and defiant approval of the guest of honour. Everybody who went would be committed either to avowing his belief in Marsac's innocence or what would be worse, if perhaps not quite so *bête*, to condonation of and even to sympathy with his crooked standards. Harry Menteith, in spite of ten European years, had lost none of that extreme sensitiveness to his neighbour's opinion which is one of the characteristics of an enlightened democracy. He suffered acutely from the voracious Cerberus of liberty, equality, and fraternity. For him, as for so many millions of Americans, individualism could only be practised in secret like a vice. Even in Sirene he was not free from this pressure of the 'bunch' upon his own mental space.

Arrived in the Piazza, Menteith handed his little girls over to the care of their nurse and walked up the steps by the Duomo to call on Scudamore at the Villa Parnasso.

The scholar was no nearer to beginning his great work on Roman morals than he was four years agő, and if it had seemed tralucent then, the emaciated bearded face above the grey dressing-gown now verged upon transparency. His voice sounded more hollow than of old, and behind his grave pedantic humour an immense weariness was perceptible as if he had become aware that he would never begin, much less complete his task, and desired death to relieve him of the burden of his own grinding honesty as an historian. Duncan Maxwell's departure from Sirene three years ago had been a great loss to Scudamore. The most fatiguing line of research had been well rewarded by Maxwell's comments, and the impingement of his ruthless vitality upon the gloomy rooms of the Villa Parnasso used to clear the air of the stifling must and dust of books. Nobody had such an unflinching sense of the fact as Maxwell and withal such a supreme capacity for lighting it up with his own electric imagination. And now Maxwell himself was almost beginning to flag in the fogs of London, where he was sub-editing a blue-nosed review of humanity's monthly progress. Oh, hell, could there but be an Elysium where Lucian, Martial, Petronius, Maxwell, and he might one day meet! And the scholar would shrink from the distasteful food that Nita was banging down before him and ponder sadly the accumulated wit and wisdom upon his shelves from which he should soon be parted for evermore.

"And I have been tempted to discover in my character an affinity with the Stoics," he would think, polysyllabic even to himself.

Scudamore enjoyed the company of the young painter, who was willing to sit and listen to his lectures on classical lore for as long as he cared to be talking. It is true that Menteith was apt to ruffle the suave exposition with some comment that would bring the scholar up with as much of a shock as if his young friend had actually slipped and badly bumped his head on the surface of knowledge over which he was skating. But anon he would remind himself stoically how idle it was to expect from the average product of modern education a more stable progress down the ways of knowledge. He would forbid himself a sigh for Maxwell's insolent wisdom and make the best of this new friend's eager and often pathetic knowingness. And then he would turn as ever to his beloved Martial:

> *tu tantum inspice qui novus paratur*
> *an possit fieri vetus sodalis.*

Would this new friend ever become an old companion in the richest sense of the word? But presently that problem would be forgotten in an attempt to torture the English language into yielding a personal noun to express the idea of sodality, and the scholar would pull down dictionary after dictionary to trace with chalk-white tenuous forefinger the fine print of their information.

"You look worried, Harry," Scudamore said, when the young painter sat wrinkling his forehead at the Villa Parnasso that Sunday afternoon.

Menteith explained the decision he should presently have to make, while Scudamore sat puffing at a very large and very foul pipe and looking like a benign wizard at a consultation.

"Do you yourself want to go to this dinner?" he asked when Menteith was through with his sketch of the situation.

"Why, I don't give a whoop one way or the other," said the other with a nonchalance that overreached itself and turned to nervousness.

"There is, if you come to consider it, something nearly sublime in the way those two old maids stick to their guns. That poor Gaul must be given the triumph of a Cæsar. By Hercules, I don't know how you can contemplate absence from such a spectacle. Why, if the old ladies invited me, though I have not been outside the Parnasso for eighteen months, I'd have to go just for the pleasure of seeing Mrs. Macdonnell curtseying to Ganymede. Surely that will be one of the memorable occasions of our time. I wish Maxwell were here to urge her *bulbis salacibus* into the more extravagant homage that Scotch witches used to accord the devil."

But Menteith was in no mood to join in the scholar's laughter, even had he appreciated the allusive ribaldry.

"It's going to give old Goldfinch a big jolt if I go to this dinner," he said.

"And it'll give the old ladies a big jolt if you don't," Scudamore added.

"Oh lord, I know it will."

"Well, that being so, I'd sooner jolt Goldfinch by going than I would the old ladies by staying away. Besides, you wouldn't miss a whale of a good dinner in that case, and I wouldn't have to rely on the mutilated text of Mrs. Ambrogio's account of the ceremony."

"But the old boy's been terribly good to me ever since I came to the island," Menteith objected.

"Haven't the old ladies been pretty good to you also?"

"Why, sure . . . oh, skittles! I don't know what to do."

And ten minutes later Menteith, perceiving that the scholar was beginning to let his eyes roam toward his worktable covered with open volumes and half-sheets of notepaper, left him to his studies and went off to visit Goldfinch, hoping that perhaps at the Villa Adonis he might reach a final decision about this fool dinner of welcome to Marsac.

The old romantic had hardly changed at all in these four years, in spite of having in the course of them fallen downstairs and broken his arm, from which he had hardly recovered when he fell down the steps by the Duomo and broke a rib. Besides these accidents he had had pneumonia two winters ago, and through the last year a chronic indigestion which tied him for nourishment entirely to Sponger's Food.

"By gad, it's fierce stuff," he used to croak. "I don't know what it's made of, but they tell me they bring babies up on it. It's horrible to think of the way we treat children. And they tell me it's a substitute for mother's milk. By gad, I call that an insult to women, and I don't believe it. No, sir! I don't believe that any woman who ever lived had milk that tasted like whitewash and hair-oil. However, Squillace says if I keep on with it for a month or two yet I'll be fine, and we'll have some great old parties again. I bought some exceptionally good wine three years ago, and it ought to be just right around about midsummer. It seems quite certain now that Sheila will be here in July. She cabled me two months ago and said there was a letter on the way giving her plans in detail. The letter hasn't arrived yet; but I've cabled again, and I'm expecting to get an answer every mail."

As a matter of fact, Christopher had been expecting an answer from Sheila Macleod almost every mail in all these four years to give him the date of her return to Sirene. It was the resolve to enjoy again the sweets of her company that cured all his ills, and to that was now added a determination to be quits with Sponger's Food.

Menteith found Christopher's room thronged that afternoon, and he was greeted on his entrance by a shout from the lingering visitors to know if it was true that the Count was coming back next week and that the Nortons were actually preparing a banquet in his honour. Christopher himself was sitting in one of his *seicento* chairs, wagging his head like a disconsolate Doge who had received news that the Genoese had captured the Venetian fleet at Sapienza. Marian de Feltre, not grown less buxom in these four years, was walking up and down the already overcrowded gold and crimson room, waving a cigarette-holder that was nearly as dangerous as the point of a parasol and drawling over and over again:

"I knew it! I knew it, Uncle Chris! What did I tell you?"

But as Marian de Feltre always did know everything nobody paid any more attention to her than was necessary to avoid being blinded by her cigarette-holder.

Mrs. Neave, seated a little precariously on a heap of rich stuffs, was looking Sunday-afternoonish and flushed with guilt because she was dallying here at Mr. Goldfinch's when Joseph ought to be taking his medicine. During these four years Joseph had finished his translation of the *Inferno*, and being at last embarked upon the first canto of the *Purgatorio* he needed sedatives for his scholarly excitement. However, in spite of the way Joseph's medicine glass was tinkling reproachfully in her ears, she simply could not tear herself away from the thrills of this discussion. There were several other Americans present, the most conspicuous of whom was a large woman with a face the colour of raspberry fool, who was addressed almost obsequiously as 'Princess.' She was the daughter of something very rich in Chicago, and she had bought Prince Marlínsky for a husband as a spoilt child might buy an enormous Teddy Bear. Scratch a Russian and you find a Tartar. Prince Marlínsky was a Russian who had been severely grazed all over. He was a huge creature with a head like a button, a squab nose, and little slanting eyes—a villain who had stepped straight out of a Sardou play and who would have seemed embarrassingly unreal in any room smaller than the stage of a theatre, if the way he thrust his overpowering masculinity upon everybody had not made him so embarrassingly real. This rastaquouère of the steppes spoke English like a Chicago gunman; but Goldfinch, who was dazzled by his wife's money, treated him as if he were Jenghiz Khan himself and was inclined to fawn upon his blatant denunciation of the wanderer's return. Indeed, if the anti-Marsac faction had not been warned by the fiasco of Aston Duplock's labours on an earlier occasion they might have supposed the Prince capable of giving the Count a jolly good knouting in the Piazza and dragging him off by the ear to Siberia.

"Hell, if we had a skunk like that in Sheecawgo," said the Prince ferociously, "he'd be tarred and feathered and flung into Lake Michigan."

"I believe you," Goldfinch croaked as reverently as if Chicago shared with republican Rome a moral grandeur never attained by any other city, as if indeed this Tartar adventurer were a second Cato demanding the deletion of Carthage.

"That's the plain truth, isn't it, honny?" the Prince added, turning to his wife, whose flabby face wobbled affirmatively while her lack-lustre pale blue eyes tried to concentrate upon fixing a date for bridge with Marian de Feltre.

"My opinion is that any man who speaks to any so-called man who speaks to this vile brute is only a so-called man himself," Marlínsky challenged. And like the tuba entering a symphony a deep "hear hear" rumbled from the corner of the room where Herbert Bookham was sitting upon a damasked tabouret between Christopher's broken-nosed Diana and a bright young American who had lost Assisi on her way down through Italy and was hoping to pick it up if only for half an hour on her way back to Paris.

"Of course, I don't expect to do everything in Europe, Mr. Bookham. But I did feel peeved that I missed Assisi. And it was all the fault of that silly porter at the hotel in Perugia. You see, when my friend and I reached Rome we found we had an extra half-day, and I said, 'Why, my dear, we've missed some place or other on the road,' and she said, 'Was it Assisi, Clarice?' and I said, 'Oh, my dear, it surely was,' and then we just sat and looked at one another."

"I'll plan out your journey back," Bookham offered. "You're jolly well not going to miss Assisi again. But to make absolutely sure I'll underline it in red ink."

"Oh now, isn't that too terribly nice of you, Mr. Bookham. Why, I think that's most terribly kind. You know I always used to hear that British people were so stand-offish. But I haven't found that at all. Not at all. But of course one of my father's grandmothers was British, so I daresay I understand British ways better than most Americans."

Bookham was on the verge of daring to observe that blood was thicker than water when Marlínsky's raucous truculence broke out anew.

"I've been talking to Arturo Westall," he said. "And he tells me that the whole island is mad at the idea of this beastly degenerate coming back."

And then the Prince became abruptly silent, because the Princess was looking at him. The Prince knew that the Princess was thinking that Arturo Westall had a good-looking and attractive wife, and he decided in view of the fact that she had recently made two heavy reductions in his allowance to say no more about Arturo Westall or visits to the Anglo-American Stores.

"I've been talking to Alberto and Enrico Jones," he continued, "and, by gard, they're feeling mighty sore."

"You bet your life they are," Goldfinch croaked. "Still, there's none of our bunch will have anything to do with him, and I guess we can make it pretty clear to the Sirenesi what *we* think of Marsac and his friends."

Harry Menteith looked across at the old painter from screwed-up eyes.

"Harry, I suppose it means your giving up your friends at the Amabile," Christopher went on.

The eyes of the bunch were upon Harry Menteith. The slave that is moulded by democracy cringed.

"I guess it does, Goldfinch," he said, blinking.

The old romantic smiled a rich paternal benison.

"My gad, he's a great boy," he murmured to Mrs. Neave. "The finest chap we've had on the island for years. I wish he and Angela would make a match of it."

Mrs. Neave's eyes lighted up.

"Why, Mr. Goldfinch, I think that's a perfectly stunning idea."

"They'd certainly make a great pair," the painter croaked fondly. "By the way, did I tell you I'm expecting a cable from Sheila every day? I reckon she'll be here by mid-July at latest."

When Harry Menteith went home that afternoon, he bit his fingers for a long time over the letter he had to write to Miss Virginia; and in the end he sent the very excuses that were most likely to enrage the old lady. He took two pages to set forth the reasons why he as an individual had no objection whatever to assisting at the dinner of welcome to the Count and then another two pages to explain the reasons why he must consider the feelings of his friends in the matter. After this he suggested as a compromise that he would meet Marsac casually at the Amabile if Miss Virginia would see his point of view about not joining in a formal celebration of the Count's return.

The old lady read this letter and rang the bell.

"Agostino," she said to the fat dough-faced olive-green boy of sixteen who answered her summons. "Portare via quello pictura subito!"

Agostino was not so bright as his brothers and sisters had been at understanding the Italian of the *signorina*. He looked round the *salone* for an offending pot of paint.

"What a great stupido you are, Agostino. La pictura on the—oh, where's the signorina Maimie?—what's wall? O Agostino, if you aren't the stupidest boy I ever did know. Qui! Qui! Ecco, idiot!" She dragged him across to the picture of Celia and Evadne Monteith on that sunny Amabile terrace.

"Portare via questa cosa. Can't you capito what I'm telling you, you silly boy?"

"*E dove debbo portarlo, signorina?*" Agostino asked, his lips quivering, tears of fright in his big eyes.

"To Signor Menteith of course. And take this biglietto, and niente risposta!"

She sat down at a Gothic bureau enamelled in white and dashed off an excommunication of Harry Menteith and of the two little girls who had been such a joy to her.

The young painter at once sent Miss Virginia a cheque for the money he had received for the picture. Although her own impulse was to tear this up, at Miss Maimie's instigation she paid it into her bank.

Four years had passed away; but those four years had not changed Miss Maimie.

Chapter 2

*solliciti sunt pro nobis, quibus illa doloris
ne cedam ignoto maxima causa toro.*

TIBULLUS

MARSAC came back to Sirene looking younger and more debonair than ever. He was now thirty-two or thirty-three, and he genuinely appeared ten years less. People began to wonder if after all there was not some elixir of youth distilled from the poppies of Benares, of Java and of Yurmam; but when they turned to Carlo they were doubtful. Carlo had aged a great deal more than four years. In fact he looked older than Marsac now, with his puffiness and sallowness and heavily-ringed eyes. On him the poppies of Benares, of Java and of Yurmam had evidently exercised a most deleterious effect, and in spite of Marsac's voluble praise of opium people were not convinced that they wanted to go to the expense of becoming slaves to it for the sake of the intellectual aloofness he promised them. However, Carlo revived rapidly in the airs of his own country, and he was a great success at the dinner of welcome, at which he sat next Phyllis Allerton and held her hand under the table whenever he had an opportunity. Mrs. Ambrogio, who was on the other side, declared that he held *her* hand too.

"Held it and squeezed it and tickled my knee," she vowed, but not in the hearing of the old ladies.

The dinner of welcome recalled the glories of the Villa Amabile in its palmiest days. The table was as long as it was on the night of the Christmas party before the Nortons quarrelled with any of their friends over the guest of honour to-night. Yet the occasion lacked something of the spirit of the old gatherings, because more than half of those present were visitors to Sirene for the season only. Jokes had to be explained and allusions to old Sirenian histories elaborated for the benefit of these semi-strangers; and when Effie Macadam began one of her ritual dances she had to be restrained, because it was felt that some of the guests might not understand that for Effie to lift her skirts above her knees and try to kick as high as Diana in the popular song of her youth's heyday did not imply a low standard of feminine morality all over the island. In order to do exceptional honour to dear Count Bob the old ladies had invited several inappropriate people—a retired Indian civilian, the wife of a rural dean, the cousin of an American senator, a decayed German baroness, and the Honourable Cerulli himself, whose brief experience as a deputy helped him to face the torrent of Marsac's rhetoric without losing one mouthful of the excellent dinner. Miss Virginia took Mrs. Ambrogio aside and begged her to make herself responsible for Mrs. Macadam's behaviour until the party came to an end.

"When she looks as if she was going to begin dancing on her own, just lead her right out and introduce her to some nice dancing man, there's a good soul. We hate to stop anybody enjoying themselves as they'd like in the Amabile, but we noticed Signor Cerulli seemed just a little bit surprised when our dear Mrs. Macadam wanted to dance around the pineapple. And we just love to have her do it. Only we wouldn't want him to misunderstand our harmless fun after what he's done for us."

"Oh, you're so right! Wouldn't do at all. Italians do not understand a bit of fun. Climate too hot. I'll see she behaves herself. Peter! Peter! Vous venn ici,

Peter. Vous dance with Effie Macadam toute la swore. Vous comprong bang, Peter?"

"But, Mauda," the husband protested. "I do not wanta for dance with Effie all one evening. I have combined to dance with many ladies. *Io non voglio ballare sempre sempre con Effie. Non è ragionevole. Sei curiosa,* Mauda."

"Nong! Nong! Moi toojer raisins! Vous dance with Effie Macadam, Peter. Don't argue. And her skirts—vous comprong—her gonnas must rester bass. Nong dwar kick her legs on haut. Vous fais comme see, or moi furious."

"Oh wella, if I musta, I musta," said poor Peter sulkily. He had had a bad morning with the quails, and he now looked like missing all the girls to-night.

"Bravo! Multer contenter," his wife declared, and turning round to her neighbour, who happened to be the decayed German baroness, she fizzed enthusiastically, "I love my husband so much. Best husband in the world. Wouldn't exchange him for any other husband. Good Catholic, so can't divorce, but wouldn't if I could. Love the darling old Nortons too."

And while she was saying this Mrs. Ambrogio was screwing up her eyes and examining the Baroness's flaxen transformation so eagerly that the owner of it was afraid she was going to bite a mouthful out of it and kept interposing her lorgnette as a defence.

The whole evening might have passed off like a Sunday-school treat if Martel, the little Belgian hunchback, had not tried to kiss Phyllis while they were sitting out between dances on the slope above the big pergola that served as the ball-room.

"You kisses me, yes, I think with pleasure?" he suggested. "And I kisses you with grand heat I think, yes?"

"No, I'm dashed if you will," said Phyllis contemptuously.

"*Pardon*, mademoiselle. I imaginate such passions underneath of this moon."

"You can imagine what you like," said Phyllis. "But you're not going to kiss me."

"I take your lips with the force, I think. It excites much to take the lips with the force."

Whereupon he clasped Phyllis to him. She struggled hard, and the two of them losing their balance rolled down the bank on to the orange tiles of the pergola in full view of half the guests.

It was only her devotion to Mrs. Macdonnell that kept Miss Virginia from ordering Phyllis out of the house. And then Phyllis plunged herself deeper into disgrace by daring to flirt with Carlo.

"It is terrible to perceive the change in young girls, Miss Maimie, since I am travelling," Marsac observed, biting his lips with rage to see the way Carlo was waltzing with Phyllis.

"My dear boy, it's perfectly disgusting," she agreed. And as Phyllis and Carlo whirled past they heard her singing:

"Will you waltz with me all the night time?
Will you dance with me till the dawn?"

"*Ah, mais ça, c'est trop fort*," Marsac exclaimed, his cheeks crimsoning, his light blue eyes flashing.

And as the dancers drew near again on their circuit he interrupted Carlo, who was now singing himself as much of the couplet as he could manage to Phyllis.

"*Assez de cette valse ignoble*," he called sharply. "*Viens ici, Carlo.*"

The young man seemed inclined for a moment to pay no attention as he whirled on with Phyllis; but his courage soon wavered. Pleasant though it was to be back in Italy, the tails of that waiter's greasy coat flapped there much more audibly than in China. He made some excuse and with obvious unwillingness relinquished his charming young partner to join his protector. On his way, however, he was intercepted by Mrs. Macadam, who had escaped from the tutelage of Peter.

"Hullo, old dear!" she exclaimed. "I say, haven't you got a partner? What a shame! Come on, I'll see you through. Hold tight."

With this she seized the ephebus in her arms and swept him back into the dance.

"Cannon to right of them, cannon to left of them," Effie muttered grimly as she drove a path through the waltzers, dragging Carlo with her. "Coo! They don't mind bumping into you, do they?" she demanded indignantly when they had sent two couples spinning off the porcelain tiles of the pergola into the bushes beyond. "Serve 'em dam well right," she growled, tightening her lumbar muscles for the next onset. "Biff!" she jeered truculently as they dispatched a third couple into the outer darkness. "Any more, and I'm jolly well ready for 'em. This *is* the Blue Danube, isn't it? Dear old tune."

"*Alors, alors!*" cried Marsac, fuming.

But he might as well have tried to push Venus into the orbit of Mars as deflect Effie Macadam from her course; and when the last dreamy notes of the waltz died away she and her captive partner were all that was left of the dancers.

"Jolly fine waltz," she said. "But, I say, I've got a whopping bump on my behind. Toora-looral! I think I'll go and look for some butter." Then taking a run and uttering a loud whoop she slid over the last three yards of the pergola into the shadow of the house.

"*Tu es vraiment dégoûtant, tu sais,*" said Marsac severely to Carlo when he presented himself at last.

"*Mais, je ne pouvais faire rien, Robert,*" he protested. "*Elle m'a pris par force.*"

"If you cannot dance like a gentleman, *alors*, it would

be much more polished that you do not dance at all, *mon cher*."

Carlo flushed, and Miss Maimie taking pity on his mortification interceded.

"Don't be vexed with him, Bob. The poor boy meant no harm."

"But I assure you, my dear Miss Maimie, that I am excessively enraged. One does not conduct oneself in such a beastly fashion even at a ball of students."

"Now, it was all the fault of Phyllis Allerton," Miss Maimie urged. "And her poor aunt *is* such an admirer of yours. She declares that you are far and away the most distinguished-looking man she ever met."

"Mrs. Macdonnell is, doubtless, a most excellent woman; but I find that her niece is nothing more than an impudent *gigolette*."

"She's all that and more," affirmed Miss Maimie, who had not the least idea what a *gigolette* was. "But don't let a silly little flippertigibbet like that spoil your evening, my dear boy," she pleaded, laying a hand on his arm. "We do so want this to be the first of lots of lovely evenings."

At this moment Effie, who had completely shaken off Peter Ambrogio, came sliding back across the pergola.

"Hullo," she exclaimed, pulling up short and fixing the Count with a slightly glassy stare. "You've been to China, haven't you?"

He bowed.

"So have I, old sport," she said; and then rushing up to Ibsen, the ladylike Norwegian, she seized him in her arms and began a violent polka, although the orchestra was indoors partaking of light refreshment and every instrument was mute.

Mrs. Ambrogio was summoned to reason with Effie.

"Furious with Peter," she spluttered. "Told him to dance with Mrs. Macadam all the evening. Where is he?

Peter! Peter! Vous venn soobiter! Too sweet! Soobiter! Vous venn too sweet, Peter, when I call you."

But Peter was panting after Miss Hannah Bilton up and down the shady slopes of the Amabile garden. Peter was hoping to live his little hour, come what might in the way of a conjugal argument on the way back to the Villa Botticelli. It is true that Hannah was much too thin for his taste, but what she lacked in acreage she made up for by accessibility.

"I wouldn't trust that woman a yard," Mrs. Ambrogio declared to Effie Macadam when about ten minutes later Peter and Hannah emerged from the shadows. "Wish I dared tell the dear old Nortons what she is. Not a bit jealous. Don't know what jealousy is. But I can't stand deceit and lies. That woman's a prostitute."

"Where?" asked Effie, fixing with a glassy stare of the sternest propriety the wife of the rural dean.

"Give anything to be able to tell the darling old Nortons that she is not to be trusted with men. Wouldn't trust her with a man on top of an iceberg."

"Look here, Maud," said Effie fiercely. "Do you want the Nortons to know about her?"

"Give anything! Give anything to show her up," Mrs. Ambrogio fizzed.

"Well, I'll go and tell them for you that she's a prostitute," Effie volunteered in the accents of one who was ready to do anything for an old friend. "*I* don't mind. Only which is she? That's all I want to know."

"Don't be an ass, Effie," Mrs. Ambrogio cried apprehensively. "Come back! Miss Virginia would never forgive me. Come back, I tell you. Here, for goodness sake come and have a drink."

"Oh, all right, old sport. Anything to oblige. But I don't mind telling *any*body she's a prostitute. Well, I mean to say, if it's true, what of it? I'm always jolly downright. That's one thing about me."

"I know you are, Effie. I know you are. But do come away."

Mrs. Ambrogio was genuinely alarmed. She had visions of a Norton excommunication launched against her and of Peter's losing the conduct of Marsac's legal affairs, such was the hold that the Bilton girls were supposed to possess over the two old ladies. And indeed it was not until the gate of the Villa Botticelli clanged behind herself and Peter at half-past four next morning that she ventured to reproach him for his behaviour with Miss Hannah.

"But, Mauda, permit to me if you please that I speaka one word. If I take one young lady for promenade the garden, I musta not to make the love with her for that."

"You did make love to her! You did! You did! I know the look on your face. Lies. Lies. Lies. Oh, thank God I'm not a jealous woman!"

Peter shrugged his shoulders and followed his wife indoors, with the prospect of very little repose before he must rise again in order to water his seedlings in the fresh morning air.

The anti-Marsac faction did not derive much serviceable scandal from that first dinner-party. However anxious they might be to declare it an orgy, it was difficult to persuade even the most credulous that the wife of a rural dean or the cousin of an American senator had assisted at such a style of entertainment. Prince Marlínsky might swagger around and, with intermittent ogling of anything that wore a skirt, call down fire and brimstone upon Sirene for its toleration of a Marsac; but he became a bore with his creased flannel trousers and his too demonstrative red bathing-suit. One heard him coming round the corner and turned the other way as one turns to avoid an unpleasant wind. And by the middle of the Summer all that one thought about Prince Marlínsky was a vague astonishment that he had escaped the Chicago stock-yards and managed to return to Europe outside a tin. There was a sigh of relief when he and the Princess left for Paris in the Autumn.

Marsac himself had learnt during his exile to be much more circumspect; or perhaps it was that opium had by now obtained such a hold over him that he had no superfluous exuberance left. At any rate, the parties at the Villa Hylas, to which the old ladies never failed to ride up from the Piazza on their white donkeys beneath scarlet parasols, were nowadays those of a dignified recluse and bore no kind of resemblance to the fantastic routs of other days. The host himself affected the air of a man who had seen and suffered much and only wished now to cry with Horace: *Hoc erat in votis*. To his guests he tried to convey an impression that in saturating himself with opium he had at the same time saturated himself with the wisdom of the East. He talked as incessantly as ever; but people were usually so tired by the long walk up to the Villa in the sun that they did not want to talk themselves and were quite glad to loll back in comfortable chairs, sipping exquisite China tea and listening to their host's incoherent philosophy. And when they were rested Miss Maimie used to show them round the villa, pointing out the various treasures and the portraits of the Count's ancestors, and even contriving by the low note of reverence in her voice to give an effect of religious frescoes to the huge pictures of sunburnt naked young men riding over the fiery terra-cotta landscape that swore so at the Aubusson carpet in the marble hall.

The trees had grown apace in those four years of assiduous watering by Gigi, so fast indeed that Gigi was always begging his employer to be allowed to thin them out. This was sternly forbidden; and, when the guests were led in single file along the overgrown paths, they used to hear as the twigs stung their faces denunciations, from Marsac in front and from Miss Maimie in the rear, of the iniquities of Sirenian pruning-hooks. The two of them spoke of the horticultural atrocities of Sirenian gardeners with the warmth of intellectual humanitarians condemning Armenian massacres.

"Our dear friend Count Marsac will not have his gardener touch a single twig," Miss Maimie would explain proudly to some visitor who was unskewering his cheek from the dead boughs of an acacia.

"Ah yes," Marsac's voice would be heard from the head of the column. "I prohibit absolutely my gardener to cut even the dead woods from my trees, because they are such rascals that all at once, I assure you, madame, I would behold a desert in my garden, which would be excessively disagreeable."

In justice to the anti-Marsac faction, which made the most of them as orgies, it may be admitted that the Count did on several occasions that Summer allow his guests to try for themselves the pleasures of opium.

It began by an argument between Mrs. Ambrogio and Mrs. Macadam. Effie, who did not feel that she was having the success at these afternoons which she was inclined to believe was her prerogative nowadays, observed to Mrs. Ambrogio:

"Here, what's all this about an opium den, Maud? Why, I've seen hundreds when Archie and I were in China."

"Yes, but you've never smoked it," Mrs. Ambrogio insisted.

"Of course I have. Hundreds of times," declared Effie.

"Don't believe it. Don't believe it. Don't believe you ever did."

"Pooh! There's nothing in that," said Effie loftily. "Not if you've been in China like I have."

"Did you have dreams?" Mrs. Ambrogio demanded.

"What do *you* think! Dreams and realities too, my dear woman, if it comes to that."

"Oh, I *don't* believe you. What colour were they?"

"Why, pink of course. What colour would you expect a reality to be?"

"Yellow. Yellow. Yellow. Yellow," Mrs. Ambrogio contradicted.

"Shut up," jeered Effie.

"I dare you to ask the Count to let you smoke a pipe this afternoon."

Effie at once took up the challenge and was sick. Then Mrs. Ambrogio tried a pipe and was not sick; on the other hand she burned a hole in one of Marsac's Persian rugs.

And then Mrs. Macdonnell announced that she was going to smoke. Vesuvius could not have announced one of his own eruptions more importantly.

"My delightful aunt," Phyllis murmured to Carlo. "I hope *she's* sick."

Carlo squeezed her hand encouragingly.

"Tell me, Count Marsac," Mrs. Macdonnell rolled out, "what drreams may I expect? I feel like Cleopatrra!"

She was led to a divan and invited to sit cross-legged, an attitude that gave her the look of a cornflour shape into which the cook had put too much cochineal. Of course, Phyllis had to smoke too; and historical honesty demands that it should be set on record that she was abominably sick on the Count's marble staircase. Legend, however, declares that it was Mrs. Macdonnell who was sick; and the responsibility for that legend must rest on Phyllis who, with Mrs. Ambrogio's help, used the evidence of her own weakness as the proof of her aunt's.

All this must sound most disgusting to fastidious readers, who will agree with the anti-Marsac faction in reprobating such orgies and in considering that the good manners of the Count's partisans had been corrupted by his evil communications.

Presently, however, these excesses were forgotten in the startling news that in the month of October the Nortons and the Biltons were going to accompany Marsac and Carlo to the East and return by way of Japan and Honolulu to America.

So much for the people who said that Miss Virginia (she was now at least eighty) was beginning to break up. Even Christopher Goldfinch and the ranks of Tuscany he commanded with such cinquecento picturesqueness could scarcely forbear to cheer.

"The Wandering Jew becomes almost credible after this," Major Natt grunted painfully. "The Flying Dutchman is no longer a myth."

"By gad," said Christopher, "those old women are . . ." But he lacked the Major's sesquipedalian vocabulary. He had no word long enough, and he could only express his amazement in an immense and (thanks to his magnificent false teeth) a most decorative gape.

"I think I'll cross over myself, Natt," he added. "It seems that Sheila's too busy to get over here this Winter. I want to have an exhibition in New York, and look up a few old friends before they die. And then I want to buy some new clothes. Yes, I think I'll sail in October."

And so he did, just a week before the old ladies set out for home the other way round.

Even those most bitterly prejudiced against the Count admitted that the proposed trip did him credit. Whatever his behaviour might have been in the past, he was showing most unmistakably his appreciation of the battle the old ladies had fought for his name. And it was no light task he had undertaken. Annam, Cambodia, Cochin-China, Siam. And Miss Virginia was talking gaily of exploring the lot on the back of an elephant!

"My sister and I are just pining to see all the wonderful places our dear boys have told us so much about. We're going right away into the jungle to explore all those old ruined temples and I don't know what not. Oh, we're just mad to be on our way. And then we're going to take a peep at mysterious China and the cunning little Japs, where we shall leave the boys and sail over the great bounding blue Pacific to lovely Honolulu and from Honolulu to romantic old Frisco, and from there we'll visit the state of Idaho for tiresome grubby old business, and then through our own great wonderful country to Philadelphia and New York and back to our own sunny wee island next May in time to shower the golden broom on our dear old silver saint. And there's only one thing that frets me, and that is what we'll do with Agostino while we're away."

Fat Agostino, in spite of her occasional impatience with his stupidity, was dear to Miss Virginia's heart. He was the youngest of the family she had bought with the original little triple-domed cottage twenty-five years ago; and, though he was now sixteen, he still seemed to her the same fat little boy who at eight years old had been handing round cakes at tea, his eyes a-goggle with responsibility, and still liable to burst the seat of his trousers as he had been bursting them at intervals ever since he first wore the white sailor suits that were the Norton livery.

"I wouldn't have him fall into lazy habits when he's just beginning to grow up," she confided to Mrs. Macdonnell who, now that Phyllis had at last gone back to England, had enjoyed making the old ladies conclude that her niece was even more wicked than they had believed her. "I wish one of our dear friends would have him to help in the house while we're a-wandering."

"That's the very thing the boy needs," Mrs. Macdonnell agreed warmly. "You're quite right, Miss Virrginia. He needs a good home and a firrm hand."

But she did not offer to supply either of them herself, as Miss Virginia hoped she might. In the end it was Mrs. Ambrogio who made herself responsible for Agostino.

And Agostino had almost as adventurous a Winter as his old mistresses.

The first day he waited at lunch in the Villa Botticelli

coincided with the moment for his trousers to crack like a lobster's carapace.

"Went off like a cannon," Mrs. Ambrogio related to Scudamore. "How I laughed! Upset the spaghetti all over Peter. Poor dear boy. So mortificarter! How I laughed! Like a cannon."

> "*Nam displosa sonat quantum vesica pepedi
> diffissa nate,*"

Scudamore quoted from a satire of Horace. Mrs. Ambrogio was almost the only woman in Sirene whom Nita allowed to frequent the scholar's company.

"Don't know what you're saying, but sure it's rude. Wish I had brains like you. Do nothing but read naughty books all day if I had. Lucky man. How I envy you!"

"Well, perhaps it is not translatable with perfect politeness," the scholar nodded solemnly.

"Knew it. Knew it. Knew it. Knew it!" Mrs. Ambrogio triumphed. "Wish I knew Latin. Only know Ave Maria. Hunted. No education."

Soon after the disaster at lunch Agostino took a charcoal brazier up to his bedroom and omitted to open the windows.

"Found him in the morning bright green. Gave me such a turn. Shook him with all my might and he staggered like a dead man. Green. Staggering. Bright green. Like grass. Staggering. Tongue green. And the poor dear boy had tied pink ribbons to the handle of his brush and pink ribbons round his looking-glass. Bless his heart! Wouldn't have him die for anything. Ribbons don't mean he's one of those. Learnt to tie pink ribbons round everything for the dear old Nortons. Sure he's a perfectly good boy. Won't ask Mr. Burlingham to lunch again. Staring at him all the time."

After Agostino had recovered from the brazier, he quarrelled with an enormous maid of Mrs. Ambrogio's called Caterina.

"Came sobbing to me this morning after breakfast and said Caterina had called him an orangatang. Sent for her and told her she wasn't to call him an orangatang again, and when he went down to the kitchen she called him a mandriller and pulled his nose. How the poor boy cried! Bellowed like a bull. Peter was furious. Had the sindaco in his office on important business. Bellowing sounded all over the house. Sindaco white as death. Most nervous man. Thought he saw his brother knocked down by a tram in Naples, and nervous ever since. Wasn't his brother after all, but just as nervous. Shook like a jelly. White as a jelly. Business impossible. Told Peter to speak to Caterina. Frightened to say a word. *Knew* he'd been making love to her."

Shortly after this Caterina, carrying a large tray, was overcome by faintness and contrived somehow, though it was never quite clear exactly how, to faint on top of Agostino.

"Flat as a pancake," Mrs. Ambrogio related. "Dragged him out from underneath as flat as a pancake. Nothing but fat. Fat goes flat like that. Shows you how cunning these Italians are. Watched for the chance, and fainted right on top of him. Buried underneath her. Enormous woman. Bones like scaffolding. Couldn't see Agostino. Thought it was Caterina groaning. Flung water over her and found it was Agostino. Caterina never said a word. Such a good servant! Get rid of her otherwise. Not safe for Peter. Sprain his ankle making love to her one of these days. Know he will."

Finally Agostino was involved with another man's wife. This was Carmelina, the mother of fourteen children, and soon to become the mother of a fifteenth, who came in twice a week to do rough cleaning at the Villa Botticelli. Pasquale, her husband, who by the way was a son of 'O Gobbetto, the original owner of Marsac's land, and if possible more like a gnome than his father, worked in Peter's garden. He conceived the idea that Agostino was trying to seduce his wife, and one evening when the Ambrogios were out at a dinner-party he arrived at the villa armed with a knife. It may be that Caterina had fed the fire of the dwarf's jealousy. At any rate she warned Agostino that his last hour had come. Agostino gave a shriek and fled for sanctuary to the Villa Amabile, pursued by the infuriated husband. In spite of continuing to shriek all the way down the steps to the Grande Marina he eluded his pursuer and reached the protection of his family, from which he refused to stir for the rest of the Winter.

"Won't come back," Mrs. Ambrogio related. "Went down and told Micheluccio his father that Peter had made everything all right with Pasquale. No use. Hid under the bed when I arrived. Done my best. Can't help it. Dear old Nortons in Kitchen-China. Catchin-China. Never could learn geography. Somewhere in China. Had a postcard from them this morning. Here it is. Read it if you like."

She presented to her audience a picture postcard of an avenue of gigantic idols in Cambodia. On the other side was written:

Wish you were here with us to revel in this wonderful place on elefant back. Our dear boys are well and happy, and our dear Bilton girls are a great joy to us. Loving messages from Virginia and Maimie Pepworth-Norton.

Nobody they cared for in Sirene was forgotten by the old ladies during their journey, and it was clear that Miss Virginia was as much in love with life as ever. One or two specially favoured friends like Mrs. Macdonnell received long letters from her, giving much fuller descriptions of what they were seeing than could be squeezed on to a postcard. Miss Virginia laid herself out to describe the tropical scene with the zest of a Pierre Loti, and what her adjectives lacked in colour they made up for with enthusiasm. Mrs. Macdonnell was so proud of these special letters that she gave tea-parties with really expensive cakes for the pleasure of sitting in a conflagration of cerise and carmine silk and rolling them out in public.

Nothing could give my sister and myself truer joy and happiness than the sweet thoughtfulness of our two dear boys, wrote Miss Virginia. *We are sorry for the poor folks who have not had the advantages of seeing the wonders and glories of this grand old earth of ours in such company. Dear Count Bob is a " mine of information," so that we feel as though we had gotten the " gorgeous East" in our blood, and all these wonderful old legends seem just as real as they can be. Our beloved Bilton girls grow nearer and dearer to us every day. We are proud to show them to the dear natives as the best type of our fine American womanhood. Next week we are giving a real Sirene lunch-party to our friend the King, who has been so polite to us. The more we see of this " dreamland " of " gorgeous romance " the more sorry we feel for the ignorance and wickedness of some Sirene folks.*

"It's grrand to think that the dear Count has shown himself sans peurr and sans reprroche," Mrs. Macdonnell proclaimed. "But I always say that brreeding will out."

After this letter came postcards from Macao and Shanghai; and then there was a silence, until from Yokohama the following postcard reached Sirene:

Here we are with our dear boys amid the fairy blossoms of lovely Japan. The Misses Bilton left for San Francisco yesterday.

Virginia and Maimie Pepworth-Norton

Nobody in Sirene had the least doubt after the damning formality of that reference to the Biltons that there had been a serious quarrel, and the next letter from the old ladies was awaited with excitement. But when it arrived a month later from Honolulu, there was no word in its pages about the Biltons, nothing but raptures over Waikiki and scarlet hibiscus flowers, with regrets that their dear boys were no longer with them to enjoy the beauties of a land that rivalled even Sirene as a setting for human mirth and happiness, those and 'aloha' to all their dear friends in 'sweet sunny Italy.'

Mrs. Ambrogio was jubilantly convinced that the Nortons had caught Miss Hannah out at last, though the details of the scandalous exposure varied with each fresh narration too flagrantly even for Sirene to accept them as authoritative, in spite of the fact that Mrs. Ambrogio within a week was claiming that she had actually had a letter from Miss Virginia herself giving her all these details in the strictest confidence. Not even Sirene could swallow being told on Tuesday that Hannah had spent the week-end in the harem of a hospitable potentate, on Wednesday that she had gone to Marsac's bedroom in mistake for Carlo's, and on Thursday that the whole trouble had occurred through her familiarity with the Chinese coolies. These discrepancies were too much even for Effie Macadam.

"I say, steady on, Maud. Here, have you ever seen a Chinese coolie?"

"Seen everything. Seen everything. Lived in Paris for ten years. Look through a hole in the wall and see everything. Worst woman in the world. Worse than the worst in Paris. Do any mortal thing. Vilest creature I ever knew. Heard all about her from Peter. Looked him straight in the face and he told me everything. So glad the dear old Nortons have found her out at last. Never went wrong myself. Missed it by inches lots of times. But always thought of my dear old father and kept straight."

"Good lord, I wouldn't have thought of him. I always thought of what might happen," said Effie.

"Never thought of that in my life. Go over anything. Take any gate anywhere. Just the same when I loved a man. Dozens of men in love with me. When I was a girl no man could be in the room with me alone for two minutes without trying to make love to me. Upset tables and chairs. All rubbish about temptation. No girl need be tempted unless she enjoys it. Never tempted in my life."

Mrs. Ambrogio may have been inaccurate in her details; but she correctly divined the fundamental reason for the quarrel, which was in fact created by Miss Hannah's behaviour. Miss Hannah began to find that the tropics were becoming too much for her feelings. Simultaneously Carlo began to find that without the anaphrodisiac effect of opium (the old ladies' energetic explorations did not allow the requisite leisure for smoking) the tropics were becoming too much for *his* feelings. What Madame Protopopesco had been able to achieve in the middle of an unusually cold winter for the South of Europe it was evident that Miss Hannah was not going to muff in the demoralizing atmosphere of Macao. But Carlo's protector was on the alert. He dropped his napkin one night at dinner, and in bending down to pick it up the blood must have rushed to his head, for when he appeared above the table again his cheeks were crimson and his nostrils were dilating.

"Now, my dear Bob, you ought not to exert yourself like that in this heat," Miss Maimie scolded gently. "See, you've quite frightened poor Carlo."

And Carlo certainly was extremely pale.

"I assure you it is nothing, my dear Miss Maimie," said Marsac, taking from his pocket a small bottle of salts and sniffing them, his eyes closed. "I feel myself already perfectly recuperated."

During the voyage to Japan the Count was gloomy, and Carlo whom he had forbidden to walk about the deck with Miss Hannah was very ill from the effect of a stuffy cabin in the China Sea. By the time they reached Yokohama the Count was saturnine.

"Whatever can be the matter with our dear Bob?" Miss Virginia asked her sister. "You don't think he's caught one of those dreadful tropical illnesses?"

VESTAL FIRE

Miss Maimie much agitated pressed Marsac on the subject of his health.

"I am sick of my heart, my dear Miss Maimie; I have suffered again a most disgusting arousement to human abominations. I am the most disillusionated poor devil who is now living. All which I cherish has turned to hashes."

"Why, Bob, tell me what it is. I can't bear to have you suffer like this."

Whereupon Marsac after a little more persuasion told Miss Maimie that Miss Hannah having successfully seduced Carlo was now trying to seduce himself. There was another version current that Marsac accused the elder of the two Biltons of attempting his own virtue. Anyway, whatever he said sealed the doom of both the dear Bilton girls.

The next morning Miss Virginia with a document under her arm marched into the private sitting-room of the Yokohama hotel, where Miss Rachel and Miss Hannah were talking about the beauties of Japan. To their surprise Miss Virginia proceeded to tear up into small fragments the document she carried, and that with such a fever of energy and such an expression of malevolence as turned surprise into alarm.

"You miserable ordinary creatures!" the old lady shrilled. "And if I could tear the pair of you up as easily, I certainly would. That paper was my will. You were written down in it to inherit all I possess one day. And oh, dear heaven, aren't I glad I've found out the kind of women you are before it was too late to start kicking myself for being such a silly old fool as I have been? There's a steamship for San Francisco sails to-morrow. Take it, and never let me see either of your shameless faces ever again."

And thus Miss Virginia shooed the Biltons out of her life as she might have shooed from a drawing-room a pair of cats which had been misconducting themselves.

It must have been difficult for Mrs. Ambrogio not to tell

the old ladies, when they came home and took a few of their dearest friends into their confidence, that she had known all along what Hannah Bilton was. That she was able to refrain may have been due to the reflection that once more the old ladies were unencumbered by heirs with all that such an open state of affairs might one day mean.

Marsac arrived back in Sirene about the tenth of May bringing with him, besides his own store of luggage, which included several trunks crammed with enough opium in purple boxes from Saïgon to last him for years, not to mention case after case of additions to his own oriental collection and a Siamese kitten, all the trunks that the old ladies had filled with their purchases during those wonderful months.

Christopher Goldfinch reached Sirene about the same time. He had had, all his friends were delighted to hear, a very successful exhibition, though somehow he had not managed to sell as many of his larger canvases as he had expected.

" But my pastels of Vesuvius went remarkably well. You know the one I call *What the Painter Saw*, the one where I've ventured to give my imagination a little play and filled the smoke coming out of the crater with mysterious shapes of nymphs ? Rather charming studies from the nude, most of them. By gad, they went great ! I used to work away up in Sheila's studio, and I did over fifty of that particular one for commissions. But the larger canvases didn't sell so well. No, not quite so well. It's this darned life they lead nowadays in apartment houses. By gad, they've no time to look at a large canvas. Still, I had a fine crowd to see my work, and it was enormously admired."

As a matter of fact it was Christopher himself who had been so much admired. He appeared on Broadway like the last of the Mohicans. The people of New York had had no idea that they possessed such a fine Tennysonian antique. He made them feel that their culture was a great deal older than English lecturers had allowed them to suppose. With the slightest encouragement they would have put him in the Bronx Zoo, and when he was dead stuffed him and set him up under a glass case in the Metropolitan Museum.

The old ladies themselves came back a fortnight later; and after a week of unpacking they invited everybody down to the Villa Amabile for the celebration of San Mercurio and a view of the lovely things they had brought back from the East.

Agostino had not even yet fully recovered from the fright Pasquale had given him; but he lost some of the sympathy that Miss Virginia might have felt by dropping a gilded Buddha on her toes while they were arranging the trophies of their Odyssey.

"Poor boy, he's so clumsy," she exclaimed to Mrs. Ambrogio as she limped round the *salone*, fanning herself with one of the many exquisite Chinese fans she had brought back. "I know he can't help it, but I'm afraid he must have been a great nuisance to you, dear Mrs. Ambrogio."

"So relieved, didn't know what to say," Mrs. Ambrogio related. "Dreadfully afraid she'd be furious over Agostino's running away. But the dear boy dropped an idol on her toes and made her forget all about it. So glad the poor old pet had something to take her mind off other things. Always say Sirene never the same without the darling old Nortons. Love them! Love them! So does Peter. Brought him back a walking-stick made of banana wood from the Straight Settlement. Wouldn't use it for anything. Hung it up over his desk. Went everywhere. Heart of the jungle, and gave me a shawl. Took it to old Cataldo and he said he'd give me five hundred liras for it whenever I wanted to sell it. Wouldn't sell it for anything. Love the old pets too much. Heart of the jungle. Brought back dear old Burlingham two dried-up Dryaks' heads. Put them in a china bowl. Looked like two old men in a bath. Showed them to everybody, and his cook had hysterics. Covers them up now and only shows them to his friends. India. China. Siamese. Japan. San Frisco. Grand Cannon. Everywhere. Two Bilton women drunk every night. So glad. Good riddance. Everything merry and bright at last. Miss Virginia younger than ever. So thin. Didn't feel the heat. Love my shawl so much. Only wish Mrs. Macdonald was dead."

There are few more dismal experiences that humanity can be called upon to endure than being shown the trophies of a voyage round the world, and it is seldom anything but an aggravation rather than a mitigation of the ordeal to be presented with a souvenir from this kind of compulsory museum. Yet when the roses and broom had been showered upon San Mercurio's venerable head and the guests gathered in the big *salone* for tea found that between every spoonful of praliné ice they were expected to admire a mandarin's robe held up by Miss Maimie or a set of ivory chessmen proffered by Miss Virginia, such was the infectious zest of the two old ladies in their voyage, there was not one of those present at the Amabile that golden afternoon who wilted even when after tea, instead of strolling out on the shady terrace and drinking whisky and soda as usual, he had to stand in a group and try to think of a fresh adjective expressing polite appreciation. It was even possible, so much did the old ladies manage to communicate of their own joy and pride in him, to tolerate Marsac's running commentary on the exhibits and his confidential revelations aside that most of what his dear friends had bought had been bought against his own advice.

"I regret excessively that so much of all these charming things are of no value to a connoisseur," he would whisper. "The jade is nearly all of it of an excessively inferior quality. Lamentably they were resolute to buy what was pleasing to them without regard to taste. I made all my force to prevent their expensiveness on little nothings, but they were excessively obstinated."

There was indeed that afternoon the breath of an argument between Marsac and Miss Virginia over a missing trunk of their treasures, which had gone astray on the voyage home.

"I assure you that I have made the most minutious enquiries at the *douane* at Naples, my dear Miss Virginia," he protested. "And there are no words of your trunk. Carlo has made a grand search equally, but alas, without success."

"Well, I guess it was left behind," said Miss Virginia, fanning away as hard as she could at the faint pink spot of irritation on her cheeks.

"Allow me to say that I do not think so, my dear Miss Virginia," Marsac contradicted.

"Well, my dear boy, either it was left behind or it's in Naples now."

And Miss Maimie, looking anxiously across at her sister and perceiving that she was on tenterhooks trying to keep from an explosion, came hurriedly along with a mandarin's robe of turquoise blue embroidered with rose and coral flowers and with crimson birds; and with this she draped the old lady's shoulders, which were beginning to wriggle in the way they did when she was on the verge of losing her temper.

"Ye look grrand, Miss Virrginia," declared Mrs. Macdonnell. "Ye have the real impeerrial air."

And then, of course, Mrs. Macdonnell had to be dressed in a mandarin's robe, in which she stalked about the room looking like the Widow Twankay as portrayed by a beefy comedian in a pantomime.

"I will drream to-night that I am an Easterrn Prrincess," she avowed.

"The woman's a damned fool," muttered Mrs. Ambrogio.

"Damned idiot," responded Mrs. Macadam.

Thus, through Miss Maimie's anxious tact, the argument over the missing trunk was forgotten and nothing jarred upon the serenity of the assembled company when, exhausted by the praise of oriental fabrics and ware and the attempt to say something new and sensible about native curios, they lolled upon the shady terrace and sipped crême de menthe frappé or whisky and soda, watching a world enambered.

A world enambered indeed, a world now lost and as if it never was except in the mirage of a painting by Turner or Claude . . . and four weeks later, on a breathless June day when the island glittered like a sorcerer's palace through a haze of blue and silver, when it towered in a hush of dreams from a sea as calm and lucid as a gem, there was a murmur that the Archduke Franz Ferdinand had been assassinated at Serajevo. And it seemed of such slight importance in that exquisite weather.

Chapter 3

nunc ad bella trahor . . .
quis furor est atram bellis accersere Mortem?

TIBULLUS

DURING that Summer and Autumn of 1914 the dogs of war barked nowhere on Sirene so fiercely as they barked and growled and yapped in the Villa Amabile and in the Villa Adonis. The English and the German residents were too uneasily aware of being the guests of a country which, although neutral for the time being, might at any moment emerge as a combatant on the opposite side. There were, indeed, several dignified and restrained demonstrations of patriotic emotion, as when Herbert Bookham appeared in the Piazza wearing a purple crape mourning-band for a sister-in-law's second cousin who had been killed in action, or as when Mrs. Ambrogio first gave the cut direct to Madame Minieri, the German wife of an Italian painter domiciled on Sirene these twenty years and more; but it may be claimed that nothing was done by the representatives of the warring nations to imperil or even to embarrass the neutrality of the country that was harbouring them. And let it be set on record that in Sirene at any rate Italian neutrality was most strictly watched. When one of the doyens of the English colony sent a telegram in code to his commission agent in London, putting a sovereign accumulator on three horses running at Newmarket, the Secret Service in Naples spent a fortnight in unravelling the mystery, so deeply did they suspect an attempt to revictual a submarine at the Piccola Marina; and in the room of two Russian exiles a samovar was arrested by the *carabinieri* on the charge of being a wireless equipment.

In the neutral villas of Christopher Goldfinch and the Pepworth-Nortons there was not a vestige of neutrality. If anybody had worse to say about the Huns than Miss Maimie, it was Christopher Goldfinch; and if anybody could outvie him in denunciations of American delay, it was Miss Virginia. Yet, though the war had brought these old antagonists spiritually closer than they had ever been, they remained as implacable toward one another as they were toward the Germans. And poor Christopher would have enjoyed himself so much down in the sympathetic atmosphere of Hun hatred at the Villa Amabile in those days when his other compatriots in Sirene were continually dismaying him by a callousness which they had the effrontery to exalt as cool judgment.

"Gad, I can't stand Scudamore's blasted pro-German talk," he groaned. "Here it is in the paper that they've just crucified twenty-five women in Belgium, and he has the impudence to tell me that he doesn't believe it. Gad, I believe those swine are capable of anything after what we know they have done already. Why aren't I ten years younger? I'd be right over in France by now. I tell you, Neave, I'm darned near ashamed to draw my pension."

Christopher was still receiving a few hundred dollars a year from Washington for the part he had played in defending the Union over fifty years ago.

"I'm quite as anxious as you are, Goldfinch, that our country should come in on the right side," Joseph affirmed. "But perhaps this isn't the moment."

"Not the moment?" the old romantic exploded. "Not the moment, when these filthy German brutes are slaughtering women and children every day? This comes of electing a blasted college professor President of the United States. I tell you, Neave, that big-mouthed Democrat is dragging the Stars and Stripes in the dust. Oh, why aren't I ten years younger? I'm just too old to do anything. I'm over eighty. I wouldn't be any good. I tell you, Neave, this is the toughest moment in all my life. And I fell downstairs again this morning. Just when I was thinking that perhaps after all I might do something for the Allies I fall down the blasted stairs. I tell you, Neave, not being able to handle a musket when I'm wanted has aged me twenty good years. And Jack Scudamore a pro-German! My gad, it's fierce!"

"But he isn't a pro-German. He's trying to keep an open mind and be reasonable," Joseph argued.

"Reasonable? Hell to being reasonable at such a time! You let loose a mob of ruffians all over Europe violating women and slaughtering children, and you have the nerve to talk about open minds and reason! If that's an open mind, give me an open drain. If that's reason, blast reason, say I, and blast everybody who talks about reason in these days."

With this the old man rattled his teeth in their plates and was even so far forgetful of his wonted courtliness as to cram his hat down over his white curly hair at a filibustering angle before he stalked out of Joseph's study in the Villino Paradiso.

Not only was Christopher unable to go to the war himself, but he seemed to have no friends by whose valour he could play a vicarious part in the struggle. It was humiliating.

The old ladies were informed of their enemy's anti-German feelings; but that did not make them the least bit more kindly disposed towards him.

"I guess he'll feel worse about it yet," declared Miss Virginia, "when our dear Bob who he's persecuted with his vile old tongue all these years leaves for the Front."

"Our dear boy," Miss Maimie murmured, the tears in her eyes. "But he'll come back to us safe. Right always wins in the end, sister."

"It surely does," Miss Virginia agreed; yet, something in the sweep of her fan, as she said this, might have tempted a cynic to suppose for an instant that she was not perfectly convinced of this proposition and that perhaps she was indulging her beloved sister in thus assenting to it so readily.

With Marsac liable to leave for the Front at any moment, Miss Maimie thought it outrageous that some of the English people on the island should not be leaving too.

"I don't see why we don't put it into their heads to volunteer," she said grimly.

And a few minutes later she showed Miss Virginia the postcard she had written to old Burlingham:

Do please let us know when you and Mr. Cartright will be leaving for the Front as we are so anxious to have you both come down to the Amabile for a farewell lunch before you both go. Count Marsac leaves us all next week.
Virginia and Maimie Pepworth-Norton

To be sure, many years ago Anthony Burlingham had been a subaltern in the Ninth Dragoons; but he was well over sixty now, and his eyes became more globular than ever, himself more like a huge elderly baby, when he read this call to arms.

"If I *did* go to the Front," he told Mrs. Ambrogio in that voice of his which sounded as if he was speaking inside a cupboard, the door of which kept opening and shutting all the time, "I jolly well shouldn't go with *Cart*right. He'd *bore* me to *death*!"

Cartright, who was well over fifty and who, in spite of still frequenting the Villa Amabile, was not at all in sympathy with Burlingham's point of view over some things, said to Mrs. Macadam in his deferential bedside tones:

"Good morning, Mrs. Macadam, I hope you're feeling better. I heard from Westall that you had not been quite yourself lately. The weather . . . yes. I've just had a rather peculiar postcard from the Miss Nortons suggesting that I ought to leave for the Front with Burlingham. Of course, I'm most anxious not to offend either of the ladies, but if I do manage to get out I'd really rather not go with Burlingham. I'm sure you'll understand my reasons. I have nothing against Burlingham personally, but . . ."

Effie covered the embarrassment of explaining further with one of her enveloping winks.

"What ho, eh?"

"Quite. Yes, quite. Exactly, Mrs. Macadam," said Cartright gravely. "That's rather what I feel myself. Though at the same time I hope to do my bit." And he did get as far on his way to the Front as asking most people he met what they thought he would be able to do when he got there. Among them was Natt.

"What *could* I do, Major? You're a military man."

"I laboured under the miserable impression that I was," the Major barked painfully, "until I wrote in to the War Office for any kind of obscure employment and received an answer to say that they regretted they did not know of any position in which my services could be usefully employed. We deserve to be beaten, Cartright. We embark on a war against the most powerful military nation in the world like a lot of old women fighting to get on to an omnibus."

Of course, it was reported all over Sirene that Major Natt had called the Germans a powerful nation.

"The man's a trraitor to his country," Mrs. Macdonnell avowed to Miss Virginia.

"Well, I do certainly feel for you to have a British officer behave so," Miss Virginia agreed. "But what else would you expect from such a great long-legged scarecrow as that mean grumpy old Natt? I hope he'll be ashamed when he sees Count Marsac away off to fight for his country next week."

"When I heard of the dear man's gallantrry it brrought the tears to my eyes, Miss Virrginia."

But Marsac did not leave next week. It appeared that

the French Government was anxious for him to stay in Sirene for the present.

"I am horribly disappointed," he told everybody. "I can assure you that I am aspiring with all my heart to venge myself upon these *sales boches*, who have ruinated all my properties on the frontier. Oh yes, madame, I shall soon be without any money at all and I am excessively thirsty for my *revanche*."

It was true that the Germans had seized the great Lagerström steel-foundries near Nancy, and it was true that the Count had begun to make economies up at the Villa Hylas. Perhaps it was also true that the French Government had recommended him to stay where he was for the present. But several people shook their heads. And one or two of the anti-Marsac party declared that they would believe the Count was at the Front when they saw his name as a casualty.

The first Autumn of the war darkened into the first Winter, and perhaps the only sign that Miss Virginia let slip of her impatience with the French Government for not calling upon the Count's services and so giving her the right to point proudly at the incontestable vindication of himself in the eyes of the world was one day when she returned to the subject of the missing trunk.

"I can't understand how it is you've never been able to find it," she said to him a little peevishly.

Marsac shrugged his shoulders.

"I regret that my researches have not been rewarded, my dear Miss Virginia; but I can assure you that I have done all which could be done to find it. I fear that these beastly Italians who will not march with us have robbed it. I find the conduct of Italy in not declaring war against the *boches* more and more disgusting. France which has saved Italy so many times is violated by Germany, and Italy her sister will not do nothing to aid her. Oh yes, it is quite abominable. We may perhaps forgive America, but we shall never forgive Italy. *Ah, non*, that is impossible

I can tell to you that Carlo weeps every evening tears of degradation for his country."

"Well, of course, we all hope our bella Italia will strike a blow for the good cause in the sweet springtime," said Miss Virginia, sitting up as stiffly as she could. "And I get letters from home every mail saying nobody can understand what old President Wilson thinks he's about. But this I know full well myself," she proclaimed with a toss of her head, "we won't be able to keep Old Glory much longer from waving beside the blessed flags hoisted for freedom."

"*Je l'espère, mademoiselle*," said Marsac, bowing as ceremoniously as if his country incarnate in him were receiving the homage of the civilized world.

"I do feel so mad about that poor old trunk," Miss Virginia insisted, "because the lovely fan you gave my sister is packed away in it, and she wouldn't have lost that fan for anything."

"I shall send Miss Maimie another fan this evening as soon as I shall be at the Villa Hylas."

So he did, and a very beautiful fan it was; but it could not mean as much to Miss Maimie as the fan he had chosen for her himself that sunny day in China before the war.

February with almond-trees shedding their waxen blooms gave way to March, when the whole island was flushed with peach-blossom; but Italy still delayed, and Miss Virginia was still burning President Wilson's speeches in her inability to burn him. April broke in a tangle of wistaria and creamy Banksia roses; but Italy still delayed, and Christopher Goldfinch was threatening to cross the Atlantic and, as a survivor of Gettysburg, ask what in hell President Wilson thought he was doing. And then at the end of the month Harry Menteith made the old man the proudest figure on Sirene by telling him that he had gotten a job with the American Red Cross in France. To be sure, he would not have an opportunity to kill many Germans in such a position;

but he would be near the Front, and when America did come in, why, Harry would be on the spot.

"Gad, I'm delighted you're going, my dear boy. I honour your resolve. And now you have your Aunt Hester here, the little girls will be fine. I will miss you, Harry, but thank God, you're going to do your duty. And by Jove, I hope you'll have a chance to kill some of those infernal swine. And if we hadn't gotten a blasted college professor at the White House you would have."

Perhaps Miss Virginia's belief in the Count was being shaken by the way the French Government kept on declining his services, or perhaps it was merely a spontaneous gush of pride and joy that a young American on the island was mindful of his country's honour. Anyway, she raised the ban and invited Harry Menteith down to a farewell lunch at the Amabile.

"What's past is past, Harry Menteith," she said, fanning herself nervously, for it was not a sentiment that came easily to her lips except when it referred to her own age. "We'll not say a word about it, if you please. Only, my sister and I couldn't have you go away on your fine mission without wishing you godspeed. And we've asked our friend Count Marsac to meet you," she added defiantly. "He's naturally proud to meet any man who's away off to help his poor country in the hour of her need."

"*Enchanté de faire votre connaissance, monsieur,*" said the Count, with his most aristocratic air and with a little extra urbanity to show that he was completely indifferent to Menteith's discourtesy in refusing to attend the dinner of welcome. "You are excessively fortunate to have the privilege of serving my poor desolated country. Myself I shall probably be parting for the real Front next week, or at latest the week after. I am awaiting anxiously for my instructions from the Minister of the War."

Miss Maimie smiled at him with a mother's pride.

"Poor Count Marsac's been fretting his heart out to

be in the thick of things," she explained, as Agostino announced lunch.

"Oh, is lunch servitoed ? Come right in, Mr. Menteith," said Miss Virginia, gathering her lace round her and leading the way to the dining-room, her shoulders wriggling.

Italy declared war on Austria in May, and the fact that it was referred to in the press as *La Nostra Guerra*, as a kind of war within a war, a proprietary war, and that while the Bohemians on Sirene were dragged off to internment camps the Prussians continued to strut about without the mildest invigilation did not spoil the occasion for sterling patriots like Mrs. Ambrogio. She rushed about the island, producing the effect of an overheated overexcited Britannia. Had she possessed a trident, she would certainly have used it to some purpose on her national enemies.

"So glad my dear Italy has come in on our side. Always knew they would. Such a sell for that vile old Madame Minieri. Saw the old hag all by herself on the cliff beyond the Caprera. Know she was signalling to spies. Push her over into the sea if she isn't careful. Hate traitors ! "

Madame Minieri was a comfortable, blonde, middle-aged Prussian whose two sons were already on their way to the Trentino with their regiments. It was a bad time for Germans married to Italians ; and Madame Minieri used to seclude herself as much as possible, praying for the Fatherland and the safety of her two sons fighting against the ally of the Fatherland. To be sure, Madame Minieri had herself been eloquently bloodthirsty in the first days of the war when the Fatherland was trying to adopt Belgium, and she was known to have written an ode to the War Lord, for which it was rumoured she had received the Iron Cross and a personal letter of thanks from his Imperial Majesty. By this date, however, she had become a taciturn, middle-aged, blonde Prussian woman, taking solitary walks to distract her mind from the conflict of emotions within her ample breast.

"I'll give her God staff England," Mrs. Ambrogio threatened. "Ought to be shut up in gaol. Disgraceful to let her go wandering about supplying submarines. A dirty German spy. That's all she is. See it in her face. Love my country. Put my tongue out at the old pig every time I pass her."

But Mrs. Ambrogio was not the only Englishwoman swelling like a gourd in the warmth of patriotism. Mrs. Rosebotham rushed about the island in a convulsion of loyal hydrophobia. So English was she, in spite of now admitting kinship with a noble Polish family of extreme antiquity, that none of the other English residents was sufficiently English for her, and she used to write letters to the War Office denouncing them as pro-Germans, spies, and traitors. Bookham himself did not escape the calumny of her pen. Even he, who was as English as an illustration in *Punch*, figured as a continental suspect in the myth-enveloped files of Whitehall. Add to the rabid nonsense of Mrs. Ambrogio and Mrs. Rosebotham the extravagant and ferocious balderdash of Mrs. Onslow, Mrs. Gibbs, Mrs. Macadam, Mrs. Macdonnell, Mrs. Bookham, and the Miss Coopers. Add to that the sentimental anti-Teutonism of Mrs. Neave and other American matrons. Then multiply the result by the shrill hate of the Nortons, and you have an idea of what Sirene was like in the first year of the great war for civilization.

The competitive denunciation by Mrs. Macdonnell and Mrs. Ambrogio of one person after another as a pro-German emptied the hospitable rooms of the Villa Amabile far more successfully than the social war over Count Marsac ever did; and then, perhaps luckily for Mrs. Ambrogio, because when it came to remorseless lying Mrs. Macdonnell was more than a match for her, Mrs. Macdonnell herself began to worry about the possibility of Italy's being overrun by the Austrians and decided to return to Scotland.

"Have you heard that beastly Macdonald woman has

gone?" Mrs. Ambrogio crowed. "Lucky for her she isn't really a German, or she'd be boiled down and used for poison gas. Staggered by her lies. Made me gasp. Made me gasp. Couldn't say a word. Said 'Oo! Oo!' Couldn't think of anything else to say. Hope to goodness she gets torpedoed."

"What?" Mrs. Macadam exclaimed scornfully. "Torpedoed? Her torpedoed? Good lord, a torpedo wouldn't touch her with a barge-pole."

Air-raids had not yet become a menace to the civilian population, or the two of them might have hoped for Mrs. Macdonnell's extinction by a German bomb, even with a measure of confidence by one of the anti-aircraft shells.

And what of the Count during these days of noisy patriotism?

Carlo was called up a week after Italy entered the war. Marsac's income had already been much diminished, and if the war continued for long it was likely to shrink almost to nothing; but he spent every franc he could collect on bribes to secure Carlo a position in Naples, and for a while he was successful in doing this. He took rooms at the Grand Hotel Eruzione and spent his time bemoaning Carlo's dreadful fate in barracks without any opportunity to smoke opium. As a matter of fact, the deprivation of the drug was the best thing that could have happened to the young man, who rapidly improved in health under the hard regime, so rapidly indeed that he was sent up to the Front in spite of the way his protector scattered about what money he had left to keep him in safety.

In the Autumn Marsac returned to Sirene and his opium dreams in the solitude of the Villa Hylas, where he had to cut down his monthly household expenses to a sum that in old days would not have paid for a single lunch. Apparently the French Government still maintained their inexplicable prejudice against accepting his services.

"I am a broken spirit," he told Miss Maimie. "I never expect to behold my poor Carlo again. This savage epoch has distracked me. I wish for nothing now except to die hurling myself against the enemies of my country."

"I can't understand why they won't let you go," Miss Maimie said, wrinkling her sombre eyes in puzzled anxious compassion.

"No more can I," Miss Virginia snapped.

"There is certainly a conspiration to prevent me from dying with glory. My soul starves itself here," he sighed.

"Well, if I was you, Count Marsac," said Miss Virginia sharply, "I'd go right off now to Paris and just insist on having something to do."

"Count Marsac?" he echoed. "And why must I no longer be Bob, mademoiselle?"

"Did I call you Count?" the old lady replied. "Oh, well, I guess old Wilson's gotten me so as sometimes I don't know what I do say."

And then Peter Ambrogio, to whose help the Nortons had appealed to trace that missing trunk, found it in a dusty corner of the Naples *dogana*, where it must have been lying for eighteen months or more.

Mrs. Ambrogio, already much elated by the triumph of witnessing Mrs. Macdonnell's departure, could hardly contain herself. She did not as yet venture to criticize *her* too directly; but when she found that Miss Virginia was mild enough under her cautious denigration of Marsac, there began to dance through Mrs. Ambrogio's mind, perhaps a little out of focus but still definite enough, the richly attired possibility of inheriting one day the whole of the old ladies' splendid fortune.

"Found the trunk at once. Knew he would. Told you he would. Advised you to ask Peter at the start. There it was. Quite safe. All corded up. Thank goodness Peter's honest. Might have taken everything out and brought over an empty trunk. Wouldn't do such a thing.

Couldn't. Too honest. Never have married him. Hate lies. Can't think why Count Marsac isn't at the front. So sorry for him. Know he's longing to be there. Our brave boys, bless them! Wonder why they won't have him. Can't think why he didn't find the trunk. So easy. Peter found it in a moment. Staring him in the face. Cleverest lawyer in Italy."

When the opening of the trunk restored to Miss Maimie the fan that Marsac had given her what now seemed a century ago, she sent him back the beautiful substitute. It is possible that in doing this she was implying a criticism of his present behaviour, but there is really no need to suppose that she was actuated by anything except sentiment. Marsac, however, chose to believe otherwise and returned the fan to Miss Maimie with a note to say that he should consider himself excessively affronted unless she kept what had been a little gift offered with all his heart. Something in the way he expressed himself in the letter touched her pride and, Miss Virginia sternly encouraging her, she sent the fan back again to the Villa Hylas, whither Agostino on the tip of his turned-in toes, his eyes squinting with the carefulness to which he had been so earnestly adjured, carried it.

The fan was a frail ivory thing, the vellum of it inscribed with polite sentiments in Chinese ink by courtly Celestials of long ago. Marsac dipped his pen to add another sentiment that should touch Miss Maimie. Then he frowned and tossed his head.

"*Ah non*," he murmured, "*elle ne se moquera pas de moi*." And he sent the fan down again to the Villa Amabile, this time without even a verbal message.

"I can't understand what's come over the Count, Maimie," Miss Virginia snapped. "If the old fan arrives down here again, tell him you'll throw it in the fire, honey."

Miss Maimie could not bring herself to send such a cruel

message; but she did return the fan to the Villa Hylas without a word, and that to Marsac in his present mood was as bad. He put the fan in his pocket and walked down to visit Burlingham, who had abandoned Anasirene for the upper part of a small house in the Via San Giorgio close to the Villa Botticelli, where, in these straitened times of war, he was rather too frequent a visitor at meal-times to be always welcome. Most of the inside of Burlingham's quarters was occupied by a grand piano; but there was a large terrace on which he exercised what was left of his bulk to exercise after practising Chopin and Brahms and Schumann for six hours a day, by watering a collection of flowers, mostly geraniums and nasturtiums, in an extraordinary variety of pots which included every kind of receptacle from a petrol-tin to a dishandled jordan. In Winter, when the nasturtiums were dead and the geraniums did not require the attention of the watering-can, he strolled up and down the Piazza for two hours, speaking to nobody, always dressed in the height of fashion of twenty years ago in an endless variety of wonderfully preserved suits and wearing usually the colours of the cavalry regiment to which he had once belonged round his straw hat on sunny days or on cloudy days as a tie.

The walls of Burlingham's rooms were covered with photographs in silver and plush frames of people in the 'eighties, and the number of musicians among them seemed entirely in keeping with the rosewood grand piano. Although Burlingham himself was not in the least like the owner of such a concert-hall ante-room, as soon as he began to play you forgot the appearance of this great globular-eyed military gentleman and were transported by the technique of his performance back into the world of which those photographs were the ghosts. You were inclined to think Brahms a little too ultra-modern while admitting that he was keeping just within the bounds of classic art and at any rate not corrupting the world like that fellow Wagner. And then you found that Burlingham himself had been one of the original guarantors of Bayreuth and you felt a little embarrassed by such gamey company and began to wonder if some of the queer stories you had heard about his tastes might not after all be true. You were oblivious of the present in that externally hideous world of the pianoforte, dreaming, dreaming, until you looked up and saw on the wall above the player's immobile chub's eyes that stared into those flashing rapids of music by which he was surrounded the portrait of an unusually handsome young man with wavy flaxen hair and a flaxen moustache; and as you listened it was the portrait playing and the gross elderly man he was to become had vanished. The music stopped. Old Burlingham was back in the present with his piano and his photographs and here and there a few silver ornaments as relics of a wasted fortune and souvenirs of a wasted life, while heavy upon him hung the loneliness that an abnormal obsession casts upon age.

After Carlo had gone away, Marsac fell into the habit of seeking Burlingham's company when he was not busied with his own dreams in that luxurious subterranean den at the Villa Hylas. The walk did him good, and he found his new friend—for until now Burlingham had been but a tea-table acquaintance—an excellent audience, because a silent one. The musician used to sit back in a plush armchair, smoking a *minghetti* cigar, which resembled at any rate in shape the Havanas he used to smoke twenty years ago, and listening to Marsac's endless stream of rhetoric; sit there as a chub hangs motionless in a deep pool at the side of a half-open sluice-gate. Marsac had tried hard to convert Burlingham to the pleasures of opium, and having failed to do that he was now trying to convert him to the beauties of Ravel and Debussy, of Granados and Albeniz.

"I'm *much* too old to care for *them*," Burlingham objected, shaking his head with a monumental negative that would have discouraged anybody less complacent than Marsac.

"Ah, but I must explicate to you, my dear sir. . . ."
And he was off on the rhetorical switchback of artistic jargon.

"Wagner is as far as I care to go in *one* direction, Brahms in another," Burlingham replied firmly, when the lecturer paused. "And I really enjoy Chopin the *best* of them *all*."

"*Mais*, Chopin," Marsac protested with a wry grimace. "You must permit me to point out, my dear sir, that in Paris we no longer consider Chopin even to have talent."

"Here, I say, wait a minute!"

And rising from his chair Burlingham buried the remains of his cigar in one of his flower-pots before charging into Marsac's arguments at the head of a polonaise.

"Yes, but I must be permitted to propose that such music lacks all suppleness . . ."

"I sup*pose* you mean subtle*ty*?"

"It is the same for me."

"It isn't the same for anybody else then," Burlingham declared stolidly.

"It is, *si vous voulez*, a very agreeable triffle, *mais, mon cher*, there are in Debussy deepths which perhaps only a Frenchman is capable to appreciate."

"The French *aren't* a musical nation. They never *have* been, and they never *will* be."

"Please do not let us jest about this, my dear sir."

"I'm *not* joking. I'm in *deadly* earnest."

"If it was another person than you I assure you that I would consider myself abominably affronted by such a *bêtise*," said Marsac all lily-rosed with indignation.

However, in spite of their differences of opinion over music, there were other subjects on which they were in complete agreement; and it was to pay Burlingham a compliment that Marsac entrusted him with the fan that Miss Maimie had refused.

"Do you mean to say I'm to keep it?" Burlingham asked, opening his eyes very wide.

VESTAL FIRE

"It will one day be to you the souvenir of a tormented spirit," Marsac sighed.

"Yes, but I really haven't got *room* for any more things here."

"That is all ones to me. Do what you please with this fan provided I never see it again."

"Well, do you mind if I give it to Mrs. Ambrogio? I've been lunching with her *rather* a lot lately and I *think* she's inclined to *resent* it. Only I found it *so* convenient not to have the smell of cooking here in the middle of the day."

"Give it to who you will. It is for me a dead leaf."

But no sooner had Marsac reached the Villa Hylas than he sent down a note to Burlingham to say that the fan had too many memories for him of a dear friendship and that after all he thought it would be better to keep it himself. So, it was put into a glass-topped table with a dozen other specimens of Chinese art.

Burlingham, who wanted to go on lunching as often as he could at the Villa Botticelli, told Mrs. Ambrogio that he had intended to present her with the fan; but as the story reached Miss Maimie, it was Marsac who wanted to give it to her and she who had refused.

And then the two old ladies feeling discouraged by the emptiness of the Villa Amabile in this drear time of war went off to Rome for the Winter.

Chapter 4

tantane, fallax, cepere oblivia nostra,
. . . . . .
ut neque respiceres nec solarere iacentem,
dure, nec exsequias prosequerere meas?

OVID

IT was natural that an old romantic like Christopher Goldfinch should be impressed by the splendour of the women during the war. When he read in the newspapers of their doughty resourcefulness, he used to nod his head in what one hesitates to call senile agreement. The fact that he had been the lover of so many of these splendid creatures procured him a sentimental participation in their superb deediness. Dreaming in the museum-like shades of the Villa Adonis he beheld dozens of his former mistresses discard the nightgown for the apron and lay down the lipstick to pick up the red pencil.

"By gad, Scudamore," he croaked, "there's no doubt about it. The women *are* splendid."

The scholar sucked at his pipe and nodded a meditative assent.

"Sure, they're splendid. They dress the wounded and undress themselves with equal devotion."

Christopher raised his beautiful hand in protest.

"Now, don't go knocking women. I won't stand for it at a time like this," he proclaimed.

"I was considering this morning," the scholar went on equably, "the contrast between the respective positions of prostitutes and pleasure resorts in a time like this."

"Eh? What do you mean? More of your darned sneering, eh?"

"The Paphian flourishes like a munition-worker. Paphos itself is abandoned. Ligeia, Leucosia, and Parthenope are sleeker than ever; but you cannot find a single bone upon their strand."

Christopher marched out of the Villa Parnasso, crying out against cynicism.

"There's nothing a blasted pro-German's ashamed of," he told everybody. "Beat 'em in an argument and they pull Latin and Greek on you, which is just the darned cowardly trick the Germans themselves would like to play. The sort of trick President Wilson would play."

Yet it was difficult for a Sirenian like Scudamore not to become sentimental over the down-at-heels condition into which his island had fallen. The iridescent bubble had burst, leaving nothing behind except a spot of soapy moisture. Ridiculous and perhaps offensive though such a suggestion will appear, it genuinely did shock one more to hear that the little barber on the Piazza who had shaved one under his father's critical eye had been killed than to see the name of a dear friend in the casualty lists. Is it in *The Master Builder* that Ibsen makes the heroine able to weep for her burnt dolls but not for her burnt children? The empty echoing hotels, the wind-swept Piazza, the few disconsolate figures in uniform playing cards in Zampone's, the uncockaded *carabinieri* in the dingy green uniform and service caps of war, the filthy little boat that rolled over twice a week from Naples instead of the spruce *Regina Elena* every morning (and she rumoured to have been sunk by enemy gunfire), the scarcity of food, the famine of tobacco—these shadows were dismal enough; but over the whole island hovered a shadow blacker and bigger than any, and that was the doubt whether Sirene would ever be itself again.

In the Summer of 1916 there was a rumour that the British Government had decided to make the island the headquarters for hundreds of convalescent officers, and for a fortnight the Piazza was cheerful. But the officers never arrived, and gloom descended again upon a community which had never imagined the possibility of a world deaf to the song of the Sirens. Hundreds of convalescent officers with wax-filled ears, and the British Government bound to the mast by the covetous French steering them all past Sirene to the Riviera! The French were blamed, but it transpired later that Mrs. Rosebotham had written to the War Office to point out that Sirene was not a fit place for convalescent officers on account of the temptations to which they would be exposed there at a time when they would, as she was alleged to have put it, 'just be feeling their legs again.'

Deaths among the old members of the foreign colony added to the feeling of insecurity about the future. Their empty villas haunted the imagination of the Sirene shopkeepers. '*Questa brutta guerra*,' they groaned, shivering in the horrors of a black *tramontano*. Simon Pears left the Villa Eolia for Rome where he died of pneumonia, and his granddaughter, who had not cared greatly for Sirene since that afternoon in the Villa Amabile, vowed she would never return to the island. Joseph Neave died before he was able to revise even the first canto of the *Purgatorio*. Those who had laughed most at Joseph were the sorriest of all to hear of his death, for there are no friends so fondly remembered as those at whom we were always able to laugh. Elsie Neave braved the peril of submarines to return home; and Beatrice Mewburn had not tired of mapping out for her a woeful future as the slave of all her relations on the other side of the Atlantic when the doctor's three bloodhounds died in quick succession.

"Of course, the loss of his three beloved old friends will kill my poor father," she bemoaned.

The old Cambridge professor did die soon afterwards; but acute bronchitis was held to be the cause. His daughter left Sirene and wrote from England several letters that took the gloomiest view of Dorothy Daynton's ability to cope with the strain of hospital work in Great Yarmouth.

Thus of the four who in a tontine would have started with equal chances only Christopher Goldfinch survived. He fell out of bed and broke his collar bone; he slipped down one greasy day in the Piazza and bruised his hip; he was prostrated by a severe attack of influenza; his old enemy indigestion gripped him again, and with the impossibility of obtaining Sponger's Food in wartime he was kept for nine months on gruel; but he showed no sign of dying. On the contrary he talked confidently of Sheila's getting over as soon as the Germans were beaten, and of the bully parties they would be having at the Villa Adonis to celebrate the victory of right over might. The entry of America into the war gave him superlative joy, and though it would be an exaggeration to say that it put new life into one who had such an abundance of life in him already, it did serve as a fine tonic after his influenza. He was worried for a while because Nigel Dawson was not immediately sent off the island and up to the front-line with the first American troops that arrived, and the news that Harry Menteith had been given a commission did not quite compensate for Nigel's seclusion.

"Gad, he and that skulking brute Marsac ought to be tied together and shot," he declared.

The Count was still in Sirene; but he could no longer pretend that the French Government spurned his services. Indeed, the French Government was now making a great effort to obtain them. The arrangement by which England, France, and Italy were pledged to comb out each other's eligible objectors to active service was a serious matter for Marsac. Harrowing scenes occurred. And actually an English poet was dragged away from Sirene by *carabinieri* and put to the job of emptying slops in an hospital at Florence with as little compunction as an Italian waiter hiding in Soho might have been set to work with a labour battalion in the middle of Warwickshire.

It was when this agreement was reached between the Powers that the Count first discovered how weak his heart really was. He discovered at the same time that the more opium he smoked the weaker it became. A panic seized him that with the growth of the inquisition all over Europe the police might raid the Villa Hylas and confiscate his store of the drug. He pondered a hiding-place. The natural place to choose was the Villa Amabile; but the two old ladies had just retired again to Rome after an empty Summer at Sirene when they had had to depend almost entirely on Mrs. Ambrogio for company. Marsac had been down to see them two or three times, before the weakness of his heart made such a long walk inadvisable; but there were no donkeys left on the island, on which they could ride up to pay him a return visit. Marsac attributed their lack of courtesy entirely to the machinations of The Ambrogio who he was convinced was never losing an opportunity to make mischief between him and them. And yet, such was the malice of fortune, Peter Ambrogio had been appointed *pretore* of Sirene, so that an open quarrel with his wife at such a crisis in his affairs was too imprudent to be considered. The possessiveness of The Ambrogio would make the Villa Amabile an unsafe place in which to store opium while the real owners were away, even if he cared to ask a favour of the old ladies themselves.

So, Marsac approached Burlingham on the subject.

"*Four* trunks of *opium*?" the musician gasped. "But where could I put them? I haven't got room for another *hat*box. In fact my top hat *is* in the bath at this moment."

"I regret excessively, Monsieur Burlingham," said Marsac, "that you find yourself unable to disconvenience yourself on my account. I offer you my most sincere excuses for presumpting upon which until this disillusioning moment I had imagined to be a friendship."

"Don't talk such *utter* bosh," said the musician. "Can't you see that it's a physical impossibility to put four trunks in these two rooms? Why I haven't even got a w.c. indoors. I've got to go out in *all* weathers to a kind of *beehive* at the corner of the terrace, and last Sunday in that gale we had the whole place was *trembling like an aspen*."

"It seems that when a man is in misfortune," Marsac sighed, "his friends forsake him very easily. If I had not to live on what my mother can afford to give me while my properties are in the hands of these vile *boches*, I would hire a house for myself."

"Oh, don't talk about money," said Burlingham. "It's *some*thing *dread*ful."

Marsac frowned.

"I wish to you good morning, monsieur," he said coldly, and head in air he marched out of the little house in a huff. Burlingham took off his coat, pulled up his well-creased trousers, and sat down to his daily scales.

Scudamore was the only other person who might offer sanctuary to the opium, for his villa was so large that even if the police did search it, which was not likely, they would have some difficulty in finding the trunks. Nothing had changed much in the Parnasso. The rooms were dustier. There were more tabs sticking out of the books. Nita had lost the few remnants of her dark-eyed beauty. The scholar's dressing-gown was grubbier, and the ashes of his pipes had burnt a number of new holes in it. He himself was nearer to being a skeleton. The first sentence of the History of Roman Morals had not yet been written.

"Why, sure," Scudamore said cordially. "Store anything you like here."

"I will have to send the trunks by night with the extremity of cautiousness," said Marsac, frowning like a conspirator.

"That's quite all right. I'm up the whole night working. And it's mighty discouraging these days. This blasted war's upsetting the book-mail. I can't get a-hold of a derned reference nowadays in under a month."

Marsac shook his head sympathetically.

"We worshippers of Apollo are all of us grounded down beneath the treadings of the antipathic Ares."

"Talking of that particular aspect of Ares, how is our young friend going along?"

"Carlo?" Marsac sighed deeply. "Alas, I am of the impression that I shall never see him again. One perceives very plainly the beastly result of forsaking the Greek ideal. In Greece he and I would have stood with our shields as one against the Persians. I have no hesitation to say that if we civilized nations had not forsaken the Greek ideal we must have conquered the *boches* by now."

Scudamore went across to his table and made a note on a half-sheet of paper: *Effects of Hom. on mil. strat. Jul. Caes. etc.*

"I dare say you find it a bit lonesome up there?" he suggested.

"I am the most solitary being on earth," Marsac replied eagerly, so eagerly that Scudamore looked apprehensively at his work-table. It seemed as if his visitor intended to talk for at least half an hour on the topic he had so rashly started. And Scudamore was right.

"Well, you mustn't let me keep you from your dreams," he said at last. "I'll see the opium is put in a safe place. And I hope you'll have no more trouble with your consul," he added, steering Marsac toward the door. "We put people with weak hearts into the line and people with weak heads behind it, and then we are surprised by this Caporetto business."

With this the scholar managed to get his visitor outside the big nailed door of the Villa Parnasso, and in the mood suggested by Caporetto he turned back to pore over the account in Livy of some great Roman disaster.

Carlo, who came through the Caporetto business unhurt,

was able to spend a few days' leave in Sirene before Christmas. He looked a great deal better than he had looked for years, and he was rather depressed to be told by Marsac that he had death at the back of his eyes. He refused to touch opium, which let him in for an evening of retrospective jealousy over Madame Protopopesco. Perhaps he was glad to leave the gloom of the Villa Hylas. People noticed that he seemed debonair and happy on the dirty little boat crossing over, much more debonair and happy than the Count who crossed with him to spend a few days arguing with the French consul in Naples.

It really did begin to look as if he would have to join up at last. He was forced to undergo another medical examination.

"I most disgustingly was compelled to unclothe myself and stand entirely naked in a line of abominable *crétins*," he confided in Burlingham, with whom out of a need to talk he had made friends again. "And now I await for my call to arms."

He was so sure that he would have to go that he wrote off to Miss Maimie in Rome, telling her that in spite of his weak heart he had managed to persuade his country to give him a chance to die fighting and that he hoped to say goodbye to her and Miss Virginia on his way through Rome.

He received an answer from Miss Virginia:

> HOTEL VENTI SETTEMBRE,
> ROMA.
> *Dec.* 15, 1917.

Dear Bob,

We were glad to hear your news, but my sister was struck in the chest by a tram as she stepped off the sidewalk yesterday—and though all goes well the doctor says she is very badly shaken—but your news was a real happiness to her. How grandly our beloved Italy is holding up after that damnible Capporetto! We are so proud to be here in this grand old eternal city and able to help a wee bit here and there with the poor wounded. Our American help is slow in coming and let us hope that old Wilson is feeling ashamed of himself, the old villain. But we hear from all our friends that by the " sweet springtime " we will be able to do our share in driving the vile Hun out of " the fair land of France."

With greetings from my sister and myself.
      Your old friend,
        Virginia Pepworth-Norton

And then Marsac managed to have so violent a heart attack in the hotel at Naples, where he was waiting for his final orders, that the French consul began to think that his might be a genuine case after all. However, he was sent to a hospital to be under the observation of a German-Swiss doctor, and here he remained for three months, and incidentally occupied the vigilance of a sentinel *carabiniere* day and night to guard against his smuggling in any opium. The entry of any official into his room was the signal for attacks of hysteria, in which he would shriek and clutch the bars of the bed, imploring them not to drag him away in his pitiable condition. Meanwhile, the Villa Hylas was searched and, nothing of the drug being found, he was allowed to return to Sirene on condition that he presented himself every week at the French consulate to display the state of his health. He prepared for these visits by immersing himself in the subterranean den at the Villa Hylas and smoking incessantly. While he was in Naples he found there a dusty old French marquis whose relations had taken advantage of the war to keep him out of France by allowing him only enough money at a time to prevent his actually dying of starvation. No doubt Marsac genuinely pitied the old nobleman's destitution and the abasement of his ancient name; but he was extremely useful as an intermediary between the opium hidden in the Villa Parnasso and the smoker hidden in the Villa Hylas. Moreover, he was ready to listen for hours to the narrative of Marsac's dreams, and that nobody else was prepared to do nowadays —not even Burlingham without refreshing draughts of Brahms and Chopin at intervals, and certainly not Scudamore who once besought him: "*aut vigila aut dormi, Nasidiane, tibi*"; but Marsac, who did not follow the Latin, thought that he was being paid a compliment, whereupon Scudamore, to protect himself, took to going to bed later in the morning and not getting up until it was quite dark.

"I'm rather *sorry* for that poor old marquis," Burlingham said to Mrs. Ambrogio. "Marsac *brings* him down to see me and introduces him with about a *dozen* titles and then *hustles* him off to the Piazza in a most *frightful* wind for a pound of carrots."

"Had a long chat with the marquee this morning," said Mrs. Ambrogio. "Poor old fellow so pleased when I told him I'd been so much in Paris. Nearly cried. Never see the Count nowadays. So glad. Hate cowards. Never comes to the Amabile nowadays. Miss Maimie terribly ill. Count's behaviour killing her by inches. Feel so furious with him. Told the old dears about his being watched by a carbineery to keep him from smoking opium. Miss Maimie put her hand up to her side. Such pain. Won't live much longer. Hear Mrs. Macdonald's been killed by a Zeppelin."

"*Has* she?" Burlingham exclaimed, his globular eyes bursting from their sockets.

"Hope so. Hope so. No papers yet. No lunch to-day. Having lunch with the dear old Nortons. So sorry! Can't do without me. So glad! Love to be useful to people. No good for anything else nowadays."

It was not true that Mrs. Macdonnell had been killed or indeed that she had been within four hundred miles of a Zeppelin; but it was true that Miss Maimie was seriously ill.

The old ladies had returned from Rome as soon as Miss Maimie appeared to have recovered from her accident.

The gusto with which Mrs. Ambrogio related the history of Marsac's humiliating behaviour did not serve as a tonic; and now on her seventieth birthday the blue March sky was for her clouded over by the bad news from France. She leaned back in her arm-chair and let a sheet of note-paper tumble from her tired hands on the porcelain tiles of the big *salone*. It was a letter from Marsac in Naples to wish her many happy returns of the day.

> GRAND HOTEL ERUZIONE,
> NAPOLI.
> le 26 Mars '18.
>
> *My very dear Miss Maimie,*
>
> *I send you with a bundle of carnations my most profound and affectionate salutes to your birthday, and I am wishing so many years of happiness to you. The doctor assures me that if I endure as I am to be without the opium to which I am ashamed to be a miserable slave I will soon perhaps be able to fight for my poor country in her new distress. One does not wish to abuse one's allies, but I must certainly permit myself to declare that the English have behaved with such a most abominable egoism that I am excessively suspicious of what they are plotting against us by permitting the boches to march immediately against my beloved Paris. Poor France has indeed been maltreated by her friends. I hope so soon to hear from you a little word that you are much better.*
>
> *Always your most devoted*
>
> *Bob.*
>
> *I regret to inform you that my heart is still excessively weak, but perhaps with my cure it will be better in the same time.*

But Miss Maimie's own heart was excessively weak, hardly seeming to beat louder now than a butterfly's wing, as she leaned back wearily in her arm-chair and listened to the canaries singing out in the *entrata*, and the logs crackling on the great fire, and the click of Miss Virginia's fan, and the sigh of the wind round the minarets of the Villa Amabile in the March sunlight.

"It's nice to think that our dear Mr. and Mrs. Ambrogio will be here for your birthday lunch, honey," said her sister.

Miss Maimie opened those sombre eyes that still glowed faintly and smiled her pleasure.

"I'm only so sorry I haven't felt like going down into the kitchen this morning."

"Why, sweetie heart, don't you fret yourself about the old kitchen. We know so well our dear Alfonso will give us a perfectly bully lunch. But I wish it was more than just us four for your birthday. It seems kind of dreary to have nobody but you and me and the dear Ambrogios. But they won't know how old you are."

"Bob writes he'll soon be in France now."

The other's fan quickened.

"I guess he will. Look, honey," she said, pointing with it to the view of the garden beyond the pergola, "see how big the cypresses have grown over our little temple, and see how they wave in this real Italian weather."

"I guess we never thought we'd love Italy quite so fondly," Miss Maimie sighed. "Not when we used to wonder and wonder what it was like, away over at home."

"Four years now since we've seen the old folks," Miss Virginia reminded her.

They were silent for a space, Miss Virginia rocking back and forth in her old cane-bottomed chair and Miss Maimie gazing from half-closed eyes at their little temple so white against the richness of the sky. Perhaps she was thinking of that blue Roman weather in a March of thirteen years ago when they first met the Count, or perhaps she was thinking of ruined temples in the jungles of Cambodia, or perhaps of ruined temples in the recesses of herself.

The voice of Mrs. Ambrogio was heard above the singing of the canaries in the *entrata*. She came rustling and spluttering into the *salone*, dressed in her best for the birthday lunch and followed by Peter.

"Many happy returns! Many happy returns! Brought you a bunch of carnations. Wish I could have brought you something better. Too poor. Too poor. Lost all my money since the war. Belgian railways. Never mind. Don't care. Starve in the gutter so long as we beat the Germans. Paying guests at the Villa Botticelli. Five liras a day profit. Worked it out. Must do something. No money. Peter no money. Judge can't make money. Others all do, but Peter too honest. Nay pas vrai, Peter? Troppo nesta! Bravo!"

Fat Agostino came in to announce that lunch was served.

"Bonn jaw, Agusteena. Senta bene? Bravo! How that boy grows! So fond of him. Fat as butter. Love him so much."

Agostino felt deeply the absence of festas at the Villa Amabile in these days, and he had taken advantage of this miniature occasion to set temptingly close to Miss Virginia a bowl of peach-blossom he had stripped from the trees that morning. And, when toward the close of lunch Peter in response to violent double-eyed winks from his wife made a little oration of birthday auguries, Miss Virginia did dip her hand into the bowl and scatter the rosy petals upon her sister and upon her guests.

"That foolish Agostino thinks this is a real old Amabile party like we used to have," she said, half apologizing for her demonstrativeness.

But after lunch Miss Maimie put her hand up to her side and the two guests had to help her back to her chair.

"This is the first birthday party we either of us ever kept," Miss Virginia admitted, "and I was an old fool to suggest it. How do you feel now, honey?"

"Oh, I'm fine. I just feel it sometimes where that old tram bumped into me. But my gracious, it's just nothing at all."

The guests went away presently, and Miss Maimie leaned back in her chair, listening to the merry crackle of the fire and the click of Miss Virginia's fan; but the canaries were silent, for the sun had moved round and was no longer shining on the palms in the *entrata*.

When tea came in, Miss Maimie roused herself to follow with her eager watchful eyes the course of Agostino handing the cup she had poured out for her sister.

At sunset Miss Virginia went across to the french windows that opened on her favourite loggia.

"I never saw our dear smoky old mountain look so beautiful, honey," she said; and Maimie to please her got up a little uncertainly from her chair to stand beside her where she could see across the bay the cloud upon Vesuvius lie soft and rosy as a flamingo brooding.

In the morning, when Rosina came to wake Miss Maimie, there was no reply as she pulled the curtains and let in the sunshine, crying:

"*Bella giornata, signorina!*"

And on the table by her bed was the tattered copy of an old American magazine open at a poem which must have appealed to Miss Maimie, for it had been double-scored at the side with a blue pencil.

> *Warm summer sun,*
>   *Shine kindly here!*
> *Warm southern wind,*
>   *Blow softly here!*
>
> *Green sod above,*
>   *Lie light, lie light!*
> *Good night, dear Heart,*
>   *Good night! Good night!*

And this was the epitaph that Miss Virginia had carved upon the marble stone that stood on one side of the romanesque window cut in the wall of the cemetery. She put up at the same time her own stone on the other side, but there was no inscription upon that as yet.

Marsac arrived in Sirene an hour after the funeral was over. On the terrace of the funicular he met Burlingham marching solemnly up and down in a frock-coat and silk hat, looking as if he had stepped out of a boudoir photograph of 1891.

"I have been betrayed by The Ambrogio," Marsac exclaimed. "She has made a *complot* to keep me from arriving to the funeral of my beloved friend. I am written for *demain*, and I arrive to find myself betrayed. What I will not tell to that ignoble cow! But first I must go at once to have an explanation from Miss Virginia. I am enraged as I have never been in all my life. I am in such a furiousness that I assure you I would find it excessively easy to commit an assassination on those vile intriguing Ambrogios."

"You're *not* proposing to go down and see Miss Norton now?" Burlingham gasped.

"Oh yes, indeed, I must not avoid another moment. There must be an explication of my treating. This is the *comble* of injuries which I am suffering for more than three years. *Ah non*, I cannot remand this explication."

"But I say, look here, you *can't* go down and upset the old lady at this moment. You can't really. She was taken out of the cemetery in a state of *utter* collapse."

"By the courteous and solicitudinous Madame Ambrogio I may presumpt?"

"Well, I daresay she helped. But they've got a kind of nurse-companion over from Naples, and Mrs. Ambrogio told me that Miss Norton wished to be left quite alone."

"*Donc*, that harpy is not with her?"

"No, she has invited me up to tea at the Botticelli."

"Perhaps you are right," Marsac muttered. "Yes, I am convinced that you are right. I shall not disturb her to-day. I shall suffer in my desolation of spirit in the solitude of the Villa Hylas. And nobody is knowing that which I suffer."

Yet, incredible though it must sound, within an hour Marsac had changed his mind and was demanding to see Miss Virginia.

She received him not in the big *salone*, but in the *salotto* that stored up the morning sunlight, where she used to sit and fan herself while Miss Maimie went through the accounts and interviewed the various members of the *famiglia*. It was a cosy little room lined with sentimental English and American novels, and it was dear to the old ladies because it was the first addition they had made to the original triple-domed house among the vines.

"My dear Miss Virginia," he cried, hastening forward and bending over to kiss her hand, an action which once upon a time had never failed to bring the ghost of a girlish flush to her ivory cheeks. But now her cheeks were white as bones and her hand was icy cold.

"Oh, so you've come, have you?" she said tonelessly.

"I must expose at once the malicious *complot* by which I have been betrayed. When I have sent my telegram to know the day of the funeral of my adored Miss Maimie, I receive from Madame Ambrogio a response that the funeral is to be on to-morrow."

"I know. I had her telegraph to you the day and the hour."

"Then she has betrayed us both, because she has waited so long that I am not receiving the telegram in time to take the boat."

"There was a boat last evening."

They argued for awhile about the boat, and then Miss Virginia said sharply:

"I don't know why you think I would believe you now, Count Marsac, after the way you've lied to us all these years."

"Mademoiselle, I do not permit even you to say that I lie," Marsac exclaimed, folding his arms in melodramatic fashion.

VESTAL FIRE

"Yes, fold your arms," the old lady sneered. "My, you must be used to folding your arms by now."

"Ah, Miss Norton, I did not come here to have your insults."

"You lied to us years ago, and we believed you. A pair of foolish tiresome old maids, I suppose we were. But we did believe you, and I guess we gave folks lots of fun the way we—but oh, dear heaven, that's all dead and done with!" she cried.

"It pleases you to repeat that I lie, mademoiselle," said Marsac, trying to look as grim as the old lady.

"It certainly does please me to repeat that you are a liar; and a slave to your vile habits; and ugh! a coward," she stabbed slowly. "Now leave this house for ever, Count Marsac."

"Ah, but I will not go until I have told to you that you have with enormous deliberation plotted to divide Miss Maimie from myself. You and your friend Madame Ambrogio have most vilely separated us with infamous suggestiveness. And why? Because you were jealous. Ah yes, you were always jealous of our sacred friendship. Do you think I was not perceiving so when you made that trunk an occasion to wound me to the soul? You were entirely aware that I was incapable of military service; but with your poison you have made my adored Miss Maimie conceive that I was a purposeful *insoumis*. And now when she is dead you show me your malevolence. It is you, mademoiselle, who is the coward, because you would not dare to address yourself to me so when Miss Maimie was alive."

"Leave my house," the old lady shrilled, rising to her feet and ringing the bell.

"I shall leave your house with an infinity of pleasure, when I shall have told to you what you are. You are like all the women of earth, mademoiselle, all the women except my mother and my adored Miss Maimie, from whom you have not hesitated even to rob me in death. . . ."

Frightened members of the household stood in the doorway.

"Il conte deve andare via—subito—subito!" she commanded. "Fuori la porte! Fuori! Fuori! And never to aprire the porta again. Oh, hell, what's 'never' in Italian?"

But though Miss Maimie was not there to remind her of that word she always forgot, the servants understood well enough that to her Count Marsac was dead.

Whatever one may think of the Count, it is probable that his behaviour saved Miss Virginia's life, rousing her as it did to such a passion of hate that she was snatched from the stupor of despair into which she had fallen.

Miss Virginia stayed in Sirene long enough to see the great rococo tomb finished; but when a relative who had been cabled for arrived from America she agreed to return with him and stay there at any rate until the war was over.

The Villa Amabile was closed, except the original little house underneath, where the *famiglia* lived. The valuables were locked up in cupboards and presses. The keys were left in charge of Peter Ambrogio, but at his request every receptacle was sealed. Before she went away Miss Virginia bought the adjacent plot in the cemetery, which she caused to be paved with a mosaic of broken Roman tesseræ. On this she fixed a small marble stool, and every day and all day in the May weather she sat on this stool, staring out through the romanesque window cut in the wall of the cemetery at the azure bay and dreaming that Miss Maimie was beside her. But in June she sailed to America, and nobody in Sirene expected ever to see her again. Miss Virginia was eighty-five now.

Chapter 5

*O bone, num ignoras? . . .
insignem ob cladem Germanae pubis*

*. . . oleum artocreasque popello
largior.*

PERSIUS

intereunt partim statuarum et nominis ergo.
LUCRETIUS

THE promotion of Marshal Foch to command the military forces of the Entente had a most beneficial effect upon the Count's health. The succession of victories through the late Summer and Autumn was evidently the right treatment for his malady. In fact by the end of October he appeared to be definitely cured, and the prospect of an early armistice was distasteful to his recaptured health. He walked buoyantly about Sirene, his rosy cheeks aglow with ardour, his blue eyes flashing with gallantry.

"Aren't you glad to think that this loathsome war may be over quite soon?" somebody asked him.

"*Ah non, par exemple*, I am by no means so content," he replied. "I find it absolutely necessary to continue as far as to Berlin. I assure you I am excessively enraged by such *faiblesse*. *Ah, oui, c'est idiot*. Oh, yes, madame, the only place where we must dictitate peace to these vile *boches* is in Berlin. It has been my sacred dream for all these years."

Italy, luckier than the Count, did manage to secure a spectacular triumph over the Austrians and beat the armistice by a neck. Vittorio Veneto brought another person out of seclusion. This was Nigel Dawson who issued cards inviting the Mayor and Corporation together with the leading residents of Sirene both native and foreign to celebrate the occasion with a grand *brindisi* at Zampone's immediately after the Te Deum of thanksgiving in the Duomo for the success of the Italian arms.

There were of course a few uniforms among the guests; but it was the superb enthusiasm of the black-coated civilians that made the occasion remarkable. One comprehended what a weight of solid flesh had stood behind the spirit of the combatants throughout these weary years; and a lieutenant of *alpinisti* present whose breast wore the blue ribbon of the cross for valour must have felt that the arm he had given in exchange was well lost to preserve the tongue of Dr. Squillace, who in an oration lasting twenty minutes and containing several hundred five-syllable abstract nouns voiced a nation's pride. His eloquence did not merely arouse a storm of ' *bene* ' and ' *benissimo* ' and ' *bravo* ': it fired the municipal counsellors on either side of him to kiss both his cheeks when he sat down, and half a dozen more along the table who were too fat to reach his beard with their lips to lean over and shake him warmly by the hand in congratulation.

Nigel at this date was getting discouragingly near to forty, and he was shocked to see how much younger than himself Marsac continued to look, when they passed one another in the street with haughty indifference. As he sat in Zampone's this evening he thought regretfully of his vanished youth; and when there were calls for the host to reply to the speech of the *sindaco* thanking him for his hospitality as the representative in Sirene of the noble American nation, Nigel replied with a lament for the sacrifices youth had made during the war, which roused many among his audience to tears.

There were one or two other Americans present who,

while agreeing with all the compliments the *sindaco* had paid their country, felt that Nigel Dawson was not the typical representative of it they would have chosen. He seemed to lack some of the personality of a George Washington or an Abraham Lincoln. America was being taken very seriously by the Italians at this date, and when the Italians take anything seriously they always change the names of their streets, so that for a time in even the tiniest village you would find a Via Woodrow Wilson, not one of which survived the conference at Versailles. The way Nigel was standing champagne this evening seemed to be an earnest of the way America would be standing champagne to Italy in the thirsty days of peace-making. When the magnum of Fiume was emptied into the glasses of the Serbian delegates at Versailles, President Wilson became a No Thoroughfare in Italy, much to the relief of Latin lips, which champ at the letter W as a horse champs at an uncomfortable bit.

But although this evening Nigel might shine with the reflected milky radiance of Wilson's benevolent teeth, every one of which seemed to stand up like a lighthouse in the murk of war, his long hibernation had been too much for him. He never recovered from it; and after flitting round for awhile like a faded butterfly of last year in the cold and cruel light of Spring, he left Sirene without letting anybody know his destination. Rumour was busy for a day or two after his departure. Some said that repenting of his life he had become a Trappist monk. Others suggested economy as the explanation of his disappearance, and one or two would be content with nothing less than suicide. Three months later the mystery was solved. He had been growing a beard; and he who had once been used to being told that he reminded people of the Naples Narcissus was more than grateful nowadays to be told that he was not unlike a Velasquez. There were many to suggest that Nigel had grown a beard to assume a masculinity he did not possess. But they wronged him there. A double chin, not a double life, was the inspiration of the change.

"*Autres temps, autres cœurs,*" Marsac sniffed. And that was more witty than true.

Nigel may still be seen on the Piazza. He is close on fifty now, and he is known to ribald English visitors as The Bearded Lady.

Harry Menteith arrived home, much to the delight of Christopher Goldfinch. The old romantic was making extensive alterations in the Villa Adonis to accommodate Sheila Macleod, who had written to say that nothing should stop her coming to stay with her darling Chris in the Spring.

"She talks of going to Paris while the conference is on," he croaked. "But I reckon she'll be here on and off most of the year. I'm knocking my bedroom and the room next it into one so that she can have a comfortable room, and I'm putting a bath in the other spare-room."

"And where are you sleeping?"

"Oh, I'm moving down into that little room on the ground floor next the studio. I had water laid on there a few years ago to clean my brushes. And of course as I've had to give up painting at last, owing to my eyes getting so queer, it'll suit me fine."

Marsac was most cordial when he met Menteith on the Piazza. One might almost have supposed that by quarrelling with Miss Virginia he considered that he had entirely rehabilitated himself in the eyes of Sirene.

"Ah, I am enchanted to see you again, Monsieur Menteith." He stared at the young painter's buttonhole. "I perceive I must congratulate you on a charming little piece of red ribbon you are wearing. I am excessively pleased to think that my country has made you this compliment."

Shortly after this Marsac awarded himself the rosette of the Legion of Honour, which he wore, or rather with which he juggled for several weeks, slipping it surreptitiously out of his buttonhole when he saw somebody coming who might raise his eyebrows. It looked as if opium had begun to attack his mind.

The Winter of the armistice was by no means the joyous season that Nigel Dawson's *brindisi* had promised to inaugurate. The visitors whom the Sirenesi had been expecting to come as the quails came in May and September remained as rare as they were during the war. A panic seized the owners of the hotels and the keepers of the *pensions*. They had been sustaining themselves all these years with a dream of peace and plenty, and now when peace had arrived they were worse off than ever. They had felt that in postponing the hordes of German tourists for a whole bashful year they were perhaps erring on the side of caution; but who would have supposed that their own allies, the English, would have betrayed them by not taking the first opportunity to visit their island? Prices were rising fast, and the whole burden of expense was being borne by the empty hotels. It was not astonishing that, when a syndicate of Milanese profiteers arrived to buy up all the hotels and *pensions*, the owners were only too delighted to sell them. Old Luigi Zampone had died during the war, and Ferdinando was glad to be rid of the Hotel Grandioso with its crushing burden of mortgages. The white elephant which was intended to give rides and annoy Don Cesare Rocco with the sight of its populous back had turned on its owner and trampled him. But his rival himself did not live to enjoy the triumph long, and Don Cesare's widow was happy enough to be relieved of the Hotel Augusto, the empty rooms of which were haunted by the spectre of her capable husband and already reeked of bankruptcy. The example of the chief proprietors was followed by the lesser ones. Scarcely a *pension* remained in the hands of the family which had created it. There was still Zampone's Café to preserve some semblance of the old Sirenian life; but even upon Zampone's a lethargy seemed to be gradually descending. Ferdinando slept over his ledgers, and Donna Maria's head nodded and nodded behind the counter.

Carlo was not yet demobilized and Marsac, feeling that it was time he did something to impress Sirene, decided to become a Catholic. He was still supporting existence on what his mother could allow him while the commercial affairs of Europe were being tidied up. He could not afford to travel, even had there been the facilities. He required a change after the strain of the war. He wrote, as he would have written to a doctor, and asked the *parroco* to give him an appointment.

Don Pruno seemed strangely unelated by the prospect of receiving the Count into the Church. Marsac, supposing that his temporarily straitened circumstances were leading the priest to imagine that he was no longer rich, reassured him.

"But this is not a question of money," said the priest in French.

"*Ah non, mon père*, I am not suggesting such a thing. But naturally I should wish to express my appreciation of the Catholic Church by some slight gift—a new chapel, the endowment of a school, extensive benefactions to the poor—oh, there are many ways in which I perceive that I shall be desirous of assisting you as soon as I shall be in possession of my properties again."

Don Pruno took a pinch of snuff and bowed.

"Far be it from me to discourage a penitent sinner from trying to give practical expression to his remorse," said the priest. "But the Church requires from a soul his heart. She is not content to pick his pocket."

"*C'est entendu*," said Marsac cheerfully. "So, please make the necessary arrangements for my immediate reception, which will give much pleasure to my mother, who is already a Catholic."

"There will have to be a long instruction," said Don Pruno.

"An instruction in what?" Marsac asked in lofty surprise.

"A doctrinal instruction."

The aspiring neophyte chuckled complacently.

"I think that is not very necessary in my case. I am already acquainted with the doctrines. I have examined the claims of Catholicism with much care, and I was startled to find how closely they accorded with my own ideas. I assure you that I was most agreeably surprised to find how much of what I have thought for myself has been adopted by the Church. Oh, yes, I can certainly congratulate the Church on its intelligence."

One had an impression that he was patting the Pope's head; but Don Pruno took another pinch of snuff.

"And the long instruction will have to be preceded by a sign that you are serious, *monsieur le comte*."

"But naturally I am serious, *mon père*. I am not accustomed to waste my own time or the time of other people."

"*C'est bien*," the priest replied. "And first of all I shall require an assurance from you that you will dismiss your secretary."

"*Pardon?*"

"It would be impossible to consider your request as serious unless the association between you and your secretary came finally to an end."

"Am I to understand, monsieur, that you are permitting yourself to plan my future life? Let me tell you that nobody has ever dared to tell me what I must do. I imagined that you would welcome the intellectual surrender of a man like myself, but I perceive that you are incapable of esteeming the sacrifice I am willing to make. No priest shall ever arrange my private conduct. That, I venture to say, is entirely my own affair. Indeed, I can assure you that I find your suggestion excessively impertinent. The suggestion that you should instruct me was merely *bête*. At that I could afford to laugh. But when you presume on my good will to attempt to manage my household . . . ah no, that I find a little too strong."

The Count marched back to the Villa Hylas, head in air, and as he sat down at his desk to pour out in verse his indignation he muttered:

"*Ces Chrétiens ne sont que des Juifs. Ah, oui, ils sont des vrais Juifs. Mais je n'accepterai jamais la circoncision de mon cœur . . . jamais! Carlo, mon Carlo,*" he groaned to the empty air, "*tu sais combien j'ai souffert pour trouver un cœur qui comprenne mon âme désolée, tu sais qu'ils m'ont couronné d'injures à cause de toi. Reviens, Carlo! Je te veux. Je dois vivre tel que tel ils m'ont conçu. Reviens, reviens, et reste encore auprès de moi! Cherche, si tu veux, Aphrodite! Aime qui tu voudras! Mais reviens, et reste encore.*"

The *parroco* was not aware when he made the dismissal of Carlo an earnest of Marsac's repentance that Carlo himself was at this moment questioning the possibility of returning to Sirene. He would indeed have welcomed with all his heart the faintest excuse for not returning. The tails of that waiter's coat had ceased to flap in his ears since he had been in uniform. Marsac's mad egoism led him to see in the demand of the priest a plot to separate him from Carlo, and coinciding with Carlo's own evident hesitation to return made him more than ever resolved that Carlo should return. He threatened suicide. He taunted Carlo with abandoning him because he was temporarily poor. He offered him complete liberty. He pleaded the death of Miss Maimie, his only other friend, and his persecution by the malevolent Miss Virginia, now his greatest enemy. Carlo, already demobilized, lingered in Verona. Marsac sent the dusty old marquis back to France solely that he might deliver a personal message to Carlo on the way. That he did not go to Verona himself was due to his dread of being humiliated by Carlo's refusal from his own lips to return with him to the island. And then another of Sirene's tragic farces effected what all his eloquence had failed to effect.

The termination of the completely unnatural existence that Scudamore had been living for so many years seemed at last fixed. People had been saying for such a long time that the scholar could not continue to persecute his health indefinitely; but every year, growing leaner and leaner, paler and paler, he had worked incessantly all night (in which was included the task of eating the food that Nita prepared and left out for him) and sought during the daylight a feverish unrefreshing sleep. Apart from the irregularity of the book-post the war had not much affected him, unless that perhaps his meals became even yet a little more unpalatable. That now in the early Spring after the armistice he should be clutching at his counterpane to fight the agony of the gastric ulcers which had been diagnosed by Dr. Squillace could not be blamed upon the war. No illness that ever overtook a man was ever more his own fault. Yet the physical pain he suffered was as nothing compared with the mental pain he suffered on account of Tiberius. Whatever Dr. Squillace might say, Scudamore knew that he was dying with the final rehabilitation of his hero unaccomplished. The pains of indigestion had never until now been strong enough to deter him from the most arduous pursuit of a cross-reference. There had been plenty of moments when in a spasm of agony he had clutched to his breast the great musty folio he was carrying from the remote confines of the library, as a mother might think to save her child from the peril of her own weakness; but now he could not have reached up to the nearest shelf and carried thence a duodecimo volume as far as his own work-table.

He tried to divert his mind from the reproachful countenance of the slandered emperor by translating an epigram of Martial, which appropriate to the occasion was running in his mind.

Nuper erat medicus, nunc est vispillo Diaulus:
Quod vispillo facit, fecerat et medicus.

"*Squillace once a doctor now an undertaker,
 Works just as hard preparing people for their maker.* . . .
No, that's clumsy . . . *the undertaker undertakes what once
the doctor undertook* . . . no. Perhaps the other will go
better.

> *Chirurgus fuerat, nunc est vispillo Diaulus,
> Coepit quo poterat clinicus esse modo.*

"*Squillace once a surgeon now an undertaker* . . . *baker,
faker, maker, quaker* . . . oh, hell, I can't concentrate . . .
and then there's that epigram about who it was who'd
been an *ophthalmicus* and became an *oplomachus* . . . one
might work in something there about the glad eye and the
gladiator . . . queer thing for an eye-specialist to turn
gladiator and give old Martial a chance to say a distinction
without a difference. Now did I refer to that epigram
in my proposed chapter on the games?"

He rang the bell beside his bed, rang it again, and then
again before Nita appeared.

"O Nita, you might go to the third drawer on the
left of the table in the far corner from the window in the
second room and bring the drawer right up here."

"I'll do no such thing," she said. "The last words
Dr. Squillace told me was to keep you still; and still you'll
stay, or there'll be folk in Sirene to say Nita murdered you."
She tossed her head. "Ah, don't I know 'em? Jessir,
I certainly do."

"Don't be so foolish, Nita."

"Foolish?" she screamed. "And an't I worked myself
to the bone for you all these years? An't I quit my own
country for your sake? An't I been treated like a dog by
all your friends? An't I half daffy because of you lying
there so sick? Answer me that?"

"Well, if you won't fetch me the papers I want, I'll
go myself," he said, thrusting from the bed a leg as thin
as a toothpick and then writhing in the agony that the
movement set up.

"You dare to move," she shrilled. "Move, and I go right around for Mr. Menteith or Mr. Goldfinch to call them to witness before the God you mock that I'm not to be held responsible for you no longer. I won't *be* held responsible. No, I won't. I've given you all a woman can give a man. I won't *be* held responsible."

Scudamore closed his eyes wearily, exhausted by the pain and the voice that were rending him.

"Drink your milk, man alive," she adjured. "What's the use for me to search the whole of this cursed little hole of an island, if you won't drink the milk I find for you? 'Latte, latte, latte,' says Dr. Squillace to me, as if I was nutty and didn't know what latte was without him chattering it at me like a monkey. 'Oh, go along with you, you an' your "latte, latte, latte,"' I said, as I pushed him out on the street." She drew near the bed. "Say, would you believe it . . . now listen to what I'm telling you," she added roughly, for Scudamore was still lying with closed eyes that seemed to exclude her from his world. Her voice dropped again to a horribly suggestive whisper. "Say, would you believe it, but that old doctor tried to take liberties with me. He's like all your friends. There's not one of 'em that don't try an' take liberties with me. Goldfinch, Menteith, all of 'em. Animals, that's what men are. Animals. Oh, don't I know 'em? But *you*?" Her voice rose in contempt. "You jest lay there all dried up by work and you don't care nothing about it. Yet you were a man once yourself. Oh, gee, you certainly was some man once, but now I could sleep with anyone who asked me and you wouldn't give a nickel. . . ."

While this tirade went on Scudamore was lying back and pondering the first sentence that should open his great History of Roman Morals.

"*Living as we do in an age when man appears to be severing the last cords that bound him to* . . . no . . . *when man at last appears to be struggling free from the meshes* . . . no . . .

the deterrent meshes of medievalism, the study of Roman morals assumes an additional importance . . . no . . . is identified with the . . . no, no . . . I can improve on that if only this derned belly-ache would let up for a while."

The pain that was rending him and the clatter of Nita's voice were merged in his consciousness, and he bribed her to leave him by drinking a glass of the milk on which Dr. Squillace insisted. He felt that if she would only leave him she would take the pain with her and that the first sentence of his life's work might assume its final shape. But when he was alone again his mind refused to contemplate that sonorous opening he craved to settle, and turned instead to the problem of his own epitaph.

John Bendle Scudamore
Natus Novo Eboraco
Civit: Foed: Amer:
A.D. IV Id. Iul. MDCCCLVII
Mortuus Sirenibus . . .

"Mortuus quando? Before the Kalends of March, MCMXIX, I guess," he muttered, filling up the vacant date of his death with various figures. "I guess I'd better put *ante diem* instead of A.D., or some blasted hayseed mentality will think I meant *anno domini*."

Then he put out his thin white hand and picked up a small vellum-bound volume of the Annals of Tacitus.

"*Cum laude et bonis recordationibus facta atque famam nominis mei prosequantur,*" he read aloud with a hollow chuckle. And had he possessed the strength he would have smacked his leg in jubilation at finding in the most deliberate slanderer of Tiberius a sentence from one of the Emperor's own speeches which inscribed on his own tombstone could be used to the glory of that Emperor. "My name," he muttered. "His name! Our name! With praise and . . . now how would one translate *bonis recordationibus*?"

Then the fever ran high again, and from the floor round

the scholar's bed great gilded heads of Tiberius, the eyes wet with tears, rose and slowly swelled until they burst to make way for others. Sown these heads by the dragon's teeth of remorse for a labour never finished. *Opus imperfectum ! Officium inchoatum !*

When Marsac heard of the state of Scudamore's health he was perturbed for the trunks of opium stored in the Villa Parnasso. They would be safe again at the Villa Hylas now that the war was over, and the sooner they were brought back the better. Yet, having at the moment enough to smoke and having been for so long accustomed to the dusty old marquis's fetching and carrying, he postponed action. Besides, he felt incapable of meeting anybody while Carlo's return was still uncertain.

"*Oh, mon Carlo, reviens. Sois, si tu veux, dédaigneux, sois cruel dans ta beauté ; mais reviens, je t'en prie, et donne à ma douleur au moins ton sourire illusoire.*"

Thus he cried aloud across the night, standing upon his white terrace that overhung the Tyrrhenian; and for answer like a mouse the wind scuttled uneasily through the *macchia* on the cliff's face. The moon came gazing huge and tarnished above the distant Apennine. The sea turned over with a lover's sigh toward the land.

"*Ah, Carlo, si tu reviens, je serai si jaloux de t'avoir, si jaloux et si frileux d'effroi en pensant à te perdre un jour que je serai ton esclave à me croire un vainqueur. Grande lune de printemps,*" he invoked, "*dis-moi que tu ne mens pas pour me griser d'espoir. Rend-moi le despote que j'aime. Rend-moi son âme lointaine, son âme future, son cœur-inconnu. Ce soir, grande lune, tu n'est plus un nénuphar. Tu n'es qu' un pavot, fantasque et lourde d'opium. Alors, rend-moi mon rêve.*"

In the hope that the moon invoked with such passion would be kind, Marsac retired for a week into his subterranean den after giving orders that he was not to be interrupted by any news of the outer world. He had now as sole servant an elderly and rather lazy cook who was only too glad to see his master retire to his divans and be spared the trouble of making his bed or laying the table for meals. Marsac had planned with himself that Carlo should return and wake him from one of his drugged trances in much the same way as the Prince woke the Sleeping Beauty. However, at the end of a week Carlo had not returned, and his stock of opium was very low. He roused himself to pay a visit to Scudamore.

"But the *signore* of the Villa Parnasso is dead and buried," the elderly servant informed him.

"*Que je suis un homme infortuné!*" Marsac cried. "*Une haine implacable me poursuit.*"

He hurriedly divested himself of the deep blue robe threaded in gold with the Chinese symbols of longevity in which he had been dreaming and donned his ordinary clothes. It was astonishing how fresh he always looked after one of these bouts. A pale violet beneath the eyes, a faint puffiness, and that was all. The almond-blossom seemed very rich in the fading grey light of the February afternoon as he hurried along the narrow walled *viali* toward the town. By the time he reached the Villa Parnasso it was dark and the unlighted patio was chill and eerie. Nita opened the door. By the flickering candle she held up to see who the visitor was Marsac perceived that her eyes were red and swollen with weeping.

"Good evening, Madame Nita. I have only at this moment heard of my poor friend's death, for I have been excessively ill myself."

"He's dead!" she cried, sitting down with the candlestick in her lap on the marble steps that led up into the villa from the door. "He's dead, Count Marsac. He's dead and buried."

"Tranquillize yourself, my poor woman," said the Count, assuming the grand style of sympathy.

"Oh, I haven't slept since they put him in his grave. But come right in, Count Marsac. His friends are my friends. I've been so misjudged. They said I tried to keep his friends from him. But never! Never, Count Marsac! It was Tiberius kept them away. It was that dirty old heathen, not me. So, come right in."

She led the way into the first of the dead scholar's rooms. The work-table once covered with half-sheets of notepaper and open books was now covered with unwashed china.

"I haven't had the heart to wash up a thing since they took him from me. But let me get you a cup of tea. There's still plenty of clean cups, so it won't be any trouble."

Marsac declined her hospitality.

"Will you have some whisky?"

"Nothing, I thank you."

"A drop of Canadian Club? Come on now."

"Indeed no, I assure you, Madame Nita."

"He's left me well provided for, Count Marsac.'

"But naturally."

"Only, *I* don't want the dollars, Count Marsac. I'd give every dollar he's left me to have him back. And I looked after him. I was his slave. Milk he was ordered and milk he had. But he'd overdone himself. He couldn't make a fight. That dirty old Tiberius had sucked the life out of the poor man. And of course when the ulcers started perforating it was nothing at all for them, because he wasn't much thicker than a two-cent stamp."

"Poor fellow, poor fellow," Marsac murmured impatiently. He wanted to talk about his trunks of opium.

"I'd have ground my fingers to the bone for him, Count Marsac," she moaned. "And yet there's folks here'll say the contrary, the wicked liars that people are on this mean little cork of an island."

"I must excuse myself for intruding upon your sadness, Madame Nita . . ."

"Oh, I welcome a bit of company," she broke in effusively.

"You are most obliging . . . but you will without doubt remember that I have deposited here there are some months two trunks, from which I have often sent my friend the Marquis de la Tour des Bois to extract packets of my requirements."

"Oh, that smutty little old marquis! The liberties he tried to take with me. I had to watch his hand like a cat watches a mouse."

"*Bien, bien, bien!*" Marsac chattered impatiently. "The Marquis has departed. I shall send the *facchini* to fetch these trunks to-morrow morning."

"But you can't," Nita told him. "Everything in the house is sealed up until the lawyers have finished. Why, even I mayn't touch a thing. That comes of dying in a place like Sirene. These dagos are such thieves themselves, they can't believe in anybody being honest. They're afraid I'll try and sell his books." She laughed hideously. "Sell his books! As if I wanted his books! If ever a man was choked by books, it was surely him."

She began to weep again.

"But excuse me, Madame Nita, it will be easy to explicate to the lawyers that these trunks are mine."

"Count Marsac, of all his friends I like you the best. Now that's talking from my heart . . . oh, my heart. Feel the way it's going." And before Marsac could stop her she had seized his hand and was pressing it to her flabby breast. Had she plunged it into boiling water he could not have snatched it away more hastily, and he looked at it anxiously as if it might have been actually blistered by her scalding femininity.

"Oh, Count Marsac," she groaned. "I want consoling. Nobody understands what I'm suffering. I'm so lonesome. There isn't anybody but me in the house. Would you like to come upstairs and see the room where he died? And I'll show you my room. The bed's all untidy because I haven't had the heart to make it. But you won't mind that. Oh, if you knew what it was to feel as lonesome as what *I* do and have someone as sympathetic as what you are come and console me."

"I cannot wait now, Madame," said Marsac pale with apprehension of what she would do next. "Indeed I am feeling a little bit sick."

"Lie down on the sofa. Lie right down, there's a dear man, and I'll . . ."

"*Non, non*, I cannot," he almost shrieked.

"What blue eyes you surely have! Why, they're jest as blue as a cute lil' baby's."

"Madame Nita, *je vous en prie*," Marsac protested.

"Oh, I'm in such a state, Count Marsac. Maybe it's the indigestion. I've been drinking too much tea. I don't know what I'm doing. Don't go away and leave me. Nobody'll come in. The front door's locked."

The Count was so terrified by this dark blowsy creature of whose gypsy beauty nothing remained except a pair of horribly bright dark eyes, and they ringed with the bloated crimson of a week's unrestrained sobbing, that any thought of rescuing his opium was swallowed up in the need to rescue himself.

When he had escaped from the Villa Parnasso and stood outside, breathing in the frore air of the February night, Marsac felt like a child who has escaped from a witch's tower.

The next day when he came down to lunch he found the dining-room at the Villa Hylas full of bunches of narcissus. He was furious, and rated his servant.

"I have given orders that I will not permit the flowers in my garden to be picked," he fumed.

"Excuse me, *signor conte*," said Domenico. "These flowers are not from your garden. They are a present from the *signora* of the Villa Parnasso. She brought them up herself."

The Count sank down into a chair, and mopped his forehead with a scented handkerchief.

"The *signora* wished to speak to you personally," Domenico continued. "But I did not think you would wish to be woken. The *signora* asked me to tell you that she had been to see the Avvocato Galuppi and that the Avvocato Galuppi could not permit anything to be moved at present. The *signora* . . ."

"*Mais, basta con tua 'signora,'*" Marsac screamed. "*Mon dieu, non si da 'signora' alle puttane.*"

Domenico bowed his head politely as a token that he accepted the Count's ruling.

"*Quella donna* said that she would be at home from five to eight if the *signor conte* would go down to see her."

"Lock the gates!" Marsac cried.

Domenico bowed.

"Bolt the doors!"

Domenico bowed again.

"Close the shutters! Fling those disgusting flowers over the cliff. Fetch my revolver. Go down into Sirene with this telegram and tell Gigi to come up at once and to bring his gun with him. Go to the *maresciallo* and ask him to send at once two *carabinieri* to protect the villa."

Domenico bowed again and retired with the telegram.

On his way down to Sirene he met Gigi Gasparri followed by two slaves loaded with plants for the garden of the Villa Hylas.

"*Buon giorno, Gigi.*"

"*Buon giorno, Mimì.*"

"*È uscito pazzo.*"

"Who has gone mad?"

"*Il conte.*"

"No!"

"*Sì!* He says that he intends to shoot anybody who comes near the villa."

Gigi clicked his tongue.

381

"Then, I'd better not do any planting to-day."

He turned to the slaves and bade them carry back their baskets to the nursery.

"He told me that you were to bring up your gun," Domenico added.

"Bring up my own gun to be shot? Thanks! He's not going to shoot me with my own gun," said Gigi firmly.

"He has telegraphed for the secretary."

"What does the telegram say?" Gigi asked, reading it through. "Do you think he wants to shoot him too?"

"Who knows?" said Domenico shaking his head.

The gardener paused reflectively.

"Well, if he wants to shoot somebody," he said at last, "it would be better to shoot the secretary. I shall send him a telegram myself and advise him to come at once."

"To be shot?"

"Naturally I shan't tell him he's going to be shot. I am not an imbecile," said Gigi scornfully.

And it was the gardener's telegram that fetched Carlo back to Sirene.

Qui tutto disordinatissimo conte Marsac ammalatissimo venite prestissimo

Luigi Gasparri
Orticoltore
Sirene.

Where Marsac's emotional appeals had failed to touch Carlo's heart Gigi's superlatives reproached his secretarial conscience.

As a matter of fact the Count never did recover his store of opium, for when finally the legal formalities were concluded and eight porters groaning, sweating, and cursing brought the trunks up to the Villa Hylas, they were discovered to be full of Scudamore's books instead of the priceless narcotic. A piece of paper inside explained the reason:

VESTAL FIRE

I am sending you some of HIS books because I know he would like you to have them instead of giving them all to that college which he said to do in his will. Lawyers may be smart, but this child am smarter.

Even the language the porters used when they were ordered to carry back the trunks without so much as a glass of wine to refresh themselves was hardly as strong as the language the Count used when Nita sent another message to say that she could not find the opium.

And to this day nobody knows what happened to it. It is one of the few Sirenian mysteries, for islands in that clarity of southern air do not breed gothic terrors.

Instead of making the best of a compulsory cure and trying to build up some kind of an edifice out of the ruins of his futile existence Marsac now set out to make his happiness dependent on cocaine.

Nita, after the Villa Parnasso was sold to an American family and she found herself in full control of the money she had inherited from Scudamore, stayed on for about six months in Sirene, buying a new hat every week and a variety of gaudy clothes. Then she went back to America.

And the mistake that Scudamore dreaded was after all perpetuated upon his tombstone, for Harry Menteith and Herbert Bookham who had charge of it did get confused between *ante diem* and *anno domini*, so that the scholar lies for ever under a piece of bastard Latinity. Tacitus was avenged for the defiant theft of that sentence from his Annals.

Chapter 6

orba est, dives, anus.

MARTIAL

FOR the next year the Milanese Hotel Company disgorged some of the profits of war in what they called bringing Sirene up to date. Their avowed intention was to rescue it from the unpleasant bohemianism of manners and morals for which the island had long been notorious and convert it into a fashionable health resort. So, the wives and daughters of the directors in guaranteed Parisian models hobbled about the roughly paved alleys with high heels. The air seemed heavy with large hips and rice powder and the languors of Latin vulgarity. A notice board was fixed to the baroque tower giving the statistics of the temperature, the distance of every famous belvedere from the Piazza, and the prices that the drivers of the *carrozze* were entitled to ask. If the Company had acquired an hotel surrounded by a fair old wall over which sprawled a tangle of roses and wistaria, it pulled down the wall and put up iron railings in the convulsive Munich style; it put up the prices at the same time. The death or departure of so many old Sirenian figures and the destruction of so many old Sirenian buildings by the hard-headed Milanese, whose sense of beauty did not extend beyond the notion of a fat woman in bed, made all the survivors of old-fashioned days lament the way the island was being spoilt. To be sure, Sirene was changing, yet perhaps not quite so profoundly as the veterans of bygone pleasure supposed. Newcomers

VESTAL FIRE

who would evidently maintain the reputation of the Sirenian stage for comic excellence were already making their first entrances among the temporary nobility of the place; but diverting though the pursuit of these new protagonists would be we must stick to what is left of our own protagonists, for their play is not yet over.

Mrs. Ambrogio was one of those who felt that the old life was disappearing.

"Everybody dying. Feel so old myself. Hate these Napolitans who've come for the Summer. So dirty. The old woman at the bathing-place told me the sea's quite black every morning. Wrote last week to dear old Miss Norton to say all's well at the Amabile. Haven't had an answer yet. She's probably dead herself. Never come back to Sirene. Nearly a hundred. So glad old Goldfinch has got his friend Sheila Macleod with him for a few weeks. And Major Natt's quite happy because he can have his beloved Germans again. Never forgive him for the way he spoke against my poor old England during the war. Ought to be ashamed of himself. Go to tea at the Capo di Monte, but never feel the same towards him. Saw Carlo yesterday. Looking so worried, poor boy. Told him all lies that Peter and I made the split between him and the Nortons. Says the trees so thick at the Villa Hylas now they can't walk in the garden at all and the Count won't have one cut. Got his money again at last. Sure he tried to get hold of the darling old Nortons' money. Everybody after it except Peter. Thank heaven, Peter's honest. Goes down twice a week to the Amabile to see that the seals haven't been touched. Wish I could run over to dear old England now the war's over. Can't afford it. Lost all my money. Two paying guests. Young Napolitan married to an Egyptian princess. Jealous. Frightfully jealous. My God, you don't know how jealous that woman is! Beats him on the head with the heel of her shoe when he comes home late. Making love all over the house. Can't help it, poor boy. Beats him if he won't. Never mind. Pay their bill every week. Couldn't live otherwise."

This, with a few interjections from her audience, was Mrs. Ambrogio's summary of the state of affairs in Sirene that Summer.

And indeed it did seem improbable that Miss Virginia would ever come back from America, so improbable indeed that when that Autumn in various shops pieces of Oriental fabrics and embroideries were offered for sale, although people had an uncomfortable notion that they were extremely like some of the fabrics and embroideries they had seen in the Villa Amabile, they could not resist buying them. What they felt was that, if they did belong to Miss Virginia, the old lady was never likely to come back and miss them and that, if they did not belong to her, they were being sold much too cheaply to let strangers take advantage of such bargains.

"Well, I haven't been inside the Amabile for so many years," said Mrs. Dawson to Mr. Bookham, "that I really can't be expected to know where they do come from. Old Cataldo told me he bought them from a wandering Indian who wanted to pay his fare back to Ceylon."

"I bought my wife a kimono with which she's delighted," the churchwarden admitted. "Oh, by the way, we've got a chaplain coming out in December, Mrs. Dawson. It's a shell-shock case, poor fellow, so the Bishop is delighted to do something for him."

"Why, I'm truly sorry to hear that, Mr. Bookham. Dear me, what with Nigel growing a beard and me with my hair snow white, what we have all been through! Well, you think it'll be quite all right if I buy this perfectly stunning old shawl?"

Mrs. Dawson was now a white Brahma-Dorking, and Bookham's hair was brindled like a Plymouth Rock; but Major Natt, thrusting his long neck between them, was outwardly the same old gobbler that he was that Sunday in May on which this tale began.

"Good morning, Mrs. Dawson. Good morning, Bookham. You're both perpending, I see. I confess I have been tempted to acquire some of these barbaric splendours myself. Rumour says they are the fruits of that circumnavigation of the globe just before the war. People are continually stealing my books, but I don't know that I can make that a legitimate excuse . . . and yet if we don't buy them somebody else will."

"Why, how perfectly true that is, Major Natt," Mrs. Dawson agreed.

"But if they were stolen, who stole them?" the churchwarden boomed.

"Who stole them? Good lord, who do you think stole them, my dear man?"

It was Mrs. Macadam who had joined the little group and who stood there eyeing it with a gaze that the most sophisticated detective might have envied.

"Oh, come now, Mrs. Macadam, these innuendoes are monstrous," the Major exhaled.

"Monstrous yourself," retorted Mrs. Macadam indignantly. "I haven't accused anybody, have I?"

"Indeed you certainly have not, Mrs. Macadam," Mrs. Dawson put in hastily.

"If anybody's innuending it's Major Natt," Mrs. Macadam continued. "Good lord, now the damned war's over let's have a bit of peace on Sirene. That's what I say. Here, did you know that geese can't make love without a pond? Peter Ambrogio told me that yesterday. So that's why I haven't had any young ones since I started keeping them when my dear old boy crossed the road for the last time. Eggs, yes. But, you know; they're not tutti frutti. What?"

This was too much for the chafferers and chatterers outside Cataldo's shop. The bazaar broke up.

"Silly fools pretending to be shocked," Effie murmured to herself contemptuously as she watched the departing figures. "And now I suppose it will be all over Sirene that I said Maud Ambrogio stole the stuff from the Villa Amabile."

She turned to old Cataldo.

"Senter, signor Catalder," she began, assuming again that concentrated gaze of the detective. "Quester coser sonner . . ."

"*Molto belle cose, evvero, signora?*" the dealer interrupted, rubbing his hands over the fabrics he was offering so cheap.

"Yes, I know they're multer beller. But who brought them in to you? Chi portata? Io so bene." She thumped her chest in case her Italian might have failed to convey the accuracy of her intelligence.

Old Cataldo shrugged his shoulders and looked puzzled. He had no intention of understanding what Mrs. Macadam meant; and indeed there was, grammatically, no reason why he should.

"Voi capeeter bene. Si, si, si! Multer forber. Si, si, si!" Then she picked up a pair of embroidered slips of faded green silk. "Quanter coster, eh?"

"*Venti lire, signora.*"

She pitched them back on the counter.

"Tropper caro. Io non millionaria. Here, I'll give you ten. Dieci."

Cataldo shook his head.

"*Mi dispiace, signora, ma non è possibile. Per Lei diciotto. Eightatin, perchè Lei è stata sempre gentile, sempre buona. Allora per Lei facciamo un prezzo speciale.*"

"Eighteen a special price? Shut up! Here, I'll give you twelve. Dochi."

Cataldo shook his head.

"Oh, then keep your rotten old chin-chin-chinaman rubbish. I've been in China myself," she said, marching out of the shop.

On her way down the Via Caprera Effie met Mrs. Ambrogio.

"Hullo, Maud. Here, do you know what everybody's saying?"

"Don't know. Don't care. Never listen to gossip. What are they saying?"

"Why, they're all saying that you've been selling the stuff from the Villa Amabile round Sirene."

Mrs. Ambrogio sat down on one of the seats thoughtfully provided by the *Società Pro Sirene* to deal with crises of this nature in the Via Caprera.

"Oo! Oo! What disgusting lies! Oo! Everything locked and sealed. Peter keeps the keys in his safe. Who said I'd stolen them?"

Effie Macadam pondered a moment.

"Well, Marian said to me only yesterday that somebody had told her that old Catalder had sold Mrs. Dawson a mandarin's robe that was awfully like one Miss Maimie brought back with her from China."

"That beastly woman! How I hate her! *How* I hate her! And I've been so good to her! Stuck up for her through thick and thin. Knew she was in bed with that young Dutchman the other afternoon when I called. Didn't say a word to anybody. Loyal. Always loyal to my friends. Told everybody I didn't believe she was in bed with anybody. Tried to tempt Peter. Said she had a mosquito-bite on her knee. Nothing but an excuse. Came into the room. Peter red as fire. Oh, I gave her such a look! Cut her dead after this. Never speak to her again. Never take her part again. Sleep with anybody she likes. Shan't put out a finger to help her. Sirene not what it was. Never will be. Never was. Everything sealed up. Lies! Lies! Lies! Go mad if I stay here much longer. Must get over to dear old Blighty next year. Everywhere else except England nothing but lies."

Had Sirene felt that Miss Virginia would ever come back, it would never have enjoyed suspecting Mrs. Ambrogio of having despoiled the coffers of the Villa Amabile, because in that case the matter would have drawn far too near to the world of reality that the world of scandal so genuinely abhors.

And then as Mrs. Ambrogio, with a sequence of logical thought that could only have been evoked by intense emotion, exclaimed:

"If they think I stole the things, why are they all in such a damned hurry to buy them?"

However, gradually the pieces of Oriental stuffs, the rugs, and the robes vanished into private houses or the trunks of transient visitors, and before Christmas it would have been a dull dog that would have ventured to discuss whether or not Mrs. Ambrogio had had anything to do with the matter. No lees indeed remained in the tea-cup where such a storm had been brewed except Mrs. Ambrogio's ignorance of Mrs. de Feltre's existence and Mrs. de Feltre's amazing unawareness of Mrs. Ambrogio's overpowering presence.

"Here, what's this everybody's saying about you going for a week to Naples with that young Dutchman, Marian?" Mrs. Macadam had asked her.

"I like Van Loon very much," Mrs. de Feltre replied in her most ponderously conceited drawl, "but I don't think I've quite reached the age for making a fool of myself over a boy of twenty-two, my dear Effie."

"Well, I was told you went to the Hotel Erupshione with him in Naples and never came down from your room the whole week except for dinner."

"My dear Effie, I haven't been over to Naples since Van Loon came to Sirene."

"Well, there you are," Mrs. Macadam ejaculated in tones of the profoundest satisfaction and relief. "It only shows what people will say. I'll tell Maud next time I see her she got the whole story wrong."

"Oh, it was Maud Ambrogio who told you this, was it? Well, that's the end of Maud so far as this child is concerned.

And when I think of the times I've said 'no' to Peter for her sake. My dear Effie, do you wonder I'm a cynic?"

"Well, I wouldn't want to be a sinner with Peter Ambrogio! Good lord, I'll get something better than that if I ever go off the deep end."

And when next Mrs. Ambrogio and Mrs. de Feltre found themselves in the same *salone* they were as unresponsive as two of the arm-chairs.

"Silly asses," said Mrs. Macadam. "Good lord, if I'd stopped to listen to half the things they say about me on Sirene, I might as well go into a deaf and dumb home right off. Are you going to dine at the Villa Adonis to-night? I intend to jolly well enjoy myself, whatever other people do."

So she did, and reaching her little house on the slopes of San Giorgio about four in the morning she let herself quietly into her wardrobe with her latchkey; and while Maria, her little maid, was scouring Sirene for her next morning, she emerged about noon from the heap of skirts in which she had wrapped herself and was cooking lunch when Maria returned.

"Here, do you know what I did after I came home from dear old Chris Goldfinch's dinner last night?" she asked at Zampone's where various friends were having tea. "I got mixed between my front-door key and the key for my wardrobe, and I thought my wardrobe door was the front door. I said 'damn it, this house has got jolly small since yesterday.' Good job I didn't think my front-door was the wardrobe, or I might have undressed in the street and hung up all my frillies on the knocker. And I slept awfully well. But the joke is my little maid Maria was sure I'd been out all night on the razzle, because she couldn't find me when she came in with the coffee. I thought that was rather funny, I must say."

Sirenian life was continuing, and Effie Macadam was maintaining the tradition of ancient eccentricities against the efforts of the post-war generation to impress itself upon an island which had beheld so many post-war generations.

And then in the Spring the news came that Miss Virginia was actually on her way home from America.

"So happy," Mrs. Ambrogio declared. "So glad the old pet's coming back. Never thought she would. Made up my mind she'd die in America. Can't forget all those lies they told about me in Sirene last Autumn. Wounded my quick. Didn't say much, but felt it frightfully. Cried my eyes out every night. So did Peter. No paying guests this Spring. Starve in the gutter presently."

There was nobody to welcome Miss Virginia's return in April except the Ambrogios and the members of her own household who had been living in idleness at the Villa Amabile since the old lady went away nearly two years ago. Indeed, there were no other old friends left nowadays, except Effie Macadam, who was in Rome, and Burlingham, who was seriously ill.

Miss Virginia did not seem changed. She carried herself as straight as ever, though she was now drawing very near to ninety. Her eyes were not less keen. Her fan cleft the air not less sharply. She arrived with a companion —a pleasant colourless woman called Miss Hazell, whom Mrs. Ambrogio viewed with the profoundest suspicion and therefore treated with effusive cordiality.

Before she entered the Villa Amabile that morning Miss Virginia drove on in the carriage to the rose-hung gate of the cemetery, and here alighting she bade Miss Hazell wait outside while she went in. One or two curious visitors who had been gazing at the epitaphs turned round to stare at the ivory-pale old lady sitting on that marble stool beside the big tomb, sitting there in the April sunlight and gazing out over the azure bay through that window cut in the cemetery wall. They wondered who she was, those strangers to her passionate proud life.

Ten minutes later, Miss Virginia rejoined Miss Hazell in the carriage and drove down to the villa.

"My, how sweetly our dear little birdies are singing," she said, as she paused a moment by the big gilded cage to greet the canaries. "And looking so fat and well and happy too," she added with a smile of congratulation for the various members of the *famiglia* who were following at her heels.

In the *salone* Peter Ambrogio assumed his most official manner in order to hand over to her the keys of her house. She thanked him and bade him and his dear wife to lunch the next day.

"You'll pardon me if I don't ask you to stay right now and have lunch with me. And I wonder if you'd drive Miss Hazell up with you, dear Mrs. Ambrogio, and show her a bit of our beloved wee island? I just feel I'd like to be all by myself till after tea-time."

At six o'clock Miss Hazell, a little bewildered by the hours she had spent with Mrs. Ambrogio and deciding that Europe was a great deal more unlike America than she had imagined in her most extravagant dreams, came back to the Villa Amabile and heard Miss Virginia's voice shrilling as in all the months she had been with her she had never heard it at home. She hurried upstairs and found the old lady standing in the middle of the *salone*, the *famiglia* huddling away from her wrath.

"Miss Hazell," she cried, "go right back up to Sirene and fetch Mr. Ambrogio! Tell him we've been robbed of everything we had. He's to bring back the carbineeri right along with him."

"The what, Miss Pepworth-Norton?"

"The Italian police, girl. Our silver's gone. All the precious things we brought back from China are gone. The cupboards are empty."

There were, of course, plenty of people to say that the

Ambrogios had robbed the old lady. Who else, they asked, except Peter could have removed the seals he had himself affixed ? Who else except him had the right keys when they were removed ? And how was it, they reminded one another, that when the Oriental rugs and robes were being openly sold in the second-hand shops neither of the Ambrogios suspected a robbery unless they themselves were the robbers ?

Indeed, the case looked so black against the Ambrogios that for the first time in the memory of Sirene Mrs. Ambrogio was dumb in her own defence. Yet her dumbness, could people but have realized it, was a strong argument in favour of her innocence. She had been in the wrong so often, and always in order to silence the clamour of her own conscience so volubly in the right, that to find her now without a protest should have made people hesitate now before they condemned her.

The inquisition by the police was a long and wearisome business. The stuff sold in Sirene was easily traceable, and all those excellent bargains of the previous Autumn had to be surrendered. Yet, nothing could shake the united testimony of the shopkeepers that they had bought the goods from a wandering Indian. It was true that a Hindoo had passed through Sirene, but that he could successfully have broken into the Villa Amabile and stripped the sealed-up chests and cupboards of their contents was unbelievable. The important part of the loot could not be traced at all. The silver and the valuables had certainly not been disposed of on the island itself. This produced another theory of the part the Ambrogios had played. It was suggested that they had stolen the real valuables and as a blind allowed the servants to steal and sell locally the Oriental stuffs. Peter Ambrogio had naturally made many enemies during his magistracy, and again it was surely a sign of his innocence that not one of these enemies could manage to implicate him.

Christopher Goldfinch had a theory that the Count had committed the burglary.

"Why, it's as clear as daylight," he croaked. "A mean-spirited skunk like that, why, it's just the very way he'd been revenged on that poor old woman down there. You remember all that trouble there was with Nita over those trunks he'd stored at poor Jack Scudamore's? Why, it's as clear as daylight. Only, Nita was one too many for him. I guess she was wise to what he'd done and took the stuff away back with her to America."

But attractive though this theory was for an afternoon, general opinion condemned the Ambrogios. Poor Peter went about looking pale and worried, crossing over to Naples almost every day to interview the Commissioner of Police, coming back to Sirene looking paler and more worried than ever. His wife visited Miss Virginia boldly every afternoon or morning for a month until Mrs. Macdonnell arrived back in Sirene, and she found Miss Virginia becoming stonier and stonier every time she called.

"That disgusting Macdonald woman is telling lies about me. Know it. Feel it," she confided in Effie Macadam. "Well, let her have the Villa Amabile when Miss Virginia dies. She's wanted it all these years. Let her persuade Miss Virginia to leave it to her. Don't care. Hate the place now. Can't sit down on a chair without feeling she thinks I'm trying to get up with the cushion. Hot bricks all the time. Hope she does leave the Villa to that vile beast of a woman."

And in the big *salone* down at the Villa Amabile Mrs. Macdonnell sat in crimson and cerise like a funeral pyre consuming all Miss Virginia's dead friendships.

"Ha-ha," laughed the Count up at the Villa Hylas, inhaling the white dust of cocaine. "I am a little afraid that our friend Madame Ambrogio will not inherit Miss Norton's money after all. She has poisoned me, and now she is being herself poisoned. *C'est rigolo.*"

However, the innocence of the Ambrogios was at last proved when the robbery was traced home to fat Agostino. Toward the close of the war he had become wildly enamoured of a kind of Carmen who lived in the *basso porto* of Naples, and it was she who had instructed him how to remove the seals with a hot knife, who had supplied the skeleton keys, and who had disposed of the silver for him. His father and the rest of the family were suspected of complicity, and it was probably they who, feeling quite sure that Miss Virginia would never return to Sirene, had sold the fabrics and robes, perhaps using the wandering Hindoo as an intermediary.

So, Agostino, who had been Miss Virginia's own special favourite out of that family she had cherished for close on thirty years, was loaded with chains and led away from Sirene to trial and sentence and long imprisonment.

Chapter 7

eheu quam Marathus lento me torquet amore!
deficiunt artes deficiuntque doli.
parce, puer, quaeso, ne turpis fabula fiam,
cum mea ridebunt vana magisteria.

TIBULLUS

IT was not Miss Virginia's habit to wrap her toga about her and fall when she was stabbed by a Brutus. The treachery of Agostino, on whom she had lavished so much fondness, was perhaps the cause of prolonging her life. Just as she had recovered from the death of Miss Maimie by having to express her hatred of Marsac, so now, when everybody declared that she had merely come back to Sirene to die and find eternal rest beside Miss Maimie in that tomb, she had been galvanized into a fresh frightening vigour by the outrage of the robbery and the behaviour of the fat youth she had cherished from babyhood. Her pride sustained her to show the utmost mercilessness of which she was capable. But of Miss Virginia presently. . . .

Marsac, becoming all the time more and more dependent upon cocaine, continued to live his futile existence at the Villa Hylas. There is little interest in following the psychological progress of a drug-taker whose mental symptoms reproduce with a cloying monotony the symptoms of all those who have taken drugs before him. It is a common superstition to believe that a man can be ruined by narcotics; but such a man is always ruined before he allows them to take possession of his character. You seldom find the foul freckles of henbane very far from the rubbish of human habitations; it does not thrive with the honest weeds that haunt the tillage.

In fairness to Marsac it may be said that he did not pretend that he might have been other than he was without the poisonous influence of narcotics. On the contrary he was inclined to attribute whatever he fancied he had added to the sum of artistic achievement to their aid. Whenever he could, he obtained fresh supplies of opium; but nowadays cocaine was his chief guide among the mazes of unreality.

He still wrote a great deal of verse, mostly variations on one theme. Formerly he had drawn many attractive pictures of his friendship with Carlo when that friendship set free from the bonds of passion should achieve the perfect serenity of human intercourse. But now, when Carlo had returned to him from what was only a deep sense of duty and loyalty, Marsac spent all his emotion in appeals to resume the old manner of life. There was no longer the least hint in his verse of that calm eventide to which he had once looked forward so eloquently. There was nothing but the hyperbolical expression of thwarted passion; and not the richest embroidery of words or phrases could make anything but disgusting the sores with which this beggar of love tried to win alms.

There were many times when Carlo was on the verge of abandoning Marsac. The war had given him a new confidence in himself. Since he was a boy of thirteen he had never been separated from his patron except for a few weeks during that Winter when Madame Protopopesco ruled at the Villa Hylas. The waiter's tail-coat was no longer a nightmare. Even should that be his ultimate lot, it no longer seemed such a hard one. He had learned during the war that physical discomfort and physical pain gave back to a man as much as they took away. He could now only bring himself to endure Marsac's alternate reproaches and self-abasement by reminding himself that he had been able in the past to put up with his own self-abasement. He was in fact discovering for himself that penance was founded not upon the counsel of interested ecclesiastics, but upon a tremendous desire and profound need of the human mind.

A cynic might argue that Carlo's penance was an easy one. His life was superficially enviable enough. He ate well and drank well. He had clothes and entertainment. He met plenty of amusing people, for Marsac made no pretence of being a hermit in these days. The new society of the island was empirical; there were enough houses where they were welcomed to create the illusion that the ambient wherein they moved was the essential Sirene. The war had begotten at any rate a spirit of tolerance, though whether that spirit was the result of moral exhaustion, or an apology for allowing humanity to relapse into barbarism, or a genuine attempt by the imagination to reach out toward a wider comprehension of life, it would have been hard to decide. Besides the advantage of a comfortable existence at the moment, a cynic might add, Carlo could suppose that he was securing for himself a comfortable existence in the future.

Yet it is certain that none of these considerations weighed much with Carlo in consenting to remain at the Villa Hylas. He was now over thirty. He had learnt to feel compassion without youth's dread of being thought sentimental. He regarded Marsac as a madman incapable of protecting himself. Aware that the world had no longer the right to despise him for what he was, though it might continue to despise him for what he had been, Carlo had no qualms about looking the world in the face. In old days he had avoided the curious glance, and even in the presence of those presumed to be sympathetic he used to speak rarely. Now it was Marsac who was glum and Carlo who sustained the outward forms of polite intercourse. In old days, when the Count with his head in the air of a self-conscious aristocratic hauteur had marched through the town, Carlo had always seemed to drag shamefacedly a yard behind him. Now they marched abreast, and whereas once Carlo had always raised his hat a second or two after the Count, now their two hats came off with the simultaneous precision of a couple of military automatons. In spite of opium and cocaine Marsac had lost none of his boyishness of carriage. His complexion, too, was as clear as when he first landed on the island. It was impossible to believe that he was drawing very near to forty. And from his blue eyes the tragic follies of a wasted life vanished in the glow of a superb self-importance that added to his general air of youthfulness, because it is from the eyes of youth that vanity always shines out most brightly. Much of Marsac's verse had formerly been inspired by the need to express his perpetual condition of being misunderstood by the mass of mankind. Now he wrote entirely about Carlo's failure to understand him.

"You have been blunted by the war," he told him. "You have lost the power to appreciate the subtlety of a nature like mine."

"I am more than thirty years old, Robert. The time has come for me to be my real self."

"*Mon dieu*, you were far more yourself when you only lived in and by me than you are now."

"My mind is made up," Carlo insisted obstinately.

"Your mind? Ha-ha! I find the idea that you have a mind a little droll. Your mind, my friend, is a receptacle into which for the last four years the mob has been pouring all its rubbish. Your mind is become like the minds of all except a few superior spirits, a mere wastepaper basket. If you had this mind of your own, you would at once be able to comprehend my need. But no, you are now no more than a beautiful bronze incapable of responding to the salute of my soul. I receive more sympathy from the phantoms that haunt my own dreams than I receive from you. Ah, that is my tragedy—that only in myself do I find a response to myself. Into your outward beauty I could have breathed the half of myself and of you made a human being more perfect than Cellini's David. You transformed by my genius might have conquered that Goliath, the world."

Carlo shrugged his shoulders. He had had enough of conquering the world up on the Piave.

"I have been thwarted all my life," Marsac cried. "*Grand dieu*, I have never been allowed the illusion of even a moment's happiness. My childhood? Lonely and misunderstood. *Le lycée?* An eternal horror. My mother whom I adored and who, by the way, is coming to stay here with my sister next week—you will have to arrange to find a maid for her—my mother whom I adored and who is indeed a very charming woman was, alas, entirely occupied with herself and utterly incapable of appreciating me. And then my military service! *Mon dieu*, what I suffered in those lousy barracks. I did not comprehend my temperament then. I wandered through the hideous fogs of Lille like a damned soul. I fancied that I must love a woman, and I had an idyll with the daughter of a *petit négociant*. And then I discovered that she, whom I had imagined to be icily pure because she was enshrined in my own purity and innocence, was indeed by no means pure. Listen how abominably I was betrayed."

Carlo listened as earnestly as it is possible to listen to a tale one has already heard a hundred times.

"I found her in the arms of one of my comrades. Yet she was the means of revealing to me that I despised women, and for that I forgive her. For that I even forgive all women. Yes, because when I surprised her in the arms of my comrade I found that I was angry with her for robbing me of his friendship. Of my sufferings when I was unjustly condemned in Paris I will not speak to you, who were once my second self. I sought relief upon this enchanted island from Man's persecution. I dreamed—*rêveur de demains que je suis*—that here you and I would by the perfection of our united life together turn the world back from the filthy road of Christianity along which it has been wallowing for nineteen hundred years. *Mais non!* I must again be persecuted and driven forth. Again by my indomitable will I conquer and return in triumph, and fate launches against me this atrocious war. I struggle, bereft of you, deserted by all. I struggle on. My adored friend, who alone of women was capable of understanding me, falls ill and is poisoned by that old witch Miss Virginia. And why? Because she was jealous of me. She comprehended that under my influence Miss Maimie would elude her own vulgarity. But still I struggle on, saying to myself that he who was torn from me will return in the end. Alas, I have yet to suffer my greatest disillusionment. You have returned; but you are a stranger. Your eyes that were once blue islands set in unfathomable seas are now tawdry mirrors which reflect the disgusting rotundities of displeasing *cocottes*."

Then the rhetorician fell upon his knees:

"*Carlo, Carlo, pleurant à tes pieds et t'aimant comme je t'aimerai toujours, je t'assure que je n'attend que ton baiser pour revivre.*"

"*Mais, Robert, ce que tu demandes n'est plus possible. È impossibile, caro amico mio,*" he pleaded, plunging back into his own tongue in the embarrassment the humiliation of his friend was causing him. "*Supera le mie forze. Supera la mia intelligenza. Non ci pensiamo più. Perchè vuoi tornare sempre sullo stesso argomento?*"

Marsac rose from his knees and eyed him gloomily.

"I perceive," he said, "that I have now only one more disillusionment left, which is to find that even my death has been deprived of all its sweetness by the intrusion of a disgusting immortality. *Du reste*, I am convinced that this disillusionment is close at hand."

"Don't talk like that," Carlo begged.

"Talk? Talk? *Mon dieu*, I have forgotten how to talk since the atrocious suffering that your return has brought me."

In the end the Count's mother did not manage to make the journey to Sirene, much to the relief of Carlo, who had encountered her once or twice in Paris, and was not at all anxious to taste again that concentrated hostility of a whole family which a French matriarch knows better than any woman how to express. However, one of Marsac's sisters came, and the brother conceived the astonishing notion of marrying her to Carlo. Madame de Grancy was muffled in the heavy crape of Latin widowhood, her husband having been killed in the last Autumn of the war. She was about three years younger than her brother and remarkably like him in appearance; but she greatly alarmed Carlo by her attitude of contemptuous criticism; and when Marsac suggested that a marriage might be arranged he nearly tumbled backward off the marble balustrade of the terrace into the peacock-blue Tyrrhenian, seven hundred feet below.

"I shall speak to her on the subject to-night," Marsac announced. "I have decided that it is the only way to save you from making a fool of yourself with the first wretched young girl who opens wide at you her insipid eyes."

"Robert, I beg you will not speak a word to Madame de Grancy. I assure you that she regards me with *mépris*."

"Permit me to know better than you how she regards you," said the brother haughtily.

"Listen, Robert," said Carlo, "if you make this suggestion to Madame de Grancy I shall leave Sirene at once and never return."

"*Mais, c'est de la folie*," Marsac raved. "Why do you take this pleasure in thwarting me at every point? Why have you this sadistic delight in tormenting me? When you departed to that abominable war, you departed as a shepherd might go to seek his lost sheep. You were a sensitive and gentle creature—a sunburnt youth cast in bronze by some Greek artist whose immortality was secure in your beauty. Mantegna might have painted your youthful grace for some Scaliger tired of love. Bazzi might have chosen you as the model for his Saint Sebastien. You return from the war like some foul ascetic of Zurbaran or dark dream of El Greco or like a god carved by a savage from poisonous wood in the green murk of the jungle. The crystal goblet you once were and that I clasped between my hands I lift again to my lips, and I find it brimming over with blood."

Carlo did not have to carry out his threat to leave Sirene, because Madame de Grancy was so much insulted by her brother's plan that she at once left the island herself.

"It is strange," said Marsac pensively as from the terrace he watched the boat for Naples cut like a glazier's diamond the vitreous surface of the bay on a breathless afternoon of Spring. "It is strange how utterly I find myself out of sympathy with the aspirations of my female relatives. *En effet elles sont des petites bourgeoises.*"

For a year and a half after Madame de Grancy's brief visit daily existence at the Villa Hylas continued as before. Just as the garden was now a wilderness of overgrown and crowded trees, the dead undergrowth of which made it impassable, so was the mind of its maker. Just as he had refused to prune a single twig in that garden, so all his life through had he refused to check a single mood. He had attributed preciousness to everything connected with him; even when he had his hair cut he could hardly bear to see the barber sweep the clippings away into an ignominious corner of the saloon.

And then through all that tangle of futility death cut sharply.

Marsac and Carlo had been spending a few days at Amalfi.

From this *villegiatura* they returned to Sirene on a golden morning in early November and walked up from the harbour to the Villa Hylas. After lunch Marsac was taken ill. Dr. Squillace and two rival doctors, snarling at each other over the sick man like three dogs over a bone, decided that the cause was an overdose of cocaine. Carlo had been wise to call in every doctor in Sirene, for that night his friend died.

Gigi Gasparri, the gardener, who was present at the end, declared to everybody that the Count died *repentitamente*. He had been so much awed by the unwonted silence of the sick man that his quick Southern fancy had to snatch at some explanation of it. Moreover, Gigi had a queer streak of Calvinism in his Catholicism, and he welcomed an opportunity to rub in the possibility of a dying man's repentance without the help of priests. He was also much struck by the mortification of Dr. Squillace on being brought face to face for the first time with the richness of the villa's interior.

"It gave him a lesson," he said. "Perhaps next time he will not be quite so quick to take part in deputations. *È stato molto mortificato. Si vedeva chiaramente una fortissima gelosia.*"

Marsac had left such full directions for his burial, including the design for the tombstone and the inscription upon it, that people began to talk of suicide. There was not the least reason to suspect him of that. It was in perfect keeping with his character to provide carefully for his eternal resting-place. So, to the little Protestant cemetery came an immense oblong block of granite which was surmounted by a great block of white marble foliated in the manner of an ancient Greek tomb. Within the marble was set the urn containing his cremated ashes. The inscription was simple:

Baron Robert Marsac Lagerström
n. 1. 4. 1881
m. 3. 11. 1921

It was then that for the first time people realized that

Marsac had had no more right to the title of count than he had had to the rosette of the Legion of Honour. They had been so busy in attacking his reputation that his title had escaped uninjured.

Old friends and old enemies, English, Americans, Germans, Swedes, and Dutch, residents of many years, transients who came for a week and dying on the island will remain there for ever, all of them lie very near to one another in that little cemetery. The mighty tomb of Marsac, which occupied a double plot, was as far away as it was possible to be from the resting-place of Miss Maimie; but it cast a shadow across Miss Virginia's path when every day she went to sit on that small marble stool; and she never passed it without looking coldly ahead of her, the way she and Miss Maimie used to pass excommunicated friends on their rides up from the Villa Amabile to the Villa Hylas. The vacant plot of earth next to the Count's tomb (for in spite of the inscription a count he will remain to contemporary Sirenians) was reserved for Major Natt.

"I'm rather surprised, Bookham," he exhaled painfully, "that you've allowed Marsac to erect that brobdingnagian sarcophagus. I shall lie between him and my neighbour on the left like a weevil between two biscuits or a bookworm between two folios."

"I offered you the double plot, Major," the churchwarden reminded him.

"Yes, I know you did at what I considered a most exorbitant figure."

"I can still let you have a double plot on the other side of the cemetery. Only, you'll have to pay more for it now. Prices have risen considerably since the war."

"Ah well, I suppose I must pay the penalty for having lived in a house too large for me by cramping myself in eternity," said the Major, retiring with a grimace.

Marsac bequeathed to Carlo the Villa Hylas and all

that it contained. The rest of his fortune went to his family, and how Carlo was to live in the Villa Hylas he omitted to suggest.

Marsac's inspiration for this arrangement of his property was a posthumous jealousy. He wanted to tie Carlo to the Villa Hylas. He was convinced that if he left him money he would at once marry and bring some odious girl to be mistress of that Tiberian cliff. In his dreams he saw her pruning the trees, putting fig-leaves on the statues, and using his subterranean den as a store-room. "*Ah ça, jamais,*" he had cried. And his embrangled mind conceived this ruse, which, had he still possessed a vestige of logic, he might have foreseen would be the surest way to drive Carlo into searching for a dowry large enough to feed the white elephant on whose back he had been hoisted by his friend. If he did not marry, Carlo would either have to sell the contents of the villa to live in it until it was empty and then try to sell the villa itself or, which would be more prudent, sell it at once with all its contents to some profiteer who wanted a ready-made civilization.

However, Carlo had scarcely had time to contemplate his future when the Lagerström family made an attempt to solve it for him in a very unpleasant way. They saw no reason why the man who, as they told themselves and everybody else, had ruined poor Robert's life should gloat luxuriously over them in the Villa Hylas. They were convinced that Carlo must either have been left a large sum of money or that the contents of the villa were even more valuable than was supposed. To them it seemed obvious that Carlo had murdered poor Robert, so obvious that they could not understand why the idiotic Italian police had not immediately arrested him. So they wrote to the authorities and expressed their astonishment at the hurried way in which Baron Lagerström had been cremated and buried without apparently any inquisition into the cause of his suspiciously sudden death.

The Italian police are famous for their conscientiousness, and few will expect to hear that they paid no attention to this sinister communication. They did not actually arrest Carlo; but they badgered him with questions every day for at least three months before they decided that there was no evidence he had murdered his friend. Then the Lagerström family threatened to launch a civil suit against him for improper influence, forging codicils, and anything else that disappointed legatees can sue over. In the end, after protracted arguments and wearisome negotiations, a cash offer was made to buy Carlo out for the equivalent of £10,000. He slid down the trunk of his white elephant with alacrity and retired immediately from Sirenian life, into which he has never penetrated since. He is probably married now, and happy.

Chapter 8

turpior assessu non erit ulla meo,

. . . .

*vel cui iuratos cum Vesta reposceret ignes,
exhibuit vivos carbasus alba focos*

*causa perorata est. flentes me surgite, testes,
dum pretium vitae grata rependit humus.*

PROPERTIUS

MISS VIRGINIA survived Marsac nearly a whole year; and until two months before she died she visited Miss Maimie's grave every day, sitting beside it on that small marble stool fixed to the path she had had paved with fragments of Roman tesseræ. She sat there to tend for a little while yet the fire she had tended for ninety vestal years, dimly though to her clouded eyes the flames seemed to be burning now. She never flinched from her pagan creed. She never paltered for a moment with the fancy that she might meet Miss Maimie again in another world. She who had tied so many pink and pale blue ribbons round life tied none round death.

A mere thirty of such lives as hers placed one above the other would have stretched beyond the security of human history. The old woman sitting upon that marble stool in her long flounced skirt of dove-grey silk, a lace fichu round her shoulders, a scarlet parasol held up against the rays of the Italian sun, holding a fan whose slim old ivory handle seemed a part of the old ivory fingers that urged its motion, was a thirtieth of comprehensible humanity.

She sat there finding her way back along the margin of the winding stream of existence into the past, deaf to the noise of its swift and swollen waters in the present. It is true that Mrs. Macdonnell primed her with horrifying tales of the new Sirene that was forming itself after the war; but she listened as one might listen to a tale of Babylon, or Nineveh or Tyre. Once, as she was driving up to the cemetery, she did turn to look curiously at three owl-eyed young men of the moment with solemn and intelligent faces and dank devitalized hair—votaries of Athene who scoffed at romantic passion, looked askance at humour, and found a footnote of Dr. Ernest Jones as stimulating as cantharides.

"And do you mean to tell me, Mrs. Macdonnell, that those homely little students I saw walking up from the Grande Marina this morning are all so many Nigel Dawsons?" Miss Virginia asked later on.

"Immorrality on Sirene was never so rife," Mrs. Macdonnell declared with unction.

"I guess I've lived too long," the old lady sighed, "and maybe I've always been foolish and sentimental; but I think that a man with queer ideas ought to look kinda bold and bad and picturesque."

Yet Nigel Dawson, who was just half Miss Virginia's age, felt as much out of the present as she, when sitting at one of the tables in Zampone's and surrounded by a group of these ruthless young moderns he was asked if he had been up at Oxford with Oscar Wilde. And they did not even pay either him or Wilde the compliment of pretending to be interested in the answer.

The hotel-owners and tradespeople need not have worried about the future of the island. Sirene was again as full as ever; and there was one observer who derived the very greatest satisfaction from a contemplation of this microcosm of European culture in the years that immediately succeeded the war, because he found there the most exquisite material on which he hoped one day to weave a pattern of that confused period. But not now. Let the creatures of this tale recede while Miss Virginia still sits upon that marble stool beside Miss Maimie's tomb, which will soon be opened for her. Let no new intimacies of romance be formed. Let the living world send a few of its representatives across these pages; but let them be no more than snapshots on the glazed paper of an illustrated magazine.

Here is the genial Marinetti arrived for the Summer, his futurism already bobbing about behind him like a bustle of 1888. He holds conferences and recites his war poetry. He fails to shock anybody. He fails even to astonish anybody. One converses with him, leaning against the parapet of a terrace incandescent-seeming under the August moon, a terrace whereon the shadows of the tranced guests lie like cloaks of jetty velvet among pools of silver fire. Behind upheaves a frozen cataclysm of diamonded rocks, a stupendous lunar cliff whose cold fantastic edge five hundred feet above jags the pansy-deep sky, the warm and tender sky, while as far below spreads the relucent sea out of which rise black and steep as a sorcerer's stronghold the twin towers of the Faraglioni. Beauty tempts this herald of modernity with a Faustian vision, fuses for him in a sublime flash all classic calm and gothic ecstasy. His essentially gentle and academic spirit succumbs for one wistful moment and then, before he swoons utterly away in the Siren's embrace, he cries aloud in desperation:

"I shall not be content until we have a café-concert and electric light on the top of the Faraglioni."

And not a coffee-cup stirs uneasily in its saucer.

The owl-eyed young men who have awarded a green apple to Athene, who have smacked Hera's monumental behind and tweaked her imperial nose, and who have put Aphrodite on the dissecting-table under the impression that the female form there stretched out is naked Truth,

these young men are not likely to be shocked by Marinetti.
And the rest of us, after four years of war and three years
of Milanese profiteers, think ' why not indeed ? '

" Much as I love this island," Marinetti confides, " I
distrust its effect upon my art."

And presently he rushes away to Milan as a man in a
country lane hearing the roar of an incoming express runs
to catch it.

Here is Casella upon that same moon-blanched terrace,
disposing in his own grave style of all that has been in music.
He consents to play for the pleasure of the murmurous
company, and as he steps out of the moonshine into the
golden haze of the candle-lit studio the Siren follows him.
She sits beside him at the piano and, whispering in his ear,
lures him into a nocturne of Chopin, which he plays as
almost only he could play it.

A young French intellectual, whose brain will presently
scatter the shrapnel of its prose upon the page, presses a
hand to his brow and groans:

"*Mais Chopin! Chopin, vous savez. C'est dure!
C'est dure!*"

And the owl-eyed young men, who do not intend to be
chloroformed by the moon, groan in sympathy. They
feel as if somebody had laid a wreath of sham flowers upon
the naked form of Truth.

A few days later Casella, who has realized that he too
must beware of Sirene, flies back to the noise without which
no modern composer can feel sure of escaping from the
poisonous exhalations of the dead past. And Malipiero
soon follows his example.

Prampolini arrives and holds an exhibition of his pictures;
but he too retires as much baffled by Sirene as every painter
who deserts the oleographic style.

One after another the apostles of modern art arrive,
and one after another they retire before the unimaginable
touch of time.

Pesce cani, tedeschi, americani, automobili, lesbiane, nazionalisti, and finally *fascisti* all land in turn upon that fantastic rock.

English authors arrive to fatten upon the stimulating pasture, and the air is full of their plaintive bleatings about royalties and reviewers. Their works are sold in Zampone's as a natural product of the Sirenian air. They are sold like serpentine paper-weights at the Lizard or cakes on the platform of Banbury station. At Zampone's the name endures; but while Miss Virginia was still alive it ceased to be Zampone's.

After old Don Luigi's death Ferdinando and his mother kept it, what it had always been in the memory of living Sirenians, the focus of the island's life. And then dear fat Ferdinando succumbed to a complication of maladies and died. Donna Maria sold the property to some Italians speaking English with an American-Italian accent instead of a German-Italian accent, and this transfer was symbolical of the new Europe. It may be admitted that the German tourists used to guzzle their soup very noisily, but their arrival in Spring shed a more genial atmosphere than that of the hordes of small-town Americans inspecting a world made safe for their democratic adventures and gloating economically over the exchange.

As a matter of fact the Germans did come back for a couple of Springs and scandalized everybody by drinking champagne while they were arguing about their capacity to pay the war indemnity. But what a relief it was to see other people than profiteers drinking champagne with such gusto!

Miss Virginia stood by the gateway of the Protestant cemetery watching the long funeral procession of Ferdinando Zampone move past upon its way to the Catholic cemetery beyond. She pondered the crowd of mourners—the *facchini* staggering under the burden of that twenty-stone corpse ; the immense laurel wreaths, some of which took a couple of men to carry ; the long trail of empty carriages with their hoods raised in token of grief.

"I wonder why these poor folk fret so over dying," she said to Miss Hazell, " when all the while they believe they're going to dance around the mulberry-bush for evermore."

LUTTO CITTADINO. The shutters of the Sirene shops all closed. Donna Maria, who had wept in sympathy with so many, weeping now for herself. And presently Zampone's would pass into new hands. The pictures of Serene Highnesses who had drunk there in old days, the faded photographs of groups of bygone Sirenians, the framed parchment nominating Luigi Zampone Chevalier of the Order of the Crown of Italy—these indeed remained, because the new proprietors bought the place lock, stock, and barrel in a laudable desire to maintain its character. But how soon it changed in a hundred small ways, and little it stands for now in Sirenian life.

On the afternoon of the funeral Mrs. Macdonnell came to call at the Villa Amabile.

"I feel so sorry to think that Ferdinando Zampone is dead," said Miss Virginia, rocking gently to and fro in that old chair. "Oh, I know he was a vile pro-German all through the war ; but I suppose, the way he had so much of his education in Germany, it was to be expected and maybe forgiven."

Mrs. Macdonnell opened her eyes at this, the first sign of weakness in Miss Virginia she had yet perceived.

"His Maker may forrgive him," she said sternly. " But we would never have been able to forrgive him. So perhaps it is as well that the man is dead. He had his conveniences in many ways, I'm told ; though he never put himself out to be of the least serrvice to me, and I considered it more patrriotic to deal with Westall."

"And do you really believe, Mrs. Macdonnell, that there's a funny old gentleman sitting up aloft like a judge and giving long vacations to some and hard labour to others ? Why, to me it's just foolishness to believe any such thing."

"I trrust in my Maker," Mrs. Macdonnell affirmed stoutly. Her profession of faith might cost her the Villa Amabile, but she felt bound to be true to her Presbyterian ancestry. Moreover, the amount of money she had made out of munitions was enough to prevent her running any risk of losing that.

"I believe we go back to the old earth from which we came," said Miss Virginia. Then she turned a little irritably to Miss Hazell who was pouring out the tea. "Mrs. Macdonnell takes three lumps of sugar," she said, trilling her fan. The companion smiled apologetically. She knew that Miss Virginia could not help resenting her presiding over the tea-table. She had once been told sharply not to take a certain chair, and afterward she had found out that it was the chair in which Miss Maimie always used to preside over the tea-table.

Mrs. Ambrogio was announced, and made a blusterous entrance, because she always felt ill at ease in the Villa Amabile when she found Mrs. Macdonnell with Miss Virginia. It seemed to her that they must always have just stopped talking about herself. That she continued to call upon Miss Virginia at intervals was due a little to her fear that people would still whisper that she and Peter had not been entirely innocent in the matter of the burglary; but chiefly it came from a deep and disinterested affection. She had long abandoned the hope of inheriting anything from the old lady, or even of spiking Mrs. Macdonnell's guns. She had tried to do so once or twice; but the glitter in Miss Virginia's eye and the hawk's swerve of her fan had warned her to refrain.

"So upset about poor dear Ferdinando," she spluttered. "No, I won't have any tea, thank you so much. Didn't come down for tea. Came down to see Miss Norton. Didn't come down for tea. Ferdinando always against

Peter. But so sorry he's dead. So glad to see you looking so well, Miss Virginia. Marvellous woman. Constitution of iron. Poor old Goldfinch deaf as a post. Can't understand a word I say. Shout at him with all my might. All the things on his mantelpiece rattle, but he can't hear a word. Going blind too. Building a new room at the Villa Adonis."

"For Sheila Macleod, we suppose," said Miss Virginia setting her lips. "Dear heart alive, you'd think he'd be ashamed of himself at his age. Well, well, if he isn't the scandalous old reprobate."

"How lovely the Amabile's looking this afternoon," Mrs. Ambrogio spluttered on. "Wouldn't like to live here myself," she added hastily. "So fond of the dear Botticelli. Wouldn't live anywhere else if I'd put all my money in munitions instead of Belgian railways."

"It's a grreat pity ye did not have somebody to advise you a little more prrudently about your investments, Mrs. Ambrrogio," said Mrs. Macdonnell tartly.

"That loathsome Macdonald woman gets more awful every day," Mrs. Ambrogio told Effie Macadam when she met her in the Piazza that evening. "Saw her card in the hall. *Always Ready*. Leaves a card every time she goes. Such damned affectation."

"Of course," Effie agreed. "The woman's a dam snob."

"Says we're all too bad to live on this beautiful island," Mrs. Ambrogio spluttered on. "Only she has the right even to bathe in the sea."

"Dam cheek," Effie growled indignantly.

"Told the bathing woman she wants her cabin cleaned out and whitewashed when anyone enters it after or before her. Sends her maid down to do it for her, and which of course she doesn't."

"Good lord, I wouldn't bathe after her with the end of a barge-pole," Effie avowed.

"Poor dear old Miss Norton! Lives in the past. Lives

in the past. So do I. To live in the past is beautiful. Thank God I have a past to live in! Not like that prancing Mrs. Macdonald. Never had a past. Never will have."

"Do you know what my darling old Archie used to call her?"

"Dear old boy!" said Mrs. Ambrogio warmly. "Wish to goodness he was here now. All the nice people go. Only the rotters hang on."

"He said to me the only time he met her, 'Effie, you mark my words, that woman's a spiteful old bitch.' I must say, I thought that was rather good. What?"

"Splendid! Describes her perfectly."

"Archie was a jolly good judge of human nature. You know: he had the knack."

"Dear old boy. Dear old boy. So fond of him. And now poor old Burlingham's very ill."

"So I hear."

"Never recover. Can't possibly recover. Sleeps in a tweed cap every night. Puts it on last thing before he turns over. There it is in the morning in exactly the same place. Never walk again. Afraid of draughts."

"We shall soon be the last of the old brigade, Maud."

"Live in the past. Both of us live in the past. We can do that, thank God."

"What? Rather! Why, my past would be a jolly good future for some women," said Effie fervidly.

Thus with their dreams let us leave Mrs. Ambrogio and Mrs. Macadam, and wander back with Miss Virginia across the Atlantic even as far as Idaho, while sitting on that small marble stool in the Italian sunlight or alone in the big *salone* of the Villa Amabile she dreams that she is riding again on her white horse and urging the whiskered young cavaliers to spur their own steeds to overtake her. And now she has come East with her father the Colonel, to whose kindly questions a little girl in frilled pantalettes and a chequered frock is muttering shy answers. She has taken that old daguerrotype of Miss Maimie from the faded violet of its worn leather case with pinchbeck clasp. She holds it slantwise in the window, peering to catch the faint rose with which the cheeks are tinted and the pencilled eyebrows and the pale blue ribbon in the smooth hair. Old Falls come back to her when there was golden-rod in all the fields and when the woods glowed with so rich a crimson above the blue mist of the valleys. The Colonel is dead now. She and Miss Maimie have landed at Cherbourg to visit Europe for the first time after so many years of planning. Ah, those years of planning, which always come back to her fancy as one sunny morning in Spring, with herself rocking to and fro on that old chair and Maimie listening to the plans as from time to time she turns a sombre eye in the direction of the awkward new hired-girl shuffling back and forth past the lilacs in the door-yard. And now Maimie and she are hurrying along the platform of that little Cherbourg railway-station among the trees; and now they are sitting opposite to each other in that dusty grey second-class compartment vowing that there can be nothing in the world so cosy and comfortable as these funny little old European trains. And now Italy . . . and now Sirene. "My! isn't that the sweetest little cottage you ever did see, Maimie?" And the vines . . . and the wistaria in the old Albergo Odisseo. Still alive that wistaria, yet perhaps twisted and contorted though it be, not yet so old as the dreamer herself. And the wine . . . and the olives . . . and the pink, blue, and yellow houses huddled along the edge of the Grande Marina . . . and the letter to say that there was enough money coming in now to let them stay for ever on this beloved sunny island. Miss Virginia's eyes are closed for a moment. She is thinking of disappointments. She is remembering that *cochiere* they wanted to help and who repaid them by telling everybody that they had expected him to make love to them. She is remembering the lawyer who swindled them, and Marsac, and Agostino, and the Biltons, and a dozen others. But she waves aside these derisive phantoms, and she sits again by Miss Maimie in the Temple of Vesta, pointing to the butterfly boats on the dancing bay and the long curve of that classic shore and the swan-breasted cloud above Vesuvius. And away up the winding road among the lemon-groves and lush young vines they hear the music of San Mercurio's procession and the bangs to greet the old silver saint coming back from his grand throne in the Duomo to the niche in his own little basilica. They are surrounded by so many friends now, and they are leaning over the balustrade of the terrace above the road, leaning over and clapping and waving and showering genista blossom and red rose-petals upon the throng. And now they are alone together in their new loggia, through which the summer *maestrale* blows with such a life-giving freshness when the sun has dropped behind Monte Ventoso, whose towering bulk casts a shadow upon the Villa Amabile. 'Oh, Maimie, doesn't Vesuvius look a great old boy this afternoon? And my! isn't it good to be alive, honey?'

Thus, reaching back and back, the old lady stretches forward to the end.

An inscription beneath the romanesque window in the cemetery-wall says:

> *Within this bit of foreign earth*
> *there lies*
> *The dust of Two*
> *Who loved this Italy.*

There is neither the date of their birth nor the record of their death upon the headstones of Miss Virginia and Miss Maimie. They brought with them the puritan fire of old America and quenched it in the pagan earth of ancient Europe. There is neither nationality nor surname upon their headstones. MAIMIE is carved upon one, beneath it the sentimental verses she chose from that tattered magazine:

Warm summer sun,
  Shine kindly here!
Warm southern wind,
  Blow softly here!

Green sod above,
  Lie light, lie light!
Good night, dear heart,
  Good night! Good night!

Beneath VIRGINIA upon the other stone is carved her verdict upon life:

> *Happiness*
> *is the only Good*
> *and the*
> *Greatest Happiness*
> *Consists in*
> *Making others Happy.*

And the small marble stool is still fixed to that pavement of Roman tesseræ.

As old as Miss Virginia, Christopher Goldfinch outlived her. He had just had a cable from Sheila Macleod to say that there was a letter in the mail. He was expecting her in the Spring, and he was hoping to feel a little better by then. He had bought some really stunning wine, which would be in its prime about Midsummer.

" I'm afraid it won't be quite ready when Sheila arrives," he croaked regretfully. " Still, we'll all drink hearty in the Summer. She tells me she may go to Paris for a while, but I fancy she'll be here for most of next year. I'm getting along great with my new dining-room. I find the one I've had all these years is just too small nowadays."

The Lagerström family had by now emptied the Villa Hylas of its treasures. It stood empty and forsaken in that impenetrable thicket of mimosas and pines and casuarinas. The Lagerström family had never noticed the lifesize bronze of Carlo as Hylas gazing down into the lilypool, so much overgrown was it when they took possession. That statue and the old gnome who had once owned the land kept each other company. 'O Gobbetto was happy in the new straw hut so like a bee-skip he had built round the gnarled trunk of a carob tree. He growled a malediction upon Alberto and Enrico Jones when one afternoon they drove a way through the thicket like two determined ruminants.

"In a year or two," Enrico was saying, "they will be glad to sell for half of what they are asking now."

Alberto shook his head. He lacked some of his brother's idealism.

"Too far from the Piazza, *caro*," he sighed.

And down in the deserted garden of the Villa Amabile the boughs of the cypresses have met at last above the domed roof of the Temple of Vesta.

CAUSA PERORATA EST